THE WEIGHT OF
Indifference

"How fortunate they responded so quickly," Monty said. "Go on."

"Reggie freaked out when he heard about the double-tap. He made me wait in the living room while he and Barry got Martha out of the closet and into the hearse. Reggie said it was all over. But it wasn't. Not by a long shot."

Monty tapped the file. "Mark, the paperwork says you didn't embalm."

"No. Martha and I talked about it, you know, before. We think it's important to return to the earth. I made that clear to Reggie at our first consultation. Instead of a headstone, we're planting an apple tree. The kids want to bake pies."

"Well, there you have it. Not embalming is risky, Mark. It prevents—"

Bernie leaned forward. "I know what you'd like us to think it prevents, Monty, but we don't believe in embalming or the Easter Bunny because we're not dummies. Embalming's a scam. It's another way to rip-off the bereaved."

Monty exhaled and silently counted to three before speaking. "Bernie, it's not—"

"Don't 'Bernie' me like you're God Almighty or Morgan Freeman, Monty. The problem wasn't the lack of embalming; it was the sub-standard temperature of your coolers."

"That's ridiculous. Our coolers are kept at the regulation 38 degrees!"

"Yeah, unless the power goes out and back-up generators fail. The morgue went dark the evening of May 11th Monty. We know. Barry squealed."

"How dare you. I'm not going to grace that accusation with a response."

Bernie pounced. "And then there's the timing, Monty. The funeral was scheduled for the twelfth, a Saturday. Reggie claimed it was the next available time slot, but really, it was because you charge extra for Saturdays, don'tcha?"

"We try to accommodate—"

Bernie cut him off. "The seventh to the twelfth! Do the math, Monty! Burial within three days is the law, and for good reason."

"The three-day rule is not law, just a common misconception based on old wives' tales. Resisters don't always rise after the third day."

Bernie went for the jugular. "But Martha did, Monty. She did because you let her body warm up. One and done, my—"

"Enough, Bernie," Mark said. "I think Monty understands where we're coming from."

"I hear what you're saying, and I feel for you, but I don't think you understand your culpability in all of this. Embalming makes time, temperature, and all sorts of other things non-issues. Not embalming is highly irregular—"

Mark said, "But so is coming back! Resisters don't happen in places like Farmington, Monty. They happen in places like Haiti or Zimbabwe or—"

"San Francisco!" Bernie said.

"Right!" Mark said. "Weird places. In Farmington, it's not normal for the dead to do laundry."

THE WEIGHT OF
Indifference

by D.H. Robbins

First electronic and bound edition published 2019
Second edition published 2023

ISBN-13-978-1-7330722-7-4 (Print -paperback)

ISBN-10: 978-1-7330722-4-3 (Kindle e-book)

All trademarks are the property of their respective owners.

Published by D. H. Robbins

Cover photos, treatment and design by D. H. Robbins
Part opener photo collages and design by D. H. Robbins
Book design by D.H. Robbins—Typeface: Garamond 11/14

Edited by Bonnie Gauthier
Editing Ink
West Hartford, CT

3456

To Carl

Who served in-country
and will remain my very best friend.

Acknowledgments

Thanks to all those who encouraged me along the journey of writing "The Weight of Indifference." A special recognition goes out to the West Hartford Fiction Writers Group, and Amy, one of my readers, for their often insightful and constructive criticism. Also, a special recognition is due to my friend, Norm Green for his always helpful encouragement. An extra special thanks to Bonnie Gauthier, my editor, for her fine work on the book. Also, thanks to those at the U. C. Berkeley Archives for making themselves available during my research.

I used my own recollection and a number of books and journals to research the Vietnam, era, most notably, Stanley Karnow's "Vietnam—A History"; Michael Herr's "Dispatches"; Mark Bowden's "Hue 1968"; Philip Caputo's "A Rumor of War"; Karl Marlantes's "Matterhorn"; David Halberstam's "The Best and the Brightest"; Seymour Hersh's "My- Lai 4"; and many other books and commentaries and video clips about the war and military structure.

"My own eyes are no more than scouts on a preliminary search,
for the camera's eye may entirely change my idea."
– Edward Weston

"The camera is an instrument that teaches people how to see
without a camera."
— Dorothea Lange

PART ONE

Daniel

CHAPTER ONE

The thing in the box

Watts, Los Angeles--August 11-12, 1965

Los Angeles might as well have been someplace else, like Morocco. Daniel Lilienthal supposed L.A. was one of those places that had that kind of effect on someone like him. It had challenged his virility even more than San Francisco had. He felt like he was viewing the motions of his life from underwater, deprived of the delicate right to drown.

At first, his relationship with Jared had been more about the convenience of something that passed for affection until nothing mattered. For the last two months, some inner force had compelled him to endure this half-life of being with another man. He didn't care if he had liked it; he'd become too emotionally paralytic to care about anything, much.

He puffed out his cheeks and wiped his brow as he leaned on the railing of the second-story porch and heard the dry thunder of a jet ascending from LAX. This August morning there were more pressing things to think about. Like air-conditioning. Or the lack of it. The over-taxed window unit in the living room had once again ground to a halt sometime during the night's iron weight of stagnant heat.

Aside from the air conditioning, there was a rebellion writhing eight blocks away.

Last night's news reports had deemed the outbreak of Black protesters in Watts as contained and under control; but now the turmoil was louder and closer. He squinted across the street at a shirtless sinewy Black teenager in greasy chinos carrying a newly pilfered portable TV on his shoulder as he ran down the sidewalk. He was spurred on like a sprinter by some neighbors from their porches, as two cop cars rushed past in the opposite direction and toward the the riot.

Daniel glanced toward the chaos. Three clots of smoke roiled white and dark grey against the aluminum sky. The incessant yowl of police sirens pierced the swells of distant crowd noises, which sounded like taunts from the wild. A strange undercurrent of sweetness barbed by the taut pungency of burning tires permeated the hot atmosphere. He wanted to be there. To be in it, maybe as a sociological thought-experiment. His famous sociologist father would approve. Or not, as he was 3,000 miles back east, bull shiting his class of grad students at Columbia

Daniel felt a wave of dull nausea as Jared's cool hand glided over his shoulder. Its smooth skin was the color of milk chocolate. "Yeah, hi, Jared" Daniel said in a crinkled morning-voice.

"It doesn't look as though it's gotten any better." The rich sound of his slight Anglo-Caribbean accent was easy and hypnotic.

He drew his hand away as he probably sensed the little spike in Daniel's tension. Daniel breathed a sigh of relief. "This really sucks."

"We're in Watts, brother. What you're seeing has been brewing since the nineteen-twenties. With all that went down in New York, Newark, and Chicago last summer? This was bound to happen."

"But in L.A.?"

"What? You think sunny California is immune from all this shit? Just look around you. You're the only bright white skinny red-haired human out here. Actually, I find that bizarre, myself."

Others in the neighborhood had begun dribbling out from their apartments and toward the epicenter of the action. Daniel looked down at another looter supporting two cases of beer: one on each shoulder. "Look at that guy carrying all that Miller. I would have at least gone for the Heineken."

"That's because you're white. Heineken's a white man's brew. We drink Miller...or Budweiser."

"*We?*"

Jared sighed and inclined his head toward the smoke of the riot. His gaze turned thoughtful. "I'm with them today," he said "Anyway, Dan, you'd best stick with me while all this is happening."

"For protection?"

"No. I don't know, maybe. Just stay out of sight. Okay?"

He knew that Jared didn't share the experience of the African American Blacks as they kindled the fires of their tortured frustrations out in Watts. Jared was Trinidadian, born into the privileges of a banking family in Port of Spain. He was prep schooled at Choate. From there he went on not to Yale, as a typical "Choatie" might, but to U.C.L.A.'s School of Journalism. He nurtured his talent enough as a writer to land an entry-level associate reporter job at *The Los Angeles Tribune.*

A film-studio helicopter swooped low from behind and hovered close enough for them to see a cameraman perched precariously on one of its skids. He controlled a cumbersome industrial-strength camera sporting a huge film magazine. The riot was being Hollywood-ized. And why not, with Hollywood and Disneyland so close by, making L.A. the Center of Surreality?

Jared's voice sounded distant. "I just don't want you going out into all that shit."

Daniel stiffened at the conviction hidden in his message. "I don't know, Jared. The sociologist in me says I need to go get involved with it."

"As some sort of study for your father's next book?"

Daniel cringed over the remembrance of working with his father. "Shit, man, I don't know. I hope not. Maybe."

"You don't sound very convincing, Dan."

"This thing out there really calls to me. I need to check it out."

"And maybe get yourself killed in the name of some sociological research."

Daniel rolled his shoulders and cast Jared a patronizing look. "It's my course of study. Maybe I can get a subject for my thesis…even my dissertation someday."

"Sure, Dan, if you live that long," Jared said. "Look. I'm a journalist. Going out into this kind of shit is what I do. I *have* to document this."

"You're a new hire at the *L.A. Trib*, Jared. A junior reporter. It's not worth getting yourself killed out there, either."

"But it's okay with you if you do."

"Maybe I have a death wish." Daniel tried to make it sound like a joke.

"I get paid for this. Journalism drives me out there."

"So, Jared. You get my point. I'm driven to go out there, too."

Jared shook his head in resignation. "Okay, then, Dan. But I don't want you going out into all that without me." His feather-light kiss on Daniel's cheek registered as a shudder up his spine. "We'll figure something out."

Jared had been taking an increasing number of doses from his inhaler as his chronic asthma became weighted down by the humidity. Caged by his determination to cover the growing riot, he treated the event like prey on which to pounce. Through the afternoon, he paced to and from the porch to the living room to glance at the anxious reports from the TV. Daniel lounged back on the couch indolently sipping his beer as he watched The Six-O-Clock Evening Newshour.

Tonight's Viet Nam story featured a Marine helicopter assault in the Elephant Valley just south of Danang. Then there were some interviews with a platoon of shirtless Marines waiting for the fight to begin. They relaxed near their hooches, playing cards and smoking cigarettes. This was followed by footage of Marines and Seabees leveling some land for a base golf course. After a commercial break for BaBo Cleanser and Shake n' Bake chicken seasoning, the reports became more explosive as they cut to aerial views of the burning warzone of Watts.

Daniel felt the bounce of something dropped next to him. He glanced down at a box containing the 35-millimeter Pentax camera gifted to him by his father for his birthday two months before. He'd studied the thing for about ten minutes; just enough time to find it too confusing, then packed it back up to give to charity later.

"Thank you, Jared. Why have you unearthed that camera?"

Jared eased down next to him, nursing his rum and Coke as if it were the sweetest concoction on earth. "You need to start using it. I found a few extra lenses with it. A couple of telephotos and a wide-angle still in their boxes. You have a state-of-the art camera system, here, man, and you've never even used it."

"There's a reason for that. I don't have the head for it. Besides, it was a present from my father."

"So, you're not supposed to accept gifts from him?"

"Believe me. Nothing from him is a gift. There's always some sort of caveat attached." Another jet rumbled overhead, accentuating the silence between them as Daniel stared down at the box. "What do you want me to do with it? I can't use this stuff. I'm only wired to be a sociology major, not a photographer."

"Yeah, but you're not happy with your major and you know it. That was only what your father wanted for you. You once told me he'd kept you in his box like some sort of god-damn prisoner. You need to try to find something else. Besides, I might need a wingman."

"A wingman," Daniel repeated.

"Look. I've decided. I'm going out there tonight." He reached into his breast pocket, brought out his inhaler and took two quick hits. "You're staying here tonight."

"No fucking way! You don't know what's out there, man. You need me to keep you from getting fucking killed. Besides your asthma's hanging all over you in this heat." He tensed again as Jared placed his arm around his shoulder and drew him close.

"Ah, my little guardian angel," he said in a voice tightened by his medication. "Always looking out for me. It's what I love about you."

Daniel hoped Jared couldn't read his thoughts every time he told him he loved him. It all seemed so unnatural, although at times, reassuring. "Yeah, well, I'm going with you."

"I'm going, not you. And what I want you to do while I'm gone is to learn this camera, especially quick loading the film. A while back I pilfered a few twenty-packs from the *Trib.* And left them on the bed for you."

"Jared, what the fuck are you talking about?"

"I told you. This riot isn't going to end tonight, I just know. I'm going out again tomorrow and I'll need a photographer." He kissed him on the cheek. "And tag. You're it." He stood up to leave.

"Yeah? Well, I'm going out there to get some material for my thesis. I've been piecing it together in my head for the last few hours."

"You'll learn more if you take pictures of it, Dan. If we cover this together, we'll keep each other safe."

"Oh, great. So why can't I go with you now?"

"You need this time to learn that camera," Jared said as he flung the strap of his cassette tape recorder over his shoulder. He held the recorder's mic to his lips for a sound check. "Testing...Testing. Peter Piper picked a peck of pickled peppers and got pickled." He swiped a passing kiss across the top of Daniel's head. "Bye," he whispered, twitched a brusque smile, then set out toward the belly of the beast.

Daniel stared at the TV, then down at the camera box as if it was an unwelcome stranger. He placed his hand on the box and felt its veneer, then picked it up and began to open it as though he was diffusing a bomb. The camera itself was a beautiful instrument that fit well into his grip. He brought it to the kitchen table to study it, repeatedly working the film advance lever until it felt natural.

He scanned the twenty-page manual cover-to-cover once, then again with just as little understanding. He loaded and reloaded a film cassette and changed the lens. It was a delicate process as he fumbled with lining up the fine screw-mount threads to tighten the lens to the body. He practiced focusing as he squinted through the viewfinder. He set the film speed to 400, then worked the speed and aperture settings to adjust the through-the-lens light meter.

He loaded a roll of film, shot a picture, rewound it, and reloaded it; each time quickening his pace. He was mildly amused and amazed at how swiftly he had picked up the technology and mechanics of the little camera. He stood and drew the camera up like a sharpshooter's six-gun again and again. He took some shots of the lamp on the end table, throwing off the focus to re-focus. He felt the gentle recoil as he took his shot and advanced the film: *saddack-thwip...saddack-thwip...saddack-thwip.*

He became acquainted with the camera over the next three hours until Jared returned breathless and lit up with excitement. "Holy *shit*! I've got some *great* stuff!" His voice was constrained by a mild asthmatic spasm. "You have *got* to come with me tomorrow."

"Okay."

"Hell, yes!" he said as he sat at the kitchen table and busied himself with the workings of his recorder. He continued to cough, and then pumped in a few shots from his inhaler. " I might have been the only *Trib* reporter there." He rewound some tape and pressed down the play switch. "Just listen to this..."

An anxious cacophony of sirens blaring over the shouts of rioters crackled through the tape recorder's little speaker. Chants like "Kill whitey!" "Burn, baby, burn!" "Death to the Little Man!" and "Blood Power!" rose above incessant swells of commotion. Then there was Jared's far-away voice: "Tell me why this is going on."

Another voice, this one desperate and breathless over the crowd noises: "Shit, man. *You're* a blood. You tell *me*! " Then a pause. "You a reporter, or sumptin'?"

Jared's voice, even more distant: "I'm from the *L.A. Tribune*."

Frustrated Negro: "No shit?"

Jared: "No shit...(illegible)...you are here?"

Frustrated Negro: "'Cause we bin here too long. Stuck in falling-down houses an' no jobs. We bin down long enough, an' we want our say!"

Jared: "And you think throwing rocks, looting stores and burning cars in your neighborhood... (indiscernible)...is going to help?"

Frustrated Negro: " Hell, blood! I don't live *nowhere* near here. I live over on 118th. I was there las' night when the white cops, they pull out that Black kid for drunk drivin' an' then this all started. Been wit' it since. 'Sides we ain't burnin' and looting the brother's stores. We only burnin' down *whitey's* stores! I tell you, blood, we had e-nough! Look aroun' at all the cops. They all *white*! And they been beatin' us down all these years? We ain't gonna take it no more in whitey's world. We earn our right to be free a hunnerd years ago. An' now we finally *esspressin'* it! We want our *own* justice!"

Jared clicked off the tape recorder. "And there's more like that. This is going to be a freaking amazing story! What's going on out there is going to be happening for days!"

Daniel hadn't been listening, as he was more concerned with Jared's short, jagged breathing. "Jared. You're breathing really wierd."

"Hell, yeah, man! My heart's racing! We're going out there tomorrow to cover this. Tonight, there were about a thousand people in the street. Tomorrow, there'll be three times that many. This is *big*!"

"Calm down, man. Take some deep breaths and sit down. I'll get you a beer."

Jared fanned a hand like he could wave away his asthma while he walked to one of the puffy living room chairs and fell back into it. "Did you learn how to work that camera?"

"Yeah, I played with it a little," Daniel said from the kitchen as he drew out a couple of Heinekens.

"Well, bro. You're gonna need it. Tomorrow we're going in as a team."

Daniel stared down at his beer bottle and heaved a sigh. "Yeah, right."

"You're gonna be camouflaged to blend in out there." Jared said then let out a short wheeze.

"Take a hit from your inhaler, man," Daniel said. "You're starting to worry me. And if I go in with you, I'm going in as no other person than myself. No disguises. No pretensions." He was overcome with an electric wave of excitement as he concluded that going out into the riot was the only thing he wanted to do. And to hell with everything else.

CHAPTER TWO
When Night Falls

Heat and humidity mingled with the sweat and anger in the streets. Passenger jets rumbled unseen above the billows of smoke and smog as they departed eastward from LAX toward a saner world. The diminishing banshee whine of their engines added a horror to the anarchy-spiced confusion that raged below. There were no leaders, just rampant frustrations hotly expressed by 10,000 souls.

The message of overwhelming force was clear. A police helicopter swooped low through the motionless fumes and crackling fires. A cop in riot gear holding a machine gun was perched in the open doorway, poised to shoot down at any Negro torching the street. It didn't matter that the bullets were rubber and meant only to maim; to perhaps incapacitate a person for the rest of his life.

Daniel knew from his studies for his father that clashes like these ended as quickly as they began. Tonight may belong to the rebellion, but tomorrow or as soon as the riot ran out of breath, all that remained would be the mopping up by the L.A.P.D. Nothing would have come from it but deeper resentment. The victors would be the ones showing the more unified image of power, and the L.A. cops, were masters of maintaining the status quo of raw force—certainly more than their counterparts back east who at least pretended to answer disillusionment with a show of justice.

Daniel feared he might have made the wrong decision, but it was too late to back out. Even from a distance, he stood out as a grungy neighborhood whitey in a black t-shirt, worn-out jeans and a frayed Dodgers ball-cap pulled low to shadow his face. Weirdly out of place with his camera strapped just close enough to his body to allow for its mobility gave him a special presence. Jared had been right; Daniel felt safer being near him.

He realized that Jared, consumed by his mission for a story, was unaware of his own tightening gasps for breath. The acrid smoke and other smells from burning buildings, cars and crude hand-made explosives was asphyxiating. Nearby flames robbed the air of precious oxygen, heating it beyond the ninety-six-degree temperatures stifling the rest of the city. Daniel was startled by a swift whizzing past his ear, as a random rubber bullet fired from above just missed him.

"Jared! We gotta get the *fuck* outta here!" he cried.

"No, brother! We gotta get the fucking *story!*" Jared took two spritzes from his inhaler and crouched down into a swift walk. "Take some pictures! Just start shooting! It'll get you away from all this."

Daniel hunched behind Jared as he made his way to a doorway where they could be relatively safe. He snapped a picture, probably of nothing; and then another. Across boulevard, a supermarket was being gutted by swarms of Blacks who made their way out with armfuls and shopping carts of food. Daniel aimed his camera at the looters and snapped a picture, then another, then another, and another: *saddack...thwip... saddack...thwip... saddack...thwip...* until he realized he might quickly run out of film. A plume of flame burst from a building down the street. A rioter preparing to throw a Molotov cocktail into an empty store stood two doors from where

Daniel aimed his camera.

Saddack...thwip...saddack...thwip...saddack...thwip.

He took three pictures, one of a rioter in mid-aim, and two others of him in mid-throw as the flaming bottle left his hand. His eyes were wide open in frenzied determination. He found a quick fraction of a second to compliment himself on the shot before he took another of the burning supermarket.

He crouched in a walk away from where he and Jared had huddled, and then quickened his pace, mimicking the soldiers he'd seen on the news scurrying from helicopters in Vietnam. They carried M-14 rifles, while all Daniel had was a camera and his wits for protection. He had started to feel detached from it all—invincible. He focused on the riot through the viewfinder—an oddly comfortable little window out onto the fiery world around him.

Saddack...thwip...saddack...thwip...saddack...

He was becoming one with his camera. His picture taking, though not precise, felt more intuitive.

Saddack...thwip...saddack...thwip...sa-ack;
saddack...thwip/saddack/thwip/saddack.

He swung around and took pictures of a burning liquor store. He heard the shattering explosions of its stock of heated bottles bursting on their shelves as if they were bombs themselves. The pulse of flame light illuminated the intensity on a rioter's face.

Saddack...thwip/saddack/thwip/saddack...

Sensing Daniel near him, the rioter quickly turned to face him. "Yo, blood! You take a pitcher o' me?" He crossed his arms and leaned back against the brick front of the burning store. In one hand he casually grasped a Molotov cocktail.

Saddack...thwip...saddack...thwip...

"Man! Are you, like, some sorta reporter?"

"*L.A. Tribune!*" Daniel shouted nervously over the rhythmic *thwop* of the rotors of a chopper hovering three hundred feet above.

"No shit! Here...do me doing this." He lit the cloth sticking from the neck of the beer bottle half-filled with kerosene. He held it toward Daniel as though serving it to him while the fuse flared.

Saddack...thwip...saddack...thwip...saddack—

"You gonna throw that thing, buddy?" Daniel shouted.

The rioter lit a cigarette from the slowly burning fuse." 'ventually."

Saddack/thwip/saddack/thwip/saddack...

Three white cops in full riot gear were approaching from behind. The rioter glanced down at the fuse as it burned more rapidly toward the neck of the bottle. "Better duck, brother!" he said as he flung the burning bottle back over his shoulder toward the cops he knew were coming up on him.

Saddack...thwip...saddack...thwip...

Just before the bomb exploded in front of the cops, they backed away to shield themselves against shards of glass from the explosion. The rioter dashed toward Daniel, who quickly pivoted out of his way. "You tell yo' newspaper Malcolm Jackson was here!" he called back over his shoulder.

Saddack/thwip/saddack/thwip/saddack...

The advance lever drew taut at the end of the roll. Daniel anxiously rewound the film as he ducked into the shadow of a nearby alcove to load a new cartridge. It was an exercise in fumbling in the dark. He extracted the canister of rewound film, dropped it onto the doorstop and grabbed it up as it nearly rolled into the street. He shoved it deep in his right pants pocket and drew out a fresh roll from the collection of film canisters in his left. Threading it into the camera was a trial of patience and anxiety. He wished he had practiced this with his eyes closed the night before.

He snapped the camera-back shut and whirled around to run back out into the action. He felt a hard, stinging blow to the back of his knees, accentuated with a seething shout of: "God-damn fucking NIGGER!" He felt another blow; this to his lower back. "You black fuckin' piece of SHIT!"

Breathless, Daniel rolled over on his side. Out of the corner of his eye he saw the lead cop of the three patrolmen who had been the target of Malcolm Jackson's Molotov cocktail. They must have mistaken Daniel for their attacker. No matter to them. He was one of those trying to burn down L.A.

The lead cop with the baton had removed his helmet to reveal his blond-haired, smudged white face with fat lips twisted in hate. He raised his baton to strike one more time as Daniel rolled over and aimed the camera at him. The cop froze in position, poised confusedly with his baton held high for another strike.

Quick-focus. *saddack...thwip...saddack...thwip/saddack.*

Then the cop lowered his baton to his side. "Shit!" He squinted a piercing look at Daniel. "You ain't no *nigger*!" He turned to his buddies. "What th' *fuck*?"

Daniel rose painfully to his feet. His right leg felt like burning liquid as he sensed he might fall. "No. I'm a photographer for the *L.A. Tribune.*"

Saddack...thwip.

"And you're gonna be on the front fucking page of the morning edition!"

Saddack...thwip...

Daniel limped back to frame a three-quarter frontal of the policeman against a backdrop of surging flames. The cop placed his left hand on his hip and hid the right arm holding the baton behind his leg. He showed the semblance of a smile, as though to say: *I got things under control here.* Daniel focused into the fluttering light.

Saddack...thwip. Saddack...thwip...

The two other cops, still in their visored riot helmets, crowded behind him, wanting to be in the picture. The lead cop folded his arms to proudly cradle his baton. The pearl handle of his custom .44-caliber side-arm glimmered in the firelight. A flare from a burning car behind Daniel illuminated the cop and his surly smile. Catch-lights glinted off the dark visors of the helmets worn by the two behind him.

Focus... *Saddack...thwip…saddack...thwip...*

He backed away taking more pictures holding the cops at bay as if the camera was a gun. He tugged his ball cap back down over his eyes. "Thank you, gentlemen," he said as he limped away to search for Jared.

Jared was two blocks away among a confusion of rioters. He was interviewing a police sergeant standing in front of a small phalanx of other cops in their riot gear. The sergeant's expression was taut with tension, or hate, as he waited for the opportunity to charge his men into the surge of rebels and looters who had seized their plunder from abandoned shops.

Jared felt the wave of angst and discomfort that often preceded one of his anxiety fits. He tightened his jaw in defense and cleared his throat. "How long have you been out here?" he asked, as he moved his mike closer to the sergeant's stony face.

Not wanting to be spotted talking to a Black person, even if he was from the *Tribune,* the sergeant glanced around. "Thirty-six hours. Without sleep." He focused his gaze on something over Jared's shoulder.

"Do you feel you're making any progress?" His anxiety fumbled around within him, tingling and numbing his nerves.

"Look around. What do *you* think? Just when we think we got 'em contained, even more of them nig—Negroes show up. Never thought L.A. had so many. They're like monkeys in a zoo." A police helicopter wheeled overhead. "But we got 'em out-forced, an' out-gunned. These monkeys can rob all the gun stores they can, but we got the force to take 'em down...and we are right. We're the good guys here."

"You don't think all this proves you otherwise?"

"Hey, *we* are the good guys," he repeated succinctly as he leaned into Jared's mike. "We're here to protect this city from this kind of cannibalism. It'll all be over by morning, I damn guarantee it."

Jared tried not to let his seething anger show and concentrated on not throwing up from his mounting anxiety and asthma. "You think these people are *cannibals*? Is *that* what you said?" He started to cough and put the hand holding the mic across his mouth.

The cop squinted keenly at Jared. He emphasized his point by lightly tapping his baton against Jared's chest. "Ain't it a fact, *boy*? Weren't allaya shipped over here from a band o' African cannibals? What the FUCK! " He jumped back as Jared let loose a torrent of vomit on his spit-shined shoes.

"Cannibals!!" Jared coughed as he wiped some phlegm from his lips. "What the *fuck*, mothah-fuckah? *Fuck* you!"

"Fuck you an' wat'cure mouth, boy! An' I do mean *boy!*"

"You think we're all fuckin' *cannibals* and monkeys?" Jared said, then coughed. He let the mic cord slip through his hand, then grasped it and swung it around like a bolo and caught the cop's cheek with the weight of it.

"SHIT! God fuckin' *damn* you, nigger!" He placed his hand on his gun and drew it.

Jared didn't hear or see any of this as his rage took him hostage. He whirled around to face the cop and then swung the mic again to catch the cop on the forehead, drawing a trickle of blood. "Fuck you! *Fuck* you! FUCK YOU!"

The cop ducked as he raised his gun and assumed a firing stance. He then fired.

Jared felt a dull thud in his shoulder, which pirouetted him around. The cop, also in a rage, fired again. This shot found its target in Jered's throat. He dropped the recorder as he crumpled into a heap. As he writhed on the ground, the cop fired a third bullet into his right lung.

Jared lay helpless; paralyzed on the pavement, mouth agape, gasping for the precious breath that was leaving him as he took in mouthfuls of smoke and grime. He managed a weak cough and tried crying out to no one in particular. He wheezed as he raised his wounded arm for his inhaler. He whispered for help with a dying breath into the roaring oblivion around him. His body was consumed by the shivering fury of a hard chill. His blood, glistening in the firelight, billowed more rapidly across his shirt until he stopped breathing altogether.

The cop looked wildly around. "Jeezzus H.!" he blathered, uneasy that this would be pinned on him. "Shots came from up *there*!" he shouted as he pointed up to a rooftop. "*Shit*!" He looked up at his platoon, then at the pistol in his hand. "I din't do this!"

"We know that, Sarge!" said one. "I sawr the whole thing. It was self-defense, sure as shit!"

"We gotcha covered," said another.

"You're right, Sarge. It was sniper fire!"

"Thanks, boys!" The sergeant called back at them.

He might had tried mouth-to-mouth resuscitation, but this monkey was a Black; maybe one of the agitators. Shit, yes! He was black and had to have been an agitator posing as a reporter. Relieved over this justification, he looked back over at one of his men. "Higgins! Radio in some EMT's and get a meat wagon in here!"

Daniel was drawn to the commotion building around an ambulance as it inched forward through a crowd trying to overturn it. Its sirens bleated out four short blasts to break the dam of shouting people. Another promising photo. Focus... *Saddack...thwip... saddack...thwip.* He moved closer as the ambulance made its way toward another close knot of Blacks gathering around a cop crouching down and backed by what seemed to be a dozen men in riot gear; their visored helmets reminiscent of those of German Storm-troopers. *Well, why not*? he reasoned as he pieced together his next thesis. *Is this any less than* Kristallnacht? *Were the chances for the Blacks any more hopeful than those of the Jew in 1938 Berlin*? This could be the sociological study that would free from the specter of his father. Focus... *saddack/thwip — saddack/thwip.*

He could see now that the cop was kneeling over a bleeding body as though protecting it. Focus... *saddack/thwip.* Then through his telephoto lens, he recognized the body as Jared's.

He stiffened in disbelief. He hugged the camera close to his chest and rushed to the scene, pushing aside some rioters as he approached. Oblivious to his own pain; oblivious to the rioting; oblivious to it all; he crouched down over the body and gathered it to him. Jared's corpse fell back limply. Daniel couldn't help himself and began to weep.

"What? You *know* this guy?" the Sergeant asked.

"Shut up!!!" Daniel bellowed at him. He stroked some blood from Jared cheek and turned to address the seething throng. "Shut the fuck up!!!! ALL of you!!" Their shouts only grew more desperate as they advanced.

"Kill the pig! Kill whitey! Kill the whitey cop!"

Surging flames, stinging smoke and the weight of the heat hung everywhere, closing in like the fires of Hades. The sergeant stepped back as his troops advanced. Daniel protected Jared's body as the cops fanned out around him in their synchronized march toward the crowd. The smack of their batons against their shields sounded out in a rhythmic tattoo. *Tap...tap...crack...tap...tap...crack...tap, tap, tap...tadap, tadap,tadap!*

Daniel stared into Jared's eyes. They were open wide with surprise. He drew the lids closed, then straightened out his shirt. Suddenly something that felt like a large bag of potatoes rolled against his back forcing him to fall back down over Jared's corpse. Looking off to the side, he saw that the body of the police Sergeant was lying wide-eyed on his side with a clean bullet hole through his forehead.

Ahead, and unaware that their battalion leader had been killed, the phalanx of cops advanced across the Boulevard toward the crowd. The formation of cops broke up and they ran amuck through the crowd. Now instead of using the batons against their shields, they used them on the rioters.

Daniel had never seen a dead body before, and now he moved his gaze from Jared's body to that of the dead cop. He saw the portable tape recorder in its case lying a little beyond Jared's reach vowed he would finish the story he'd begun to write. He grabbed the tape recorder's strap and draped it over his shoulder as he stood. He continued staring down at the bodies as he backed away rigid with restraint. He was caught between the desire to rush back to Jared and to blend away into anonymity.

The ambulance finally reached the scene and EMTs rushed around to heft the two bodies into its bay and get the hell out of there. They worked in haste, oblivious to everything but their task, which lasted only a minute before they slammed the ambulance door shut. The siren crescendoed to a wail as the vehicle inched its way through the crowd. It bolted free and rushed north into the relative clear.

Daniel felt a rock graze his back and spun around to confront the the Black kid who threw it. He instinctively raised his camera and took a picture of the boy, who posed proudly as if he'd singlehandedly won the riot and had appointed himself King of Watts. Focus... *saddack/thwip; saddack/thwip; saddack/thwip; saddack/thwip; saddack/thwip*. Tears stung his eyes and blurred his vision. He cared about nothing except exhausting the rest of the roll on that one kid as he danced through a range of quick poses.

Daniel's raw panic and grief over Jared being shot manifested itself into an obsession with taking pictures. The camera had become a part of him. His picture-taking had become a seprate and controlling force driving what was left of his emotion to channel its way out through the camera.

Feeling the tug of the roll's end, he set off in a crouching run toward the darkness of a nearby doorway to reload. Film loaded, he rushed from the doorway into the crowd and the cops with their batons and guns. Focus... *saddack/thwip; saddack/thwip; saddack/thwip; saddack/thwip; saddack/thwip; saddack/thwip;*

saddack/thwip; saddack/thwip; saddack/thwip; saddack/thwip.

He continued to shoot pictures well into the night until he'd run through 14 rolls of film—more than 500 pictures. Even when the film had run out, he continued shooting purely by instinct.

Aching with emotion, Daniel arrived back at Jared's empty apartment at 2 a.m. He stared at the reflection of his dirt-streaked face in the little mirror in the hallway. He detested the disconnected person in the mirror. He began to cry in silent heaves from the depths of his loss and loneliness, while he tried to decide if he had truly loved Jared. Watching helplessly from a distance as he'd shedded no tears while the Jared's body had been unceremoniously shoved into the ambulance was perhaps the closest he'd come to feeling love.

His only solace was to sit at Jared's typewriter and stare at the small pile of pages Jared had begun yesterday morning. Then he turned on the recorder to piece the story's ending together.

CHAPTER THREE

Sleepwalking through Gomorrah

Daniel had no idea where to start, so the eternity of the next hour he just listened to the recording until he heard enough to begin typing. First, there was an interview with an insurgent who had helped to overturn a taxi driven by a white man, then with another who had torched the cab, and another who had beaten the cabbie unconscious. There was a second set of interviews with a gang of looters, and a third with an inconsolable black man whose family market had been mistakenly set on fire. There was one with a breathlessly terrified white man who was running from the melee. Jared had tried his best to console him, maybe to imply that not all Blacks had it in for the white man. And then came the fatal interview with the cop, cut short by the three thuds of the bullets that took Jared away. The tape was still running when the cop tried to clear his action with his men, then ordered: *"Higgins! Radio in some EMT's and get a meat wagon in here!"* Daniel's crusted voice came through so choked-up he didn't recognize it: *"Shut the fuck up!!!! ALL of you!!"* And the tape ran on, capturing the raw emotions of the prisoners of Watts. *"Kill Whitey!" "Kill the Little Man!" "Blood for Bloods!!"* The tirades were short of breath; tightened by the weight of humidity, smoke, and futility.

He turned the tape player off and tried to settle back in the desk-chair. Jared's apartment, once so familiar, had become a cell, calcifying him in place in the grip of isolation and estrangement. He began to type; to let his emotion translate onto the page. Writing the article was a catharsis. He pulled his last page from the platen, and laid it face down upon the others.

Dawn light had finally crept up through the darkness. He stretched to a stand, then limped to the kitchenette to make a quick pot of coffee. The sizzling of the water up into plopping of perks soothed his mind. It was a distraction from the occasional pain throbbing in his calves from the cop's baton he'd been dealt ten hours and so long ago. The smell of fresh coffee seemed to make everything feel right and normal. Cup in hand, he went back to the desk, leaned over the dispatch, and adjusted his glasses. He took another sip of coffee and started re-reading what Jared had typed yesterday morning before he had gone back out into the rebellion:

While Watts Burns
by Jared Solombier

Watts District, South Central L.A., August 12-13, 1965
I've spent tonight ducking for my life around South Central Avenue and Avalon Boulevard. I see burning stores, burning cars and some Molotov cocktails being thrown through shattered store windows to set some of the white-owned shops ablaze. The fires are only a ferocious metaphor for the frustration in the street. I must remind myself that this is not some battle raging in Vietnam, Santa Domingo, or even Newark. And I am not watching it on television. This is L.A. This is Watts in real time, and I am standing in the middle of it. And it is out of control.

What began last summer as an eruption in places such as New York City's South Harlem district, Newark, New Jersey, Rochester, New York, and Chicago has now blown out on the Santa Ana winds to South-Central Los Angeles. The blight has emerged from the hot shadows of Watts and set it afire. Its flames are fanned by the desperation and pent up-anger of the Negroes holed up there; many of them transplants from the east.

They have come here to escape the oppression layered upon them through Jim Crow Laws, which, although swept under the rug, are felt in full force now even here. They have fled to relative freedom from the likes of Birmingham, Alabama's Police Commissioner, "Bull" Connor, Governor George Wallace, and all of that Deep South mentality. They started moving to the promise of Southern California generations ago and have been sequestered in the caldron of Watts ever since. The promise has evolved into nothing but a lost paradise devoid of jobs, decent schooling, and cruel tumbledown turn-of-the-century housing to which the Negro has seemingly been sentenced for life. Add to this the growing existence of an oppressive white police force heavily equipped with thick hickory bats, shotguns, and even machine guns to keep order among the rabble, and we have the makings not only of a riot—but of an insurrection. It has been only a matter of time.

More rioters have attracted more cops, and bigger and more guns. Some Negro snipers have taken to the rooftops to shoot over the heads any skin that looks white while chanting: 'Die, whitey! Die!'

The riot has nearly consumed itself in disorder, like the flames consuming cars and buildings. The tension in the air makes it difficult to breathe. That same air hangs stagnant in the humid, stiff, charcoal smell of burning wood, oddly sweetened by the pungent smells of kerosene and gasoline, and burdened by the weight of the heat. Even without the flames, the air temperature never goes below ninety. A virtual furnace, the stagnant, drenching heat hangs at around 120 degrees down at street-level. Fire-hose water drapes the air and blooms like a plague into the crowd, which has grown from one to five thousand in the four hours I've been here.

And this is only the second night. Reports predict the crowd may swell to ten thousand, as the media does its part to fan the flames. This rebellion, as some of my interviewees refer to it, is going nowhere. It is a feeding frenzy. The chants tell the story.

"Kill whitey!!'

"Blood Power!'

"Death to the Little Man!" (in reference to whites in general)

"Burn, Baby, Burn!" (a term popularized last year by a local disk jockey to praise pop hits)

The blight has been waiting in the shadows for decades. This riot is unlike those back east, which are ostensibly calling for pure justice. The riot in Watts is directed almost solely against whites, and this blind aggression is what is turning the riot into an insurrection.

At around 12:30 a.m., I witnessed a white man being pulled out of his burning car and beaten as he tried to crawl away, while kerosene-fueled Molotov cocktails were hurled through shop widows, bursting the dry-heated timbers quickly into flames. Snipers have taken to the roofs and are randomly firing whatever guns they own or have looted from the many pawn and sporting goods stores in the burning neighborhood. The Negroes accuse the snipers of being white cops, while the cops accuse the snipers of being Negro rioters. Each is condemned by, and to, the color of his skin.

Why the rebellion? What are the denizens of South-Central Los Angeles fighting for? Not for justice, for there can be no justice in an angry, uncontrolled mob fighting in an insurgency that has started to swallow its own tail. Justice may be too much for the Los Angeles Negro to ask for now. As one rioter told me, 'We're fighting for air.'

That precious air, more than any Molotov cocktail, is what is fueling the flames.

Daniel placed the pages back down on the desk, and recognized the passion in Jared's account, energized by purpose. What he'd described was not Daniel's father's brand of sociology—that dull, empirical study sampling of society, like a focus group. Jared had described a culture roiling up from desperation. The frustration raging in Watts was urgent and palpably real, in this city built on image, myth, and illusion. The rebellion in Watts was so much larger than what had happened to Jared and to him.

Through each sip of his coffee, Daniel came to a greater understanding that his uncertain life with Jared had no significance to whatever he was truly seeking. He would miss Jared deeply, but he knew now he really hadn't loved him. True love was too much to ask for in his struggle to survive for himself. And true love was something Daniel now realized he didn't deserve.

He recalled some of what he had seen through the camera viewfinder. Certain images might have been powerful, but who was he to know? What he did know was that his picture-taking had gifted him with a new sort of purpose; maybe even the semblance of an identity to protect him from his fear.

His thoughts turned back to the promise of the thesis he'd write as he slipped the pages into a filing envelope and put it into the tape recorder case. He looped its strap over his shoulder, then left for the *Tribune's* offices. He never wanted to see that fucking tape recorder again.

The rioting had exhausted itself with the arrival of National Guard Units and the rumor of more to come. Some fatigued protestors were trudging back to their apartments, carrying ridiculous booty—Victorian clocks and dying houseplants—mainly for the sake of having pilfered something.

It seemed safe enough for him to drive uptown. He found his six-year-old, grey VW Beetle with its scabs of rust on the rocker panels parked safely in Jared's apartment driveway. His car was so ordinary even the looters had ignored it.

Daniel had shown up a few times at the *Trib* to meet Jared for lunch. Phyllis, the dowdy receptionist up in editorial, recognized him...sort of. "Daniel?" she wondered. "Is that you?"

He noticed his reflection in the window behind her and saw that his face was still smeared with striations of dirt. His eyelashes and lips were crusted with ashy soot. "Oh, yeah, Phyllis. It was rough out there in my neighborhood last night."

She gave him a perplexed look. "So we know. Almost surreal. Jared's not in yet."

"I know." He glanced down at the envelope sticking out from the recorder case. "Is your city editor in?"

"Larry's out flying over Watts. Tony's here, though."

"Can I see him? Jared wanted me to, uh, drop a story off at the city desk."

"Come on in. I'll take you to him. You sure you don't want to wash up a little first? Maybe a cup of coffee?"

Somehow, he felt comfortable in his disguise of grime.

"No. No coffee. I'll wash up after I talk to ...who is it? Tony?"

A quiet anxiety meandered through the antiseptic routine of the *Tribune's* editorial department. A clattering of typewriting and the sounds of staffers rushing around within their glass enclosures accented the confusion as Phyllis led Daniel toward the row of editorial offices.

Clutters of pre-edited articles in their worn-out file folders surrounded Associate City Editor Tony Russo's desk and visitor's chair. An aria from an oversized hi-fi off in a corner softened the edges of the tension. Phyllis introduced Daniel as Jared's friend, and then left the room.

Beneath time-and-worry-worn features accented by his oversized dark-rimmed glasses, Tony Russo had the face of a twenty-year-old. His nervous manner seemed as urgent as the deadline he personified, as he engrossed himself in correcting a dispatch. "Don't have a hell of a lot of time, here. Wha'cha got for me?" he muttered.

"I'm Jared Solombier's roommate." Daniel replied.

Tony redlined something in the piece he was proofing. "Good. He's an okay writer. A little too much flourish, but he's learning...Jesus!" he complained quietly to the article he was editing. He penned something in the margin without looking up. "So. You're his roommate."

Daniel pulled the envelope from the recorder bag and placed it down on Tony's desk. "He wanted me to give you this."

Tony glanced from his task and at the envelope. "Couldn't he bring it in?"

"No."

"Oh-kaay," Tony murmured as he drew Jared's story toward him.

"He wrote it."

"I can see that," he said as he started to read.

"It's about what's happening in Watts. We live there."

Tony held up a hand to silence him. He reached absently for his red pencil and made some scant corrections as he read. Daniel remained quiet for a few minutes until Tony finished editing then laid the pages back on his desk. He looked up at Daniel for the first time. "Shit, man. You look like you've been through a fucking mud bath. What happened?"

"Never mind. What about Jared's article?"

"He was right in the street down there? In the soup?"

"He was."

"We couldn't get anyone in on the ground. And our guy Jared was there all the time. He was there last night during the shit storm? Why didn't he call this dispatch in, so we could've run it this morning?""

"The phones were out. What about the article? Will you publish it?"

"Of course. He was our only guy on the street."

"Do you like the article, Mr. Russo?'

Tony tapped the pencil on his desktop. "Call me Tony, for Christ's sake. Of *course* I like it! Just about the best stuff I've seen from him. The second half might-could use a little more attention, though. A little too personally intense for my taste. Maybe he was just tired."

"I'm glad you liked it."

"I guess he's still out covering it, hunh? That's why he sent you?"

"No. He was...killed."

Tony's expression bloated into that of a landed trout. "WHAT? Holy fucking *SHIT!*" He squinted at Daniel. "You fucking *sure* about that?"

"Shot by a cop, I think. Maybe a sniper. I don't know. He died. They took him away."

"Who?"

"The ambulance. The 'meat wagon,' the cop called it."

"What cop?"

"The cop Jared was interviewing when he was...he was killed. And then the cop was killed. By a sniper, I think." He glanced down at the cassette recorder in its case. "It's all there on the tape. Do you want the tape, too?"

"Fuck, yeah, I'll take the tape."

"I was with him. Here." Daniel put the tape recorder on Tony's desk, then stared out the 24th-floor window overlooking downtown Los Angeles. Harsh sunlight hit the facades of the skyline, setting it off clean contrasts of shadow and muted pastels accented by glints from the glass. The view seemed so pristine here a world away from the smoked-up, burned down guts of Watts. He felt he had come here from a place across town that defied logic. He glanced back at Tony. "I was his wingman. I was taking pictures. Do you want my pictures?"

"Shit, yes, man."

"Yeah. Well, maybe you can use them. Maybe not. I don't care," He placed a wrinkled paper bag containing the twenty rolls of Tri-X next to the recorder case.

Tony scooped the film into a rush pack to send down to the lab for processing. He clicked his intercom on and called for a runner. "Look. Sorry. I didn't get your name at first. How can we reach you if we need to?"

Daniel conjured up a sad smile. "I'm Daniel Lilienthal, Jared's friend and roommate. I guess you can reach me at his place for the next couple of days. I think phones will be back up by noon. I saw some utility men working when I left. I suppose after that you can find me up at Berkeley. I'm a sociology grad student there."

Tony thought his comment over. "Lilienthal. Sociology. Are you related to that guy Roger Lilienthal, the sociologist?"

"He's my father."

"I've read some of his books. Brilliant guy...if you like that sort of shit."

Daniel's feeble attempt at a smile fell flat. "I don't, really."

Tony suspected Jared had maybe been more than a friend to Daniel. "I'm real sorry for your loss, Daniel. For all our sakes."

The office runner peeped in through Tony's open door. "You need something, Tony?"

Tony held up the bag of film. "Yeah. Get these down to processing." The runner took the bag and left. "I'm gonna aim to get Jared's story on the front page tomorrow morning. Above the fold." There was a somber reverence in his tone as the loss of his best cub reporter continued to sink in. "It's the least and the most we can do…to honor his loss."

"Yeah. Thanks, Tony."

A merciful tension had numbed Daniel into a weird sort of indifference — or maybe it was exhaustion. He could do little else but sit on Jared's couch and stare catatonically at a baseball game on the quieted television. He lit a cigarette, got up from the couch, and went to the kitchen to get himself a beer.

As the head on his beer settled, he stared down at the filigree of its foam, trying to read into its significance. He took one sip and then another while the phone rang four times. He took a healthy chug, then went to answer it.

CHAPTER FOUR

The Decisive Moment

The thick voice on the other end of the line was abrupt and muffled "Dan Labenthal?"

Daniel cleared his throat to break up the bite of the cigarette smoke. "Lilienthal."

"Oh, right. How do you want your photo credit to read?"

"Who *is* this?"

"Yeah. Sorry, kid. This is Larry Graham, city editor of the *L.A. Tribune*. Look. I got the contact sheets of your Watts photos, here. Gotta tell ya, they're really good. You mind if we use a few?"

"That's why I left them with you. How did you like Jared's article?"

"Jared's artic—oh yeah, the guy who wrote it."

Daniel tightened in offense. "Yeah, Mr. Graham. But that 'guy' died getting the story. I thought you should know."

Larry answered after an awkward silence. "Yeah, Russo told me. He was a real asset to us. The kid showed a helluvalot of promise. And it's a helluva good piece. We're running it on the front page of the morning edition. Just below the fold. With your pictures. 'S why I need a photo credit."

"Just call it something like: 'Photo by Jared's friend' No. 'Jared's Brother.'"

"You his brother?"

Daniel pondered this. "Yeah...once removed."

"Well, kid. We can't do that—we need a name. Daniel Lilienthal? Dan Lilienthal? Danny Lilienthal? What?"

"Okay, then. Dan Lilienthal. Use that."

"And so we will. Anyway. That's not the reason I called. Usually, I have Russo call over things like photo credits." Daniel heard the flick of a lighter as Larry paused to light up. "Listen, kid. I got a proposition for you. Your photos, like I said, are real good. Who are you working for now?"

"Working for?"

"Yeah, what paper? Something up there in San Francisco near Berkeley, where you told Russo you're a student? You're not with *The Chronicle*, I hope."

"No."

"Oh, you're a freelancer, then. Good."

"Not that either."

"Oh, well. How long you been a photographer?"

Daniel thought this over. "About two days?"

Larry was becoming annoyed, and Daniel could tell that wasn't exactly foreign territory for him. "Don't toy with me, kid. I know you been shooting around the riot for a few days. What I mean is what kinda experience have you had?"

"Seriously, Mr. Graham. Jared just handed me the camera a few days ago and I started taking pictures."

"Well, then, Dan. If you shot this stuff right outta the gate, then you got the gift. Stuff's amazingly good. Good enough we wanna use more of it in next Sunday's magazine supplement. You mind?"

"Of course not. Go ahead."

"Okay. There's something else. You're up in Berkeley? On campus?"

"Uh, yeah."

"There are some student demonstrations goin' on up there? I mean like that thing last May?"

"Uh, yeah. Sometimes."

"Okay. Look. I'm gonna pass your contact sheets on to Marty Bloomfield on our San Francisco office. He's looking for a stringer. You game?"

"Well, yeah. I guess. I'm not sure what it is you want me to do."

"You're shittin' me kid. With *your* eye? The kinds of pictures you take?"

"Mr. Graham. I've got to tell you. I'm a sociology grad student. I'm not a photographer."

"Yes you are. Can you write?"

"A little I guess."

"Good. 'Cause we can edit." Daniel heard Larry's intercom the background: *Mr. Graham. Marty Bloomfield for you.* "Tell 'im I'll call 'im right back," he grumbled off to the side. "Bloomfield'll want an answer about this, Dan. He'll wanna talk to you about you being our man in Berkeley. The pay should be more than enough to keep you in beer. The exposure's the real payoff, though. What do I tell Marty, Dan? You with us?"

He thought about Larry's offer, then answered: "Sure. I'll give it a try."

"Good. Listen, the National Guard's goin' into Watts to keep some order there. Can you get out again today and tomorrow to shoot some more pictures? You can drop your film off on Monday morning. That way, you and me can talk a few more specifics. You gonna need any more cameras? I think we got a few spares lying around I can messenger over to you."

He looked over at his Pentax on the coffee table. "No, Mr. Graham, thanks, though. I've got the camera I need for now."

"Great, kid. Sociology, eh? Any good at it?"

"Passable, I suppose."

"How's that goin' for you? You happy in it?"

"I don't think so."

"Then take some advice from a twenty-five-year newshound who knows a good eye when he sees one. You're missing out on a gift. Change your major to journalism and photography."

"I'll give it some thought."

"Do more than that, Dan. Go do it. Welcome aboard, kid. And don't forget to call Marty Bloomfield with your contact info when your feet hit the dirt in San Fran.

"Thanks, Mr. Graham. Thank you very much."

"Bye, kid. Monday, ten a.m. See you then" Larry gruffed, then hung up the phone.

For the first time in months, Daniel felt an inkling of hope and relief. He lifted his beer from where he'd placed it next to the phone and took a sip

He went out to the balcony and stared down at the street. A military Jeep-led a convoy of one troop truck, followed by a column of fire trucks with Guardsmen toting their M-14s riding shotgun on the running boards. Some of the firetrucks carried a Guardsman poised behind a tripod-mounted machine gun among the coiled hoses in the back. He rushed back in, plucked up his camera and a few leftover rolls of film and then rushed toward the door.

Marty Bloomfield, patrician-looking and very fit for someone in his late-fifties, leaned back in his chair set caddy-corner to where Daniel sat sipping bad institutional coffee from a paper cup. Daniel's build was slight, and the couch in which he sat overwhelmed him.

"Loved your work from Watts. You certainly have an eye, and a gift to capture the emotion of your subject. 'The Decisive Moment,' Cartier-Bresson called it." In contrast to Larry Graham — a gruff and overweight chain-cigar-smoker who worked in shirtsleeves while he dug through the grit and muck of hard news — Marty had an easy, professorial, old-school manner about him; the type that might be accentuated by a pipe and patches on the elbows of a tweed jacket.

"Who?"

"Henri Cartier-Bresson, a famous French photojournalist from the 30s and 40s. Surprised you don't know his work. You'd probably recognize it. He's regarded by some as the father of photojournalism."

Daniel managed a nervous smile. "I don't know if Mr. Graham told you. I've had no background in photography. This is my first attempt."

Marty looked down at the contact sheets and then shook his head a little. "Remarkable."

"I'm a sociology grad student."

"I know. Up at Berkeley. Daniel, would you be willing to jump ship and change majors if we took you on here at *The Los Angeles Tribune*?"

Daniel tweaked an uncertain smile over this perfect opportunity for him to finally rise from his father's control. "Mr. Graham suggested that. I've decided to switch my major, yeah."

"I think that's a good choice for you. It's not really a stretch, just a different form of sociological study. More from the inside of culture. You should be able to port over what you've learned. To your advantage, and by extension, to ours."

"I'll need four faculty recommendations to change majors."

"I can get you two, and I'll have the *Tribune* write an endorsement. That should do it. You may need to get a recommendation for yourself from the sociology department."

Daniel proffered another scant smile. "I hope I can get one. They've been giving me certain...compensations."

"I know. Your father's good clout for them, I suppose. That'll have to be your fight. Berkeley's Sociology Department might not be too anxious to lose you. "

An office runner knocked on Marty's doorjamb. He held up a file folder. "From the photo lab, Mr. Bloomfield. I overnighted a duplicate set to Mr. Graham."

"Ah, thanks, Bob," he said, leaning from his chair to reach the short distance to take the file. "Your contacts from late Saturday and yesterday." He opened the file folder with five contact sheets from the experimental assignment he'd given Daniel a week before—photos of some homeless people in the Mission District. He took a photo loupe-magnifier from his pocket, and quickly examined some choice frames. "Really good work," he said. He stopped to examine one of the frames more closely. "The expression you captured on this this person's face is compelling." He looked up from the sheet and leveled a light blue-eyed gaze at Daniel. "I regard a good photo as more powerful than film, where the image is lost. The motion picture serves to record events in time. The single frame is lost. A photograph is indelible because it preserves a *moment* in time—a single image you can remember and call upon. I see lots of good images here. You'll be an asset to the *Trib*. So. Let's get you started in journalism, shall we?

Daniel smiled naturally. "Yes, Mr. Bloomfield, we shall."

CHAPTER FIVE

Our Man in Berkeley

Tony Russo met Daniel for lunch during the few trips Daniel made down from Berkeley over the following weeks. The first time he presented Daniel with the printed *Trib's* Sunday Magazine supplement featuring his Watts photography and the copy that Tony had re-written from the tape recordings, Jared's editorial and Daniel's notes. The interim between their meetings was peppered with phone calls as they became fast friends. Their third lunch meeting was in a deli where they immersed themselves in the clattering din of conversation punctuated by a baritone infusion of orders called from the counter to the kitchen.

"Has your dad gotten over the shock of you dropping out of sociology?" Tony asked as they sat hunched over a too-small table. He bit into his sloppy corn-beef on rye.

"Ah, Antonio. All of life is sociology," Daniel replied as he tried to will away the pervading redolence of spent old grease. "At least that's what I told him. I also told him I'd spend my career documenting culture from within. I think he liked that. For the next week at least. Then he got pissed when I told him I'd be too busy to research the rest of his book." He made a sour face as he gazed at some fennel he'd speared with his plastic fork, then slipped the questionable leaf into his mouth.

"Busy on what? Your studies?"

"Not really. Those are easy. Journalism's like sociology, but a whole shitload easier to learn. It's all the same kind of bullshit, anyway. It's all theater."

Tony had been glancing furtively at a willowy young woman sitting by herself. "Ah, the true moral of life. Everything is bullshit, like some sorta sideshow," he said distractedly as he kept her in his sights.

"Absolutely. Anyway, they matriculated some of my previous classes. Thanks to Larry's influence and my Watts photos, they put me on a fast track toward a journalism degree by the summer of sixty-seven."

Tony raised his pilsner glass in a toast. "Our Man in Berkeley. Here's to The *Trib*'s philanthropic efforts to advance the cause of higher journalism."

"Hear, hear," Daniel said as he sipped the remains of his beer. "And to your friend and mine, Marty Bloomberg and all his clout."

"Yeah. Marty, too. As long as we can educate him on all the cultural changes since the Battle of the Bulge. He's very old school." He held up two fingers in a V to a passing waitress signifying two more beers. He stared at his hand. "Hey, there you go. Churchill's 'Victory' gesture."

"Hold your fingers like that and turn your hand around so you're looking at the back of it."

He did. "What's that, Daniel? Some sorta Jewish 'fuck-you-very-much' gesture?"

"Sort of. It's a peace sign. We're seeing that a lot around campus since the Vietnam Day Committee teach-in last May. "

Tony put his hand down. "Sort of an inversion from Churchill's victory-through-bombing-the-hell-out-of-the-Germans   indicator. Guess there's a symmetry there." He took another bite of his sandwich. "You gonna be marching in that crowd next week?"

"I have Marty's blessing to cover it. Along with his reserved enthusiasm."

"That's the most you'll get out of him...reserved enthusiasm. Hell, he doesn't even lighten up for the office Christmas party."

"Yeah, well I may have certain...connections to get me in tight. It might make for a good inside story. It's planned to be a big deal."

"Well if you're gonna tape anything, don't use that same crappy recorder Jared used in Watts."

"I gave that back to you. I never wanna see that thing again."

"Just as well. That clunky old thing and its cheesy little mic made everyone sound like they were on helium in a submarine. I'll get you a better and smaller recorder from the 'cage,' where the *Trib* keeps its spares. I'll also get you one of our cool field vests. It'll mark you as a bonafide journalist."

"Why that would be very nice of you, Antonio."

Tony became pensive as he stared down at his sandwich. "How're you coping after, you know, since Jared...?"

Daniel felt a surge of dismay creep in as he thought about his answer. "Coping...trying to erase it all."

"I, uh, sensed you two were very close, Dan. I'm so sorry. I can see the pain in your face from time to time."

"I guess we were close for a while. I didn't think it showed."

Tony paused, considering his response. "Not everybody notices, buddy. I just know because I've, uh, been there myself. I lost a woman I thought I loved and knew. She died from heroin." He looked down at the remains of his sandwich. He was brought back into the moment as the waitress placed two beers on the table. "Thanks, doll."

She shot him a dark glower. "Don't call me *doll*," she grumbled, then added: "...you dumb jerk," as she walked through the greasy air toward the kitchen.

Tony took a final bite of his sandwich. "My kinda woman. Anyway, if you ever want to talk about it, just know you can."

"Thanks, Tony. Really"

"Consider it done. Oh!" he suddenly brightened. "Did I tell you I've put in for a transfer?"

"Really. Where?"

"International desk. Assistant managing editor. I guess maybe I'll be editing the war if I get the job."

"That's great, Antonio. That war needs editing."

"Yeah. It'd be good career move for me. Even though Larry's a little pissed he'll lose me as his batman on City Desk, he thinks it's for the best. Like he told me: 'Only a kid like you young enough to be fighting in the trenches of that mother-fucking war can really be crazy enough to understand it enough to write about it'. Words to that effect."

"Well, then, Larry's very wise. Hear, hear to Larry. Again"

"Hear, hear, to Larry...and that mother-fucking war...and the stories it tells," Tony said, and then swigged his beer.

Two weeks later Tony and Daniel pored over some prints from the Vietnam Day Committee demonstration Daniel had covered at Berkeley a few days before. Tony selected a photo of the crowd being held at bay by a line of police behind their riot shields. One of the cops was yelling something at the demonstrators. "Shit. This looks a little imposing."

"Actually, the crowd was uneasily peaceful. Mostly, they just stood there and chanted like that's all they needed to do."

Tony examined another photo—this one of Allen Ginsberg and Ken Kesey leading a circus of teens draped in bright-colored rags. Ginsberg's hair was tied in a loose queue atop his head. "Who are these nubile kids?"

"Merry Pranksters. They came up on Ken Kesey's psychedelic bus from his commune in La Honda. They were all pretty well tripped-out on LSD."

"They look it." He narrowed his gaze at a tubby, shirtless bearded man. "Oh jeeze, is that...?

"Allen Ginsberg. He's gone native."

Tony shook his head. "He looks more like a welterweight sumo wrestler." He selected a third photo showing some motorcycle toughs launching into the protesters. "Looks like it's getting a little ugly here."

"Yeah. When the cops held back some Hell's Angels, things did get kind of rough. The bikers got off on it a little."

"What about the demonstrators?"

"They just watched and cowered." Daniel pointed to an enraged figure in the crowd with an unruly mass of curly black hair over his eyes. "There's Jerry Rubin."

"No shit," Tony mused.

"No shit. And he gave us a gift." Daniel held up couple of joints.

"Hey, buddy, as much as I'd wish they'd change the rules around here, there's no joint-smoking in the offices. Cigarettes, cigars and other crap that might kill you quicker are fine. Just no weed."

"I know," Daniel said as he set the joints on Tony's desk. "It's for you. For later. Rubin's a weed connoisseur. This particular brand is from his private stock imported from Tijuana."

Tony's expression brightened. "Really? For *me*? What a thoughtful bribe. Thank him for me, would ya, Dan?" He put them in his shirt pocket and then lifted another photo. It was a close-up profile showing Ginsberg staring down a Hell's Angel. The biker's gaze was perplexed as the poet flicked his finger cymbals together near his face. "What the hell is this?"

"That's Ginsberg pinging his little Hare Krishna cymbals at a Hell's Angel."

"Well, that's some sorta paradox, to say the least. It would make a helluva story if the biker ended up punching Ginsberg's teeth in."

"Actually, it turned out to be the other way around. Ginsberg, Kesey and some of their Merry Pranksters went to the Hell's Angel's president's place."

"Hell's Angels has a president?"

"Well, it *is* a democracy after all. Anyway, they shared some weed and LSD along with some Hare Krishna chanting. Then, the next morning, Ginsberg and Kesey emerged as honorary members of The Hell's Angels."

Tony sputtered a laugh. "Hell's Angels chanting Hare Krishna? Jesus Christ, that is fucking surreal!"

"'Tis the season, I suppose. Strange days, these."

Tony stacked the prints together. "Guess I'll have to interpret these for Marty when I send them to him." He patted this shirt pocket. "Meantime, buddy, this shit's burning a hole in my pocket. Since we I can't light up these things in here, I say we go out to Echo Park and toke on 'em. Then we can grab some lunch — on me for a change."

"I thought you'd never ask, Tony."

"Yeah, well, you've done some great stuff for the *Trib*, and the word's out. Even your writing's improved—a little—thanks to my efforts, mostly. Stick with me and someday you and I will make a great team."

"Someday. Have you heard anything about your bid for the international desk?"

"No. And Larry hasn't even mentioned it. He wants to keep me right here."

"He probably just doesn't want you to get killed in Vietnam. I get that."

"Shit, I'm not gonna get killed. I'm The Press. I'll have a whole army to protect me." A *Rigoletto* aria from surged from his hi-fi. He swirled a finger around in the air as though he was conducting an orchestra. "Here it comes. Wait for it…wait for it…" The aria's refrain tore through the relative tranquility. "Ahh, masterful! My man, Verdi."

"Jesus-Louise-us, Tony. How can you stand all that cat-screeching?"

"I'm Italian, man. I *have* to love it. It's in my DNA."

"Have you tried listening to Dylan?"

"I don't know. Is he Italian?"

A faraway smile flowed across Daniel's lips. "No. He's Jewish. And that's in *my* DNA."

CHAPTER SIX

Father and Son

As Daniel sat across from his father at Fabrizio's Fish House, he watched him pour another oyster down his gullet like a bird swallowing a worm. The atmosphere of the place featured wet, old seafood fragrances weighted by drawn butter. Daniel was normally impartial to seafood, but here in Roger's presence he hated it. The smell of it. The taste of it. The petty annoyances of the place only amplified his discomfort as father and son sat facing each other like wary strangers. The sounds of silverware against china clinked politely through the air as Daniel dabbled his fork around his salad. He reminded himself he had to remain cool here on the battlefield, and not expose the soft underbelly.

"You haven't touched your dinner, Dan."

"Not hungry."

"Um," was all Roger said.

Roger was done up well in his three-piece grey suit and red paisley tie, playing the part of businessman-sociologist. He had grayed at the temples since Daniel had seen him last, most likely to look more distinguished than his son knew him to be. He'd even traded his thick, black-framed glasses for wireframes to be California hip.

Daniel broke the ice. "How was your conference in Sacramento?"

"Same as last year. Too many eggheads and not enough objectivity."

"Okay. Good, I guess. How's mom doing? She and I haven't talked in a few months."

"You really should call her, Dan. She asked about you when I talked to her a few weeks ago."

"I suppose I've been too busy. It's nice to know you two are still talking, though."

"Too busy romping around with your camera taking pictures?"

Daniel felt the chill of his father's remark as he concentrated on moving a few lettuce leaves around with his fork. "Well, it's what I do, so… Anyway, how is mom?"

Roger daubed some oyster juice from his lips with his napkin. "Last I heard, she'd moved from Skokie to Racine. She complained that Chicago was becoming overrun by Nazis, and unsafe for Jews."

"So, she moved to Wisconsin?"

"And she's lactose intolerant, so figure that one out. I guess she reasoned that there'd be no Nazis there because no one knows Wisconsin exists."

"So, it's gotten worse. This whole Jewish thing."

"She's been bitten hard by the faith. If she were any more Jewish, she'd be shaving her head and donning a *shietel* and a black headscarf. I could never really figure that out. Women shaving their hair off to wear a wig, and then wearing a scarf to cover the wig." His voice fell off as he was distracted by the looks of a high-cheeked twenty-something girl-woman sitting alone at a neighboring table. Her face was framed by a soft, long curtain of auburn hair. Daniel knew enough about his father to surmise what he was thinking: Roger liked women with long auburn hair and voluptuous lips. Maybe this one would like some company.

Daniel shivered his shoulders. "To each her own, I guess, Roger. I'll call her."

"Call who?" Roger said distracted.

"Your ex-wife. My mother. I'll call her."

"You really should call your mother more often, Dan."

"Yeah, I will."

"Do that," Roger said into the distance.

Daniel glanced over toward where Roger was looking. "Jesus, Roger. She's young enough to be one of your freshmen. Speaking of that, are you still dating that teenager? Have you taken her to the prom, yet?"

Roger shot him an accusatory glare. "Bite your tongue, Dan. Robin is three years older than you." His glare turned thoughtful. "And, unlike you, she's preparing her dissertation. She'll have her PhD from NYU in two years."

Daniel sipped his beer as he let Roger's snark slide by. "Sounds like she's dedicated. Is she gonna end up teaching, like you?"

Roger sipped another oyster down. "Umm. No. She wants to go on to do field work."

And probably to be away from you, Daniel reckoned. "What's her specialty going to be?"

"Children and the adaptation to their culture. Strictly Piaget stuff. She's thinking about starting in the Middle East, then she wants to go to Africa."

"So, she'll be leaving you to dry out all alone back at Columbia?"

Roger held his fork and its oyster halfway to his mouth. "What the hell is *that* supposed to mean?"

"Nothing really. Just that you'll have more free time on your hands. I mean, there's only so much squash you can play."

"I'll get by okay. It'll give me more time to write my books."

"Working on any now?"

"Yeah. It's one about the cultural stigma of Jews and banking. I'm calling it 'The Plight of the Gilded Jew'."

"That sounds intriguing."

"Yeah, I guess. If not a tad bit trite. My editor wants it done by next March." He looked provocatively over the rim of his cheap wireframes. "I can't see that happening if I have to write it alone."

Daniel ignored Roger's innuendo and forked a lettuce leaf.

Roger concentrated on trying to capture a Brussel sprout rolling around like a pinball on his greasy plate. "So, any little dalliances you want to tell me about? Any pretty surfer girls you've hooked up with?"

"Surfers are a little bit south of here. Near L.A. mostly."

"Okay. Anyone in your life now?" He speared the Brussel sprout. "Ah! Got you, you son of a bitch." He popped it in his mouth.

"You'll be the first to know. So, how's your teaching going?" It was a prickly question that Daniel regretted asking even as it came out. He braced himself for the answer.

"Why don't you apply to Columbia's sociology department and find out?"

There it was. Roger's *raison d'etre* for meeting with his son. "I don't want to. I'm happy where I am, thanks, Roger."

"I could fast track you into the master's program right away. And then into NYU for your doctorate."

"So I can help you research your books."

"Yeah. That, too, Dan. We made a pretty good team, don't you think?"

Roger spooned out his final oyster and let it slip into his mouth, causing Daniel to cringe. "No thank you, father."

"No thank you, *father*? We've known each other long enough to be on our first name basis."

"I call you that because you *are* my father. And I am your son, not your protégée."

"Look, Dan. I think I know why you changed your major. It was to prove your point to me. Well, point taken."

"Really? And what was this point?"

"You didn't think I was giving you enough exposure for the work you helped me with. I get that, and I'm sorry. So, here's what I can do. I'll put your name under mine on my book covers as co-author. That should give you a lot of clout to get into NYU."

"That's big of you, Roger." Daniel replied, then jabbed his fork into a slice of tomato.

Roger sipped on his martini. "Now you're just being ungrateful. You can't be happy running around taking snapshots for a living. You belong in sociology, and you know it, Dan."

"No, Roger. I *don't* know that."

"Sure, you do."

Roger had always been an expert at keeping his cool. It was probably what made him such a good professor, which led his students to respect him more than Daniel could. Roger's patience just aggravated Daniel more. It was as though his father knew he had the upper hand. Well, not this time.

"Thanks for thinking about me, Roger, but I'm happy doing work for the *Los Angeles Tribune*. I believe I've found my true niche."

"Taking pictures for *that* rag? Hell, they backed *Goldwater*. Look, if you come to Columbia, I can lock you solid into a student deferment."

"I am now. And I have a heart murmur, remember?"

"That's not going to stop them from nabbing you. The draft will be going for the more wasted majors such as yours. That's how Johnson's running things, now."

"'Wasted majors?'"

"Yeah, yours. The arts and crafts ones. Sociology's a crucial major, enough to protect you from going into that God-damn war."

Daniel tensed his jaw. *Arts and Crafts*? "For all you know I might be going over there, anyway. There's a reason the *Tribune* is pushing me through for a journalism degree. They really like my work and want me to be a photographer on their payroll. And soon. I think they have it in mind to send me to Vietnam as one of their photojournalists."

Roger put his fork and knife down and took a deep breath as he collected his thoughts. "The fuck they *will*! I didn't prepare you all these years to go over and get killed in some rice paddy in the name of that senseless war." He moved his napkin with thoughtful deliberation from one side of his plate to the other. "I'm not asking you, Dan. I'm telling you. I'm bringing you back with me to New York and away from that God-damned conservative rag of yours. I'll pay them their price to take you back to where you belong and away from that Boschian situation you've put yourself into. You are not going to that war! No way in hell."

"No, Roger. I like it here in San Francisco, four-thousand whatever miles away from y—from New York."

Roger dismissed this. "Pack your things. You'll be flying out with me the day after tomorrow."

Daniel pounded his fist on the table. "You think you've got my life all planned out just like before, don't you, Roger?" His chair scraped loudly against the terra-cotta tiles as he shot up to a stand. "No fucking way you're doing that to me! Not again. Never again."

"Sit down, son. You're making an ass of yourself."

"Fuck you, man! This is San Francisco, and I can make as much of an ass of myself as I want!"

Some guys at a neighboring table applauded lightly.

Daniel turned to go, and his vision was caught by the auburn-haired girl-woman's curious gaze at them. "Hey there," he leaned toward her to confide. "See this old guy here? He wants to take you home tonight, and then to New York." She smiled coyly in response, first at Daniel, then at Roger.

"I *love* this fucking town!" the guy from the neighboring table gushed.

Daniel realized he did, too. But loneliness can be the curse of independence, and without Roger he felt numb and alone as he strode toward the door.

"Call me when you come to your senses, Dan." Roger called after him.

"Fat chance," Daniel muttered as he wended his way through the smoky gloom and fish smells.

He stepped out the door into an alien world that existed beyond Roger's sphere of apathy—that soggy place where love had been merely a weak concept to break a man down.

From the safe distance of the sidewalk, Daniel stopped to peer through the restaurant window at his father sitting alone and staring at the remains on his plate. He eventually summoned a waiter and ordered another drink as if nothing had happened. Watching Roger sip what was left of his martini, Daniel now understood how much he'd cheated himself and how, for twenty-three years, he'd allowed it to happen.

He yearned to experience unselfish love at least once in his life, and perhaps to finally love himself. Beyond the confidence he was finding through his photography, he longed for a person to love him.

He looked deeper through the window to take a parting glance at his father, who was now being joined by the smiling girl-woman. Daniel knew that even she wouldn't be enough to cure his father's insecurity and loneliness.

He framed him through the camera in his mind.

Focus. *Saddak-thwip…*re-load…re-focus.

PART TWO

Johanna

CHAPTER SEVEN
Swimtime

Burdened with the sour cocktail of boredom and her fear of the unknown, Johanna Montaigne lounged poolside at The Waldo Point Yacht Club. She tightened her gaze toward the glimmers off the wavelets in the club's swimming pool as she fretted over the shadow on the base of her brain that Dr. Kornfield had told her not to worry about. That was all of two weeks ago, before he went to Puerto Rico to attend to the more important matter of his golfmanship. Through another fluttering headache, she felt the damp weight of swelling behind her tired eyes, then another vague choke of dry tears. *Now, girl, stop that!* she told herself, *It's not like you're already dead—at least not yet.*

But that thing looming in Johanna's brain took her back into the moment though another spike of headache. She craved a solution to take away her dread, not so much of dying anymore, but of dying alone. *Stop that, Johanna! Just* stop *it!* She forced her thoughts away and off into the possibility that maybe Dr. Kornfield was right; that she shouldn't worry, at least not for today. Instead, she vowed to eat more beets and take a swig or two of Geritol in deference to his diagnosis of iron-poor blood.

She placed the earpiece of her transistor radio into her right ear and then patted a plait of her hair over it. No! She would *never* let the treatment for this fucking thing take her hair. She turned up the music loud enough to absorb her anguish:

> *"Hot town! Summer in the city!*
> *Back o' my neck feeling dirty and gritty…"*

She let the sunlight caress her as she fell into a precious sleep for a few minutes, which stretched into a quarter-of-an-hour.

The ice in her morning grapefruit juice had melted into a murky obscurity flecked with rind as she woke to the din from her radio. She cringed slightly as she sipped the bitter remains of her drink. Some dribbled down the front of her beach shift.

"Shit," she muttered.

She yearned for a carefree moment to distract her from the grasp of her depression as she sang off key to "Rainy Day Women":

> *"They'll stone you when you're walkin' on the floor*
> *They'll stone you when you're walkin' to the door*
> *"But I would not feel so all alone…"*

She raised her arm and twirled her hand in the air as her voice rose discordant and coarse in defiance of her mood:

> "Everybody *must get stoned!!*"

"God, Jo! Take some singing lessons, already! You sound even *worse* than Dylan."

She squinted through her sunglasses at who said this. "You shut up, Nathan, you creep. You go take some lessons in not being such a dickhead." Her hair fell by degrees in a short disarrayed skein to her shoulders as she crooked a knee and supported herself up on her elbows. She swiped a quick glance at the guy standing behind Nate, who was adjusting his over-sized aviator glasses as if he was trying to hide behind them.

Her hand took on its occasional tremble as she raised her sunglasses to her forehead and pouted impishly to accent her dimples. Her tightened expression morphed into a burst of adolescent wonder. Her lips, set in a feigned severity, curled up mischievously on the verge of a feral smile. A glimmer rose in her crystalline aqua-blue eyes.

"Hello, anyway, Nathan."

"Hello, Miss Montaigne."

Johanna looked down at the grapefruit dribble on her white chintz tunic. "Oh, *shit*!" she recalled. "I spilled my fucking drink and ruined my pool-shift!" She tried to daub the stain out with a napkin—an exercise in futility.

"That's 'cause you're a total klutz, Jo," said Nate as he stole one of her Salems from the pack on her chaise-side table.

"Oh, sure, Nathan, go ahead and steal my cigarettes. What's mine is yours, you dweeb," she muttered while concentrating on the stain. She looked up and cast a sideways glance at his friend as Nate lit his cigarette.

"Take pity on me, Jo. Lynda and I have split up and I feel like shit."

"I know. I heard. I'm happy for Lynda"

"Well, I feel like shit." He took a long drag and made a sour face. "Criminey! How can you smoke these menthol things?"

She held up a hand and scissored her first and second fingers. "You are welcome to give it back, then."

He handed it to her, and she inhaled on it while taking a closer look at the two guys standing there like lost souls blocking her sun. They looked as though they might have been manufactured in the same batch. Their lean and hungry looks relayed the appearences of having wandered though some private but separate desolations. They had similar musses of hair; Nate's a dusty blond-brown, and his friend's the color of cured copper; almost like hers, minus the blonde highlights. He had a provocative confusion of forelock covering half his forehead. She liked that.

In the moment she felt comfortable for the first time since Dr. Kornfield's muted prognosis tore her away from the carefree girl she used to be. "You two look like brothers." She cocked her head toward Daniel. "Are you dim-wit Nathan's long-lost twin brother? Anyway, hello. I'm Johanna."

His friend seemed at a loss for words. Nate nudged him and said, "And *you* are...?" Then to Johanna, "You'll have to pardon my friend here, Jo. He's a little shy because he's Jewish."

The other's glower toward Nate turned into a searing glare.

"Oh. That's nice," she said as she continued to worry over the stain soaking into her shift.

"Uh...Dan-Daniel?" he answered numbly. "I'm Daniel?"

Her smile turned crooked as she glanced up at him. "Are you asking me?"

"Yeah, Jo," Nate confirmed for him. "This is my friend, Dan. Watch what you say. He's a reporter."

"Really," she replied with feigned interest.

"Yeah," Daniel said. He glanced around at all the surrounding Protestants. "And I'm also not Jewish. I'm a Unitarian."

She twiddled the delicate gold pendant hanging from her thin necklace. "So? I tried being a Druid once. But by birth, I am half-Brazilian and half-Jewish, at least on my mother's side." She felt a choke in her voice as she referred to her mother.

Nate surveyed the deck for lonely-looking young women because he'd become desperate since Lynda brushed him off. "And how'd that Druid thing work out for you, Jo?" he quipped.

"Not very well. I got bored by all the tree-worshiping but got a kick out of the pagan stuff." She lifted a tube of suntan oil from her beach bag and daubed some of it on her nose and cheeks, and then on the tops of her breasts.

"Including the human sacrifices?" Daniel asked.

She looked up at him and flickered another coy smile. "Mother of God! How to kill a moment!" She jabbed a puff on her cigarette. "So, Dan-Daniel. You are a reporter?"

"Uh, yeah. Photojournalist. For the *L.A. Tribune*?"

She sighed out a languorous stream of cigarette smoke. "You're asking me again? Okay, then. You are a photojournalist for the *L.A. Tribune*." She glanced over at Nate. "I like him. He's cute, but he needs a little work. He's not married or anything, is he? You think he might ask me out?"

"I don't know, Jo. Why don't you ask *him*?"

The line of conversation had momentarily stunned Daniel. "I, uh. I don't know." He looked helplessly over at Nate. "Do you think I should?"

Johanna snickered. "There he goes again. Asking."

"Jeee-zuz, man! How come you're asking *me*?" Nate groused. "You two are all grown up. Make your *own* sense out of it!" He sipped his beer empty and then glanced sadly at the bottle as though he had killed off a friend. "I'm gonna get another beer," he announced as he walked away. "You guys want anything from the bar?" He didn't wait for an answer as his voice followed him away.

Johanna squinted at Daniel as if trying to choose what dress to wear. She had met men like him before—the lost type who wanted to, but hoped against hope not to be approached. She'd felt that way many times before—such as now—and felt drawn to him as she sensed they had their separate sad secrets.

"Okay, Dan-Daniel," she decided. "I'll answer for you." She blew out a final stream of smoke and decisively tamped out her cigarette in a tin ashtray. "You are going to ask me out for dinner. I can see you need some fattening-up and I like Chinese food. "

"Oh, *yoo*-hoo!" came an uncomfortably familiar sing-song voice from a few lounges down.

Lynda approached carrying her traditional glass of beer and ice cubes stuck with a straw. She'd once told Johanna that she put ice in her beer to lose weight. Fat chance. She waved enthusiastically as though she was greeting a returning troop ship. "Oh, shit," Daniel said, awakening from his diffidence. "Look. I need a beer. Do you want anything from the bar?"

Johanna found his reaction perplexing. Had Lynda doused him, too? "No," she said. "Stay." Her imploring glance inferred: *please*.

"*There* you are!" Lynda's voice gushed as she approached. "I've been looking alllll *over* for you, Jo."

"I've been here for the last few hours, Lynn. At my usual spot."

Johanna cringed as Lynda planted a passing kiss on Daniel's cheek. "I *love* this guy!" she said as a blush reddened his face. Johanna lowered her sunglasses and lay back on the chaise to escape the farce that seemed to follow Lynda wherever she went out in public.

"Yeah, hi, Lynn. I didn't recognize you with your clothes on,"

Daniel said as he gazed at her in her scanty — sooo cute — pink bikini, "such as they are."

"What?" Johanna gasped as she quickly swiped up her sunglasses and squinted at Lynda and then at Daniel. A shadow of aggression crossed her face and ignited a glint in eyes.

Muffled echoes of pool splashes swelled the rhetoric of the ensuing silence.

Lynda smiled mischievously and tousled his hair. "He's *sooo* sweet! Anyway, yeah, we all went bare-naked sunbathing and swimming from Peter's boat a few weeks ago," Lynda gushed again. "Danny's got the *cutest* buns and a little birthmark right here." She brazenly poked a finger high up on his inner thigh.

"Danny?" Johanna said.

"Alright, Lynn," Daniel blushed. "That'll do."

"Yeah, Lynn," Johanna simmered. "That *will* do." Then she looked at Daniel. "It is interesting to know, though."

"What? That I have a birthmark?"

"Well, that, too," Johanna said as she rolled to her side to face them. "And that you go skinny-dipping…" then sourly: "…with Lynda. God, girl. I thought you were all done with exposing yourself in public like that. It's so cheap. And needy."

"Why, Jo, sweetie, you sound a little, I don't know, *jealous*?" Lynda taunted as she sipped her beer. "Anyway, who *doesn't* love swimming naked? I mean, like, we were born that way. No reason we can't *live* that way!"

Johanna spied Peter Moran approaching from the pool bar carrying a glass of beer. He stopped to speak with a group of chums. "So, dearie," she said to Lynda, "how long have you two been — ?"

Lynda played into Johanna's evident dismay. "Dating? Since I dropped Nate for being such a bore. But this one makes me ultra-happy!" She absently tousled Daniel's hair again. "I can't help doing this. He's sooo kee-*ute!*"

"Come on, Lynn," Daniel griped. "Knock that off!"

"He's taking me partying tonight, isn't that right, Danny?"

"Yeah, I suppose," he answered dourly.

Johanna her kept her gaze trained on Peter, wishing he would hurry over and take them all away so she could sink back into her protective cacoon of depression. "Oh," she replied as she began to fumble with the fallen transistor radio earpiece. "Well—I hope you two have a *lot* of fun." She replaced the earplug and lay back and listened to the closing refrain of "Good Lovin'."

Lynda's plush smile broadened. "Oh, we will," she assured as Peter appeared at her side and lighted a kiss on her cheek.

"You're late, hon," he told her and then looked at Daniel. "She's always late."

"Late for *what*, sweetums?" Lynda said.

"Lunch. We're meeting Chris and his crowd for lunch before you and I head off to that beach party tonight. Remember?"

"Well, Peter. Of *course* I didn't forget about the beach party."

Johanna sighed and daubed her upper lip with her tongue. "Are you going to wear clothes for this one, Lynda?"

Lynda pondered this as Peter answered. "Maybe not. It might liven things up, a little. It promises to be pretty fucking dull and upsetting otherwise—sitting around a bonfire *kumbiya*-like and singing folk songs. Hence our plans to get soused this afternoon."

Lynda stroked the back of Peter's hair as he sipped his beer. "Well, they're *your* friends, sweetie."

"The children of my father's college buddies are not necessarily *my* friends," he sulked. He looked over at Daniel. "It's something I told dad I'd do," he explained. "You know. *Noblesse obliges.*"

"Oh, I know, Pete," Daniel said. "I've been there myself over the years."

Johanna relaxed her mouth into a relieved smile. She looked toward Daniel, then nestled her cheek against the ribbing of her lounge chair. "Anyway. How nice for both of you."

Peter put his arm around Lynda's waist. "Come on, hon. They're waiting. You coming, Daniel?"

"I, uh, think I'll stay here. Catch some rays."

"Awww," Lynda pouted. "We'll miss you tonight, sweetie. Don't be a party-poop. Try to show up and make a thing of it."

Peter shook his head in resignation, glanced down at Johanna, and then at Daniel. "Probably best you, uh, catch some rays, then, bro."

Lynda repeated her mantra as Peter ushered her away: "He's sooo kee-*ute!*"

Daniel perched on a neighboring chair and tried not to stare at Johanna as she adjusted herself to lie back on the lounge. Finallyhe asked, "You a student, or something?"

She flicked the earplug from her as she tried to act nonchalant. "Once. Clearwater Art College in Florida. Did more partying than painting. How long have you been with the *L.A. Tribune?*"

"About a year. Since I covered Watts."

"You were there?"

"I was."

"Interesting. You must have been the only white guy there, except the cops."

"No one seemed to care." His tone fell off in reflection. "Nobody gave a shit. It was a bad scene all around."

The muscular guttering of a boat engine rumbled from the near distance of the club docks. Johanna inhaled the light, cool brine of saltwater tinctured by the unctuous scent of petroleum and the ubiquitous hint of coconut oil. "So. Chinese food. Seven-thirty. I'll meet you near the front door of this place."

"Hunh?"

"You have forgotten about our date already?"

"Our date. Oh. Yeah."

"Don't be late." She noticed Daniel's concerned expression. "And don't worry, Dan-Daniel. Unitarians are welcome here. And so, sometimes, are we Jews."

Nate came from behind and tapped Daniel on the shoulder. "Sorry, Jo. I need to borrow Dan for a minute."

"Hunh?" Daniel said.

"Yeah. Jack's over there rounding up a poker game and we need a fifth."

"I'm not any good at pok—"

"Well, you are today. Come on." He turned to Johanna. "Sorry, Jo. I'll bring him back soon…and maybe a little richer."

He dragged Daniel off toward the snack-bar. "No need. We're finished here," she mumbled to the departing pair. "For now."

Another little blip of a headache reminded her that there were larger things at stake, as her thoughts rambled back to her worries. She lit another cigarette then placed her earpiece back in and nestled into to the latest release by Paul Revere and the Raiders.

"…And the kicks just seem getting harder to find…"

CHAPTER EIGHT
Subtle Secrets

Johanna lay on her bed contemplating the crack in the ceiling. She wondered what the hell she had just allowed herself to get away with. She had never done a one-night stand before; never even screwed on a first or even second or third date. She could have felt like a cheap floozie, but tonight she felt only ripples of guilt, and had no one to blame but herself. Maybe this had happened from a recipe conjured up in her subconscious, and this guy, Daniel, was just there at the yacht club at the wrong time. The poor chump.

She wasn't sure if the last six hours meant anything at all to her, but there was no telling how much lifetime she had left to make love—or at least to enjoy it. Sure, she reckoned, she could get a follow-up analysis from a different doctor, but what if it was bad enough to solidify her fears? At times, she even found some sordid solace in the feeling of suspecting without knowing; maybe she even felt the spice of excitement. Then, in the tender silence, she renewed the memory of her mother withering away from an assault of brain cancer.

Tears weighted her eyes as a slow breeze through the opened balcony doors carried the cozy fragrance of warm bread from the bakery next door. The scent insinuated that the shop was preparing for the day, so it must have been after 4 a.m. She stared out the doors into the night as the random *swiff* of passing traffic helped to soften the strain of her anxiety. She eased herself up against the headboard, lit a cigarette and channeled her vision out into the bay to focus on the navigation lights. A few fishing boats were coming into the Sausalito docks, as a greater number of them headed in the opposite direction toward the Golden Gate for their morning runs. She listened to the reassuring chimes from the buoys in the harbor. A foghorn bellowed soothingly in the distance.

She glanced over at Daniel lying next to her; his slim, freckled form draped in the twisted bedsheet. His snores were muffled, short, and comforting. Though their having sex had numbed her to what it all might have meant, she thought about how well they blended. She'd served her part of the dutiful, warm and responsive lover, well-grounded in the natural buoyancy of sex. Daniel had seemed tenuous when they started as though he had gone a long time without. He acted anxious to get it over with and leave but became unselfish as he settled into a tenderness which belied his mysterious need. He remained solidly asleep as she reasoned he must be one of those types who, unlike her, could nap through a bomb blast.

Johanna the floozy tried to justify that she needed a little more time to sort things out. Johanna the nurturer hoped that once Daniel woke, he might find that being with her had meant something to him. She decided not to lean over and give into her nagging temptation to kiss him on the cheek. She tamped out her half-smoked cigarette and heaved an unsettled sigh. She slid out of bed and then tip-toed to the shower to wash away her guilt.

Bracing herself against the tiles of the shower wall, she leaned into the water slithering down her back and stared down at her toes tensed against the tile floor. The muscles tightened in her calves. Further up, past the strain she felt in her thighs, was the thin, light brown little thatch which described her entry, and then her flat belly which would never bear a child, and her firm, small breasts peaked with rosy areoles and thickened nipples that would never nurture a baby. It was no longer a question of *"might never;"* her intuition told now told her—it was more *"would never."* She rested her forehead against the wall and stood that way for a few precious minutes.

She imagined her body from above poised like a misty phantom through the steam of the shower. She saw herself clenching her hands into fists then quietly pounding the tiles in bridled frustration, seeking some sort of answer. Her apparition faded away as she turned her back to the wall and slid down into a crouch, knees drawn to breasts, oblivious to the warm tickle of shower water over her body. She felt sucked back into reality by a sense of something new: a different sort of sharp, surging stab followed by a numbing nausea from that thing in her brain. This new message implied it meant business.

As she dried and brushed her hair, she imagined small thickets of it wound through the bristles of the brush. She raised her eyes to stare at the reflection of a pale, dry, hollowed-out version of herself, and let out an abrupt cry. Her head appeared bald, save for some gossamer tufts of what was left of her hair, and her breasts were wrinkled and deflated as two dead little sacks.

The brush slipped from her loose grasp and clattered into the bowl of the sink. She brought a fist to her mouth and bit into a knuckle, then shut her eyes, deciding she had tormented herself enough. Maybe Dr. Kornfield's new x-rays at her next appointment would show the tumor was gone. She opened her eyes to her reflection. She was once again her whole child-like self.

She heard Daniel's voice: "You okay in there?" Apparently, he wasn't such a sound sleeper.

No! —"Uh, yeah, okay. I'm fine, thanks! I'll be right out!"

"I thought I heard you scream."

"It's just…I saw a water bug! Oookie! I'm flushing him down the toilet, now!" She flushed the toilet, then wrapped herself up in a bath towel. She tried a quick grin at her reflection, then padded out into the bedroom. She huffed out a nervous laugh. "That was one big fucking water-bug. Hi."

"Hi," he said through a broad smile that looked forced to her.

"Uh, sleep well?"

"Yeah. I, uh, guess."

This conversation was leaning awkward. They acted like two wayward, fragile souls wandering through a fog while trying not to knock into one another.

"Hmm," she stifled through a laugh as she shuffled over and sat on the edge of bed. "Okay. Umm…I need a cigarette. You want a cigarette, too?"

"Uh, no thanks. I mean it's not that I don't smoke."

"I know. You smoked some last night."

"It's just that I don't want one now. Thanks, anyway." His tone was roughened with morning drowsiness.

She leaned across and fumbled her hand around her bed-side table for a cigarette, found it, lit up, then plinked the match into the ashtray. She groped around the tangle of the sheets for her thick-framed everyday glasses then slipped them on to get a closer look at him. "Do you go by Dan, or Daniel?" She tweaked a quick, matronly smile. "Not 'Danny', I hope."

"I prefer Daniel."

"Daniel it is, then."

He sat up and leaned against the headboard. "And you? Johanna or Jo?"

"My friends call me Jo. And I guess after last night you're officially a friend, so Jo is fine." He nodded. She interrupted the uneasy silence. "You sure you don't want a cigare—?"

"Really, no thanks, Jo. I'm fine. It's too early for me."

"Coffee, then. I can make us some coffee." She shrugged around and rose from the bed as she grasped the top of the bath towel. "I'll go make some."

She tried to keep her free hand from shaking. He took it in his and squeezed. "Not quite yet, Jo. Let's talk."

The last thing she needed now was a heavy conversation. She recalled the phantom in the bathroom mirror and drooped her head in a thoughtful silence. "Would you like to look at me?" — *while there's still something to look at?* —

"I *am*. Looking at you."

"I mean the rest of me. It was dark when we—Well, I don't think you really saw my body."

"Uh, sure. Okay."

She sensed his apprehension and tightened her expression. "Really? You don't sound very— "

His reply came too quickly. "I do, Jo. Honestly."

She flickered an uncertain smile and let the towel fall. She thought about what a dumb thing she'd just done in front of a stranger. His examining gaze made her feel like a lab specimen. She leaned down to reach for the towel gathered around her feet. "Sorry, Daniel. I didn't mean to do that. I feel really stupid."

"No, Jo, don't," he said. "I *want* to see you like this."

She cleared her throat. "Umm…really? Do you, uh, like my body?"

"I do. You're beautiful."

"You honestly think so? Even with my hair still all wet like this? That I'm, uh, beautiful? I mean not just cute or pretty, but beaut—?"

"Beautiful, Jo," he affirmed with a quick nod.

"Thank you, Daniel. Maybe I should—" She bent over and picked up the towel to hold it over her body. "I'll go make us that coffee, now."

"Jo?"

"Yeah?"

"I'm a photographer."

"I know. And I'm really impressed."

"I'd like to photograph you. I mean, not just portraits, but your body."

She tilted her head and tensed her expression. "You mean like…*nudes*?"

"Photographers call them figure studies, but yeah. I hope you're not thinking that this is some dumb sort of male come-on. There'll be nothing porn about them, I promise you. They'll be strictly professional. I'll even give you the negatives." He reached for one of her cigarettes. "Okay if I have one of these now?"

"Uh, sure."

"It would really be more of an experiment for me. I've never tried figure studies befo—"

She held up a trembling hand as if she was stopping traffic. "Daniel?"

"What?"

"Yes, I will do it," she said. "But there is a condition."

"Sure. What?"

She worried over how their relationship was entering a shaky, more intimate territory. "You let me take some pictures of you. Naked."

He blushed and recoiled in thought.

"Well?" Johanna pushed as she walked toward him to sit back down on the edge of the bed. "It's only fair play, you know."

"If you're using one of those Instamatics, Jo, forget it. The lab won't print pictures of naked people, especially men. You'd be branded as a pervert."

"I have been branded as worse I suppose. Anyway, we wouldn't have to worry about sending the film out, or anything. My father gave me one of those Polaroid color cameras for my last birthday."

Daniel thought it over. "Okay, Jo. You can take pictures of me."

"Really?" she gushed. "Cool!" She lifted his hand to her lips and kissed his fingertips.

"I want to take them outdoors," he said. "Maybe a rustic background near the ocean."

She relished the idea of having her body preserved for posterity in a photograph before it withered away into an eighty-pound shadow. "I'm beginning to like this idea, Daniel," She gazed at her bedside table as if considering it, then opened its drawer. There, wrapped like tiny mummies lying next to each other, were five rolled joints. She picked one out and brought it to her lips. "I might know just the place. A little nude beach about twenty miles north of here. Very natural and very private." She lit the reefer and inhaled.

"A nude beach. You've been there?"

She gazed over at the Marlene Dietrich poster on her wall.

"Once. I went with Lynda and a few other girlfriends from my high school class—just to see what it was like. A lot of fat, wrinkled-up naked old people. Actually, it was pretty gross."

"I'm sure Lynn enjoyed it."

She adjusted her glasses upon the bridge of her nose and proffered a little nod. "Yeah. She goes back there a lot. I'm pretty sure that's where she and Peter went yesterday afternoon." She giggled. "Maybe they sat around a bonfire in the buff, singing Kingston Trio stuff. Eeee-yew!" She then looked into Daniel's eyes as though seeing him for the first time. "There is something sad about you, no? I hope you don't mind my saying that. But there is something hidden in there." She wondered if he had noticed the same about her.

His expression softened as if he had. "It shows? I'm sorry, Jo. I hate to feel as though I'm dampening any sort of moment, here."

She felt drawn to his sadness. She reached out and stroked his cheek. "No, hon, you're not. You don't have to tell me…"

He looked down at the furrowed bedsheet on his lap. "I lost someone very close to me about a year ago. A dear friend."

Her mouth turned up into a soft, sweet smile. "I am so sorry for you, Daniel. I know what that can be like."

His eyes teared up. "You've loved and lost someone too, Jo?"

She nodded solemnly. "Yes. My mother. Ten years ago. I loved her so much, and I've never shaken it."

"I'm really sorry, Jo. How did she die?"

She couldn't tell him. Not yet. Instead, she leaned over and gave him a trembling kiss on his lips. She gazed at him as her smile turned sad. She wanted to cry; to let loose the tears of her frustration. She felt some imaginary force—some need bridging their sorrows—which would somehow make everything seem okay.

Snapping out of her concentration, she took a quick jab on her joint, handed it to him and then stood. She flung an oversized shirt across her shoulders. "Are you going somewhere, Jo?"

She leaned over and tousled his hair, then kissed his forehead. "I'm going to make us some coffee. And then you will take me out for breakfast because I hate to cook."

CHAPTER NINE

Weir Beach

Johanna wondered if the trip had been worth it. After leaving her place at around 10 a.m. for what should have been a 45-minute drive north to Weir Beach, Daniel's car got snarled up in traffic. By the time they got there, the Beetle's engine was stuttering suspiciously as though suffering from dry heaves. Then there was the one-mile trudge through the bug-infested, late morning damp, down the dirt road to the seclusion of the nudist's corner of the beach.

The time Johanna had spent with him over the past three weeks served to subdue her fears enough for her pretend to play the joyful girlfriend. Sometimes—like today—she took it to extremes as she flung out her arms and twirled ahead of him as he slowed against the stress of his knapsack weighted down by camera gear, a blanket, and four warm Lowenbraus. She realized her act of buoyancy was only a pretense against the numbing fear created by her compounding dread.

They came upon a good spot—a clearing near some low dunes, scantily protected by a tall thicket of ground cover. What little sunlight there had been was now misted over by a fogbank that dropped the temperature another 10 degrees. The clammy chill had not made the place any more enticing for nude sunbathing than it did for photography.

Daniel put his equipment down as Johanna sidled her backpack off and peered ahead. The beach's colorless sand had been pounded flat by the slow motion of the dour-colored Pacific waves, as they crashed down and then sizzled away in a frothy retreat.

"There are no naked people out there. Not one." She lamented in a childish pout.

"That's because there's no sun," Daniel said as he busied himself with loading film into the Rollieflex he'd borrowed from the *Trib's* equipment cage. He glanced west toward the ocean where the thinned-out sunlight had begun its descent into the afternoon.

"Well, Daniel?" Johanna quipped from behind him. "Are we gonna do this or not?" She stood naked with her arms and legs akimbo, with her dark framed glasses adding an absurd accessory to her nudity. A little pendant hanging from its gold strand around her neck winked out a glint as she rolled her shoulders against the chill and then hugged her chest. "Come on. I feel ridiculous standing here in the cold like this. Me first. And then I take my pictures of you."

He looked down at his camera. "You sure you want to do this?"

She challenged him with a defiant glare. "Are you kidding me? After all this planning? Besides, I don't just drop my shorts for nothing." She stooped down, lifted a cigarette from her backpack and held it cupped in front of her face as she lit it. She then stood back up and glanced around. "Now. Where do you want me to stand?"

She had come to realize how much she needed this relationship and was certain she had fallen in *like* with Daniel, as tenuous as he'd sometimes acted toward her. She marveled at how, after only three weeks, their friendship already showed signs of growing cozy, comfortable, and lasting.

Her kvetching and stage directions hadn't made his picture-taking any easier. Once he was done, she was grateful to get out of the chill as she hastily slipped on her panties, shorts, and tennis shoes. She slipped her un-buttoned shirt over her shoulders.

As for her taking pictures of him, all he had to do was to stand in front of her while she flicked some Polaroids. She waited a very long minute for each to develop, then peeled the print from its backing, shook it dry, squinted at the result, shook her head, then took another almost exactly like the previous one. Through her breathless haste and mounting frustrations, she had trouble holding the camera still, and her pictures of him turned out like bad, blurry forensic snapshots. Once she'd finished, Daniel dressed, then sat on the ground. He leaned back against a boulder, and then shuffled though her snapshots with mild interest.

With her hair tied back into a flimsy ponytail, Johanna relaxed with her arms folded across her chest. She leaned against the side of the rock and savored a joint. A sharp headache attack from the base of her skull where the incision had been made for her biopsy a few weeks before. She cringed and tried to divert her attention from the pain in her head and the impending doom of the results.

She stared over toward a cluster of seagulls squawking in hoarse complaint over some morsel on the beach. In defiance of the growing chill, a pair of flabby, uninteresting-looking middle-aged women lay naked near the tideline to catch what little warmth was left of the day. A thin, pallid, flat-chested woman with big feet and the physique of Olive Oyl lay on her stomach in the closer distance. Johanna glanced down at her body, and felt a flush of relief that Daniel had immortalized it before it wasted away.

She took another deep toke in defense of a gust which also caused her to draw her shirt collar tight around her neck. She leaned over and picked up a small antler of bleached driftwood. She examined it, squinting as she turned it this way and that to catch the light. She brushed away some wind-tousled strands of hair from her cheek, then slid down next to Daniel. "Finally, the sun decides to come out," she mused at the driftwood, "at least a little bit." She placed it back on the ground and gazed sadly at it as she lifted the blanket and wrapped it around her shoulders. She felt another sharp pain in her head. A swell of breeze caused her to draw knees up closer to her chest. Remembering the bottle of beer tottering near her feet, she raised it to her lips and took a demure sip.

"We should get going," she heard Daniel say from faraway.

"Not yet, Daniel. I'm really liking it out here. Let's stay just a little longer." She leaned closer to him and offered him the joint. "Here, smoke this and relax." As he reached to take it, she held fast onto his hand, then brought his fingertips to her lips and looked up at him with a hint of desperation in her glistening eyes. She turned his hand up and traced his palm with the nail of her forefinger while staring at his long lifeline. "Shit!" she snapped in a dry whisper as she she squeezed his fingers at another stab of pain.

"What's the matter, Jo?"

"Nothing, really." She said as she sighed the pain away, then thought about what to say next. "You know, Daniel? I really like you."

He felt trapped by the conviction in her tone, then replied the only way he could: "Me, too, I think, Jo. About you, I mean."

She loved his clumsy shyness. "I know just what you mean." She let go of his hand and sidled against him. She leaned her head on his shoulder. "So what do we do about it, hunh?"

"Uh....I don't know."

I do not want to die alone—she thought. She kissed his cheek. "Well, I think I do. I think we should go ahead together though all this."

"All ...what?" he said apprehensively.

"Jesus, I am sorry. I don't know how to put this." She looked up into his eyes, then leaned close to whisper: *"Predi-suda. Puztaluminya."."*

He drew in hard on the remains of the joint, then tamped it out. "Uh, putsi-what?"

She smiled coyly. "It's Russian. I said: 'Come here and kiss me.'"

"Well. You could have just said that in Eng—," he began as she hugged him into a desperate kiss. He felt like he was being smothered, and tried to push away, but she only clung harder to him. She eased her lips from his as he gasped out a burst of air with a filigree of pot smoke.

She nestled her head into his chest as she pulled the blanket back around her. "Did you like that, Daniel?" she breathed heavily.

"Well, yeah. I did. But why'd you do that? What's the occasion?"

She bit her lower lip, then conjured up an easy smile. I think we should be together."

"We are together."

"I meant you and me...together."

"Jo, you're not making any sense. What the hell are you driving toward?"

She wasn't used to playing the submissive role and realized she'd been undone by a force larger than herself. She huffed out a breath to collect her thoughts. "My life is creeping in on me, Daniel. I can feel it." She twiddled her necklace as she glanced toward Olive Oyl on the beach, now dressed and gathering her stuff to leave. She pitied the woman's loneliness. "I just don't want my world to shrink to the size of my apartment," she mused.

"Maybe take a trip?" he offered to diffuse what he feared might be coming next. "I hear Greece is nice this time of year. I mean, if my course load weren't so chock full, we could go togeth—"

"Shut up, Daniel!" Johanna snapped. "We've been seeing each other nearly every day now for over three weeks." She glanced over and down at her Polaroid snapshots of him. "We've seen everything we need to see about one another. I'm telling you I think we should move in together."

"You're kidding, right? Where?

"My apartment. Not yours—I don't respond well to dorm life."

He shifted away and took a pull on his warm beer. "We've been dating only three weeks and now you want to do this? What, Johanna? Did I get you pregnant or something?"

She felt her body numb into a hard freeze. "No. Now that's ridiculous. I'm not pregnant. Of course I'm not. Jesus!." She flicked a smile to hide her annoyance. "Anyway, it's okay. I guess you're not ready."

He thought about when he lived with Jared. "It's not that. It's…It's something else."

"What? Maybe we could talk about it."

"I'm not so sure, Jo."

She smiled and stroked his cheek with such gentleness she

could feel the response of his warmth through her fingertips. She felt him ease to her touch. "Please, hon. You can tell me."

He sighed in thought. "You remember when I told you I lost someone dear to me? "

"Yes. A close friend."

"He was shot to death while we were covering the Watts riots in L.A. I watched him die and there was nothing I could do."

She felt his cheeks tremble beneath her touch. "It's okay, Daniel." She kissed the top of his head. "Cry if you feel like it."

"There was nothing I could do, Jo, but let him die.".

"Here, hon. Come to me." He nestled his head in her shoulder. "No," she whispered. "There was nothing you could do, but you did not let him die if he still lives in your heart."

"We lived together, Jo." He sniffed. "We were lovers."

"Really?" She said after some thought while she continued tenuously stroking the back of his neck. "You …loved…this man. As in… *love.*"

"I don't know if it was love. I don't think so. Do you hate me for leading you on?"

"*Have* you been leading me on, Daniel?"

"No, Jo. I have not. I'm pretty sure that was just a passing phase. I have genuine feelings for you. Deep feelings."

"Even though I'm a woman?"

He pulled back. She stared into his gaze. "Maybe *especially* because you're a woman. Maybe I now need a woman in my life. And she is you."

"You can do that, honey? I mean, switch like that? After you…you know, and men?"

"Don't fret, Jo. I've been with women, too. But I feel there's something special about you."

Her lips curled into a sad, sardonic smile. "I bet you say that to all your girls…and guys."

"It's something about what we share. It's like a certain sadness that draws us together. That's a strong bond."

She drew him into another hug. "There is. I feel it, too." A deep sigh trembled her body. "I was close to my mother." She drew away and shivered as she looked down at the ground. "The truth is, my mother, uh, she died." She fumbled to button up her shirt.

He placed a hand on her shoulder. "I know. You told me and I'm so sorry, Jo. How did she—?"

"Uh, she had—she had brain cancer. Six years ago. It was awful to watch, and I miss her all the time. She loved to take pictures and they were good. You would have liked her."

"I'm sure I would have."

She looked back up at him and raised the blanket like a wing. "Here, share this with me. I feel like I'm stealing it from you." She huffed out a sad laugh. "Now my stepmother, Tamara, she's a totally different person than my mother was. Tamara is kind of, I don't know, cold. Angry. I'll never know why my father chose her, but they got married about a month after they met. It's like they met and then hoped to develop some sort of love, or at least dad did. Tamara never seemed to give a shit. I think she just wants his money." She sniffed and shivered. "I just miss my mother so much."

"You two were really close, hunh?"

"More than you know." She reached over to touch his cheek again. "And we're close, too. Right, Daniel? I mean I feel really close to you." She looked sadly at the ground. "There's something else you need to know about me."

"Of course, Jo. You can tell me. Now that we've become like best friends."

"Lovers, maybe?" She felt his tension defuse the moment. She looked up at him. "Daniel, do you think we could be lovers? I think we could."

"I like the idea of friends. They're more trustworthy. But, yeah, in time, maybe lovers. Now, Jo, what is it you want to tell me…as a trusted friend?"

She sniffed. For a moment, she'd been emboldened to tell him about her cancer, but the thought just as suddenly passed.

"Nothing, really," she tried to convince herself. "It was nothing. Listen…" She cringed back another sharp jab of pain.

"You okay Jo? You jolted a little like you just got stung by a bee."

"I'm okay, now. With you here. Daniel, I trust you and I…uh…I love you."

He answered through an uncertain sigh, and kissed the top of her head. She nestled closer to him and tightened the blanket around them. "Maybe I've said enough." She shivered as she felt his warmth join hers to ripple through her body. "Just for now, this feels comfortable."

"Jo?"

"Yeah?"

He stroked her hair and felt the stiff bandage it didn't quite hide. She'd told him it was there because she had a mole removed. "Okay, Jo, let's try living together. For now." He felt the gentle force of their mutual need. "And I love you, too."

PART THREE
Liars in Love

CHAPTER TEN

Whirlwind

Tamara Volskolnikov Montaigne was a one-person extravaganza. She posed like a frumpy 19th century bar nude as she lounged in the couch on the sun porch of the Montaigne home. She was fully clothed, of course. Very fully clothed. The floral print of her silk caftan blended into that of the couch across from where Daniel sat apprehensively in a wicker chair. Her wrists were festooned in clusters of jewelry which jangled louder than they should have as she moved her arms—usually just to raise her third vodka and grapefruit of the morning to her puffy lips. Her big hair was bleached flagrantly blonde, and she oozed out the fragrance of last night's and this morning's booze along with a lot of Chanel No. 5 to cover it up. Her speech was ponderously Slavic, with a crude delivery hardened by her sour memories of being a bourgeois Soviet-Czech. Perhaps because English was her second language, she economized her words as she strung them out to emphasize her point: "So, Mistrah Daniel. You wannew marry my daughtrah."

Daniel smiled politely. "Step-daughter," he ventured. "And we're not getting married. We're just living together."

She gazed out the picture window of her home high in the wooded Sausalito Hills overlooking the boat-dotted bay. In the southern distance, fog curled around the north tower of the Golden Gate Bridge. "Johanna ees my daughtrah, now" she muttered with stoic conviction.

"Yes, Mrs. Montaigne."

Tamara sipped her drink. "I am not convinced this is right," she said over the rim of her glass, then skewered him with a sudden glare. "You are Jewish." This came out as if she'd wished to say: _Because you are a Jew._

"You peeked," he quipped.

"What?"

"Nothing. It's an in-joke."

"What is this thing, 'in-joke'?"

"A colloquialism."

This confused her more and she shook his comment away like as she retreated to the sanctity of her drink. She held the glass to her lips and gazed out a corner window and past the terra cotta patio where Johanna played with Jeepers, the family golden retriever. The whole backyard seemed to precariously overhang the steepness of the hill from which an earthquake might easily the tumble house into a free fall. "Do you lahv her? Or do you just pretahnd you do?"

"Pretend?"

"_Da._ I know the difference."

"I love Johanna completely, Mrs. Montaigne." His admission didn't seem real to him, as though someone else had said it.

Tamara sighed and leveled an accusing gaze at him. She nestled back into the couch, then stared into her glass. "You know I am from Rrrahsah." She said the name of her country very professionally, rolling the "r's".

"Yes. I do."

"Near Czechoslovakian border," she said to the melting cubes in her drink.

"I did not know that."

"I come from long line of Cossacks. They are good in gelding horses." She felt Daniel's apprehensive glance through the percolating silence. "If I find you only pretahhnd to love my only dahtrah, I will geld you like a horse and put you to pasture to rot. Do not think I cannot do this thing, Mistrah Daniel."

"I love your daughter, Mrs. Montaigne," he said again.

She smiled wryly. "If this is so, then you can call me 'Tamara'." She took another sloppy sip. "You have dark-red hair."

"Yes, Tamara, I do. Copper-colored, actually, sort of like Johanna's."

"My Johanna has copper-blonde hair. Your children, they will have copper-blonde hair with red roots." She concentrated on her nimble fingers as she fidgeted them lightly against her glass. "And you have bad sight."

Daniel adjusted his glasses higher on the bridge of is nose. "Not that bad, really. I'm just a little near-sighted."

"My dahtrah has bad sight; very bad without her glasses. Your children might turn blind, too. Copper-blonde hair with dark-red roots and bad eyesight. Maybe these things are a bad sign. We shall see."

"I don't think bad eyesight is inherited."

She slurped her drink. "We shall see."

Roberto Montaigne breezed in behind them carrying his morning martini. Unlike his wife, he took care of his robust physique, and was still short-of-breath from four sets of morning tennis. "Well, there you are, Tammy."

"Mistrah Daniel wanz to leeve with our dahtrah."

"We knew that. Should we let him?" He winked *mano-e-mano* at Daniel. Unlike his daughter's left-over accent, any inflection of his Portuguese accent had been pruned out.

"I tell him I cut away his balls if he does not treat her good."

"Good idea," Roberto agreed. Then to Daniel: "Now that you're almost part of the Montaigne cartel, how about a round of golf at the club this afternoon, Dan?"

"Sorry, Mr. Montaigne. I don't know how to play."

Roberto sipped his martini. "Don't play golf?" He served up a smile. "What good are you then, son? You'll have to learn the game. Golf is the gateway to the power broker, Dan."

The thought of going to Vietnam weighed heavy on Daniel's mind. He wondered if golf was a talent he could use in Vietnam, as he was certain the *Tribune* had it in their mind to send him there after he graduated next year. He looked out at the bay, past Johanna fussing with the putzy, lumbering Jeepers.

"Thank you, Roberto. I promise you I'll look into taking up golf."

"Right. Two things: A. Take up golf for the good of your career, and B. call me Bobby"

CHAPTER ELEVEN
Too Much Basil

Afternoon sunlight splayed across the mottled carpet of one of the *Los Angeles Tribune's* editorial conference rooms. Nancy Wegman, an associate producer from KABC's news department, had fanned out about a dozen of Daniel's photos from last week's Hunter Point Riots, and gazed at them hand to chin in rapt concentration. She had come to the *Tribune* for the day to select some stills for a montage in a documentary called "West of Detroit—Racial Tension in California". She'd already chosen several of Daniel's Watts photos from a year-and-a-half before.

She pointed to an over-the-shoulder shot of a cop in bulky riot gear aiming his assault rifle at a throng of demonstrators approaching though a haze of tear gas. "I think we can lead with this one. Yeah. Definitely this one."

Daniel didn't agree. "I like this one." He tapped a shot of a Negro community leader who had stepped out from a line of protesters with his arms extended toward an approaching phalanx of cops. A filigree of tear gas fuzzed out toward the demonstrators behind him. His stance might have been a beseeching prelude to a symbolic embrace. "It reminds me of that Goya painting."

"We could use that as a closer," Nancy said after a little

thought. "This first one is really nice and has an open area for a title slug to the right of the cop and his rifle."

The three-day riot ignited in late September, the week after Daniel and Johanna had gotten back from a vacation in Costa Rica. It had started with a cop shooting a stolen car suspect in the back as the kid tried to flee down Navy Street in Hunter's Point, a no-white-man's-land east of San Francisco's Mission District. The demonstrations quickly bloomed out past a Community Center where some black kids, presumably gang members, had been holed up.

During the thick of it, Daniel scurried from shadow to alcove like a guerilla fighter with a camera. Through the taut burn from the tear gas he had envisioned Jared dying in the street. Just as in Watts, Daniel allowed the memory and the situation to embolden his shooting. Also, like Watts, he had wanted it all to be over. He hated being there in the humidity and the pervasive scent of heated gun oil and the stink of the barricades of burning tires.

Nancy put the opening and closing photos off to the side and shuffled the remaining ones into random positions. "Okay," she said aloud to herself as she pursed her lips in satisfaction. She slid the opener and closer into place at the beginning and end of the two rows of photos to comprise an ad hoc storyboard. She nodded in approval of her handiwork. "I like this chronology."

Tony and Daniel exchanged bemused glances. Tony sighed and shrugged as if to quip: *T.V. editors!*

She turned the photos over and then numbered their backs sequentially. "Okay. Thanks, guys," she said. "We have our montages."

"Thanks be to God," Tony said. "So, when's this going to be airing?"

She gathered the photos together. "Oh, we're planning for mid next month. We'll be slotting it in the schedule next Tuesday. Anyway, we're laying down the narration track tomorrow."

"Who's doing that?" Tony asked.

She brushed a wave of her long hair behind her ear. "The narration track? ABC just hired a new guy, Peter Jennings, from Ottawa. They sent him here to get a little more exposure through V.O.-ing this documentary."

"So, this show is sort of a vehicle for the new guy," Tony said.

Nancy possessed a severe beauty she manipulated for all its worth. She tilted her head and shot Tony a knowing smirk, belying the secret that she'd spent a lot of time with him a few nights before. Tony later confided to Daniel that she was far too commando for his taste, and then winked at him.

"Drinks?" she said. "It's been a long day and I owe you," she said as she slipped the photos into a manila envelope.

"I've got to drive back to San Fran tonight, and I'd prefer to do it in a straight line, but thanks, Nancy," Daniel said.

"Maybe later, Nance," Tony said.

"Suit yourselves, guys."

"Let's you and me do tomorrow, Nance. Then you can buy me dinner."

"Not a chance, Russo. We go Dutch, if we go at all." She gave him a friendly peck on the cheek. "Come by my office around seven. Good to finally meet you, Dan," she said as she rushed out the door.

She bumped into Larry Graham as he was lumbering his way into the conference room. "Hey, Larry," she said intent on hurrying down the corridor.

"Good to see you again, too, Nancy," Larry mumbled behind her. "I been lookin' for you two."

"What's up, Larry?" Tony said. "Have you heard anything?"

He lit up the fat cigar he'd been holding off to his side. "Yeah, I have." He turned to Daniel. "When do you finish up at Berkeley, Dan?"

"In June, but I've a few straggler courses during the summer. Why?"

Larry took a few wet puffs on his cigar. "Paul Higgins, our Asian bureau chief over in Tokyo, is pulling Schneider and Grimes outta Saigon in mid-October. Annie Farrell will be going over there to replace Tom Fox as the *Trib's* head field guy. For some reason, she wants to bring you two jesters with her. So, I said yeah. Happy freaking birthday, or whatever."

"Shit, *Yeah!*" Tony blurted. "Thanks, Larry!"

"Yeah, well, just don't go and get churselves killed in the process. I'll have a shortage of guys here as it is."

Tony punched the air with his fist. "*Hell,* yeah! Vietnam! Annie's bringing me and Dan…as a *team?*"

Larry tweaked a wry smirk at them. "You were expecting Abbott and Costello? Come to think of it, I do see the symmetry there."

Daniel froze ashen in place.

Tony looked over at him. "Yo, Dan. We're going to *Saigon!*"

Daniel hadn't expected this so soon, but realized again that this was the kind of thing he signed up for when he joined the *Tribune.* Johanna would probably freak out. He managed a faraway smile. "Okay, Tony. That's really great."

Larry rested a beefy hand on Daniel's shoulder. "You're the best rookie photog we got for this, kid. If you can cover them street riots like you did…you're a natural. Besides, you're a journalist. You'll have the whole U.S. Military to protect you."

"Come on, bro. Lighten up," Tony said. "It's you and me. It's gonna be a *blast*."

Daniel hoped the blast wouldn't come up from the ground by way of a Claymore mine.

"Okay, well," Larry said. "You two gotta report to the correspondent's boot camp near Pendleton the first week of September."

Now Tony's expression fell. "Whoa! Wait! Boot camp at Pendleton? A *Marine* boot camp?"

"Yeah." He puffed on his cigar. "What'd ya think, Russo? We'd send you into a warzone without any training? Besides," he flicked a hand against Tony's stomach, "you could use a little muscle to replace all that desk-flab you've grown."

"Shit, Larry," Tony complained.

"Don't worry, guys. You'll be among friends. It ain't like you're gonna need to do eighty-eight push-ups before dawn. It's a cushy three-week training program for journalists, set up just for us and some other media outlets. Your drill instructor will probably be some managing editor. They're just gonna show how to shoot a rifle, and some other duck and cover shit."

"Duck and cover," Daniel echoed. He wryly paraphrased Norman Mailer from a speech he'd given at Berkely before the first Viet Nam Day Convention: "Hot Damn, Viet Nam!"

Tamara sniffed the air like a she-wolf as the fragrance of baking turkey meandered through the sunroom like a Thanksgiving poltergeist. Too much basil again this year—something no one else but she would sense.

Roberto sipped his dark malt Kentucky bourbon. It was a treat he reserved for holidays, and Tamara's name day, when he needed it most. These moments deserving bourbon had become more frequent since Johanna brought Daniel into the tight little homelife controlled by Tamara. For her, it was an excuse to get drunker than usual, as she was now.

Roberto tried out a private wink at her to ease the tension she was seething. "Smells good," he said.

"*Cho*?" Tamara replied in her native Russian.

"I said, the turkey. It smells good."

"Too mahtch bas-eel."

Roberto breathed in his bourbon again like he was clearing his sinuses. He looked over at Daniel holding a foam-laced Pilsner glass in one hand and Johanna's hand in the other. "So, Dan. You'll be graduating in August?"

"Yeah."

"Of courzz," Tamara slurred. "My daughtrah's maybe feutore hahzband muzz go summer school with rest of illiterate studenzz."

Johanna wondered why Tamara showed Daniel so much contempt. "No, Tamara," she stated. "Daniel is on an accelerated program and doing really well. He starts his career full time at the *Los Angeles Tribune* in September."

The glittering abundance of Tamara's jewelry clattered like dungeon chains as she waved her hand around. "Oh yezz. I know. A job for my daughtrah's feutor hahzband, that pays not enough to support a flea."

"Your *step*-daughter." Johanna reminded her, as she lit another cigarette. "And I'd appreciate it, step-mother, if you would stop putting Daniel down so much." She cast a furtive look at him. "And no. We're not thinking about getting married…yet, I don't think. So please stop refering to him as my 'future husband.'"

Johanna could sense Daniel's discomfort as he patted her hand, then squeezed it. "It's alright, Jo."

"No, it is not," Roberto said. "Tammy? Apologize to Daniel."

Tamara's soviet stubbornness prevailed as she huffed a sigh and said nothing. "In Rahsha…we find mate and we marry. Ees how ees done."

Daniel retreated through a sip of his beer. "The *Tribune*'ll be paying me enough." He thought on how to frame his next statement. He opted to keep it simple and straightforward. "They're sending me to the Saigon bureau in September."

"Viet Nam?" Roberto gasped. "Holy shit, man! Good for you! I'm proud of you, son."

"Yeah. We just found out last week," Johanna pouted as she glanced toward Daniel. "I am, like, absolutely pissed and totally bummed over it."

Tamara's tone seemed to brighten a little, perhaps with the realization that her daughter's future husband might fight and possibly die like a proper Cossack. Then perhaps Johanna could marry a stock market executive and live through his millions. "There eez nahthing wrong about fighting for country," she said. "He will maybe kill many and be revolutionary hero like my grandfathrah, Anton, when he fighted against the Bolsheviks."

Daniel smiled nervously and concentrated on the surroundings. Despite her old-world crudeness, Tamara kept the place in a showroom state. "Yeah," he finally replied, "but I'll be shooting with a camera and not a gun."

Tamara shot him a quizzical look. "They will not give you gahn?"

"Probably. A little one," he said.

She pursed her lips, nodded, and then labored unsteadily to

her feet. "I mahst go check turkey," she said on her way out toward the kitchen. "Too mahch bas-eel."

Daniel looked out the picture window at the surrounding houses and the bay in the distance. Like the Montaigne house, the others were gouged precariously into the knobby green and dried bunch-grass mountainside like Pueblo dwellings connected by a labyrinth of narrow, wooded roads. Clouds traveled sluggishly above the hills, lifting enough to reveal the distant towers of The Golden Gate Bridge like an upcoming event. He was chilled by the realization that after next summer he might not see these scenes again—at least not in the same reassuring way. Roberto's metallic tone eased Daniel out of his uneasy thought.

"Hunh?"

"So." Roberto repeated. "Viet Nam."

"Jesus, dad. You actually sound proud that he's going over to that stupid war." She glowered at Daniel. "Where men are dying. And for what? God and country? Bullshit!"

"Now, Johanna, don't go off into another one of your little Liberal tantrums. He's going as a civilian. The *Tribune* will keep him out of any danger." He sipped his bourbon. "Right, Dan?"

"Well. Yeah," Daniel said thoughtfully. "For the most part..."

Johanna took a jabbing puff on her cigarette. "Jesus, you two! Who do you think is taking pictures of those battles over there? Robots? No. It's some photographer with a big camera and a little gun." She showed her anxiety by twiddling a fall of her hair around her index finger.

"I'll be fine, Jo. You've been too twisted up about this."

"She does get a little emotional from time to time." Roberto offered a subtle toast to her as a peace offering.

"A *little* e-mo-tional? Do you all think it's just our soldiers getting killed over there? You think one of those Viet Coms turns to another and says: 'Hey, Ming, don't shoot that guy. He is a newspaper photographer.'? I doubt it!"

"Viet Cong," Roberto corrected.

"What?"

"The North Vietnamese we're fighting are called Viet Cong."

Johanna's eyes glistened. "I don't fucking care if they are fucking *King* Kong! They all have guns," she squeezed Daniel's hand. "*Big* guns. And they know how to shoot them."

"I'll have plenty of protection, Jo. Tony and I will mostly be with the press corps in Saigon."

"Tony Russo is going with you?"

"Well, yeah. I thought I told you. We're gonna be a team."

"Mother of God! Russo!" She stopped twiddling her hair and snatched up her drink. "Well, *that's* certainly comforting to know. You and Russo out there keeping the world safe for democracy. Je-zuzz!" She belted down the remains of her drink.

Roberto leaned his head back. "I envy you, Dan. Proud you're doing your part."

Johanna sighed. "Oh, Dad! You are such a God-damned Hawk."

Tamara's choked-off voice filtered from the kitchen. "Turkey eez done. Time to eat soon." Something clattered to the floor. "*Chort!*" she said. "Gravy will be later."

CHAPTER TWELVE

Peace, Love and Loneliness

Johanna's serape billowed around her as she stood in a patch of sunlight on a knoll above the crowd. She listened to the muffled chinkle of guitar riffs from the makeshift stage at the far end of the Polo Field. She closed her eyes and breathed in some sweet wisps of pot spicing the brisk, mid-January air. She lifted a finger to a sense of a gentle tug on her cheek and touched a light crust of paint where a face-artist had rendered a daisy.

From here, the five members of The Grateful Dead playing onstage looked like blurry troll dolls. She lowered her glasses to the bridge of her nose and gazed out over the heads of the stoned-out crowd bobbing and weaving ambiguously around in a collective Technicolor swirl. The scene was billed as "The Human Be-In, a Gathering of Tribes", and it had the appearance of a Native American jamboree.

A friendly passer-by offered her a joint, which she gratefully accepted, inhaled, and offered it back, but her benefactor had twirled obliviously away into the crowd with her frail yellow chiffon scarf fluttering behind her. "Why, thank you," she said, and took another toke.

She scanned the crowd in another futile attempt to spot Daniel taking his black and white pictures of this riot of color for The *Tribune*. She wondered why everything was a photo-op for him, denying them the pleasure of enjoying events like this together. Why wasn't he here cuddling against the chill with her under the comfort of her serape, as they had cuddled beneath the bedsheets last night? Her recollection sent up a fluff of inner warmth. Last night had been good. Other nights? Not so much—the sex had become as hit-or-miss as it was sporadic.

Maybe the heartfelt surge last night had something to do with Daniel's knowing he was going out on assignment the next day, like a centurion taking comfort with his whore the night before combat to give him strength for battle. The heated joint stabbed a burn through the tip of her index finger. "Shit! Fuck!" she jolted. She took a final hit, then stamped it out with the toe of her boot.

She sensed someone close behind her and turned to face Nate in costume. She slipped her glasses down further on her nose to peer over the top of them. His violet silk shirt was unbuttoned to expose his hairless chest. He wore a big gold chain weighted down by a silver peace symbol around his neck. Her lips curled into a smile, easing the sensation of another dull headache. "Aren't you cold, half-dressed like that, Nathan?"

"Of course, but I felt I needed to share the moment with all.... whatever this is."

"Why, this is the great Human Be-In, so we can all gather together in one big collective hug."

"Oh, well, Jo, it's the great big human blooper, if you ask me. What's the purpose of all this? I can hardly hear The Dead from this far away."

She scanned the crowd again. "I don't know. It must mean something to all the spaced-out druggies here."

"What a fuckin' zoo, hunh?"

She nodded. "Yeah, really. Did you come across Daniel anywhere?"

"Yeah. I did." He motioned into the distance toward the stage. "He was taking pictures of some poets reading their junk to Timothy Leary and some other space cadets." He shivered away a chill.

Johanna took pity on him and drew the serape up over her head and held it open to display her garishly colored mini-dress and calf-high boots. "Come on in, Nathan. It's too cold for you the way you are dressed."

"Bless you, Jo," he said as he sidled his way next to her. She wrapped him closer to her.

She offered up a cunning feline smile. "And none of that hocus pocus under here." She sounded almost hopeful.

A stoned-out wanderer from another planet bumped into Daniel as he was focusing in on poets Allen Ginsberg and Gary Snider chanting away in some indiscernible language. Obviously whatever plane they were floating on was separate from the one freely delivered through the soul of the Be-In. Ginsberg was leading a drum circle on stage, batting the air to the erratic thump of the beat.

LSD guru Timothy Leary stood Adonically-sculpted behind the poets like Captain Ahab on the bridge of the *Pequod* as he surveyed the crowd. He seemed to be basking in his earlier proclamation advising the attending tribes with his mantra: "turn on, tune in, drop out. ". The backlighting around all of them through the evaporating fog was nice. It was a good shot...*saddack--thwip*.

Despite the spirit of it all, Daniel wasn't feeling very connected to the others here. Even Jerry Rubin hadn't seemed his usual impassioned self as he announced the thing. He sounded subdued as he called for all people to come together in understanding at this hallowed place.

Daniel took one more back-up shot and then turned toward the stage where The Jefferson Airplane was setting up. After some mike thumps, warm-up twangs and a few test rifts, things got organized and they launched into their new release, "Somebody to Love." Daniel reached into his backpack, lifted out a telephoto lens and mounted it. He aimed his camera into a tight shot of Grace Slick singing close into the mike as swaths of her windblown black hair swirled around her chubby school-girl face. *Saddack ...thwip, saddack-thwip.*

He took half a roll of close ups of and a few wide shots of the group until he realized he needed a beer. He turned around toward an oversized Maypole. A stoned-out dancer, with swirling long blonde hair and wearing a black mini-dress, writhed like a windblown streamer in harmony with the flow of the throng around her. *Saddack ...thwip, saddack-thwip.* He then meandered to one of the truck-bed concession stands to get his beer.

He surveyed the mass of long-haired beats, hippies, and flower children; many of them adorned with garlands around their necks and laurels in their hair. There were also more conservative-looking types: students who were there to check it out, and other curiosity-seekers who might have sought their independence but were too timid to dress for it. Even a smattering of tweed-jacketed professor-types milled around puffing on their pipes.

Daniel's attention became riveted toward a seriating voice from the stage. He looked toward the sound and saw a young girl; a kid really, with a mass of unruly mousy-brown hair muffling her face. She appeared to be eating the mike. Even though she might have had trouble singing a harmony, it was the passion in her voice belying her diminutive size that mesmerized him. He raised his camera for a closer look through his telephoto lens at Big Brother and the Holding Company while focusing on their lead singer as he wound his way toward the stage.

The charred voice behind her roiling mass of hair belted out "Bye, Bye Baby." When she finished the song, her hair finally parted revealing overly ordinary features and pocked skin. She was a rough-looking kid—pure grit...until her chubby lips bloomed into a timid but meaningful, smile as though she was scared to death to be here.

After the set, she was introduced as Janis Joplin. *Saadack...thwip.*

"When I die, I want to be buried in San Rafael," said Nate.

Johanna glowered over at him with one eye squinted against the sun. "You are not going to die, Nathan. Anyway, why would *anyone* want to be buried in San Rafael?"

"It's better than ending six feet under in L.A.," he reasoned.

"True enough, I suppose." She sipped her beer and turned her gaze toward a platinum-haired teenager strumming her guitar while she hummed then sang lightly in a tiny child's voice. She sat on the grass with her legs tucked beneath her and one little bare foot poking from beneath the hem of her white cotton skirt. Johanna was interrupted by the sound of Nate's voice. "Hunh? What? I didn't hear what you said."

"I'm just depressed, is all."

"That's why you're talking about death and being buried,

---

whatever?"

He shook his head sadly. "Never mind, Jo."

she reclaimed her brusqueness and punched him playfully on his upper arm. "Oh, come on, Nathan. Lighten up! We're at a fucking *Be-In*, for chrissake! It's a celebration of life and an excuse to be happy. So here you are, all morbid. You're no fun, today, Nathan." A shiver warmed her body as she felt the surge of another headache. She had become used to them. She pondered over the irony of telling him not to worry about dying. Her expression fell into remorse.

He read the listless undercurrent in her tone. "You too, hunh?"

"Me, too what?"

"Depressed."

"I did not say that."

"You implied it, Jo. You and Dan getting along okay?"

"Nn—yes," she corrected quickly. "Of course we are. We're together for God's sake."

"Un-hunh," he replied in a tone dripping with suspicion.

"Shut *up!*" she giggled, then she batted him playfully on the arm again, causing her beer to slop over the rim of her cup. "You made me spill my beer. You owe me one."

He wrapped his arm around her waist, and she instinctively nuzzled her head into the hollow of his shoulder. "Here we are. Two depressed and lost souls," he said.

"Ah, Nathan," she sighed. "Who knows if you're right? I certainly don't."

CHAPTER THIRTEEN
The Photograph

I t was like creating a life.

Daniel juddered the developer tray back and forth to nudge a panel of photo paper until an image materialized like a ghost in the amber blush from the safelight. First came the hair, the darkest tone in the black and white image; then the eyes—those beautiful searing dark eyes; then the shadows in the coarse runnels of the stone background; then the skin—he remembered the feel of that sensuous, cocoa-hued skin. Its soft, smooth tone contrasting to the coarse rock background.

"Good morning, beautiful," He whispered and then smiled down at his new arrival. He wondered why he'd waited until now to print from the negative he'd processed almost five months before. Perhaps the final print was to him like a gift that had to wait a while to be unwrapped.

He had mastered the art of judging the readiness of his prints under the safelight's timid glow. The time was…now. He lifted the print from the developer and slid it into the stop bath to end the developing process, and then into the tray of hypo to fix and preserve the 16x20 inch image. He breathed in the vinegary smell of the acetic acid stop-bath, tufted with the musky smell of the fixing solution. He next slid his prize from the fixer and into a running water wash to complete the process.

Daniel thought about the circumstances of the shot he took back in Costa Rica in September, and how Carlos had allowed him a kiss after. He recalled the fragrance of his breath; a taste of peppermint smoothed with that of coconut. He once again imagined the silkiness of his skin.

He turned on the dim room lights and gazed into the picture as the wash-water streamed around it. The image of Carlos had set fully though the paper and into Daniel's soul. This picture was different from all the others he'd taken. Maybe it was something in the sensuous, provocative, coal-dark eyes.

From Watts until now, his photos had been mere records of events—he was just doing his job. He hadn't seen the depth in them that people like as Larry Graham and Marty Bloomfield did. But in this photo Daniel sensed something transcendent. He could hardly believe he'd taken it. He felt a surge grip him from within, forcing him to begin seeing what he had hidden deep inside. He caught his breath and stared at the picture; into it; into himself and, for the first time, he recognized himself as an artist.

Johanna tried to make the best of her boredom as she roamed through the photo exhibit in the gallery of Doe Memorial Library. On exhibition was the "Best Photography of 1966," a coveted competition, open to all the students and faculty. Many of the pictures were of activists and protests, as Berkeley had provided fertile ground for several gritty, tension-weighted demonstrations. One of the photos was a nicely crafted study of a wild-haired Jerry Rubin. He was standing next to the somber Mario Savio backlit in sunset on the Sproul Hall steps. Jerry held his megaphone loosely at his side, detached and pensive as he surveyed the crowd of protesters filling the plaza. The photo had won a spot in *Life* magazine the previous March but landed only a second-place prize in this exhibit.

The first-place photo was a 40-inch long landscape of a Napa vineyard at dawn. It was a magnificent work reminiscent of a mediaeval tapestry depicting furrows and trestles gnarled by grape vines. They coalesced from tendrils of mist and far back into an orange sunrise.

The third-place photo had been Daniel's black and white portrait of Carlos. The print was crisp but was softened during development with the aid of a wrinkled strip of cellophane over the enlarger lens.

The photograph troubled Johanna. At first, she wondered where Daniel might have taken it, until she recognized Carlos's features as Tican. He took this on their vacation? Was this one of the things he'd been doing while she spent all that time moping around alone in the gloomy Riki-Tican Bar drinking mai-tais and munching on Fritos? She scoured her memory. Why did the boy in the photo look vaguely familiar? Wasn't he one of the waiters or pool-boys at The Toucan Resort where they stayed? Something like that.

She concentrated on what it was about this simple portrait that drew her into it. It might have been the little pinpoint glitter of anticipation in the dark eyes. She wet her lips and sipped her Chablis. She had to admit it was a beautiful photograph of a beautiful boy. And that dug in deep. The real power of the portrait was what it conveyed out—a sad, tender simplicity and the subtle passion of an unrequited love. It radiated whatever emotion that had driven Daniel to take it.

She turned to ask Daniel who the subject was, but he'd disappeared into the thin crowd as though he might not want to discuss it. She felt a flash of a cold paralysis over her vague suspicion about the man she thought she'd come to know. She needed another wine, but first downed the one she held in her trembling hands.

Daniel had wended his way to a far corner to admire a light-sepia print of a provocatively disheveled, silken-haired nude emerging from a rumpled bedsheet. Though she exuded a comfortable, slatternly bearing, she possessed the smooth, delicate features of an adolescent.

A voice carried along on the fragrance of cherry pipe tobacco came from behind his shoulder. "I know her. That's Jenny Something-or-Other from philosophy. We had a few dates last year. Got totally wasted, but that's all that happened."

Daniel glanced behind him at a student wearing a tweed sport jacket and holding his pipe at a practiced angle. "Really," he said.

"Yeah. Do you know who took this?"

Daniel squinted at the photo tag in the wall next to the picture. "Uh, Josh Benton? He's a junior."

The tweed-jacketed student inspected Jenny Something-or-Other's small, stout-nippled breasts. Her hooded eyes were relaxed, as though she'd just been laid. "Then that Josh Benton's one lucky son of a bitch." He toasted the photo with his pipe and then ambled along to the next picture, leaving Daniel to stare back at Jenny-Something-or-Other's sloe-eyed gaze.

"Hello, gaucho. Buy a girl a drink?" Though she'd tried to maintain a modicum of her usual light humor, Johanna's tone sounded fragile with uncertainty.

His features relaxed into a smile as he looked at her. "Hello, hon."

She inclined her glass toward the photo. "Anyone you know?"

His smile drooped. "No. Someone just told me she's a philosophy student." He glanced back at the photo. "As a journalist, I generally don't mix with philosophers. It cramps my style." He thought of his father, Roger the Great. "…And ruins my life." He reached out and stroked Johanna's limp little ponytail. She shivered a relieved sigh over his show of tenderness.

She looked at the photo. "She is pretty, don't you think?"

"Maybe. A little prostitutey-looking, though."

She flicked a coy smile. "Nothing wrong with being a prostitute, hunh? Next to lawyers, it's the oldest profession. For all I know? I might have been one myself in a former life."

"I doubt that, Jo." He brought his hand from her hair to her cheek as she settled into his caress.

"Why not, hon? You don't think I would have made a good prostitute?" It sounded vaguely like a challenge.

He shook his head. "For all anyone knows, you could have been a man in a former life. Maybe even a lawyer."

She drew quickly back.

"Hey, Jo, don't worry. We can't be sure if we ever even *had* former lives."

"What? We must have hope for *some*thing after we die." Another pang of headache sent out a dark reminder from the beast within her brain. "It's not like we die, get buried, then decompose into nothing. That's like one big anti-climax." She leveled a searing gaze at him. "We *have* to have hope, Daniel," she said quietly, more to herself.

He just nodded his reply, then looked back at the photo of Jenny Something-or-Other. "How did you like my photo?"

She winced as she scoured her feelings for an answer. "Yes. It's nice, actually." She refrained from saying that it was beautiful.

"Who's that boy in your picture?"

"Just…someone I met."

"He looks Costa Rican," she replied as her anger began to simmer up. "Is that where you took it? During our vacation?"

"Yeah, I guess."

"You guess? You don't *know*? Sure, you do. I think *I* even remember him. He was one of our waiters, or something, at that creepy resort we stayed in."

His voice tightened. "How could you remember that?"

Her nervousness had become spiked with bravado. "Oh, I don' know. I guess I just have a memory for faces. Anyway, it is a nice photo, truly deserving of third place."

"Yeah. It's going into the Berkeley archives—into their permanent collection."

Johanna was overcome by a cool shadow of uncertainty as she glanced toward the exit. Her boyfriend would now forever be associated with that photo of, for lack of a better designation, a queer-looking nude guy. Her expression became sullen. "Daniel. I need to go home." She winced as she felt his touch on her shoulder.

"You okay, Jo?"

"I don't really know. I feel headaches in all this chill. I really need to rest a little."

"Okay, hon. I'll drive you home."

"No, Daniel. Really. You stay. I just need to be alone right now."

He wondered if his portrait of Carlos had somehow dismayed her. He reached into his pocket for the car keys. "Okay, hon. Here, take the keys. I'll catch a ride home with Bernie over there."

She held up a trembling hand to stop him. "That's okay,

Daniel. I'll just walk a little and catch a cab."

"Really?"

She managed a tight little smile. "Really." She extended her arms out and embraced him, holding herself close to him for a moment too long.

She pulled back and stared into his eyes as she wiped some dampness from her cheek. "I just want you to know I love you, Daniel," she whispered. "I really love you so much. I always will...love you." She kissed him lightly on his forehead, then turned and shambled toward the exit.

He stood confounded as he watched her go. He realized the photo of Carlos had revealed a subtle reminder of his sexuality. Maybe it was just as well.

Johanna took another sip of her vodka tonic—her third since she'd gotten home—and then sank back into the living room easy chair. She felt the unsettling comfort of the darkness cuddle her as the glow from her cigarette accented the dim, flickering light from a candle. She lolled her head deep into pillowed backrest of the chair and closed her eyes, trying to concentrate on a fragile concerto that only she heard. She raised her glass and took another sip followed by another languid draw on her cigarette. She lowered her cigarette to rest in the ashtray and drifted into a timid half-sleep.

She tried piecing together whatever she could. Remembering the photo of the post-adolescent boy in Daniel's photo, she recalled feeling alone and useless when he'd abandoned her a few times during their vacation. She visualized Daniel and the boy chatting over sodas, not booze, as the kid was probably not old enough to drink. Her imagination surged to envision Daniel's furtive touch resting upon the boy's hand, then the boy responding in kind as they gazed into one-another's eyes. Then they embraced, maybe a kiss on the cheek followed by one on the lips. And then…then…she was paralysed by the thought of where it might have led. She let out a primal, throaty groan: "Agggh!"

Her outcry sent the usually invisible cat scampering from wherever he had been nesting in the kitchen. Barely alert, Johanna sipped her drink and then downed it. She stared into the empty glass as if it was a crystal ball. Realizing it held no answer except for what it could contain, she labored up from the chair and trundled to the kitchen to mix another vodka tonic.

An hour-and-a-half later, she heard the telltale scrape of the front door as Daniel shuffled in. The living room light blared on and she squinted in defense of its rude intrusion.

"Turn th' fuggin' li' off!" she slurred from where she nestled on her side trying to pass out in the chair. She had tucked her slender, bare legs beneath the same serape she'd worn at the Be-In.

His tone was soft and contrite. "Oops. Sorry, Jo. I didn't see you there."

"Wha' time izzi', Dan'l?" She yawned as she strained to reach to the chair side table for the glass containing the filmy remains of her drink.

He turned off the light. "I don't know. One? One-thirty?"

"Shid! Iz-late."

"I need a little light. Can I turn on the one in the kitchen?"

"Knock yerzzef out. Azlong as you brin' me a drink."

"I think you've had enough, Jo," he said as he made his way toward the kitchen area.

"Don' tell me wad I had enough of, Dan'l! Shid…I'll make my *own* damn drin'!" She put her glass back on the table, then unfolded herself from the chair. She tried to stand, but wavered in place until she collapsed back into it. "Fug-shid!" she slurred.

"Come on to bed, Jo," he said from the kitchen. "Whatever's bothering you, we can talk about it in the morning."

She stared down at her hands and clasped one over the other to stop it shaking. "Fug no, Dan'l! I'm not goan to sleep in tha' bed with *you!* You go to fuggin' bed, an' have your wet dreams about yer…whatever. I'm stayn' in the chair an' sleebin' here."

"I have no idea what you're talking about, Jo. If it's about the nude girl in that picture, I don't even know who she is."

"Okay, Dan'l. 'f tha's what you wanna believe, fine. Jus' leave me alone…I'm gonna sleep now," she slurred as she closed her eyes, then opened them as an afterthought. "But before I do, I wan' you to know I got canzer in the head. I'm gonna die soon, so lemme sleep."

"What the *fuck,* Jo!" he gasped as he lurched into the room. "You have cancer? Is *that* what you just told me?"

"How fuggin' astute o' you. Yeah. I have canzer. There, I said it, now lemme fuggin' sleep in this fuggin' chair."

He came toward her. "Oh, shit, Jo? Why didn't you tell me sooner?"

"I din't wan your pid—piddy. I don' wan *anyone's* piddy. Now go 'way an' lemme sleep. Go." She waved him off as she turned away, then curled into a fetal position in the womb she'd made of the chair.

CHAPTER FOURTEEN
Battered Pieces

Daniel gazed out through the open balcony doors of their flat overlooking the bay. The nicely furnished, spacious ninth-floor apartment was too nice a place for their nil income. It had been an unexpected gift from Roberto through a wealthy real estate client who owed him a favor. Over Daniel's protests, Johanna sided with Roberto in favor of his insistence that his daughter live in the manner she became accustomed to under his roof.

The view was impressive. The low-hanging cloud of fog shrouding San Francisco across the choppy water of the bay took on the glow from the risen sun, as the height of the Twin Peaks and its clunky radio tower rose above it all in the far distance. To his left, the trestles and spires of the Bay Bridge spanned the five miles from the Emeryville shipyards to the edge of San Francisco's Mission district.

Daniel munched on his morning ration of Wheaties and focused on the light gray sails of a ketch slipping effortlessly through the bay. He wished he was on it, and it was taking him far away from the naked truth of his and Joanna's garbled relationship.

He'd woken up to find her lying above the sheets bundled in

her sarape as far away from him as she could get. He realized her returning to bed was more a matter of comfort and convenience than any sort of desire to lie close to him.

Making things worse would be her hangover. She didn't hold them well as they only made her thornier and disagreeable. And what was all this about cancer? He knew that alcohol had an effect like sodium pentathol—drunkenness often brought out truths amid the folly.

He soon heard her coughing dryly as she shuffled about in the bedroom, and he cringed in anticipation. He'd experienced her wrath only a few times before, usually under the brutal, hot sieges of her period. At this moment, he would have preferred facing bullets in Vietnam to whatever fury little Johanna would rain down on him.

"Good morning, Daniel," she said as she came into the kitchen.

He tried to shudder away the chill disguised by the chipper lilt of her tone. He focused hard on the ketch in the bay. "Yeah, hey, Jo."

"Sleep well?"

"Uh…no."

"Well, that's great. Neither did I." She ran some water in the sink. "Coffee?"

Christ, almighty! he wondered. *Why does she sound so fucking cheerful? Why isn't she hungover and grouchy?* "Sure. I guess I should have made some, myself."

"No matter. You never do it right, anyway."

Ah…of course. The prime weapon Every lover's arsenal: the passive-aggressive approach. "Jo, about last night. What…?"

"Ah-ah-ah!" She warned as she held up a trembling hand to stop him. "We'll talk about it when the time is right. For now, I need coffee. Lots of it." She dumped five healthy scoops into the percolator basket.

Daniel held his ground with a tacit silence as he carried his empty cereal bowl to the dining table. He watched her slather some peanut butter and jelly on two pieces of toast while the coffee brewed. The weight of silence made the plopping from the percolator sound deafening.

She carried her toast and coffee to the table, sat across from him and flashed him a feline smile. She bit into her toast, leaving a smear of jelly near her mouth. "Okay. Me first" She daubed the jelly away and heaved an uneven sigh.

"You first," Daniel agreed.

"I'm sorry for the way I acted last night."

"Okay."

She held up her hand again. "Ah-ah! Let me finish." She took a sip of coffee and then thought a little. "To say the least, Daniel. I'm confused. To say the most…I'm scared shitless. What the fuck has been going on between us? You've gone out of your way to keep your distance from me, lately." She tightened her lips, as she would often do to subdue her anger beneath an attempt to understand. "It's like you're keeping some huge inner secret from me. Are you keeping a secret from me, Daniel? Hunh?" She braced herself for his answer.

Daniel started weighing his options. "What secret? What are you talking about, Jo?"

"You tell me. What do you *think* I'm talking about?"

He looked out toward the fog streaming low above the bay. The east-facing building facades had turned bright in the sunlight.

"You're not going to find the answer looking out there, Daniel," she said. "Look at me." He did. "Is there anything you want to tell me? About us. About what you were doing when you were away all that time in Costa Rica?"

He knew this might be his chance to clean things up. No, not yet. He decided. He'd already suffered too much loss in his life, and he wasn't about to risk losing Johanna. "I should have spent more time with you, Jo. That was real stupid of me."

She kept her stoic bearing and suffered an uneasy smile. "*One day would have been stupid, Daniel. But four days? That is fucking disastrous. It was our vacation for Christ's sake!*" She stopped herself from raising her voice to a frenzy. Her eyes began to glisten. "What *I* think? I think you were out taking pictures of that pool-boy, and god knows whatever else you two did. Every time I think of it, I wanna puke!"

"Bus boy," he mumbled.

"Whatever." She took a moment to sigh, and then leaned toward him. She softened her tone as she rested her hand on his wrist. "Daniel, honey. I want you to level with me. And be honest. I won't hold anything against you because I'll always love you. I promise. Now, just yes or no. No excuses or embellishments, please. Just yes or no." Her voice had started to go hoarse as she gathered her strength for her question and his answer. "Daniel? Honey? Are you…are you more attracted to men?"

"Johanna, I…"

She jerked her hand back. "Daniel? Yes or no, God-dammit!"

The sudden shift of her tone startled him back into the truth of this moment, and his resolve to keep things alive between them. "No! And that's the truth."

"You promise? I have nothing to worry about?" she said through a tight choke. "The thought of us living that kind of lie would kill me, Daniel." She felt a flurry of chill over the thought of something killing her.

"It would me, too, Jo. I really…do love you."

She considered his claim, then stood and went to him. She held his head to her abdomen and stroked his hair. "I believe what you just said. Okay. I'm sorry I ever suspected…whatever I suspected. I love you, too." She kissed the top of his head. "Let's never keep anything from one other. Okay?" He replied by tightening his hold on her. "I don't want to lose you Daniel." She sniffed.

"You won't."

"I need you so much right now. I'm so scared." He felt her shoulders begin to heave in advance of a silent sob.

He pulled back. "Okay, Jo. Now you level with me about something you told me last night in your drunken stupor. You have cancer?"

Her hands trembled. "What? No, of course not." She turned away. "You said it yourself, it was a drunken stupor. I was kidding."

He shot her a suspiciuos look. "I don't think so, Jo. People don't kid about something like that."

Johanna walked back around the table and sat back down. She worked the stem of her coffee spoon between her thumb and forefinger as she thought about her reply. "Okay. I've told no one else." Her expression fell as she swiped a tear from her cheek. "I can't keep this in anymore, anyway. That bandage on the back of my neck when we were at Weir Beach last July? It wasn't from a mole removal like I told you."

"No?"

"I had gone to see my doctor for a biopsy. I got the results a few days before then about something I already sensed. Even before I met you, I knew. So yes, Daniel. I have cancer. The same kind of cancer my mother had."

His expression hardened in concern. "Oh, shit, Jo. They can take it out, right?"

She stared at the ground and shook her head, as she felt another jab of pain—another dispatch from the thing in her head. "Inoperable," she choked. "They can't get to it."

The silence fell like a weighted net around him. "How long?" he finally asked.

"We don't know for sure. Maybe one year; maybe ten." She broke into silent sobs as if she had fully realized, and now understood, the truth. She reached for his sleeve. "I-I don't want to die alone, Daniel. Please don't let me die alone!" It was a faint plea, barely a whisper. "All I know now is that I need your support."

He went over to her, stooped to her level, and held her close. "You have it, Jo."

She sighed into his shoulder, then pulled away and tried out a watery smile. "Thank you."

"What does your father say to all this?"

"He doesn't know. It would hurt him more than help me. My mother's death is still a raw memory for him. Now I have the same thing? It would kill him. "

"He's gonna find out sooner or later."

"I would rather save it for later. Can we just keep this between us?"

"Yeah, Jo. Of course we will."

She sniffed and buried her head in his shoulder again. "Thank you, hon. All is forgiven, okay? We can start over?"

"Yeah, I guess we can," he said,. He wanted to put her mind

at ease, while realizing he'd be going to Vietnam soon; perhaps to suffer all the consequences it implied. He'd be away for at least six months, and he now knew six months could mean a lifetime for Johanna. He stroked her hair. "I love you more than I ever thought I could, Jo. I will never stop loving you, no matter what," he whispered. But his comment didn't feel real to him.

Finally, he was struck by the germ of an idea about what would be best for everyone involved. No harm; no foul. Nate was the only friend Daniel could trust right now. He would call him to meet for beers tomorrow.

He kissed her hair, but his lips didn't feel the usual warmth of the touch; only the rough strands of her hair.

"Everything'll be fine, Jo. I promise."

"I love you, Daniel."

"Everything will be okay," he reassured her.

CHAPTER FIFTEEN

Down in Monterey

With the help of a couple of Sominex, Daniel slept hard and apart from Johanna. She lay still and tried to concentrate on the blooms of illumination from passing headlights rippling across the motel room ceiling. She heaved a sigh, rolled over and buried her head back in her pillow. It smelled old. Everything in the room smelled old. She looked over at Daniel, sleeping with his back to her, snoring in comfort.

Soon after they had returned to their Monterey motel room two hours ago, an arrhythmic thumping began to filter through the cheap walls. Occasionally, some hoarse, primal cry wailed above a cacophony of muffled guitar chords. Then came some muted yelling, one time emphasized by the crash of breaking glass against the wall behind their bed. That was bad enough, but Johanna was plagued by feverish spikes of headaches, and thoughts about Daniel again pulling away from her over the past few weeks.

The photo of the Costa Rican bus boy had continued to haunt her like an heirloom she refused to discard. She knew Daniel hadn't found his own answer as to where his commitment had settled, and this bothered her nearly as much as his going off to Vietnam in September. There at least he could fight off the very real dangers of that place by instinct. But a person cannot fight off that thing he may not know about himself. For herself, she needed the reassurance of holding him…and to be held in return.

She punched then folded her pillow against the headboard and sat up to light another cigarette. The glow from the flame of her lighter filled the space and then was swallowed back away into the semi-darkness. Her throat felt poxed from all the smokes she'd had today.

Since she'd lost Daniel's intimacy, his soft and easy touch was all she could try to remember. She reached over to lay her trembling fingers on his leg but felt no flutter of response. Even a week before, he would have eased to her touch, then maybe would have responded with an awkward embrace. He must have felt the momentary jostling of the bed as she settled back against the headboard. "Everything okay, Jo?" he muttered.

"Yeah, hon," she whispered. "You go back to sleep now." She puffed deeply, then felt his light, accidental touch on her thigh. It should have felt like something more than it did. "Sorry I woke you."

"What time is it?"

She looked toward him bundled in most of the blanket. She fumbled around the bedside table for her glasses, slipped them on, and then squinted at the dimly glowing clock-face. "Two-thirty." She suppressed a delicate cough as she tamped out the remains of her cigarette.

"Go 'sleep, now, Jo," he mumbled. "I gotta be back at the fairgrounds by 9 a.m., okay?"

That would leave her about three hours to kill before the concert started back up. It would give her time to find Nate at his parking lot campsite at the Monterey Fairgrounds. She'd take him up on that cup of coffee he'd offered her last night after Simon and

Garfunkel's performance of "Punky's Dilemma" closed out the first day of the Monterey Pop music festival. "Okay," she whispered hoarsely, and then felt another flaming swell of headache as she slipped from the bed. They had become nearly as regular as the thumping through the wall.

"Warya goin', hon?"

She rounded the bed and kissed the top of his head. "Bathroom. You go back to sleep now. I'll try to be quiet."

"Uh-hunh," he mumbled, then settled back into sleep as she stole into the bathroom where she'd stashed some weed and a half-quart of Scotch.

She closed the door and rustled through the satchel for her bottle of Scotch, which she withdrew and held up to the light like a found treasure. She pulled a Dixie cup from the dispenser near the sink, filled it and took a swig. She mused over the kitschy stupidity of the printed yellow daisies around the cup's circumference. She re-filled the stupid cup, took another swig. then fished around in the satchel for a couple of joints. She went out into the bedroom and eased into one of the dinette chairs at the Formica table near the window.

She parted the cheesy drapes and craned her neck to look out toward a commotion in the parking lot. Whoever was staying in the room door had now gathered around a baby-blue microbus decorated with yellow flower stickers. She heard a hollow chinkle as a bottle was thrown to the pavement.

She gazed into the softening yellow-white illumination of car headlights and watched them retreating as red smears of tail-lights down route 110. She thought again about the discussion she and Nate had at the Be-In over six months before. He had been right. At the heart of her fear, she was deeply depressed.

The grass-clotted dirt of the fairground parking lot was cluttered with little tents, sleeping bags and the awakening groans of their inhabitants. Johanna tried to suppress the damp, double-vision fever she was feeling from lack of sleep and the dull ubiquity of her headaches. She fingered the brim of her fedora and tilted the hat a little to the side, dousing her face in the merciful comfort of shadow. She found Nate fidgeting over his camp-stove near his lean-to attached his orange Karmann Ghia,.

"Got that coffee for me, Nathan?"

He looked up at her. "Jo! What a surprise. I wasn't expecting you this early. Yeah, I was just getting some ready for...for me." He sounded sheepish.

"Daniel had to show up early," she said distracted, by a woman's maxi-dress piled on top of his sleeping bag. She drew her lips taut to subdue her anger. "I, uh, see you had company." She fluttered a good-natured smirk. "She left her dress. Is she out and running around naked?"

"I lent her one of my shirts," he admitted. "She's freshening up in the latrine over there. "

She huffed out a nervous little laugh and settled cross-legged on the ground next to him. "How noble of you," He lit the can of Sterno under the stove. A dim blue glow flared from it as he shook out the match. Johanna trained a quick gaze over his shoulder at the gnarl within gnarl of the eucalyptus tree trunks. "I guess I won't ask if you slept well. Apparently, you might not have slept at all." She realized how caustic her comment sounded and softened her tone. "Me neither. I really do need some coffee."

"Working as a fast as I can on it, darlin'."

"Well, hell-*low!*" came Lynda's tired greeting. "Look. Jo's here!"

Johanna cringed back another surge of headache. *Shit! Lynda? Fuck you, Nathan!* "That I am. I see you two have found each other. Again. How nice."

Lynda leaned down to peck a kiss on Johanna's cheek. "It's great you're here, sweetie. Now we can have a little pow-wow around the campfire. I have the peace-pipe and the magic tobacco."

"How thoughtful of you, Lynn. But no thanks," Johanna mumbled.

Lynda flashed her a glare, then mellowed her expression. "You okay, Jo? You seem, I don't know, a little riled. Love your hat, by the way."

Johanna glanced at Nate as he absorbed himself in measuring out the coffee. "Just tired, I guess. Not much sleep last night."

"Oh," Lynda said as she sat next to her. She tucked the long tail of Nate's flannel shirt close around her lanky legs.

"How strong do you all want it?" Nate said.

"Strong?" Johanna said.

"Yeah. Your coffee. How strong do you want it?"

"Oh. Strong enough. Whatever."

"Don't worry about me," Lynda quipped. "I'll just smoke the grounds."

Johanna tried to ignore her discomfort over Nate and Lynda sitting in the two seats behind her as they shared private double-entendres. Instead, she concentrated on the stage where Country Joe and the Fish were belting out their anti-war anthem, "I-Think-I'm-Fixin'-to-Die Rag."

The song reminded her that Daniel could get killed in Vietnam, and bloated up a warm bubble of anxiety in her stomach. How could she let something as paltry as a passing resentment over him overshadow that? She wanted to run down there into the undulating mass to hug him with all her might. She scanned the crowd for a copper-haired man in a yellow windbreaker wearing three cameras around his neck.

"Hey! I see Danny!" Lynda blurted. She stood up and waved. "HI, DAN-NEE!"

"Where?" Johanna said. "Where is he?"

She brought Nate's field glasses to her eyes and pointed toward the stage. "Over there! On top of the thing."

"What thing?" Nate said, then saw Daniel. "Holee shit! What a fucking idiot!"

"Where *is* he?" Johanna blustered.

Nathan placed his fngertips on her temples and turned her head toward the stage and up. "There."

Johanna steepled her hands over her mouth. She gasped when she saw where he was. "Oh, sweet Jehovah! How did he get all the way up there?"

He'd taken a perch fifty feet up on the top of the open-fronted shed covering the stage, aiming his camera down at County Joe and The Fish. He was leaning precariously forward to frame the right shot. "He's gonna fuckin' *kill* himself," Nate said.

"Anything for that fucking shot," Johanna lamented, then yelled as if he could hear her: "Daniel! Get down from there! NOW!"

Lynda scanned the crowd with the binoculars. "Hey!" she said. "There's Pete!"

"Really?" Nate said. "Peter's here?"

"Not *that* Peter," she said, "the *other* Pete. The *fun* one." She handed the field glasses back to him and started to gather up her things. "I gotta go," she said, then gave him a quick kiss on the cheek. "Thanks, darlin'…For everything. Really good to see you again. 'Bye, Jo. " Then she rushed away to join Fun Pete.

"God, I hate that woman," Nathan grumbled as he stared after Lynda until she was swallowed up in the whooping, stomping, cheering crowd.

Johanna smirked through the lingering silence. "Easy come easy go, I guess…Again," she taunted. "If it makes you feel any better, Nathan, she does that to all of her guys."

"Yeah, I know."

"I mean, you just can't pin her down for more than one ni—"

"I *know*, Jo!"

"Oooh. Touchy-touchy."

"Yeah, well," he conceded.

She stroked his arm. "You just hoped it would be different this time? You know that's the definition of insanity. Lynn has that kind of effect on her men. She breaks them when she drops them. It's kind of her brand." She eased back down into her seat but kept her eyes trained on Daniel, who finally slid himself backward on his stomach and stood up. She breathed a sigh of relief, then looked behind her only to find that Nate was gone. "Oh, for shit's sake," she murmured, hoping he hadn't gone to try to reclaim Lynda. She shook her head and settled her sights back on the stage to watch Al Kooper sing "One."

Nate reappeared about fifteen minutes later carrying four beers in a cardboard tray. "I've come bearing beers."

"Why, thank you, Nathan!" she brightened as she took one and sipped.

"I guess I shouldn't have done that."

"What?"

"That thing with Lynda."

"Sometimes we make the wrong choices."

"It really didn't mean anything."

Johanna was overcome by the now-familiar wave of numbness that followed one of her headaches. She smiled forlornly down at her beer. "Yes, it did, Nathan. It mattered to you. It mattered to…me. I guess the only one it didn't matter to was her."

"What did you mean by that?"

"What? That it didn't matter to Lynn? Well, it doesn't. That's just who she is. She lives for that sort of thing—has since junior high. Running through men is a contact sport for her."

He smiled a woebegone smile. "Okay," he agreed. He looked over at her. "But I meant, what did you mean that it mattered to you?"

"Nothing."

"Are you jealous?"

"No!" she blurted too quickly.

"You are, too, Jo. I can tell by the way you acted around her this morning."

"Well, Nathan, I *am*…not jealous." She cleared her throat. Her voice fell off. "Not jealous. No."

"Women aren't the only people with a handle on intuition."

She glowered at him. "Jesus, Nathan. The way you push this on me. It's like you *hope* I'm jealous over you and her."

He pondered his beer for a moment. "Maybe I do."

"What? You hope I'm jealous? Jeepers, gaucho, you *must* be sick. I should remind you that I'm living with your best friend." Her voice fell off again. "I'm happy, okay?"

"Yeah, Jo. You sound it."

"What is *that* supposed to mean?"

"I can read Dan pretty well and I've known you long enough to read you. Every time I bring one of you up around the other, it's like you want to make an immediate left turn. I know you guys aren't happy, even though you may just *think* you are. It's almost like you're *willing* this relationship between you, or some shit."

She lit a cigarette.

"Well?"

"Well *what*, Nathan? What? Are you asking if Daniel and I are happy?"

"Words to that effect."

"Honestly? I don't know. It's hard for me to figure him out sometimes. But you seem to have no problem with imagining what's in his thoughts."

"It's easy for me. I'm on the outside looking in on two people I deeply care about."

"Are you just saying all this to keep your mind off Lynn at my expense? Jesus!" She accented her anger with a stab of a puff on her cigarette.

"You think I went off with her last night out of unrequited love, Jo? No. Not at all. The truth is, she was a convenient outlet for my frustrations ...over *you*."

"*What?*"

"So. There it is."

She concentrated on her cigarette ash. In the distance, a crowd was stomping and cheering as The Electric Flag performed "The Night Time is the Right Time". She brimmed in anxiety as she took a slow, shaky sip of her beer. "Well. Just so you know, I love Daniel, and I know he loves me, but I'm not happy. I don't think either of us are. Satisfied?"

"Come here, Jo."

"What?" she whispered hoarsely.

"Come here. Come to me."

"Why? What do you want?"

"This," he said as he hugged her.

She hugged him back, as her angst weakened into tears. She felt a cool, wet bloom through her miniskirt where she had toppled her beer. "Shit, Nathan!" she sniffed into his shoulder. "I spilled my beer," she said through a nervous laugh. "I'm always spilling my fucking drink around you."

He stroked her hair. "Do you want to blow this pop-stand? Come on. Let's go somewhere else."

"Really?"

"Really. Let's be together tonight."

"Really?"

He smirked at her. "Would you knock it off with all the 'really's' already? Yes, *really.*"

She drew her fingertips across both cheeks to wipe away her tears. "Okay," she agreed through a sniff and a cautious little smile. "One thing, though."

"What?"

"I don't want to sleep in that same sleeping bag that Lynda and you…"

"What?"

"You know."

"Shit, Jo. You think we…? "

"You didn't?"

"No. I slept on the ground, on a tree root, and my back's killing me. Lynda had taken another tab of white lightning LSD and was too stoned to do anything but sleep. And not *in* the bag, but on *top* of it."

"Really?"

"There you go again. Yes, really. Anyway, I think I know a nice place we can go tonight where there are no fucking tree roots."

"What about Daniel?"

He kissed her lightly on the lips. "You know what? I might know him better than you think. I kind of have a feeling it won't bother him."

"Really?"

Daniel reloaded some film, then took a moment to train his telephoto lens back at the now empty seats where he knew Johanna and Nate had been. It hit him harder than he had expected. He felt cold prickles surge through his body and was flooded by a torrent of regret over what he had told Nate to do. He was engulfed by a momentary terror that he might lose Johanna, then felt a wave of cold comfort that it might be best for her if he did.

He recalled her trembling sigh in that quiet way she had of making love, as if wanting to hold on to the moment like a cherished secret. He saw again the way she had of smiling like a ten-year-old kid; a smile holding the innocence of something she didn't want to lose. Now, once so pure to him, she had become an unwitting victim at his expense.

But, he reminded himself, it was for the best.

The only act he could perform now was aim his camera; take a picture, then another then another. Even the music ceased to mean anything; the pictures became the only thing that could matter anymore.

And Johanna—she mattered more than ever.

CHAPTER SIXTEEN
Sunday Morning

Johanna considered what she'd done as she nudged her leg against Nate's; smooth against crisp; warm against cool. A frosty gust sliced the air. She shivered and cuddled closer to him, feeling the gentle slide of flannel against her skin as she pulled the cover of the sleeping bag over her exposed shoulder.

The cadence of Nate's soft snoring relaxed her. He'd worked hard last night to provide the gift she had willingly received—his easy sighs melding into her trembling ones until they climaxed into a weightless bloom of passion. She looked over at him lying on his back, then reached over and stroked his hair.

He stirred. "Wha—?" he muttered.

"S'okay, Nathan," she whispered, "I've got to get up for a minute."

"Yeah, yeah, okay Jo," he slurred. "Go in the secon' clump of rocks to the right."

He eased back into sleep as she slipped her glasses on. She rose from the bag and hugged her arms tightly against her breasts. She found a blanket, wrapped it around her body, slipped out through the tent entrance and headed for the beach.

Some of the nearer wave crests released their residual wind-blown mists as they surged up against the rocks fringing the wild coast of Big Sur. She felt the cool smoothness of the pebbles in the sand through the soles of her feet as she gazed out at the Pacific. A curtain of fog that blended into the sky swallowed up the horizon. She curled her toes into the sand and peered to her right where the beach ended at the foot of a craggy, ore-streaked palisade. In the far distance rose a layer of hills dimmed by a veil of rising fog.

Despite the morning chill, she opened her arms as though to embrace the world then hugged the blanket back around her. She carefully walked toward the shore, while trying to avoid stepping on anything that looked sharp. The frigid water sizzled around her ankles as she felt the ocean's retreat draw the sand out from beneath her feet, and then bring some back in one of nature's turns of give-and-take.

She felt the rising sun's warmth against her skin, tightened her self-hug and closed her eyes. She realized this was the first morning she hadn't woken with a headache. The absence of the headaches only reminded her that the tumor was still there. Baring her face to the sky, she began weeping through the fear of her uncertainty.

But then, for the first time in months, she felt happy. Really happy.

Nate had given up on trying to reason it all out. As he woke, he felt cemented in place by his guilt and a wave of shame over why he'd agreed to follow up on Daniel's. He tried to reconstruct how the conversation had gone two-and-a-half months before:

Why? He had asked Daniel.

Because she needs this, Daniel had answered.

That's crazy, man! She's your girlfriend!

Don't you want to? I've seen how you look at her; how she tries not to look back at you the same way.

What the fuck, Dan? Why this?

Because our relationship needs this—requires it.

"Why? Don't you love her anymore? You know you can't just throw her aside like this. No. I won't do this for you... or to her.

The problem is, he had said, *I might love Johanna too much. That's why I'm asking you to do this, Nate. You're the only one I can trust.*

That's plain fucking stupid, Dan! You can't do this to her: just push her out in front of me like this. I want to know why you want me to fuck your lover.

Daniel had to think about his answer. *Like I said. Because I trust you.*

That's not an answer, buddy. I want to hear why you'd even ask me to do something as screwed-up as this.

Daniel's lips had begun to quiver. *Because I'm not being fair to her. She needs someone to look after her while I'm away.* Another thought-filled pause. *Besides, I'm not right for her. Uh, and I sometimes sleep with men.*

Cut the shit, man! Nate had responded too quickly. *You're just using that as some sort of weird, bullshit excuse.*

No. I'm not. Really. Daniel replied firmly.

You're a fag? I mean, Are you sure?

No, Nate, I'm a bi-sexual. I like men and women.

Shit! Let it pass; you'll get over it. Jesus H. I hate all this fuckin' free love crap!

Never mind about that. Will you do it, Nate?

FUCK! Fuck you, Dan!

Will you do it?

This is a fucked-up idea.

Daniel tightened his lips. *Nate. I gotta tell you, she's not well.*

She's sick.

What? She's got a cold or something?

It's a little worse than that.

Daniel's sorrowful delivery had caused Nate enough concern for him to place a consoling hand on Daniel's shoulder. *Is she okay, buddy? I have noticed some strangeness in her behavior, lately. Like she's off somewhere else. It's nothing terminal, or anything like cancer, right? I mean you would have told —*

"No! *It's nothing like that. That's not it. She just needs someone to be with her, to hold her, maybe for just while I'm in Vietnam. She needs support. Will you do it?*

"*Damn you, Dan. Okay, I will. But you're a real asshole for this.*

Words to that effect.

Their conversation, filtered by the passage of time, left Nate feeling sorry for Johanna as he tried to justify that taking her to his bed was an act of kindness. Now he felt as victimized as she didn't yet know she was. He sensed she was out there thinking last night had been meaningful. Maybe it was. He fought back the sour lump of bile rising in his throat. He hated himself. He hated Daniel.

And yet, perhaps he'd started to fall in love with Johanna.

—————————————————

In a weird sort of trance, Nate pulled on his jeans and flannel shirt and then crouched through the tent opening. He spied Johanna walking along the shoreline with the blanket over her shoulders. She stooped to pick up a shell and held it up to the light as she walked, then broke into a short-distance jog through the softened sand of the tideline. Finally she stopped to catch her breath, then glanced over and up and waved as she came toward him.

"Brrr! Cold!" she said as she sidled up to him. "Here, feel." She took his face in her hands and kissed his mouth. "See?" Her smile brightened her features.

He noticed that her arms and legs were bristling in goose flesh. "Of *course* you're cold, Jo. You're standing here on a Big Sur beach practically buck naked in front of God and everybody." He lifted a spare blanket from the ground and draped it over her trembling shoulders.

"I know," she smiled as she clasped the blankets around her. "It's *great*, no?"

"Well, sweets, as much as I like the view, you should put your clothes on before you catch pneumonia."

"You mean what I was wearing yesterday? That mini-dress and white patent leather knee boots? I don't think they fit into this Ranger Rick scenario."

"Come on, Jo. Put something on."

"Do I *have* to? I feel so clean."

"I'm worried about you getting sick. Here…" He noticed her quick, anguished shrug as he said this. She remained silent as he dug to the bottom of the backpack, pulled out an extra pair of jeans wrapped around a flannel shirt, and held them out to her. "Here. The jeans'll be a little loose on you, but the shirt should do."

She unfolded the bundle and scowled as she held the shirt out like a dirty diaper. "I will not wear this thing."

"Why not?"

"This was the shirt Lynda was wearing yesterday morning."

"Yeah? So? It's not like it's diseased. You're shivering, Jo, just put it on." She stood and let the blankets drop around her ankles. She pulled up the jeans and clasped the waist tightly in a hand to keep them from slipping back down. The cuffs splayed out over her feet like clown pants. "Gorgeous," he said.

"This will not do. Besides, these clothes stink."

"One of the inconveniences of camping. There's a rope under my sleeping bag you can use for a belt, and you can roll up the cuffs, unless you want to change back into your go-go stuff."

"This is ridiculous, Nathan," she complained as she crawled her way back into the tent.

"Do you want pancakes?" He called as he busied himself over the little coffee pot.

"You have pancakes?" she said.

"It's not like we're stuck on the moon."

"No? We are not on the moon? I thought we were. Or somewhere else far away from here. Anyway, just coffee, thank you, Nathan. I don't trust your cooking."

Ten minutes later she emerged from the tent dressed in a compromise—her white go-go boots and mini-dress, over which she had thrown the flannel shirt that hung down to her thighs. She combed her hands through the length of her wind-ruffled hair to tame it into some semblance of a shape. "Coffee's ready," he told her as he stirred a scoop of instant into the steaming water of a chipped porcelain mug.

"Thank you." She took it in both hands and cherished its warmth. "I need a shower."

"You should have just taken a dip in the ocean when you had the chance."

"You're kidding. The water's too fucking cold." She sipped her coffee and gazed into the little blue cooking flame. "And don't tell me *you* would do that on a morning like this."

"I would," he nodded. "I'd do it every day if I could. Just find a little tide-pool in a cove and soak in it."

She stared at him over the rim of her cup. "*You* go soak in a tide-pool. Me? I prefer a nice warm shower."

"I'll take you to your hotel room for a shower, then we'll go back to the concert."

She associated the thought of the motel room with Daniel. "No. I don't want you taking me to the motel."

"Why not?"

She took another sip, then hunkered down near the cook stove. "What if Daniel's there?"

"Dan? He's out taking his pictures as likely he will be for the rest of of the day." He poured some coffee for himself, and then sipped. "Besides, you said you needed to change your clothes. I don't want him catching you this afternoon in the same stuff you were wearing since yesterday morning."

"Why, Nathan? You think it might make him suspect something? I never showed up last night so I'm sure that little sparrow has already flown."

"Right. I'm pretty sure he noticed you didn't show up."

She smiled wryly. "You *think*?" She fumbled around in the shirt pocket for her pack of cigarettes, took one out, lit it and blew out a long, thin stream of smoke. "What did you mean, Nathan?"

"About what?"

"About what you told me yesterday. That you didn't think Daniel would mind if we…and that you knew him well enough to know he wouldn't care?"

"It's really not for me to say, Jo. You'll have to ask him." He lit up a joint.

She leveled a perplexed glance at him.

"Really, Jo. Ask him. I don't think he'll even bring up that you didn't come home last night."

"Oh? You think he thinks I went off with the ladies to play an all-night canasta game? Or maybe a knitting marathon?"

"Just ask him, Jo."

She glowered at him. "I'm asking *you*, Nathan, God damnit! You're acting like you know something about him that you're keeping from me."

He didn't reply. He took a deep pull on his joint, and then extended it to her.

"Ugh-ugh. Got my own libation, here." She took another long drag off her cigarette. "Okay then, Nathan. Answer me this about Daniel." She waited for some sort of goad from him to go on. None came. "Oh-*kay*?"

"Yeah, Jo. What?" he asked.

"I'm thinking you might know the answer to this, because you two are such close friends." She allowed a pregnant pause.

"What is it, Jo?"

She closed her eyes and let out an uneven sigh followed by a little sniffle. "Did you know Daniel was attracted to men? Do you think he prefers men over women?"

He felt the nausea of guilt. "He loves you very much, Jo. I know this for a fact."

"God-damnit, Nathan! Am I in love with a faggot?"

He let the silence settle as he cherished another pull on his refer. He wanted to hold her in his arms and assure her everything was going to be okay, but he couldn't face her. "You'll just have to ask him, Jo."

"I can't do that, Nathan. I'm afraid of his answer; but I'm not afraid of yours." She sneezed and shivered away another chill.

"Okay, then," he said. "I honestly don't know."

CHAPTER SEVENTEEN

The Persistent Secret

Daniel fanned away the smoke from the cheap cigar Tony was smoking.. "Okay, Antonio," his voice was strained, "I'm ready for you to cease and desist from smoking those foul things."

"Aw, c'mon, buddy. These are a special blend shipped to me from a Tijuana whorehouse." Tony held up and examined a print of Jimi Hendrix burning his guitar on stage. "Jesus," he muttered.

"Well, it *smells* like a Tijuana whore house. Not that I've ever been to one."

"Ugh-*hunh*. Well, I'm gonna take you to one before we ship out in September."

"No, you're not."

Tony set the photo back on top of the others spread out on his desk and picked up one of The Who. Pete Townsend was using his guitar as a sledgehammer, while Keith Moon kicked over his drum set. "What the hell are these guys doing to their instruments?"

"It's The Who. They do those kinds of things. It's theater."

"I'd hate to think what they'd do to a hotel room. Okay we can use this, and the one of Jimi Hendrix."

"I thought this feature was about the L.A. music scene versus the San Francisco one," Daniel said

"Well, yeah it is."

"The Who is from the U.K."

"That's too bad. Can't we just *say* they're from L.A.?"

"No. You're weird."

"I am?"

"Yeah. And don't ever admit in public that you like opera over rock. Not at your age."

"Well, I *do* know who The Beatles are." He picked up another photo; this one of Grace Slick singing close into the mike. "This is nice."

"Jefferson Airplane. Kind of a hybrid. They're out of San Fran, but not as raw and unrestrained. They've been commercialized by L.A."

"Okay, we'll lead with that." He picked up another photo of a disheveled unwashed far-eastern man with sunken, dark-rimmed eyes. He was sitting cross-legged on a little Persian rug with his scrawny brown bare legs cradling what appeared to be an oversized mandolin. "Who's this savage?"

"That's Ravi Shankar. He played for three hours on Sunday afternoon."

"Looks like he was wrung out of a coal mine. Is he any good?"

"If you like sitar music, and you are very stoned. To me it sounded like a three-hour cat fight."

"Sounds like fun," Tony said. He put down the photo and then crushed out his cigar. "So, I'm, like, getting real psyched-up for Saigon. Yesterday I went out and bought a big backpack from Abercrombie and Fitch. Pockets everywhere. Big enough to hold my typewriter and two changes of clothes."

"Jesus, Tony. You're not going on safari with Hemingway.

You've seen the news. We're probably going to be huddled in some swampy trench somewhere in a jungle, and scared shitless."

"Not me, Dan."

"Not you," he scoffed through a wry smile. "Tony? You'll be out there peeing in your pants. Forget the change of clothes; just pack eight changes of underwear. And dry socks."

"Hell, no man! I see those fucking bullets? I'm gonna light up a stogie and charge outta my foxhole with my M-16, just like John Wayne at Iwo Jima."

"He was never at Iwo Jima. He suffered out the war on a Hollywood soundstage. Anyway, leave your typewriter behind in Saigon."

"Fuck no. I'm bringing it into the trenches with me."

Daniel sputtered a tight laugh. "Oh, okay. You'll be writing your dispatch while you're shooting at the same time." Daniel leaned confidentially across the desk and dropped his hand on Tony's forearm. He felt a little tension in response, then slid his hand away. "Tony. It isn't gonna be any sort of thrill ride out there. When I covered all that was all going down in Watts and Hunter's Point, all I had was my Pentax, and I was scared outta my gourd. I didn't have time to think of what I was taking pictures of."

"Yeah, Dan. But they were good."

"That was me and my camera on autopilot. If I'd actually been thinking about the quality of what I was shooting, my shots would have been lousy and I most likely would have been dead by now." He had a fleeting vision of Jared dead amid the smoke of teargas and fires. He cringed at the memory of the stink of burning tires. "Scared shitless," he mused.

"Stop that, bro. Now you're making *me* scared."

"Really? Good," Daniel said as he leaned back in his chair and gazed out the window at the surreal alabaster-and-glass cityscape of downtown Los Angeles. Even that looked like a Hollywood set. "That's when we do our best work, you and I, when we're under the proverbial gun. With you, it's deadlines. With me, it's been live ammo."

"That's what I love about it all."

"You're romancing a very ugly thing, Antonio."

Tony took a sip of his coffee. "Or…maybe I know that and I'm trying to make the best of it. Speaking about romance, how are you and Johanna doing? You know you should really bring her down here with you sometime. Seriously, Dan, the *Trib* could put you two up in Beverly Hills. Sort of like a last fling before the warrior goes off to war."

"Thanks, man. But Jo hates L.A."

Tony thought about this for a moment. "Come to think about it, so do I."

Daniel wet his lips, overcome with the dry sense that Johanna would probably be with Nate again tonight while he stayed in Los Angeles. For a little over week after that first night she spent with him, she was laid out and rendered useless by a wicked head cold. Then for a few nights last week, she went away. She claimed that one of her old high school friends had just moved to Napa, and she wanted to take a few days off to visit. He knew, of course, that there was no high school friend im Napa.

Nate felt the easy comfort of Johanna nestling her head against his chest her as they strolled down the Battery East Trail. Her smile broadened as he put his arm around her waist.

In a rare occurrence for August, the fog that was usually trapped in the neck between the ocean and the bay had lifted, and the spires and girders of the Golden Gate gleamed orange against the sky. "I love this bridge," she said.

The breath of her voice felt warm against his shirt. "Yeah." He said as he tried to reconcile his awareness that he might have fallen in love with her. Lynda had tortured his trust of love, and he should have known better, but his feelings toward Johanna felt comfortable. Their words had done little but pass the time, as they had reached that sweet place where the silence spoke for itself. He concentrated on the water swirling around the rocks of the Battery, then out further into the play of sunlight on the water.

"Nathan, when are you going to tell me?"

It had become her perpetual question. "I can't tell you. I'm not so sure I know, myself, anymore."

"I have to hear it from you, Nathan. I just can't fully grasp whatever it is you and I have until I know."

"*Do* you know what we have together, Jo? 'Cause I certainly don't."

"I think I do know, Nathan. But like you I'm having a hard time understanding it."

"…mmm," he conceded as they walked. The silence was interrupted by a swooping gull's *skawk*, which then dissolved away. "Do you like it?"

"Do I like what?"

"Us. What we have. Do you like it?"

She leaned away from him. "Of *course* I do. You think I've been crawling into your bed for the last few weeks just to spite my boyfriend?" She knew immediately that was the wrong thing to say. "Sorry, I didn't mean it to come out like that. Really, I didn't."

"Yeah, you did, Jo. At least a little. There are times I think we mighta both been played."

"Been played? What does *that* mean?" she glowered. "You mean by Daniel?"

"No," he defended. "But by what we've been doing, and where it's brought us. Look, I've said enough. My thoughts are getting all twisted up."

"No. You have *not* said enough, Nathan, because you haven't told me anything. Do think either of us know where we stand with one-another? Or even with Daniel? Come on, hon. I need closure to make sense of all this. What we're doing goes against my father's Catholiscism—I'm risking Hell for it. I will need *something* to say when I reconcile all this when the time comes." She gritted her teeth though another swell of headache, now accented by a dry nausea, as she feared that her time could come soon.

"That's all a myth, you know. All that standing before St. Peter at the pearly gates. It's pure bullshit mythology."

"It is?" She blustered out a giggle and punched him in the arm. "Turn around three times and say three novenas to the Holy Virgin Mother, you heathen."

"Virgin Mother is a contradiction in terms. It's an oxymoron, like most of religion."

She tousled his hair, then leaned back against him as they walked toward the bridge. "You *are* a heathen, then, Nathan. Maybe that is one of the things I like about you. Your tortured soul."

"Not really. I've just got a touch of agnosticism, is all. I'll get over it, maybe by the time Hell freezes over," He pursed his lips in thought. "If there is a Hell, of course."

CHAPTER EIGHTEEN
Indoctrination

Daniel breathed in the harsh scent of pine and the unctuous one of gun oil as he felt the rifle stock against his cheek. The center circle in the target bolted in a frame to a tree trunk 25 yards away was a blur on top of the bead on the front of the M-14's barrel. He blinked away the blur and the target crystallized into clarity. He tightened his grip on the handguard, held his breath, then fired. At first, the noise had been deafening, but over time it sounded more like a muffled crash. The blush of a bruise in the notch of his right shoulder testified to his learned acceptance of the rifle's jolting recoil.

His accuracy with the combat rifle had come naturally to him, probably due to his experience aiming the camera and his learned ability to stay steady and still. The rubber bullet shivered and flipped the metal target. The bullet's impact resounded as a ding rather than the telltale clang of a bullseye. In the last two days he had scored three direct near-center hits. He breathed in, and then took aim at the next target.

Tony, however, had been more concerned about the dirt on his elbows and knees than about where he pointed his gun. He'd grazed his targets only twice in the last couple of days, but he was good on the obstacle course. His upper body strength was greater than Daniel's and more than half of the of the 25 other journalists at Pendleton's civilian combat school. He'd sometimes challenge the other journalists to a net-rope climb, with the losers buying rounds later at the civilian club.

Daniel was ertain that the rowdy place must have seen more action than any battlefield in Vietnam. Among reporters and journalists, drinking and pot were bonds of acceptance. The correspondents were brothers in arms, energized by a latent fear of the unknown that would threaten them a month from now. Combat journalism classes had taught them that, even though soldiers and grunts in the field were united in watching one anothers' backs, journalists often worked alone. In those rare cases when they were among solders in the mess hall, they were treated as outsiders who worked for outlets that paid them *beaucoup* bucks to be there.

They were also warned that some troops they interviewed might bloat their experiences as many of the guys might be war-worn enough to believe their own stories. So always, absolutely, under all circumstances, no exceptions, they must clear any dispatches through the Public Information Office in the Military Assistance Command, Vietnam office (MACV) in Saigon, especially any stories involving inflated American body counts. MACV knew the *true* numbers. Any undocumented rogue dispatches would be denied by the military and could result in the journalist being blackballed from going out to cover the troops, as they were considered guests of the military. One last thing. Though the journalists could, at times, break away from the companies they were covering, they were on their own and no longer under the protection of the U.S. Government. Even then, they must clear whatever they reported through MACV.

"You ready to go, Dan?" Tony asked as they lolled after hours on the base's Del Mar beach sipping beers.

"No, but I'm prepared, I guess. I've got four cameras from the *Trib*, then the two of my own and a million changes of underwear, all of which I know I'm gonna need. But no gun to defend myself from getting killed."

"I guess they'll give us guns when we get there. Leftover ones because we're just journalists. Probably they won't work."

"Hence all the underwear." He took a swig of his beer. "You, Antonio? You ready?"

"I guess I always have been. But all this boot camp shit is giving me the willies and the reality of it all is starting to sink in."

"Are you scared, yet?"

"That's just it. I'm not sure." He flicked his cigarette onto a retreating wave and concentrated on it being pulled out into the ocean. "But yeah. I'm ready."

"I think I'm resigned to it now," Daniel said. "It's hard to believe that in a few weeks we'll be out there playing with live ammo…and with our lives." He thought about Johanna. "I feel like this is my last chance to go make amends for all the shit I've put people through in my life."

"Jesus, man, you're grim. Hand me another beer would ya?"

Daniel brushed his comment off with a weak smile as he handed Tony a beer. "Such is life."

Tony toasted him. "Such it is, my friend." He poked the top of the can with the little church key he kept on his key chain. "So, do ya think we should vet our dipatches with the Military Assistance Command before we file them?"

"They made that pretty clear."

"Ya *think*? Makes me wonder how much stuff they're hiding."

Daniel smirked as he extracted a joint from the breast pocket of his fatigue shirt. "It's a God-damned war, Antonio. Everyone knows that the first casualty of war…"

"…is the truth. Yeah, I know." Tony said, then found a stone and flung it toward the tideline. "What a fuck-up, hunh?"

"Yeah," Daniel said as he held out the joint.

Tony raised his beer-can. "I never toke while I'm drinking. One experience just screws up the other. D'ju hit any more bulls-eyes today?"

He took a quick puff. "Two," he blurted in a little choke.

"Two? Damn, man! You're good!"

"Might have been two-and-half. I don't know."

"She-it! I can't even hit the fuckin' target."

"Yeah, I noticed. The trees in that forest with all the hanging targets will never be the same."

"That bad, hunh?"

Daniel took another puff. "Worse," he coughed. He looked out and saw the white triangle of a sail in the clear distance. "You know, Tony? If I get out of this thing alive, I'm gonna get a sailboat."

"Fine, indeed. A big one?"

"Even bigger."

"Sure, buddy. You and Johanna can take some time off to sail around the world. You'll have earned it." He took a hearty pull on his beer.

Tony's mention of Johanna led Daniel to think again about what he had to tell her once he'd get home in a few days. She had probably fallen into a routine with Nate by now. Her call to him the night before had been cordial enough and didn't telegraph any sort of chill or apprehension. Though she sounded distracted, probably by her headaches, she hadn't come across as the good old sardonic Johanna, who'd laugh at her own dumb jokes. He already missed her easy, mischievous, childish smile; that dry rasp that accented her voice; that coquettish, feisty glint in her eye; her bad, over-spiced cooking.

He imagined the warmth in her hug, not the passive hugs of the past few months, but the ones that began their relationship. He wanted so much to reconcile himself to her and clear things up to protect her from all the turmoil growing within her. He hated that he had set Nate up with her. How fucking stupid. Hitting a lousy bullseye was easy by comparison. God, how he'd come to love her!

The sailboat was now hidden by an outcropping jetty of rocks. Daniel picked up his warm can of beer from where he'd nestled it in the sand. He toasted the gone sailboat and took a sip.

CHAPTER NINETEEN

Peeling Back the Onion

Johanna glanced over her shoulder at Daniel leaning pensively with his arms folded against the balcony railing. He contemplated the potted red begonia dwarfing the patio table. They had almost run out of the right things to say, as their relationship was hollowing out. What was certain was that he would be shipping out for Saigon in four days. She, perhaps more than he, was probably weighted down by the fear they might not see one another again.

"Daniel, there's something dragging me down, and I have to tell you."

He let this sink in as he stared at his sneakers. "You've been sleeping with Nate."

"SHIT! How did you know? He didn't tell you, did he? God-damnit, he told you!"

He looked over at her. "He didn't tell me, Jo. I..uh.. suspected."

"God-damnit, Daniel," she gasped in a caustic whisper. "It was the way you were being. I couldn't take it anymore. I felt imprisoned by your ignoring me. I just…could…not…fucking…take it."

"I'm sorry, Jo. I'm so sorry." He heard the faint rustle of her movement as she turned and leaned back against the rail next to him.

"Why did it have to come to this?"

He looked over at her as she gazed at him, as though expecting a resolution.

"Daniel? Can you tell me why we even have to *have* this conversation?" She jabbed out her cigarette. "What's happened to us?"

"I don't know," he said in a tone seething with fatique.

"Well, I *do*. I know there's something more to this. I can tell, and it's been eating you up inside." Her expression softened with her tone. "Come on, hon. You can tell me. I can take it."

Daniel bit his lower lip, as he took a thoughtful sip of his drink. He measured out his answer. "I did know about you and Nate. I set it up for him to have an affair with you. I suggested it."

She jolted in sudden surprise. "WHAT? What the FUCK, Daniel?"

"I thought it would be best."

She pursed her lips white as she glared at him. She lunged toward him and flailed her sharp little fists against his chest. "You…fucking…SHIT!" she screamed.

He let her pound him, hoping she might tire, but she only hit him more aggressively.

"I had to! I *had* to! Our marriage was suffering!" he cried.

"No *shit*! No…fucking…*shit*!" Finally, her hits became softer as she tired and pulled away from him. Her glare continued to bore into him. "Why, Daniel? Why did you set me up with your best friend? Why would *any*one do such a shitty thing? Why the fuck would he even agree to it?"

"I did it for you. For us."

"Oh that's fuckin' *rich*!"

"No, really, Jo. I didn't set this up because I stopped loving you. I never have stopped loving you. I did it because I love you too deeply. I wanted you to be happy and protected against all that'll be coming down on you. It's something you told me back in May."

"I said a lot back then. What?"

"You said you didn't want to lose me—that you didn't want to…be alone. That you needed someone to protect you."

"I think I said I didn't want to *die* alone," she said solemnly.

He sighed. "I'm going to Vietnam, Jo. You need someone you can trust to look after you. Hon, I can't live up to the responsibility of protecting you. I could be killed or wounded. And the last thing I'd ever want would be for you to have to look after me in a wheelchair on top of all you're going through. Maybe, as much as it would hurt, I wanted you to leave me." His voice shook as he choked back some tears.

"Damn it, Daniel! I would do anything in my power to look after you, just as I know you would look after me. So, okay. Let's just say you come back from Vietnam healthy and in one piece. That might and probably will be the case, and I want *you* to come back to me. Why? Because I love *you*, and here you go throwing me over to some substitute. And your best friend, no less. I made up my mind to fall in love with you over a year ago. And I do not make such choices lightly. I love *you*, Daniel, not Nathan. I could never feel about him as I do about you." She lit another cigarette. "Now I've got to ask *you* something. Do you love *me*?"

He turned her to him and held her face in his hands. "Yes. I love you, Jo. More than I ever thought possible. Before I met you, I only pretended I knew how to love. You taught me how to love completely."

She wet her lips in thought. "More than those other, uh…men you've been with? That pool boy you took that picture of and that other guy, Jason?"

"Jared. That was a long time ago. And yes. I love you. More than I could love any—anyone else."

She placed her hand on his cheek. "If you do, and I believe you, then you do have the strength not to get yourself wounded over there. I want to be with you until I...." She gathered him into an embrace and kissed him hard on the mouth. He felt the ache of his rifle recoil bruise as she burrowed her head into his shoulder. "Thank you, Daniel. Just... thank you." She kissed him again then gazed at him. "Oh, hon. I love you so much." She stoked aside a forelock of his hair.

"I'll tell you what, Jo. If...*when* I get back home, I think we should get married."

She stiffened. "What? Married? What about my...cancer?"

"We're going to take that fucking thing on, and we'll beat it together. Forget what your doctor tells you about how many years and all that bullshit, okay? We *will* beat this thing."

When she looked into his glistening eyes, she believed that somehow it might be possible. "We will, right?" she said. "Kick this fucking thing right out of my head?" She pursed her lips and fell sobbing into his shirt. "Yes. I will marry you, Daniel. We're going to see this through together and we *will* survive."

"Yes, Jo. We will. Together."

She tugged his arm. "Well, then, let's go."

"Where?"

"To our bed."

They lay facing each other half-covered in the tangle of bedsheets. He ran his hand over the curve of her shoulder. Her skin felt as smooth as a ripened plum. She looked so innocent, like the child that had always drawn him to her. For the moment, there was nothing wrong, no torment; no misunderstanding; no secrets; no Vietnam…no cancer.

"You are so beautiful."

She smiled. "Shut up." She traced her fingertips around his chest. "So are you."

He heard a harder sort of dry rasp in her whisper. He kissed her forehead. "I love you. I believe in love because of you, Jo. You did this for me. You made me believe."

Her expression turned serious. "Why did you ever doubt you could love, hon?"

He thought about his response while she lit a cigarette. "I think it started back when I was just an eight-year old kid in Chicago." There was a choke in his voice. "But that's all gone and dead."

She moved her fingertips from his chest to his cheek. "But maybe not buried. If you want to tell me about it, Daniel. You know, to release whatever it is; I'm here to listen."

He lay in silence, then said: "Ricky Taylor." There was an undercut of venom in his tone. The ensuing silence hung leaden.

"Ricky Taylor," Johanna said. "Who is he, hon?"

"I hate him. Hated him." He pursed his lips tight in an anguished remembrance. "He was a farm-boy from Idaho. I guess his family struck oil or something, because they were suddenly living well-off enough to afford the apartment above ours on Lakeshore Drive." He cringed at her touch but wished she would never stop.

"Your father could afford an apartment like that on a teacher's salary?"

"He and my mother both came from money, and his first book was a minor hit. Anyway, Ricky was fifteen, and I was eight. I looked up to him as sort of my teenage mentor. But he frightened me because he was a little backward. Anyway, he made me feel important and showed me some respect my parents never would. I felt he accepted me. I didn't know then that it was part of how he operated. "

Johanna's took a long drag on her cigarette. "Operated?"

"It started innocently enough. First a pat on the shoulder; then a hug; then a kiss on the cheek. One time he made his thirteen-year-old sister undress and had her stand naked in front of us. I remember she stood still as a statue. He told me to run my hands around her body especially her little breasts and then down below. She acted bored, like she'd done all this before. He told me to keep doing it, so I did. I guess at the time I thought it was gross, just like any eight-year-old would.

"I remember looking over my shoulder and seeing Ricky with his hand in his unzipped pants, massaging his part. 'Keep going, don't stop,' he said. So I did. I pretended I was molding clay in class, so it wasn't so bad. I remember her just standing there like some sort of prop, not responding. Like she was just part of…it all." Daniel went silent again as a tear rolled down his cheek.

"It's okay, hon. You need to get this out. I'm here."

He bit his lower lip. "Then Ricky…Ricky spun me around and kissed me on the lips as he reached down and rubbed me. I let him do it because, like I said, he frightened me, and I didn't want him to beat me up. Then he took me to his bed and fondled me naked, while his little sister watched. That's how it all began. I've even forgotten what he looked like. I only remember his contorted face in extreme close up. He had missing teeth and he smelled like a cigarette, and like garlic. He had this big patch of a scar in his cheek. I remember how it gleamed. And his breathing—that still haunts me. He breathed these loud, gasping, uneven breaths broken by his swallowing close into my ear. At first, I tried to be oblivious to all, but after a few months I got a tiny erection and began to enjoy it."

"A few months? How long did he do this thing to you?"

"Four years, until I began to reach puberty. Anyway, after a few years, not only did I enjoy it, I asked him for it until he dropped me like I had abused *him*. Finally, he moved away, leaving me hurt, confused, and humiliated. I didn't know where I stood. I was only twelve."

"Oh, honey. I'm so sorry you had to go through all that. Why didn't you tell your parents?"

"I don't know, I guess I was too ashamed. One of the worst parts about this was that even though my mother didn't know, I think my father did. I know he did. But he didn't do anything to stop it—didn't even try. He'd never thought of me as his kid, but just some sort of prop in his stage set. Maybe that's why I was drawn to that fucking teen-ager to begin with. I needed to feel wanted."

Daniel sat up in the bed and stared down at the furrows in the sheet. She eased up next to him. "Did you ever come to terms with your father?"

"I suppose I came to his terms. About the time I turned fifteen, after his second book became a big success, he started to treat me as some sort of peer. Like his minion. I helped him research his stuff as he groomed me to be a sociologist when I didn't know exactly what that was. I learned quickly enough. I was the class Marxist-socialist in high school, and I turned my frustration over my father into rage against all mankind. I trusted no one."

She sniffed back some tears as if she felt his anguish. "Did that help you forget about what happened to you when you were eight?"

Daniel shook his head as he looked out the bedroom window. "I was attracted to girls. I even had a year-long relationship with a girl named Connie Mueller when I was a high school after we moved to Iowa. But that didn't turn out too well. Something in me still craved boys—it was like I was cursed. I never followed up on it until a short relationship with my roommate in college. That's when Connie found out and dropped me."

"Did you ever see her after that?"

He weighed out his answer in silence. "No. She committed suicide. I blamed myself for having been been in that relationship with my roommate."

"It wasn't your fault, hon. Your high school fling didn't last that long. This Connie could have easily moved on. There are usually bigger things in a person's life that would lead them to suicide."

"And then there was Jared a few years ago. He might have been an experiment for me to expunge the curse of Ricky Taylor. But instead, I only ended up hating myself…" He kissed her on the forehead. "Then I met you that day at the Yacht Club and you gave me hope. I sensed something needy about you reaching out to my needs. It was our needs that brought us into love, Jo."

She gathered his face in her hands to kiss him, but then turned away to stifle a chortle. "Oh, yeah. You were *something*, all right. I thought you were from another planet, the way you acted so confused. I think I might have pitied you. I couldn't let you suffer, and I had to draw you in because I felt so deeply for you, right from then."

He kissed her. "Thanks for that. And thanks for letting me finally release all the shit that's been eating me up inside for years." She tightened her expression. "Another headache?"

"Yeah," she cringed. "They may have gotten a ltlle worse, lately. I've been starting to feel really dizzy." She placed her hand on his bared knee. "It'll be okay. I've got another appointment with Dr. Kornfield later this week. I'm sure he'll prescribe the right drugs."

"How many pills are you taking now, Jo?"

"About eight, I think."

He placed his hand on top of hers on his knee. "Is Kornfield okay for you? I mean, from what I've seen, he's a little pill-happy."

"I'm living better through chemistry," she said, then tamped out her cigarette. "But, yeah, he's okay. He'll probably send me back to the oncologist again for another test. Soon I'll be glowing in the dark from all the x-rays."

CHAPTER TWENTY

The Mahogany Pen

Dressed in her Saturday-casual faded jeans and oversized Oxford shirt, Johanna stood barefoot in the laundry closet. In a minute, the wash cycle would end, and she could add some bleach. She looked out at the living room carpet cluttered with the clothes and the personal paraphernalia Daniel would be taking with him to war.

He acted unfazed as he went about packing the Abercrombie & Fitch duffle bag with its million-and a-half-pockets that Tony had talked him into buying. Next to it were two oversized camera gadget bags swollen with gear, including his two Pentaxes and four *Trib*-issued Nikon F-1's: the official camera of the war. He seemed to be more excited about his state-of-the-art gear than concerned about where he would put it to use. But then, maybe it was a smoke screen. Maybe he was trying to hide his true fears from her.

The wash cycle for the bedsheets ended and she poured in some bleach. As the cycle resumed, she tip-toed to the living room and crept up behind where Daniel was stacking some shirts. She slinked her arms over his shoulders.

"Hello, you," she said.

"Hey," he said, and moved his hands up to stroke hers.

She maneuvered him to face her, then leaned down and kissed

him. "You know I'm going to miss you. I can't stand that you're going away. And for a whole year."

He nestled his head against the softness of her belly. "Six months. The *Trib*'ll draw me back in May. They almost insist on it."

"Still, it may as well be a year. It'll be no fun for me, and complete hell for you," she pouted in a choke. "Sometime in May?"

"Maybe late April," he said as he stood and stroked her hair.

She heaved a breath as she leaned into his touch. "Jesus, Daniel. That is too fucking long. I can't wait that long," she said in a dry whisper.

"It'll go by fast, Jo."

"Yeah. Maybe I should kidnap you and not let them send you."

"Yeah. Please do." He kissed her lips.

"You know what I am going to do first thing after you leave?"

"No. What?"

She thought better of telling him that she was going to drop by Nate's place and punch him in the stomach for not trying to talk Daniel out of their agreement. "Never mind. But you promise me some things while you're away, okay?"

He could hear the restraint in her voice as she tried to act brave. "Sure, Jo. What?"

"You keep yourself super safe." She sniffled. "You've got nothing to prove, Daniel. So don't try to be any sort of God-damned war hero. "

"Of course."

"And keep an extra couple of pairs of socks at all times."

"Extra pairs of socks. Yes, ma'am."

"I mean it. I know how you hate your feet to get wet. You

usually end up catching a cold. And then this," she edged her fingers to his forelock. "Get this cut off. As much as I love it, it can only get in your eyes." She seared her tear-filled gaze into his. "And don't you go and get yourself fucking hurt. Or anything else." She drew his head tight against her chest. "God damn. I love you so much, Daniel."

"I love you too, Jo," he croaked.

They held one another tight in a meaningful silence, both realizing that they were all they had. "I'm so scared, Daniel," she quivered out as she tightened her arms around him.

He wondered if sharing such a mutual need brought on by this fear of uncertainty was what true love felt like. Yes. It must be.

She relaxed, then peeked over his shoulder to notice the edge of a small leather-bound notebook still in its store wrapping sticking out from his gadget bag. "That notebook in your camera bag. You'll be taking your war notes in it?"

"No. It's my personal journal."

"Oh." She slipped away, crossed over to the kitchen island and brought back a mahogany-barreled ballpoint pen. "Take this with you." She handed it to him. Its steel shaft was cool, and it felt heavier than its size. "It's my special pen. Use it to write in your journal. That way whenever you write in it, we'll be together." She clasped his fingers around the pen, then lifted his hand to her lips and kissed the pen as if it were a holy relic. "And that way you'll know I'll always be with you, loving you." Then she added: "No matter what happens to…either one of us."

He saw that her hands were shaking more than usual, suggesting that her cancer might be taking greater control. "No matter what happens, Jo," he whispered into her hair. "No matter what."

PART FOUR
Hot Damn! Viet Nam!

CHAPTER TWENTY-ONE
Dire necessities

S itting wedged between Daniel and Tony in the Boeing 707 bound for Tokyo, veteran correspondent Annie Farrell closed her eyes and tried to relax back into her seat.

She knew what was coming and was anxious to get back into the shit. She recalled hunkering in-country, sweltering in the jungle, poised with her pen and notepad and her Colt .45 sidearm for protection. She often shared the wait with a huddled platoon prepared to—or for—an ambush. Usually, it never came. Covering a war was 50% boredom, 10% sheer terror and 40% lolling around and getting drunk in the sleazy bars of Saigon while waiting for another opportunity to go out and do it all again. For a war correspondent, what didn't toughen you up only fatigued you. Beneath it all ran a river of glorious, adrenaline-laced frustration.

Despite all the combat action she'd witnessed in her eight-year career, Annie still more despised flying in a passenger jet. Chopping around in a barely operational Huey one hundred feet above a triple canopy of jungle was more than okay; it was exhilarating. At least she could see the pilot and out the front. In a 707, she had no control, and that laced her nerves with anxiety. She slipped her hand into a pocket of her khaki jacket and rolled her fingers over her little El Producto cigars as if they were Rosary beads.

Daniel nestled anxiously back in his window seat as he thought about the odds of his coming back from Vietnam. Statistics had it that over a quarter of the kids bound for combat there might not return, or at least might not return intact. So far there hadn't been a reliable such statistic for war-correspondents. It was too early to tell. He gazed out at an Air France jet parked at the next gate and spied another journalist staring blankly back at him. He felt the slow rise of a sullen smile.

His Pan Am charter flight was parked among others of its kind on the dampened tarmac of San Francisco International's special transport area like school buses bound for summer camp. Many of the rear seats on his correspondent's and logistical equipment flight were cramped with duffle bags of personal gear, along with some dire necessities for the Saigon Bureau. Cases of booze were one of these necessities, and it was well known that inside information, good street grass and opium could be had in exchange for a fifth of Johnnie Walker or a few cartons of Marlboros. Small pallets of cigarette cartons were seat-belted tight as gold ingots among the cases of whiskey. The cabin was redolent with the fragrance of cardboard and tobacco dipped into a distillery.

The engines fired up from a guttural tremble to a whine and the plane began to taxi. Tony looked past Daniel and out the window as the row of commercial charter and cargo jets on the far tarmac slid from view. He could hardly contain himself. "Shit, man…here we go. Saigon!"

Annie was slouched in her seat, pretending to sleep, with her chestnut-gold hair hanging like a rumpled curtain to below her shoulders. She adjusted the bill of the ancient L.A. Dodgers ball cap over her eyes. The tone of her voice was tight. "Curb your enthusiasm, there, buckaroo. You're off to a certain kind of hell until you get the hang of it."

"Yes, mother."

She patted Tony's knee—a gratuitous gesture meant to help ease his tension.

Soon the plane was working up to speed down the long stretch of runway. Annie tightened her grip on Tony's knee. Daniel shut his eyes in defense as the passenger cabin shivered to the wheels rolling faster down the runway. The whisky bottles clinked around in their cardboard cartons. The cases of cigarettes juddered in their seats. The shuddering calmed, and the ground began to diminish below as the plane took awkwardly to the air. He and Annie jarred with the plane as the wheels thunked into their housings. Tony rested excitedly in dim attention like a kid on his first flight. The mists of cloud cover soon congealed into puffy, translucent patches concealing San Francisco and the glittering expanse of the bay. Daniel shivered away the possibility that he might never see his home or Johanna again.

Once they were above twenty-thousand feet, the stewardess placed their ordered drinks on their seat trays. She placed a coffee before Daniel.

"You're not drinking today, Dan?" Annie asked. Her voice sounded crusty. It sounded a little like Johanna's, but Annie's was more practiced, like the broadcast journalist she might have once wanted to be but never became. It wasn't that she lacked the looks. She possessed a rough-hewn mannish beauty, common to many women TV news commentators who'd been conditioned by their experience of war. But she'd admitted to Daniel and Tony over a few drinks last week that she had no confidence about being in the public eye. She preferred sitting in an operations tent or the swamp of the backroom hunched over her ancient portable typewriter like an unseen Heroine of The Word.

"Dan's a drinker, alright," Tony told her.

"I'll speak for myself, Antonio. But thank you anyway." He leveled a one-eyed pirate's glance at Annie. "I guess it's too early in the morning for any of that stuff for me. Anyway, I prefer pot. Fewer hangovers."

"Really," Annie said. She raised her plastic cup of scotch on the rocks to him. "Well then, coffee-boy, cheers to you."

"What about me?" Tony said. "Don't I get a 'cheers' from you?"

She gazed at him as she turned her mouth up in a wicked smile. She raised her cup to him, then whispered in his ear: "No." She furtively squeezed his hand.

Four hours later, Daniel looked out his window through the whorls of clouds floating high over the late-afternoon Pacific. "Where do you think we are?" He muttered mostly to himself.

"In the air," Tony yawned.

Annie peeked up over the "Valley of the Dolls" paperback she was reading and glanced out Daniel's window. "About four hours out from Tokyo, probably. Believe me, we'll need that couple of days of whatever before we wing it over to the shit in Vietnam."

"Where're we staying?" Tony asked.

"The Okura in mid-town. Phil Higgins and I stayed there on my last trip over. You'll like it."

"Well. If Phil Higgins liked it," Tony said of the *Trib's* Asian Bureau Chief. "Does he still smoke that meerschaum pipe of his with that old-shoe tobacco?"

"Sometimes it's opium, for all we know," Annie said. "Anyway, you'll like The Okura, Tony. If it was good enough for James Bond in that last movie of his, it's good enough for you, now."

"James Bond?" Tony said hopefully

Annie eased back in her seat and scrunched down behind her book, using it now as a shield to cover her eyes against the sunlight glaring through the window.

Daniel transfixed his gaze down through the puffs of clouds and their slow-moving shadows on the water. He felt the onslaught of a yawn and the gift of fatigue.

He woke halfway through the remaining flight and noticed that Annie had draped a blanket over her and Tony as they cuddled together. Her head rested up against Tony's shoulder, which crunched her features into a tragic expression. She snored out light puffs through her open mouth. His mind's eye registered her misaligned expression. He picked up one of the Pentax's he'd stored beneath his seat and raised it: *saddack-thwip.*

He reached to the side of his seat and lifted his journal to complete the letter he began an hour earlier. He caressed the cool, polished mahogany barrel of Johanna's pen. Its weight felt balanced in his hand. He missed her already. He took a glance out the window, and then began to write.

September 17, 1967:

Dear Jo,

San Fran has now faded behind me in the clouds and in time. In a week, I'll probably be crunched down in some Vietnam rice paddy with my camera taking pictures of God-knows-what. The one thing I do know is that I will be missing you so much, as I now toy with what I should have told you, not leaving you behind with so many unanswered questions.

I am scared about what lies ahead. I'd be stupid not to be. But to pretend I'm not might just keep me around long enough to be with you again. I can't really say this kind of stuff in a letter to you, Jo. Somehow a letter makes all my feelings sound schmaltzy and manufactured. Weak. But they are not— they are present enough for me to touch.

I've always been terrible at keeping journals. So instead, I'll write about what lives within me. And you are in me, Jo, through this pen you gave me. I love the feel of the pen, as I love the feel of your touch upon my heart…

The plane trembled through a patch of turbulence, and he gripped his armrest until it passed.

I'll write more tonight, once this infernal flying machine finally sets to ground in Tokyo.

The sunlight through the window caught Johanna's pen. He held it up in front of him and twirled it lackadaisically between his thumb and forefinger. He concentrated on the mahogany barrel and the burl of its grain. He narrowed his focus and let it draw him into the intimacy of the wood and into a deeper peace. He continued to rotate the pen, to mesmerize himself away from the unknowns of his future.

CHAPTER TWENTY-TWO
Saigon

Tony concentrated on the fiery bursts through the misty dusk as their plane made its sluggish approach to Ton Son Nhut airport in Saigon. He convinced himself that the glows were artillery fire, as they were under attack from the North Vietnamese Commies. Surely one of their shells would bring down their defenseless 707 short of the runway in a fireball of its own.

"We're under attack," he announced. "We're doomed."

"Be brave, little buckaroo. It's just H and I fire," Annie responded in a dried-out voice as she held her eyes closed and tightened her grasp on her armrests in her way of preparing for landing.

"What's that?" Daniel asked, trying to hold on to his bravado even as his body tensed.

"Harassment and Interdiction fire. It's from our side to let the bad guys know the good guys are here in Saigon. It goes on every night. Think of it as fireworks. It'll actually relax you once you get used to it. It's when it stops that we'll have to worry a little."

The jet continued to waver in its slow descent until the wheels touched the runway. The engines rumbled like sudden thunder and the plane slowed to a manageable roll toward the tarmac.

Annie relaxed her shoulders, heaved a sigh, and reopened her eyes. She looked out the window at the wet pavement glistening in the illumination from the tarmac lights. She remembered that it always seemed to rain at dusk in the tropics during the summer, like a prerequisite for nightfall.

An attendant outside arced his flashlights to guide their plane to its parking space. "Jesus. Saigon, again," she mused. "I didn't realize how much I missed this fucking hell-hole. Damn! It's good to be back!"

Daniel hadn't heard her and seemed unfazed as he tried to meditate his anxiety away by concentrating on the row of no smoking signs in the aisle ceiling. Tony nudged him back to the moment. He saw the other passengers grumbling as they crowded the aisle and took their carry-on gear from the overhead rack.

"Okay, Dan. We're finally here. It's time to party."

He saw Annie up ahead among the passengers waiting to deplane. She looked taller than normal because today she was wearing cowgirl boots with elevated heels. "Anne's all the way up there in line."

"Yeah. I guess she's decided to leave us on our own. She just wants off this plane. She hates flying and hates sitting still. She's a woman of action, like she wants to get this war over with. Or not."

"Or not," Daniel agreed as he wrangled himself from his seat.

The journalists in the crowd at the Ton Son Nhut terminal weren't hard to pick out. Heavily-laden with their gear, the newer arrivals like Daniel stood in a state of confused wonder, seeming to have forgotten where they were or why they were here. The returning pros like Annie traveled light and wore their time-worn backpacks casually over their shoulders as they forged toward the bank of doors leading out to waiting cabs and army Jeeps.

Tony, one of the optimistic greenhorns, had milled his way through the crowd looking for a porter with a cart on which to load their stuff. The rest of the crowd was made up of American servicemen and the weary citizens of Southeast Asia. They eddied around the dimly polished aluminum cavern of the arrival lobby. Announcements echoed in a squawk through the P.A. system, first in rushed Vietnamese, and then very broken English.

Annie recalled the carnival of the smells of Saigon; damp electricity garnished with fishy-smelling stabs through light fragrances of citrus tinged by cinnamon and orchids. It was all tainted by the sting of car exhaust. Underlying gasoline smells of napalm were carried down in the breezes from the north. The humidity of summer captured the stiff, ammoniac smells from the H and I artillery fire; a reminder that not far away another battle was raging in the hills.

Even the balmy wafts of humidity out in the parking ramp where Daniel met Annie was a relief from the swarms of people in the overly-air-conditioned airport terminal. Tony was the last one of them to escape, followed by a porter coarsely rolling two carts piled with their luggage. "Careful with that!" he warned as he placed his hand on two large boxes printed with the Sony logo. He secured the boxes back into position.

"I don't remember him bringing those on the plane when we left San Francisco," Daniel said.

"Hunh?" Annie looked over at Tony worrying over the luggage. "Oh. Yeah. He bought a stereo tape deck and big speakers when we were in Tokyo. Said he brought along some opera tapes to play."

"Oh. Right. That opera music he likes."

Annie flashed a little simper. "He likes opera?" she said as she turned her attention back to finding a cab in a line of little Citroens and Renaults left over from the French occupation. None of them would ever fit all their stuff.

"Well, he's Italian so—"

"Frankee!" Annie squealed enthusiastically as she ran toward an official-looking lanky blond Army officer leaning against a Jeep. He was as crisp as the creases on his uniform.

Lieutenant Colonel Frank Moss said nothing but perked up and rushed toward her. She jumped onto him with an embrace and a kiss. "Shit, I've missed you, Gabbie!" he said, hugging her back.

Tony looked perplexed. "*Gabbie?*" he whispered at Daniel, who shrugged his shoulders. "You've gotta be fuckin' kidding me! What the God-damned hell is *that* all about?"

"I've gotta be fucking kidding you about what, Antonio?"

Tony stiffened his shoulders like a cat about to strike. "Here we are for five goddamn minutes, like ten thousand miles away from home, and already Annie runs into some guy she knows?"

"We're talking about Annie, here, Tony. She probably has a lot of contacts from when she was here before."

"Shit!"

"Maybe it's just her brother or a long-lost cousin or something." Daniel tried to rationalize with Tony as his face darkened in dismay.

"You know that's bullshit, Dan. I thought she and I, we—" His comment fell off into a pit of rejection as they moved closer to Annie's reunion with Frank.

By the way she fawned over him, it was obvious this guy wasn't her brother, or even some long-lost cousin. "Jesus, mister.

It's so damn good to see you. What the fuck are you doing here?" she gasped.

"You kidding, Gabbie? When I heard out you were rotated back here, I had to come and see for myself." He nodded at his Jeep. "I'll be your ride into town. We can grab a quick dinner and a drink at the Continental."

"Hell and damn! Curb service!" She grabbed Frank by the hand and turned him toward Daniel and Tony. "Guys! This is my good friend Frank Moss. He's a Colonel or something. These are my strikers, Dan Lilienthal and Tony Russo."

"*Lieutenant* Colonel," he corrected. "Don't rush it, Gabbie." He smiled with an easy confidence that telegraphed to Daniel seen more of a desk than a jungle. "Hey, men. Good to meet you. Welcome to the shit." He glanced at the two packed luggage carts. "Christ. Is all that yours?"

Annie smirked. "Girl needs a lotta clothes to look her best."

Frank smiled at her and winked privately. "No, she doesn't."

She punched him in the arm. "Freakin' pervert," she whispered.

Tony grudgingly handed the little Vietnamese porter a Los Angeles-style tip of five dollars. The porter beamed and bowed his way backward into the crowd as though Tony had just saved his life.

"What's that thing, Annie?" Daniel asked her.

"What thing?"

"That." He motioned to a thick, three-foot long case among her bags.

"Ah. My private stash," she directed her attention back to Frank. "Damn, Frank. How ya been these two years?"

"You haven't gotten my letters? You only answered one, so I

gave up writing you six months ago."

Her happy look dissolved into a forlorn expression "Maybe I didn't want to find out you got yourself injured in this fucking skirmish." She winked at him. "Or by a papercut."

"I'm afraid it's more than a skirmish, now, Gabbie." He looked at Daniel and Tony standing watch over the luggage, and noticed Tony doing all he could to look away. "Listen why don't you and I take a cab to The Continental, and Dan and Ted can follow along with my driver in the Jeep."

"Tony," Tony corrected dryly. "Not Ted." He wanted to add: *You asshole.*

The Jeep was laden as a pack animal with all their gear crowding its bay and most of the backseat. Tony had wedged himself like luggage next to his precious Sony stereo system boxes and Annie's mysterious black case. The springs in the passenger seat creaked and jabbed into Daniel's rump through the jarring chunks of the gears as the driver ground through them.

"Hey, look," Tony said pointing up at a billboard featuring the front half of a Pan Am 707 fuselage aimed toward a bold headline. "It says 'Welcome to Sunny Saigon.' Like this is a vacation spot?" He glanced up at the tracer trails and H and I flack illuminating the evening sky as perpetual reminders of the war. "Ya *think?*"

"It was once," the driver recalled.

The hard case of Annie's package nudged into Tony's ribs. He knocked his fist against it as though whatever was inside would answer. "What do you think's in here? Looks like a rifle case or something. You think Annie brought a rifle along?"

"Hell, Tony, it could be anything," Daniel said over his shoulder. "Maybe it's her camera gear."

He looked at the size of the case. "Yeah, maybe from MGM Studios. Anyway, I thought taking pictures was *your* job."

Daniel glanced over his shoulder and toward the bay of the Jeep to make sure his own gear was tightly stowed beneath the flapping tarp. "It is."

The driver steered the Jeep onto the reprieve of the flat broad pavement of Doung Cong Ly, and toward the distant dim glow of Saigon's lights. He stayed quiet, begrudging this chore of driving these two civilian rubes and their luggage into town.

He was a slight Vietnamese whose hard-chiseled features belied his youth, and whose skin was the same cinnemon color as Jared's. "So, you speak English, right?" Daniel asked, and then the absurdity of his question.

The driver simpered. "Ah, so, mistah American man. My Engwish numbah one," he mocked. His tight simper broadened as he nodded his head. "Yeah, of course I speak English. I lived in Syracuse for eight years."

"How did you like it?"

"Uh, well, it was, uh, cold?"

His sarcastic attitude prompted Daniel to hunker quietly back down in seat. "Yes. I suppose it is," he mumbled.

Though the driver's manner seemed non-deferential, his mouth settled into a slight, relaxed smile. Daniel noticed the darker khaki hue of his uniform, and the red and yellow patch on his arm. "You're in the South Vietnamese army?"

"I'm an ARVN corporal. Yeah. Colonel Moss's attaché."

"I thought he said he was a Lieutenant Colonel," Tony said.

"He's going to be a full-bird Colonel in about a month."

"Oh," Tony said dejectedly as he realized that Frank's promotion might put Annie further out of reach.

"Maybe I shouldn't have said anything," the driver said. "Nobody in our unit knows yet. Besides, it's bad joss to presume a thing before it happens.".

"Well, we know the Colonel-to-be's name is Frank Moss," Daniel said. "What's his attaché's name?"

The driver deflected the question by taking on the role of travel guide. He nodded toward a brocaded, four-story block of a building. "This is where they've just finished building the American Embassy in case you ever need it. And now, up ahead is Independence Park. There's the palace, where President Thieu will be moving next week." Daniel detected a sour shift in his tone.

The subtly ornate concrete structure of the palace was built in Bauhaus functionality with rows of narrow vertical windows. It was set back on an immense lawn tended like a seventeenth green fronted by a two-tiered fountain surrounded by a circular driveway. Its entrance was barred from the public by coils of concertina wire fringing the sidewalk and high black wrought iron fence set into imposing concrete pilasters. The building was illuminated like a separate world; a festival all to itself. "Nice," Daniel said.

"Isn't it?" the driver said caustically as he hung a left and then a right at the twin-spired Notre Dame Catholic cathedral, and onto the brisk action of Tu Do Street.

The traffic was a claustrophobic tangle of pedestrians, over-burdened bicycles, rickshaw tricycles, and motor scooters weaving through the ever-present Citroens and Renaults, military vehicles. and some big American cars. Feeble dings from bicycle bells punctuated the cacophony of horns beeping at all pitches. The lights around them had grown brighter and more colorful, too. Huge billboards pitched Perlon and Hynos Dental Cremes, and similar ads were painted on the sides of some of the buildings. Daniel wondered if the only product available to the Vietnamese population was toothpaste.

The traffic in front of the Continental Palace Hotel had lessened in slow onset of night, as the sounds of the street had intensified into a sibilance of pedestrian bustle along with rock music from open-fronted bars. The humidity was scented by an admixture of fish, citrus, musky earth, and the ubiquitous taint of carbon monoxide left over from rush hour. Daniel fidgeted with a chopstick as he eavesdropped on the table conversation and glanced now and then at the Jeep. It was still laden with luggage, including his camera gear only loosely protected by the coverage of the tarp.

He might have worried about the $5,000 worth of camera equipment being stolen if he hadn't been so busy trying to avoid exchanging glances with the driver seated across from him. Occasionally Daniel would risk a surreptitious glimpse at him, and once caught his furtive glance in return. He'd just started to feel comfortable and at ease over his relationship with Johanna; and now this stranger had just showed him an uneasy, seductive smile. The quick smile had diffused Daniel into weightlessness.

Tony's voice rose up to rescue him from his confusion. "So, Frank. Where is this war happening?"

"All around us, buddy. But mostly to the north. You'll find out soon enough."

"I can't get over how anxious you are to get out into all that shit, Tony," Annie said.

He glanced at how she held Frank's hand as she sipped her bourbon while trying to act ridiculously demure. "It's my job here, right?"

"Not yet. You're still a correspondent-in-training." She looked at Daniel. "You both are."

"You've seen action out there, Frank?" Daniel asked.

"Yeah, right," Annie blurted. "Maybe around the press room."

Frank tightened his mouth as though Annie had blown some sort of cover. "I'm with the Joint U.S. Public Affairs Office," he said. "We proudly sponsor your daily press briefings."

"The Five-O-clock Follies?" Tony said.

"That's what they call it, Tom. You'll learn soon enough."

Annie patted Frank's hand as Tony quietly fumed. "Frank's my man in the system,"

The driver glanced at his watch, then rose to excuse himself. "May I go, sir?. I'm supposed to meet someone at the Rex in an hour-and-a-half."

"Mai Ling, again?" Frank guessed.

"You are clairvoyant, sir."

"She does keep you hopping, son. Okay. You're dismissed for the day. Find a porter to unload the Jeep."

"Thank you, sir." He shot another uncertain smile at Daniel, whose trepidation faded upon hearing that he had a girlfriend. The conversation moved on as the driver walked past Daniel and he leaned close to his ear. "I think we have something in common. Meet me here at the bar at one p.m., thirteen-hundred hours, next Thursday. My name is Thien."

"Thien." Daniel repeated.

The driver nodded. "Pleasure to meet you, Daniel." He then moved with purpose toward the the bank of pay phones in the smoky gloom of the bar.

CHAPTER TWENTY-THREE
Spring-loaded

The cushions on the rattan couch on the Continental Palace porch bar were thin. Daniel felt some stray tines of the bamboo frame poke into his back as he watched Thien take a long sip of his beer. "How long have you been working with Frank?"

"You mean Lieutenant Colonel Moss?"

Daniel wriggled his body back in defense against the prickling bamboo and Thien's equally prickly response. "Whatever."

"Sorry, Daniel Lilenthal…"

"Lil-i-enthal. You left out that crucial middle 'i'."

Thien brushed it off with a coy sip. "I guess I have been a little coarse with you. Sorry. It's this whole shit we're in. Nothing rapes you harder than war."

Daniel was imnpressed by Thien's casual command of American lingo. "Right. I'll probably find out soon enough."

"When are you going out into it?"

"We're slated to cover a reconnaissance operation down in the Mekong Delta next Monday, I think. Some place called Din Turong, something like that. Operation Coronado."

Thien smiled and concentrated on digging at his beer label with a thumbnail. "We've been working that one since June. It's probably a good start for you. Anyway, the Delta's a pit. Bring bugspray. The mosquitoes there are sadists." He looked up at Daniel. "So, you've been here, what? Almost a week. How do you like it? Having fun yet?"

"I don't know. It's not like I'm on vacation. It's hot, humid. I'm having trouble breathing and sleeping."

"You'll get used to it."

"What? Not breathing?"

Thien conjured up a sardonic smile. "Not breathing...not sleeping. It all becomes a high art around here. Kind of necessary when you're out on operations."

"Have you done that? Operations?"

"Oh, yeah. For about six months back in sixty-five, until I opted out to become Lieutenant Colonel Moss's lackey. I thought I wanted more to help the American effort by risking my skinny ass in my own country." He looked over a Daniel and smiled. "Too much effort for a lost cause."

"Lost cause?"

"Oh, sure. You know, Daniel?" he said after a thoughtful pause. "There's something about you that really hit me when I met you last week. Something I can trust about you. Can I trust you, Daniel?"

His austere tone put Daniel on edge. "Uh, yeah...sure."

"I'm sure you've heard this already, but America will never win this war, at least not for us Vietnamese. And most positively not for America's own gain. Don't get me wrong, I'm totally with your country's involvement with my county, but there's no way our side or your side can win this. No fucking way. Ho's troops from the north are gonna end up coming south to scoop this place up. And easily. There're no winners in a culture war. Vietnam has a thousand years of proof of this."

"You're talking to a journalist, Thien."

"I know. And I wanted you to know what's the absolute as you go out there with some misconception that 'our side' is doing the right thing." He lit a cigarette. "The difference between 'our side' and the Viet Cong is that the north knows this because they're Vietnamese. Ho Chi Minh is more than a communist leader, much more. Uncle Ho is a Vietnamese leading his Vietnamese people."

"Why are you telling me this?"

"Like I said. I feel I can trust you. I sense you and I think alike. In more than one respect."

"I think like a Vietnamese?"

Thien stared up into the lazy stram of smoke from his cigarette. "No," he said. "You think like a homosexual. Like me. A bond like ours gnaws much deeper than a war we can do nothing about."

Daniel felt the paralysis of restraint as the air took on a peculiar weight. "What the hell are you talking about, Thien? I'm, uh, I'm in a relationship…with a woman."

"And how's that working out for you?" he asked through a knowing smile.

"I love my wife-to-be. We might as well be married already."

"And I love my cat. I find comfort when she cuddles up to me. But that doesn't change how I feel inside."

Daniel stared at him. The resemblance to Jared was uncanny. Thien thought like Jared, talked like him. They had the same sallow cheeked fragile features, but Thien's had been leathered by the raw experiences of his past. Daniel gazed beyond him at the swarms of activity in the street.

Throngs of pedestrians chattered away at one another in clipped tones and clicking tongues. Many of the men were dressed in the national garb of white shirts and black trousers, which would have looked like uniforms if they weren't so casual. They dressed more like waiters. Many of the women wore the *to-dai*, a white, slotted smock over black linen pants, and flat conical *non la* hats woven of straw or bamboo. Some women had long black hair which hung neatly down to their waist. Thien had just said something.

"What, Thien? I didn't hear you."

"I said, you're going into the shit. Do you have a piece?"

"Piece? Of what?"

"A gun. A sidearm. You'll need one."

"Why? I'm not military. I'm just a journalist."

"Come on Daniel. It's a fucking war out there. You think you can protect yourself with your camera? The Viet Cong don't care who they hit. Marine grunt. Photographer. It's all the same to them. Trust me, man, you need a gun."

"I don't have one."

"Do you know how to use one?"

"Yeah. An M-14."

"An M-14 is clunky and out-dated. They're out there using M-16s, now. Anyway, a pistol's a whole different kind of philosophy. I carry an extra in the jeep. A Colt .45, and a couple of rounds. I'll give them to you."

"Thanks, Thien. But I really don't need—"

Thien interrupted him with a condescending smile. "Yeah, Daniel, you do." He tamped out his cigarette and took a swig of beer to hurry it done. "Let's go to your room. I'll show you how to clean it."

Daniel smirked at the macho-queer pick-up line. "Sure. I suppose." He was annoyed with how natural it had been to assume he'd be spending the night with him.

Thien had left at around 2 a.m. Daniel lay anchored in bed, fearing his recollection would attack him like prey. His relationship with Johanna now seemed like nothing more than an awkward experiment, as he stared at the contours of the bedsheets. They had been delicately mussed into a memory of last night, when Thien had lain there next to him, then upon him. The touch of his gentle body had only jabbed him with a remembrance of Jared and the final view of his corpse being carted away in the ambulance.

So, what *about* Johanna? What could her love mean after last night? He despised himself for loving Johanna as much as he did without knowing why. He needed her understanding now more than ever and yearned for that one thing she'd tried to show him that was now gnawing at him behind the scenes of his role as her proper lover.

The silence had become deafening even through the tenuous creak of the ceiling fan ticking away the seconds. He concentrated on a peak of the ruffled sheet still smelling of the citrus cologne Thien had worn.

He let out a primal groan and lunged for of the fucking little peaks in the sheet and tore it from the bed in a white swirl. He tried to rip it in two, but only got himself tangled in it as he fell to the hemp rug. He rolled away and lumbered toward the little bathroom where he kept his razor and its blades.

He drew his hand away from the razor as he ealized he would have many chances to die in the coming months. Best to let it catch you by surprise. He stood weakened and breathless as he backed through the door with his gaze fixed upon the open razor and its blade.

He exhaled whatever anguish he'd felt, then looked over his shoulder at the dresser. There in waiting, lay the Colt .45 pistol Thien had taught him to clean, then left with him with the caveat: "It's only for you to protect yourself, Daniel."

He picked up the pistol and stared at it, contemplating its weight in his hands. He he stared at the gun and clenched his jaw until it ached. He gritted his teeth harder when he thought about Johanna. He extracted the seven-bullet magazine and flung it at the solitary chair in his room.

He craved a woman's view.

The bleat of the saxophone chopped throughout a rough approximation of "Heart and Soul." Annie knew her playing sounded bad, but it served the higher purpose of relaxing her. She lifted her fingers from the keys to flex away their ache. She heard a timid knocking on her hotel room door, then leaned back in her chair then stretched her legs to rest on the undersized bamboo coffee table. "Yeah?" she called out.

"It's Daniel."

"Dan? Yeah, come on in. It's unlocked."

He opened the door. "I just wanted to talk about to you something," he said. He crossed the room and sat on the couch opposite from her.

She tilted her head, then shifted her single braid from her right shoulder to her left. "You look like shit, cowboy. You okay?"

"I don't know. You should wear your hair like that all the time. I like it."

"The braid? Yeah. I call it my lucky combat-do. Tell me why you look like shit. You hungover?"

He managed a dim smile. "You might say that."

"I just did."

He nodded toward the saxophone she'd rested on her knees. "So that's what was in your mysterious package. Tony thought it might have been a dead body."

She spanked its brass bowl. "My only friend. It's my solace in a world fucked up by torment. I can't play it for shit, but still, it relaxes me." She cast it a furtive smile. "Along with my cigars, it satisfies my oral fixation." She patted it again and looked at Daniel. "Enough said. Now what's the matter, Dan? Tell momma."

"I just wanted to talk."

"Let me guess. About you and Frank's driver?"

A chill caroused through his nerves and bristled out a shiver. The last thing he wanted to do was answer her.

"You didn't think I could tell? Shit, Dan. Investigative journalism has been my life for fifteen years. I'm good at it. Plus, I'm a woman, where intuition is part of *that* job description. It didn't take much. I saw how you and that guy were playing eye-footsie with each other the other night at the Continental. I catch you sometimes even looking at Tony through the lens of your secret, even though he's too needy for girls to notice a guy. He's about as heterosexual as they come, and too Catholic to think beyond that mythical conviction of marrying to carry on the species. He's not your type anyway."

"He's yours?"

She choked out a dry laugh. "Shit, no. Like I said, he's Catholic. Wife, kids, Wednesday night spaghetti and Friday night fish in some duplex suburban home. Not for me. Besides, if I ever get married, it can't be for keeps. I want the escape hatch of a divorce if things go south, which, given who I am, they definitely will."

"And he's half your age."

She glowered. "Watch your mouth! There's only about six years between us. So tell me why you're so concerned about you and Frank's chauffeur? It's probably just a passing thing, like any relationship."

"I'm in a relationship with a woman."

"A mere technicality."

"She needs me, and I love her."

"Congratulations. I'm sure you do. That makes you a devoted boyfriend." She placed her hand on his and leaned toward him. "Besides, no woman actually *needs* a man. That's just part of the dance."

"Believe me Annie, I'm sure she needs me."

"Okay. And you need her. Dan, there's no shame in what you did."

"I feel like I've cheated on her."

"No, hon. You've cheated only on yourself." She saw the glimmer of defeat in his eyes. "You've done nothing wrong." She leaned closer. "Let's try something here. Kiss me."

He smelled the light staleness of tobacco on her breath "What?"

"Kiss me. On the lips, like you'd kiss your girlfriend."

"Shit, Annie. On top of all I'm going through this morning, you're coming on to me?"

"Trust me, sweets. It's only an experiment. It'll mean nothing."

"Well, thanks for *that*."

"Okay. It could mean something. But not the way you're

thinking. Now kiss me." He kissed her. Tenuously. Then drew back. "Hell, man. Tinkerbell could have done better than that. Now *kiss* me, god-damnit. Pretend I'm what's-her-name. What *is* her name?"

"Johanna?"

"You're asking me?"

Her comment reminded him of that first time he'd met Johanna by the pool back when...Jesus. When *was* that? "Johanna," he said.

"Kiss me like you'd kiss Johanna and think of her. I won't mind. And probably neither would she."

He kissed her again with more passion, and she kissed him back. He stroked her cheek when the kiss was done as he would Johanna's.

She leaned her forehead against his, then let out an uneven sigh. She settled back in her seat and a feline smile crossed her lips. "There. Feel better?"

Daniel had to absorb what had just happened, then decided: "Yes. Actually. I do."

"Ah, then the experiment worked. See? There can be a whole universe in something as simple as a hug and a little kiss. Now go out and do good. Spend your day loving Johanna and your night rolling around in the sheets with Frank's driver. All can be forgiven. Know that when you feel like shit about this again, I'm here for you."

Daniel did feel better. He recalled the pistol Thien had left behind on the bureau in his room.

"He left a gun behind for me to use. A Colt .45."

"Ah, like mine." She absently fingered the keys of her saxophone. "Probably a good idea. You may find yourself needing to shoot some Viet Cong with more than your Nikon. You know how to use it?"

"Yeah, maybe, but I might need to refresh myself. I mean, I can shoot an M-14."

"Nah. A pistol you use up close. You can see your target's eyes, and that'll cause you to hesitate just long enough for him to shoot you. Out there, hesitation kills more people than bullets. There's a shooting range out across the river channel past the market on Le Van street. That's the one I use. It's far enough out of the way for you not to do any real damage, except to yourself if you misfire." Another little private simper. "That said, I've never used my piece to kill anyone, but I have brandished it in front of a few frisky men."

CHAPTER TWENTY-FOUR
Hunting buffalo

Daniel fidgeted with the four press passes neatly folded and tucked into their Mylar packets. He'd come to realize that the moist hot mantle of the jungle climate had become his new reality. He It had become a nervous habit. Fluffs of harassment and interdiction illumination glowed in the distance like dry lightning through the twilight. He lifted his camera. *Saddack-thwip* Closer, more distinct flares of gunfire lit up the fringes of coconut trees lining the shore. *Saddack-thwip-Saddack-thwip.* He felt no anxiety over the gunfire aimed in his direction from only 70 yards away. He was there to do his job.

In the nights before he'd left for this assignment, his second on the Mekong Delta, Thien had taught him some breathing and tai-chi exercises to deal with the stress of combat and the humidity's effect. But none of this helped to battle the mosquitoes and whatever other critters had biten him. But tonight, he refused to let those annoyances divert him.

The sluggish brown waters of the Mekong Delta tributary gleamed apologetically in the dusk light, while the power of the swift boat trembled even more under the recoil of the rotating twin .50-caliber machine guns in the bow. Third Class Gunner's Mate Brand was firing deafening bursts at nothing but the shoreline flares. The NVA regulars on the shore crouching behind their Soviet issued AK-47s fired back just as randomly. Also more for the exercise than the kill.

The engine vibrations hummed consistently through the river patrol boat's steel-plated deck over the sound of Brand's transistor radio blaring out "Paint it Black." The harsh, rapid pulses from the boat's guns had numbed the soles of Daniel's feet for the last six hours, and that numbness had now reached his hips. He felt locked into place like a human tripod as he focused in on a tight shot of the gunner's mate. He wore an oversized helmet with a couple of orchids stuck in its netting. His eyes broadcast the calm austerity he attached to his task. It had become his routine as the kid from Tulsa's manhood had savaged its way into being before its time. Even under the relentless weight of the humidity, Brand hadn't even broken a sweat.

Daniel took some more shots. *Saddack-thwip, saddack-thwip...*

Another burst from the swiftboat's bow machine guns was now joined by some rounds from the stern gun. Thin filigrees of tracers from their bullets had become faintly visible through the deepening twilight. Soon a ridge line of trees burst into sequential flame lighting up the horizon as napalm seemed to erupt into the sky from their roots.

Daniel no longer had to think about the shot. Taking pictures had by now become instinctual. *Saddack-thwip, saddack-thwip, saddack-thwip.*

Two single-prop A-1 Skyraider marine fighters with their ground-trembling-loud enigines veered off close overhead. The World-War II-vintage planes used for dropping napalm were as clunky-looking as they were powerful.

Quick, now: *Saddack-thwip, saddack-thwip...*

Daniel heard Tony shout "HOLY SHIT!!" from four feet away where he was covering the story from the boat's bridge. The two planes heeled around for another run to flush out the shoreline with a close-range spray of bullets.

Saddack-thwip, saddack-thwip…

Finally, they veered around one last time to head home to their base in Da Nang. One of them flew two-hundred feet above the boat and the pilot dipped its wings. Mission accomplished for today.

There were no more gun flares from the shoreline. Even above the guttural pulsing of the patrol boat's engines, it had become eerily quiet. Brand leaned back and relaxed back in his bow gun bucket and massaged the stiffness out his neck. Master Chief Gene Polanski, the boat's pilot, called out to his crew: "GOOD WORK, Y'ALL! Now let's go ashore and get shit-faced! I gotta piss like a racehorse, anyway!"

"Aye fuckin' aye, cap!" Second Class Machinist's mate Palance called back from behind his rear gun as he slapped the breach closed nice and neat. He prepped his gun for tucking it in for the night, then draped a rubber tarp over it.

The master chief gunned the engines as the boat veered steeply starboard, east toward Me Tho. The thick fragrances of heated gun oil and boat fuel were underscored by those of napalm and scorched coconut from the shore.

Brand looked out from under his helmet at Daniel. "You got pitchures of me?"

Daniel showed him a broad, nervous smile. "Lots of pictures."

"Can I have one when you're done with it?" He slammed shut his guns' breaches. "My gal, Jeannie, won't believe I can do this kinda shit."

"Sure, of course."

Saddack-thwip.

Daniel and Tony soon caught a chopper for Saigon. He mused over how entire war-effort seemed powered by rock 'n' roll, as "Highway Sixty-one" chopped out in full-volume from the big speaker housed under the canvas jump-seat of the Huey. Despite its volume, the music thumped faintly through the jittering whuff of the rotors and the squawk and static from the navigation radio. Hollow little stings caused by the reverberation from the thwop of the rotors shot up through his body.

For the four crew members of the chopper, this cushy mission was pure boredom. The crew chief was nearly asleep in his low-slung canvas seat across from Daniel and Tony, sending a clear message that he didn't cotton much to reporters. The four other passengers, three army grunts—two lightly wounded—and another journalist from *The Sydney Times* seemed to take it in stride as they relaxed back into their canvas seats.

The door gunner was whistling out some disjointed, imperceptible tune beneath the noise. Sometimes, more from habit than duty he tapped his M-16 magazine against the helmet on which he sat. He glanced at Tony and showed an easy, gapped-toothed grin, as if to say he was in control of this situation.

"Why do you guys sit on your helmets?" Tony shouted as he pointed to his own butt as sign language.

"AA fire comes at us up from the ground! I wanna keep my nuts in one piece for when I need 'em!"

"Ah, so," Tony said. He kicked his rucksack under his seat closer beneath him.

Daniel looked beyond the gunner and through the open door

as they flew at around one-hundred knots, three-hundred feet above the treeline. There was something hypnotic about the dusk-lit view. Flares of gunfire bloomed safely off in the distance. The spotty more stationary glows from hamlets in the clearings through the tree canopies sent out comforting signs of domestic life. The lowering sunlight beneath clouds caught pools of water in a shimmering silver glow from the basins cantilevered in the dark terraces of rice paddies. The rushing air through the Huey's open gun-door had cooled. Daniel leaned back to breathe in the moist, earthy fragrances.

His brief solace was interrupted, as the door gunner crouched to attention over his Gatling gun while shouting: "Buffalo!"

"Come again, Tyler?" the co-pilot shouted back over his shoulder. "Buffalo?"

"Yeah, buffalo!"

"Buffalo," the co-pilot repeated to the pilot.

"Shee-it!" the pilot said. "Here we fuckin' go again! Where?"

"Forty-five degrees! Three-o-clock to the right!" Tyler called back as he slapped the breach on the Gatling gun. "Hard right!"

"Shee-it," the pilot said again, cutting off his complaint with a sudden right jerk on the control stick, which lurched the chopper into a thirty-degree bank as the distant glow of Saigon slid past them. The three correspondents grabbed the canvas webbing of their seats to keep from tumbling to the deck. Daniel felt a numb bulge of suspension rise throughout his body as he fought for footing in the lightened forces of gravity.

"God damn, *shit*!" The crew chief groaned as he jolted awake. "We gotta fuckin' do this *now*? I gotta get my ass back to Saigon. My babe is havin' contractions waiting for me at Tu-Do Central for a fuck!"

"Yeah. Jackson!" the co-pilot said. "Waitin' around just for you with her fellow fuckin' co-workers! I'm sure she'll fuckin' find someone to keep her busy while she's waitin' for you! One fuck's as good as another in that chicken coop!"

"Right there!" Tyler shouted. "One klik to the right! Looks like four of 'em!"

The pilot flicked on the search and landing lights, then swooped the Huey to fifty feet above ground level.

"Shee-it!" Jackson said. "They's just a bunch a' water buffalos!"

"What's he doing?" The Aussie journalist asked.

"I have no fucking idea," Tony said. "Something about buffalos."

"If it looks like some Cong action, we gotta investigate!" The co-pilot shouted to them.

"Ain't no fuckin' Cong! Just fuckin' buffalos," Jackson griped.

"Yeah, well them there buffalos is Cong action, alrighty!" Tyler said, then cut his comment short with the jarring loud crackle of his machine gun fire. Daniel felt the pain of the noise ring in his ears. "Yeee-hah! One down!" Tyler said.

"You want I should come around again?" The pilot asked.

"Fuck yeah!" Tyler answered, as he swung his gun to take a bead on the remaining buffalos.

Daniel clenched his jaw, knowing that Tyler's sport of using the buffalos for target practice was depriving some Vietnamese peasants of more than a family pet, which was bad enough. But worse, he had deprived them of a livelihood, since the cost of a new buffalo needed to till their paddies was probably far beyond their means. He wondered if Tyler was the kind of kid who'd pull off a fly's wings or the leaping legs of a frog when he was younger.

Or had the army made him this way by providing him with a means to kill where there was no place for rationale?

"Two down!!"

"Hey, man!!" Tony called over to him. "Why are you killing those buffalos?"

Tyler thought for a moment, then grinned. "Because I *can*, man! Because I fuckin' *can*!"

CHAPTER TWENTY-FIVE
Small, pretty packages

The correspondents gathered at the Rex Rooftop Bar every weekday at 5 p.m. for the "Five-O-Clock Follies". Attendance for the reporters was an unwritten requirement, where the MACV public affairs officer could spread the boo-rah! bullshit stuff coming from the field. The level of the press's interest was cynical at best, as the breifings served also as a way for MACV to take the media's pulse. The seasoned reporters: those with keener intuition, had already gleaned much of the truth like wheat from the chaff of yesterday's rumors, anyway. Even Barry Zorthian, the military public affairs officer who led The Follies, knew it was all just so much propaganda. But he knew how to play the game, because he too had been a war correspondent back in the day.

He'd already recounted the U.S.'s continued successes in on-going operations: Quang Tin and Dinh Tuang provinces in the central coast and lowlands; the central highlands; the DMZ; and Kien Hoa, and Dinh Tuong provinces in the Mekong Delta,. Also, Route 20 along the Cambodian border — commonly known as The Ho Chi Minh Trail, from which a network of rugged dirt paths branched east into the jungles of South Vietnam. Of course, these campaigns were all just being mopped up because the U.S. had already won. The G.I.s were now returning to their bases and Bambi was once again free to frolic in the fields and jungles where bluebirds flew freely above the messiness of battle.

But this time Barry added that Operation Wallowa, a skirmish in the central lowlands, had been heating up since mid-September and might be getting hotter. Though allied body counts had been low, there was some mounting concern. The operation had been under-covered. Tony poked Daniel lightly in the arm. "Man, let's go there. Walla-walla."

"Wallowa," Annie corrected in a whisper above the light afternoon rain spattering a sizzling tattoo against the canvas stretched tight above them. "And I heard it was dicey. Maybe a little too hot for you tin-heads. But I may go."

Daniel seared a gaze at her. "Without us? Annie, you're gonna need photo coverage."

"Sean's up there already. I was thinking of letting him piggyback some of his secondary shots onto my coverage."

"Flynn?" Tony groused. "Shit, Annie. He's with *Time*. He's not going to just hand his stuff over for the *Trib* to use."

Annie showed him a coy smile. "He owes me a poker debt."

"Flynn's too busy getting stoned to play cards," Daniel remarked.

"Well, he did. Anyway, now he owes me a photoshoot."

"Jesus, Annie," Tony pouted. "You just have the hots for the guy."

Annie's smile turned privately thoughtful. "Well, there's that." Sean Flynn had inherited the same matinee rustic good looks as his famous swashbuckling screen-idol father. His approach to photography was just about as cavalier; he wasn't one to let the protocol of an employer stand in the way of getting a good shot published. "Besides. You guys aren't quite ready for the kind of heat up with I-Corps in Quang Nam, yet. Maybe in a few weeks.

But we need journalists up there tomorrow or the day after." She lit up one of her little cigarillos as she glanced at Tony. "Russo, will you please stop staring at me like some abandoned puppy? You're giving me the fuckin' *creeps*." She sipped her beer. "Oh, hell-damn-spit. Alright. You two can come. But you gotta stay close. Either one of you get killed, I'm not gonna talk to you ever again."

"Thanks, sweetie." Tony said.

"You really *are* looking to get yourself fuckin' killed, aren't you, Russo? Monikers like 'sweetie' I reserve only for guys like Frank Moss, or whatever guy I want something from. And you ain't him." She tussled his hair. "Okay, sweetie? You guys get your gear ready tonight. I'm gonna see if we can head out to Da-Nang tomorrow or Thursday." Then she added, "Hangover be damned."

Barry must have uttered some more blatant propaganda from MACV. Scattered simultaneous grumbles of "horseshit!" disguised behind fake coughs rippled through the group of reporters. Someone in the crowd called out: "You guys are full of shit, Barry, and you know it!"

That was the unofficial signal for an end to today's Follies. "Thus endeth today's briefing. Thanks again, ladies and gentlemen. As usual, I appreciate your input," Barry said from behind an agreeable grin before leaving the podium.

"It's always hard to sludge through the bullshit of Barry's sessions," Annie said. At least she could filter out some of the facts through Frank during their pillow talk. "Happy trails, buckaroos," she yawned as she rose. "I gotta go meet Frank. Make sure you're all locked and loaded to go up to Da-Nang."

"Yeah, Okay. Have fun, 'Gabbie'," Tony said as she stood.

She shot him a dirty look. "Whatchure mouth, there, Desperado."

"I love it when you're pissed," he ventured.

"Yeah?" she challenged, as she touched the tip of his chin. "How attached are you to those pearly teeth of yours?"

The clouds over the city were embroidered with the seepage of lowering sunlight, which heated the fallen rain to rising steam around the deck of the rooftop pool.

Daniel noticed a slight Vietnamese girl-woman wearing a white *ao-dai* and woven palm *non-la*. She had been standing near one of the uprights supporting the roof and was now making her way over to the pool. Her smooth black hair hung halfway down her back as she doffed her *non-la* and placed it ritualistically on a lounge chair. She opened her *ao-dai* and shed it to reveal a skimpy white bikini, then kicked off her sandals and dived neatly into the pool. Daniel had the sense that this act had been rehearsed.

Tony was too busy concentrating on his notes to have noticed her. "Come on, man," he said without looking up. "Let's go poolside. Get us a couple of chairs and I'll buy our beers."

"You mean the Trib will buy, you fucking cheapskate."

Tony snapped closed his notebook cover. "Yeah, whatever." He made his way into the shadows of the bar to get a tray of six beers for them.

"Ya know, Dan?" he said when he returned and placed the tray on the table between their lounge chairs. "Sometimes I get the feeling I'm living in a borrowed life."

Daniel squinted ahead at the Vietnamese girl-woman as she swam to the other end of the pool, then submerged to swim underwater. "A borrowed life."

"Yeah, you know. Someone else's life. Like totally foreign."

"Well, Antonio. Saigon ain't exactly L.A."

"You're right about that for sure, except here the smog is replaced by mortar smoke and napalm."

Daniel remembered the cool clarity of the September dusk in San Francisco just before he left, and the way the hard autumn light rusted Johanna's hair. "Yeah," he whispered hoarsely, "California, this place ain't."

Tony's side vision was caught by the shimmer of black and tan and white bikini beneath the surface of the pool water, as the swimmer glided toward the pool's edge. "Look at that. She must have amazing lungs to swim underwater for that long."

She surfaced at the shallow end, then tilted her head back and ran her hands down through the length of her hair. Sensing she was being watched, she turned her head and glowered at Tony. He raised his beer in a toast and smiled in return. She turned away and rose from the pool with her head canted as she made a slight spectacle of drying her hair. She wrapped a towel around her head like a turban, then slipped her *ao-dai* on over her head.

"I think I've fallen in love. Again," Tony mused.

"Yeah, for maybe what? The tenth time this week? A few days ago, you fell for that fifty-year-old mama-san in My Tho."

"What the hell? Annie won't have me."

"And she never will, Antonio. She just doesn't want to disappoint you. She'd eat you for breakfast."

He stared into his beer bottle. "You think she even cares enough about me to disappoint me?"

Daniel lounged back to catch whatever sunlight he could. "Of *course* she cares about you. Just not in the way you want her to."

"You mean like a fucking mother hen."

"Well, she *is* kind of our supervisor over here; journalist *sensai*, whatever. At least for now."

"Hell, I'm just horny, I guess."

"No, Tony. Worse. You're just desperate."

The Vietnamese girl-woman's voice flowed out with a crusty little edge to it. "Hey, Joe. Buy me a drink?"

Tony looked up and squinted at her. She was shorter than she had appeared beneath the rippling camouflage of the pool water. Just shy of beautiful, she stood her ground with a defiant authority. Her lips were pouty, on the verge of a smug smile. Her smooth, high-cheeked features were enhanced by an arresting sloe-eyed black gaze. The wide sleeves of her *ao-dai* dripped below the fragile wrists of arms crossed over her stomach.

"Me? Buy you a drink?" Tony asked.

"Seven and Seven," she decided.

In his brief time in Vietnam, Daniel had come to recognize a street-whore's come on. "He's too cheap to buy you a drink, and you're probably too expensive for him."

"I'll decide when I'm too cheap to buy a pretty girl a drink."

"Yeh, Joe," she said to Daniel, her voice clipped. "I talking to him. Not you."

"Desperation'll kill you, buddy," Daniel warned.

Tony dismissed this with a sip on his beer. "Seven and Seven?" he asked as he rose from his lounge.

"Yeh. I go with you. Tell drink-tender how to make it."

"Ok. Sure, you come with me…" He paused.

"Trần Bian. You just call me 'Bian'," she said, then nodded curtly. "And you name?"

"Uh, Tony," he answered in his professional voice. "Tony

Russo, *L.A. Tribune*."

"Ton-ney?"

"Tony," he corrected, "with a long 'o'."

"Ton-ney," she repeated.

"Whatever."

"You buy me drink, Ton-ney, you numbah five. You buy me dinner, you numbah one for me."

Daniel wondered number five what. Boyfriend of the week? Shag of the day? "Dinner it is, then," Tony answered her.

"You be numbah one, then Ton-ney," she said, then seared a glare at Daniel.

It made her look mysteriously beautiful, but Daniel had learned that the most destructive bombs can sometimes come wrapped in small, pretty packages.

Her little smile turned wicked. "You numbah ten, you, mistah," she accused, then took Tony's arm and led him off to the bar.

CHAPTER TWENTY-SIX
Operation Wallowa

D aniel had come to appreciate this bizarre environment teeming with life in the raw. Saigon was a strangely wonderful place for him. He'd started to identify with the fragile strengths the city had culled from its ancient weaknesses.

A thousand years of life's routine sizzled awake along Dai Lo Khong Tu. Its rain-coated pavement glistened beneath a confusion of drooping telephone lines. Swarms of *non-la*-hatted pedestrians, bicyclists and scores of scooter jockeys wove around one another. Daniel stared down at it all as he leaned against the open doors of Thien's rickety wrought iron balcony. The fragile doors were aged with decades of peeling yellow over blue, over orange, over green paint.

Scents of waste and cooking wafted up from the alley next door. Occasional light gusts blew in a mixture of fried smells: fish, peppers, snail, rabbit and maybe some other things too unusual to want to even think about. Except for the peppers, in the end it all tasted like chicken. And maybe there was even some of that. The brown waters of Canal Ben Nghe, which contributed its own underlying odor of damp-rot, swirled lazily by two densely packed blocks east.

He put down his tea, then stood still and began the breathing exercises Thien had taught him. *"Stand on the ground..."* Thien had paraphrased along the lines of Thích Nhất Hạnh. He curled his toes into the prickly hemp of the rug to grasp the center of the earth, while he let the rest of his body remain as weightless as air, fragile as a weed.

He exhaled through a seven-count, stood breathless for a five-count, then breathed in for a four-count. If he became distracted, he would pull gently first on this right thumb, then on his left to bring him back to a state of relaxed attention. If that didn't work, he would imagine the weight of Johanna's pen like a talisman in his breast pocket. It had become his way of turning to her; to remember the tenderness of her embrace. He would need to call on it all tomorrow once he was in the thick of combat somewhere in I-Corps with only his camera for protection. And there was the scary pistol he carried in its holster clipped to his belt. He relaxed his shoulders to re-awaken his senses to the confusion of the world below.

"I'm done here," he called behind him.

"Good, Daniel. Now do it again," Thien said.

"No. "

"Yes."

"I have to get going. My chopper leaves for Quang Tin in two-and-a-half hours."

"Okay, fine," Thien said as he strode up behind carrying two glasses. "Here. Take some iced lemon tea."

Daniel took the cool tumbler Thien handed him.

"You feel rooted and relaxed now? Ready for your journey into the shit pit?"

"I think so. Yeah, I'm ready."

Thien's expression soured. "No. You are not. Never ready. Living takes a lifetime to master. You think you're ready only to realize you've fucked it up somehow."

"Okay. I'm not ready, then. I'm scared shitless."

"Then, Daniel, if that's true, you aren't a coward. Let your fears keep you in tune." He sipped his tea. "Our Lieutenant Colonel Moss will be promoted to full Colonel next week."

Daniel smiled down at his glass. "Well, good for Annie."

"Maybe better for me. He won't be needing me as his driver anymore."

"Really? Who will you be driving around, then?"

"No. Not driving. I got a billet as a reporter with the Public Information Office. They're going to post me with *Stars and Stripes*."

"*Stars and Stripes*. That's great for you, Thien. Is it what you wanted?"

"Oh, yeah. Now I can debunk your hard news stories by reporting harmless propaganda from the field."

"You be careful out there, Thien."

"Of course. I've got all that Buddhist discipline. And I'll be writing to the Army journalism template: We went into battle. We were successful. The end. I can probably write my dispatches from a desk near an air conditioner without ever going into the shit."

"Sounds like a cushy way to sit out a war."

"Your war maybe, Daniel. Once you all leave, I'll still be fighting the war for my culture."

Daniel knew Thien was right. He focused his gaze on a thin thread of smoke rising from one of many chimneys in the cluster of terra cotta rooftops.

The big twin-rotor Chinook settled into a shuddering hover over a clearing on a bank of the Tranh River near Tra My. The two sets of rotors went into a reverse thrust that sent the fuselage rumbling into a torrent of movement. Daniel shivered against the warm vibrations coursing from the metal bulkheads and through the canvas sling of his seat back. To comfort himself, he twiddled the assemblage of press credentials hanging around his neck. He glanced into the cargo bay past Annie, who relaxed puffing on an El Producto as she studied her notes. Tony was trying to mask his fear with a trembling bravado as he stared ahead. The cargo bay was packed with basic supplies: pallets of toilet paper, soap, combat meal rations, canned goods, bags of mail, cartons of Marlboros, cases of Budweiser, light construction equipment, and, strapped to the center of the deck, a Bobcat forklift.

The aft ramp yawned open as the Chinook shivered to the ground, letting in the rude assault of construction and rotor noises through a wind-swirled rain carrying the loamy scent of mud and wet tropics. Some grunts from the 101st Airborne—"Air-Cav"—milled about in their swelled ponchos, prepared to off-load the precious cargo of beer, mail, and toilet paper.

The promise of combat fed Annie's adrenaline. "Welcome to the shit, boys!" she shouted over the monstrous noises. She crushed out her cigar on the deck with a boot-heel, then flung her braid from one shoulder to the other—a habit for luck before each mission. She donned the narrow-brimmed cloth cap she'd had for three years; since Ia Drang, where all comabt started.

"I'm psyched up!" Tony shouted back unconvincingly.

"Then try not to let it show, gringo! Shit like that'll dull your reflexes! Just play by the rules for now, okay?!"

He nodded back with a grin, while Daniel grasped his right thumb in his left fist to calm himself. He took a six-count breath as he sought out the tiny heft of Johanna's pen in his breast pocket.

"You okay, Dan?!"

"Yeah, I guess I'll live!"

She grinned at him. "You'd *better* fuckin' live, asshole!" She grabbed the leather handhold strap above her and yawed to a stand. "Now come on! Let's move our asses!" She flung a strap of her rucksack over her right shoulder. "This fuckin' war ain't just sittin' around waiting for us!"

A young, war-seasoned lieutenant greeted her at the bottom of the ramp. "You Anne Farrell?!" He shouted as he grasped his fatigue cap against the slanting rain, and the wind from the rotor chop.

"The very same!"

"I'm Lieutenant Davidson! Lieutenant Colonel Moss radioed your assignments ahead! Bring your crew and follow me to the ops tent!"

Daniel hugged his cameras to his chest as he struggled for footing in the mud.

"Yeah, watch your steps! It's been a little sloppy out her for the last few days!" Davidson warned.

Daniel could only nod. He glanced over toward the row of six supply storage tents and the milling of infantry troops waiting to board the choppers to take them into battle. Now he now clenched his left thumb in his right fist as he tried to listen for his breathing through the surrounding clamor of hammering, grading, and the whine and thunderous thwopping rotors of a dozen Air-Cav Hueys and two Chinooks.

He felt Tony jarring him in the ribs as he motioned to a line of stretchers containing bulky, rain-glistened black bags billowing in the rotor-wind. One had blown partly away to reveal a limp leg. "Holy shit, Dan! Are those…?!"

Daniel nodded. "They are," he answered in a hollow voice. He wondered over the irony of how the military sent off their dead in wrappings that looked like trash bags. He raised his camera.

Saddack…thwip…saddack…….thwip

Lieutenant Davidson shut the flimsy plywood door of the operations tent to partly muffle out the churn and rattle of the machinery outside. The tent smelled of wet kerosene, damp pipe tobacco and hemp. "Sorry for the mess. We're working to clear a landing and supply base. I'm sure you've heard it's heating up something fierce up in the hills. But that's why you're here, right?"

"That's why we're here, Lieutenant," Annie agreed.

He staddled a wooden carton behind the plank-wood table set on sawhorses that served as his desk and fired up a Coleman lantern. He took up his pipe, applied the flame from his zippo to the bowl and then offered up a sardonic smile. "Smoke-em if you got em. Joints included. We're an equal opportunity libation place here in Tra My." He unwound the string wrapped around the closure tabs of the dispatch envelope that had been lying on his desk.

"How long have you been building here?" Annie asked.

"Going on three weeks. We'll probably never be done, though," he replied as he stared at the envelope's contents. "Looks like y'all'll be going on up to join the 101st up in Chu-lai."

"The First Cavalry Division?" Annie asked.

Davidson looked up over the papers with an expression bordering on suspicion. "You know them, Anne?"

"I worked with them back in '66 when I covered…never mind. They're a pretty scrappy bunch."

He smiled wryly. "I guess that's one way of putting it." He

glanced back down at the memo. "Y'all are going to get to know them pretty good. Lieutenant Colonel Moss says y'all are gonna be embedded with them when you're in the field. They're seeing more of this war than most, I think."

Annie told Frank she wanted to play rough to get the diciest coverage and secretly congratulated herself as she thanked him. A full embed was a coveted post, where a correspondent was pretty much free to call the shots within the limits of a division's operational zone. True, First Cav got around, and she'd be seeing lots of action, but an embed was a double-sided gift. Being embedded might limit her freedom to wander independently around the country, as many reporters did.

"You two guys'll be going up to cover a platoon from X-Ray Company on recon out in the Que San River Valley. Anne, you'll be staying back with the ops base in Chu-Lai."

"*What?* Why?"

Davidson glanced down at the orders. "Because it says so here."

"I work for the *L.A. Tribune,* and they want me out in the field covering the war."

"And Lieutenant Colonel Moss is my superior. And what he says goes here. I'm sorry, Anne, you're gonna have to stay on base."

"Jesus F-ing Christ!" she grumbled.

She knew this was Frank's way of keeping her in check just because she accidentally wandered into a nest of Viet Cong back in Ia Drang. She'd been trying to grab a story from what she thought was just a hamlet of Vietnamese peasants rumored to be housing a few NVA, and they took her hostage. Two American Army grunts were wounded, compromising their position in her rescue. It had been her first rookie mistake. Though she'd learned a lesson in caution, it didn't dim her enthusiasm for getting the story. Beyond anything rational, she was a correspondent first.

She looked over at Tony and Daniel, who were looking back at her. "Sounds like a good slot," she grumbled. "Lots of action, and Dan, you'll get some good pictures."

Davidson puffed on his pipe. "We've got a chopper going up to Chu Lai in a few hours, and I'll get y'all on it." He toasted them with his pipe. "Meanwhile, welcome to I-Corps." From under his desk he produced a bottle of Jack Daniels and a stack of Dixie cups, along with a wry smile. "Let me buy us a drink."

As the chopper rose and swiveled northeast toward Chu Lai, Tony concentrated on the fading ground through the dust and mud stirred up by the rotors. Then he looked behind him.

"Shit!" he shouted and jarred back as he realized they had been crammed into a Huey with a cargo of body bags. Three of them were filled. He stared at a mud-caked boot that stuck from one of them. It was bloodied deep along the rim of its top. There was a faint odor of feces.

"Get used to it, Tony!" Annie said. "This isn't the last time you'll be hitching a ride with a couple of corpses!"

The door-gunner turned to Tony crouched next to him. "You'll get used to the stink of shit, too! Once rigor sets in, they start farting!"

"But they're, like, dead. ...right?!"

The gunner grinned back at him. His bright white teeth accentuated a coal-black face. "Don't mean he cain't still take a shit!"

Daniel watched the eastern foothills of the central highlands

---

slide by at a hundred miles an hour five-hundred feet below. The breaking sunlight accented the dense greens of the nappy snarl of trees. Strands of fog streamed through the ridges ahead. Thinner pockets of mist, probably not gunfire, rose from the clearings. He knew the firefights were farther west, deeper into the density of the highlands. That would be his ultimate destination, possibly within a few hours.

They finally put down at the Chu Lai airbase, which, though more developed than the one in Tra My, was also under construction. Rock music from Armed Forces Radio in Saigon blared out through strategically placed speakers on phone poles. Tony scampered from the Huey to distance himself from the death that had surrounded him during the forty-five-minute flight. His face was contorted in anxiety as he swiped his rucksack from the chopper and backed away, motioning Daniel and Annie to join him.

Even within the bay of the Huey, Daniel was busy taking pictures. Annie, oblivious to the body bags, was hunched over her rucksack and rummaging through it, arranging its contents to take a spot inventory. Finally, they hopped to the ground, and she directed them over to the troop truck that would take them into the uncertainty of whatever waited in the Que Son Valley. "Go on, guys! You got a war to cover!" she called to them. "And good luck. Wish I was goin' with you."

"We'll miss you, hon!" Tony said back.

"I really *do* wish I could go with you." she mourned, then stared forlornly at the ground. "Shit!

It seemed like the entire war theater in I-Corps was being developed on the fly. This small operations base had been carved into a clearing in the central southern Que Son River Valley. It, too, was under construction.

Daniel and Tony slipped from the rear of the rattling transport truck. Shaken up, they stumbled over to the wooden-walled operations tent to meet with the base Captain, a tall oak of a guy named Morrison. "Alabama Song" by The Doors crackled through the speakers strapped on poles around the settlement.

"You guys look like you've just come back from night patrol. You been on the move all day?"

"Since before dawn," Tony said.

"Well, glad to have the press here…I guess." He quickly scanned their assignment papers. *"The Los Angeles Tribune,* hunh? And signed by a Lieutenant Colonel at JUSPAO? Interesting." He glanced at Daniel. "JUSPAO usually don't side with the organized press." He re-folded the papers and handed them back to Tony. "You all get a little shut-eye. We're sending a squad out on a recon a few kliks west at zero-five-thirty tomorrow. You two can bunk here in the ops tent behind that hanging blanket."

"I could stand to freshen up a little," Tony said. "Where's the bathroom?"

Morrison's features flattened as he leveled a beady-eyed glare at him. "Bathroom? What's that, son? There's a latrine about a hundred fifty meters behind us. And if you really want some privacy, there's a mighty big jungle beyond that. Just mind the tigers."

"Tigers?"

"Tigers. We got 'em. Welcome to The Nam, son." He glanced at Daniel and the four cameras slung around his neck. "You get lots of pictures of my soldiers doing their job. My men need something to send home, other than what comes through on those bogus TV news reports. The Cav is proud of what we're doin' here. Focus on that."

"I'll try, sir."

"Only my troops call me 'sir'. You can call me Captain Morrison."

CHAPTER TWENTY-SEVEN
Nightfire

Daniel's remembrance of he day had kept him half-awake. His legs felt iron-stiff; his feet sopped and waterlogged from the muck of the river and wetlands they had trudged through all day. The throb of the feeble light from the lantern hanging between his and and Tony's cot didn't offer much warmth; just a usless ebb and flow of illumination.

Lost in his numbness of his mind, Daniel thought back on how quiet the day had been. Except for the occasional swishing of the river, the wind-sizzled grasses on the opposite bank, along with some quietly muttered complaints from Tony, the platoon spent the day progressing through an eerie silence.

They snaked single file in and out of the dappled camouflage of sunlight through the high canopies of trees. Guided by hand signals passed down the line from the point position, what might be heard took on a heightened importance over what was seen. The out-of-place rustle of a bush, the crackling break of a branch, or, far worse, the dreaded click of a footfall on what might be the trigger of a Viet Cong *đạp lôi* mine which could blow off a foot. Plus, you never knew where or when the North Vietnamese Army and the Viet Cong lay in ambush. Not wanting to project the sound of his picture-taking with his Nikon—the *"saddack"* sounding like a mine's trigger click, and the *"thwip"* like a tripwire—Daniel reverted to using the silent Leika rangefinder camera he'd won in a poker game back in the journalist prep camp. Was that really just a month ago? Time had flowed like lava from the molten core of the past.

Tonight, Tony lay three feet away in his tousled-up Army-issued sleeping bag. His little snores had faded away to silence, but not into sleep. Then, a fatigued whisper: "Did your dad take you camping when you were a kid?"

The only things Roger Lilienthal had ever taken Daniel to were sociology lectures, especially anything featuring the theories of C. Wright Mills, Emile Durkheim and conflict sociology. "No. He didn't."

"Really? How about a ball game? You were raised in Chicago. He had to have taken you to at least one Cubbies game."

Daniel smiled sardonically. "Were they the University of Chicago team? I don't think the great Roger Lilienthal ever left the campus."

"Really? Jeeze, Dan. Your dad must have been a real slug."

"He was. He was never really a father. It was more like, he was my mentor, and I was his mentee."

"Man. Were *you* deprived." He rolled over to face him. "Ya know what, bud?" Soon's we get home I'm taking you to a Dodgers game. I mean, I'd take you to a Giants game in San Fran, but they're really sucking right now."

"We'll be home in March. They won't be playing yet."

"Okay." Tony decided abruptly. "Then a Laker's game. I'm gonna be like the older brother you never had."

Daniel's teeth glimmered in a smile. "You'll take me camping?"

"We're doing that now, I guess. It's a little spookier, though. Back then all we had to worry about was a stray raccoon or two."

"Now you've got to worry about tigers….and snakes."

"You asshole. You had to remind me, I saw a few of those pythons or whatever in the swamp today. Big mombo-jambo motherfuckers." He swiveled around to sit on the edge of his cot. Light flared from a match as he lit up a joint. "Guess they figured they'd keep Annie back at the base to protect her, like from tigers and snakes."

"And from you, Antonio."

"Aw, come on. There're a lot of hornier guys in this fucking jungle than me."

"I'm sure she could handle them. And you." Daniel took the joint Tony proffered and sucked a deep draw. "I think she wanted to leave us on our own. Maybe she found something to cover back where she's being held hostage in Chu Lai."

"Well, yeah, I suppose. As long as she lets me edit her stuff." He took the joint back. "You know, Dan? Tough as she is, she writes a pretty crappy story. Grammar-wise. Can't spell too good, either."

"I'm sure that's why she brought you along."

Bursts of gunfire punctured the silence in the near distance. "Shit, man," Tony coughed. "The gooks are coming!"

Daniel didn't seem worried. Even in the short time they'd been rucking on patrol, he'd gotten used to the sounds of itinerant gunfire. "We're journalists, Tony. We need to be impartial. Don't call them 'gooks.' NVA, ARVN, Viet Cong, Charlie, maybe. But not gooks, or what is that other thing they call them? Dinks?" Thien came to mind. "It's their war. Their country. Let's show them a little respect."

"Even when they've got a fuckin' AK-47 pointed at our heads?"

Daniel took another draw on the joint. "How are you and that Mai-Bing hitting it off?"

"Bian," Tony said, "and she's made herself into a hard sell for me."

"Really? The way she came on to you, she seemed pretty easy."

"What? You make her sound like some sorta whore. Well, she isn't a whore."

"Shit, Tony. I never said that."

"You might as well have. She's not a whore. She's a Catholic."

"Ah. Then she's a virgin saving herself for the right guy."

"Maybe. I bought her that drink and a dinner. Told her a little about how I worked for the *Trib* and that I'd just gotten back from covering the war in the Delta and was coming here. That was about it. Then she rushed off to mass."

"I see," said Daniel. "Well, Tony, if she says she's a Catholic, then she must be virtuous. Maybe she wore her little bikini top as a mantilla."

"Oh, that's just bullshit. I'm not virtuous and *I'm* a Catholic. At least I was… once…I think. I'm Italian right? I must be a Catholic. So, Bian and I have that in common."

"She's not Italian."

"And she's not a whore."

"Then she's virtuous as a nun."

"Fuck you. Very much. And stop hogging that weed." Tony's voice was cut off by the hollow, metallic *thuh-wonk!* of mortar fire from just outside their tent. He jolted up. "What the fuck was *that?*"

"Sounds like a mortar grenade being shot off."

"Yeah? Why?" His tone was thick in apprehension.

"Incoming!!" Someone on watch near their tent shouted.

A return grenade sliced through the silence, dragging a low whine followed by a crackling, then a paralyzing explosion, which flapped the walls of their tent and tumbled the lantern from its hook on the tent pole as it hit a few yards away. A commotion of voices prattled all around them as the platoon readied to respond. They fired off another mortar-grenade.

"Fuck! Shit, Dan!" Tony said as he fumbled around under his cot for his boots. Daniel grabbed up his cameras.

The squad sergeant stuck his head through the tent flap. "Come on, ladies! Move your asses into the bunker!"

"What fuckin' bunker?!" Tony said, as he tried to tie his boots and Daniel flicked a film cartridge into the Nikon's chamber.

"The fuckin' bunker we just dug around them rocks right behind your tent about twenty minutes ago while you was in here getting' your all's beauty sleep! Come on! Move it!" He flashed them a grin, then flipped shut the tent flap.

"Jeeezuzz! Did you see that? He freakin' *smiled*. I think that guy fuckin' *enjoys* this!"

"He does, Antonio. People like him live for this shit," Daniel said, then scampered in a crouch from the tent with Tony right behind him.

In the bunker with its makeshift log roof, the platoon radioman was keying his handset. "Charlie-Six, Charlie-Six. This is X-Ray-One. We've been tagged! Under fire! Over."

A voice came back delayed and in pieces through the squelch and the squawk. "X-Ray-One. Charlie-Six. What's your pos?"

"Uh, Charlie-Six, wait one..." He held a penlight in his teeth as he ran a finger along a map on his lap. "Uh...we're about seven kliks northeast of the Hiep Duc river from point position Delta. Over..."

This was answered with more static, woven through an unintelligible response.

"X-ray-One. Say again, Charlie-Six?..."

"Whiskey-Eight is at point Echo, around two kliks west of you. Can you hold until they can get to you?"...

The radioman held up a fist—a sign for silence. The distant gunfire sounded less erratic and more directed. Another grenade sizzled overhead; followed rapidly by another. Their muffled impact sent cascades of dirt filtering through the overhead logs of the lean-to. There was another cry of "Incoming!" followed by another explosion right outside.

Lieutenant Hearn, a slight, weedy guy making his way up the Army chain from Biloxi, Mississippi, hunkered next to his radioman and signaled him give over the handset. "Charlie-Six. Doubtful. Repeat... doubtful. Request AC (*air coverage*). Over..."

Daniel stood away from them in rapt anticipation as he furtively attached a small strobe to his Nikon. He opened the lens one stop for exposure compensation, flicked the strobe to half-power and waited until the diminutive hum of the battery charge went silent. The pictures might turn out a little grainy, but he figured he could make some adjustments during development.

"X-Ray-One, negative on the AC. It's too soupy at mother's house (*too foggy at the Chu-Lai airbase*)." The radio hissed out into the ensuing quiet, accentuating the silence. Then: "Request you hold until Whiskey-Eight can get to you. Repeat: hold your ground until Whiskey-Eight. They've been alerted and can be at your pos in an hour…"

Lieutenant Hearn held the handset close to his mouth as if passing on a secret. "Charlie-Six. What the *fuck*? We don't know what's around us, but it's a lot of shit! We request AC. There ain't *nothing* you can send?…"

"That's afirmative, X-Ray-One. You'll have to wait for Whiskey-Eight. Defend your pos on your own for about forty-five minutes. They have been mobilized to you…" The whistling swoop from a mortar-launched grenade ended in another quick explosion followed by the human cry of someone being hit. This was followed by a barrage of local machine gun fire.

"Shit!" Hearn spat. He soured his expression into the handset, as though he could telegraph it back to Chu-Lai. "Roger, Charlie-Six. Make it quick. X-Ray-One over and out."

Saddack/FLASH…thwip.

"God damn *fuck*!" he shouted at Daniel. "What the *fuck* you doin', boy?"

"Taking a picture."

"No. You ain't. You're giving out our position with that god damn flash bulb of yours!"

Another whizz and an explosion.

Daniel eased his way back toward the poncho liner that had been serving as a door flap. He saw Tony retching off in the musty darkness of the bunker. No wonder he had been so silent. "Uh, I think they already pretty much know where we are, lieutenant," he said, then crouched low and backed out through the door-flap.

The crackle of gunfire was almost constant now — a deafening wall of sound. Daniel could feel the vibrations through the earth beneath his boots. The slight, unctuously saccharine scent of cordite rising from the M-16s and M-60s hung suspended in the stifling humidity. Machine gun fire ripped through the night, lightening the darkness with its flashes. Daniel felt the mist heating his skin as he kept the camera viewfinder to his eye like it was his only connection to planet earth. *Saddack/flash! -thwip; saddack/flash!-thwip; saddack/flash!-thwip.* Powered by adrenaline, he hardly knew what he was shooting. His camera had taken control of the chaos, organizing it into a tight sequence of shots.

Saddack-thwip. Saddack-thwip. Saddack-thwip. Saddack-thwip. Saddack-thwip.

A grenade team loading rounds into their cannons. A close-up of a soldier's sweating face against the backdrop of night, his expression a combination of determination, duty, and fear as he shoved a grenade into a launcher tube. A three-quarter shot of same, as the grenade was fired. A machine-gunner against the penumbral mush of the nearby tree line meeting the blank sky, his face lit by the blasts firing from his weapon, as he shot randomly at flashes in the trees 150 yards away. Lieutenant Hearn directing four of his men where to aim their fire. Another of the lieutenant, his face glistening in sweat, flanked by his corporal radioman as he talked frustratedly into the handset. A medic attending to a wounded man who might have already been dead. A dark-lit, three-quarter portrait of sergeant Andre "Battleship" Washington, one of the platoon's two gunner-scouts, bare-chested and draped with bandoliers as he held up an Ingram Mark 10 machine gun balanced on one knee, and an M-79 on the other. He wore a green sweat-dulled bandanna tied around the top of his bald head like a crown, looking like one of Pancho Villa's raiders. A leather thong tied around his bicep secured a pack of Luckies, and maybe a few joints.

Daniel saw Tony, his face ashen through the dark as he interviewed some soldiers, then ducked back into the bunker to write his notes. He would return to the clearing, interview another few soldiers and repeat the process of stealing back into the bunker to write. Daniel was starting to feel a little more in tune with it all. It was like Watts on steroids, but this time, the attackers were unseen.

CHAPTER TWENTY-EIGHT
Checkpoint Kilo

The firefight went on for four more hours. The mist had become heated, accentuating the scents of cordite and ammonia from the gunfire. Daniel's right thumb felt heavy and numbed from all the film advances; his right index finger cramped in the joints from all the shutter releases. Changing film was now an automatic task, which he was able to to do left-handed as he worked his aching right hand to loosen it up.

At first light, the shooting died down. After sun-up the Viet Cong would usually retreat into their camouflaged tunnels and bunkers to rest up for the next nighttime assault. The dawn light revealed two men dead and six injured—nearly half the platoon's strength—and still no sign of Whiskey-Eight. Charlie-Six's only hope had been that Whiskey-Eight would find them before daybreak to double their strength. Muted sounds of rapid gunfire in the distance explained why they hadn't—they were caught up in their own firefight.

Smoke rose with the light that filtered in dusty long rays through the trees. Some of the men of the platoon hunkered over their weapons and equipment in dead fatigue; a few others were hunched over in prayer. One wiped away a tear and smudged his face as he fondled his rosary. He couldn't have yet been out of his teens. *Saddack-thwip.*

The order came to take an offensive position, advance up the hill toward the source of the Viet Cong fire and wipe out any resistance to clear a landing zone. Getting to the clearing would be the toughest part. The jungle up the hill was so dense that hardly any sunlight reached the ground through the hundred-and-fifty-foot-high canopy blocking out the sky. Felling the thick gnarls of vines twisted around twenty-foot-tall bamboo stalks would be an arduous task, even for twenty men with machetes.

"Where's Battleship?" Lieutenant Hearn called out in a voice hoarse with exhaustion. "Get Battleship over here!"

Though Battleship Washington may had instilled a degree of confidence, there had been no relief—no choppers, no artillery, no reinforcements. He walked tall from behind, his gear clattering as he moved. "Here, lieutenant."

Hearn leaned toward him in confidence. "I need you to recon two kliks up that hill, there. See that plateau about halfway up?" Battleship nodded. "That's where we need to be. We'll be clearing an LZ there so a firebase can be built, but if we can reach that flat area, maybe we won't have to do too much fucking work. Also do the usual. Check for any gook activity."

"As usual, sir," Battleship said in a rasp that sounded as coarse and rough as he was.

"As usual." Hearn echoed before he turned to look at him. "You'll be traveling light and'll need to shed most of your gear. And dress for it. I don't want some damn fucking mosquito taking out my best recon man. You can bring Harrison with you."

"I'd rather go alone, L.T."

"No. You'll take Harrison. You'll need some sort of back-up, and he knows how to snipe."

"Harrison, he talk too much. This gotta be silent, you know."

"You'll do as I tell you, Washington. We had a long fuckin' night and I ain't in any mood to be questioned. If he starts talking just gag him with your headband."

Battleship fingered his bandanna. "Yes, sir."

"Good. Now get Harrison and go." He turned back to the platoon. "Okay, ya'll…" *saddack-thwip*. He cast a sharp-eyed glare at Daniel. "Can you just fuckin' stop with that for one fuckin' minute?" Daniel put his camera down. "Thank you. Okay, men. Now listen up. We're going up that hill to take it and clear an LZ."

This was met with a chorus of responses: "Aww man?" "Shit!" "Fuckin' A!" "You gotta be fuckin' *kiddin'* me!" "Charlie's all over that fucking shit hill!"

Hearn held up a hand. "I know, guys. It's been a long night. But if we're gonna get any air and artillery power in here, we gotta clear an LZ." He peered toward the back of the gathering. "What was that, Morton?"

"We've got two dead, two wounded bad, and four walking wounded. We haven't got the troop strength to make that hill, lieutenant, much less fight Charlie."

"We carry them," Hearn said.

Another refrain: "Aww man?" "Shit!"; "Fuckin A!" "You gotta be fuckin' *kiddin'* me!"

"We gotta carry 'em?" Morton asked.

"Right. We carry our dead and wounded. We never leave our men behind for the dinks to find. All the more reason to clear an LZ to get them outta here."

"I wasn't suggesting we leave them, sir," Morton said.

The lieutenant shook his head. *College kids!* "What were you suggesting, then, Morton? Not going? "

"No, sir. I don't know. I mean up there don't look any more habitable than here. I was just thinking, maybe up the river a little, we'll find a clearing."

Hearn knew from the topo-map that there was no riverbank clearing. Even if there were, the Viet Cong would have nested there for a certain ambush. The rougher the terrain; the less chance of that happening. "No. We're humping up that hill to clear a zone and chopper out our dead and wounded." He turned toward Daniel and Tony. "You guys, too. We're getting' you out of here."

Tony looked relieved. Daniel, still fired up by his photography, had more work to do. He'd become one with his purpose here through his baptismal firefight. He knew now that Thien had been right. This war was not going away soon.

Hearn had circled the plateau on the recon map and labeled it "Checkpoint Kilo." During his progress toward the plateau, Battleship had radioed down that all was clear. The Viet Cong had retreated into their underground dens, at least until nightfall. Whiskey-Eight, now following in their trail one-and-a-half kliks behind, and in radio contact, could help defend the position.

The real enemy had still been the overgrowth; not as bad as Hearn had expected, but still a formidable foe. Once a small clearing had been made to set down the two stretchers laden with the body bags, and the open stretchers where two of the wounded lay. Those who could, took up their machetes and hacked laboriously at the undergrowth. Even Tony had swung a machete to chop some vines away. Daniel continued to take his pictures, some from behind the tines of young bamboo, as the men toiled through their sweating and cursing.

They made it to the ridge of the plateau by 10:30. It was a nice clear space three-quarters the size of a football field. There were large patches of dirt and ground cover clumped with coarse carpets of ankle-deep weeds and elephant grass. Hearn radioed to Da Nang airbase to send a couple of choppers with building materials and canvas along with meal packs, medical supplies and yes, some cases of Budweiser. He also requested rocket launchers, artillery and some mortar cannon to set up a solid defense position at Kilo before dark, when "the Cong would want to come out and play."

By noon the first Huey arrived, stocked with the med supplies, meal-packs and two cases of beer, which the men wasted no time digging into. "Just two cases?" Battleship grumbled. "Shee-it, Man! We gonna need more than that. Two cases ain't even enough to get *me* going. *Shee-it!*" Once that chopper was emptied, the dead and wounded on stretchers were slipped aboard. One of the walking wounded was also huddled into the Huey. He'd drowsily claimed he could stay and fight, but then collapsed to his knees.

The heavy whopping of a Chinook drew some eyes skyward. Its lowering bulk cast half the platoon in shadow as it hovered, swinging an M-105 Howitzer a foot off the ground, then six inches, where it was released. The big chopper turned and settled down off into a corner; its two massive rotors swirling up a cloud of dust to join that thrown up by the first Huey as it lifted. The Chinook was also packed with lumber, construction equipment, and skids of bags to fill with sand. A second Chinook arrived, loaded down with communications equipment, tents, and the manpower to build an army-proper command post. Once empty, the three remaining walking wounded lumbered aboard. Tony happily jumped into a Huey about to depart. Daniel set his gear into the bay, then took time for a last look just as Whiskey-Eight finally joined X-Ray-One. "Bring some more beer!" Hearn shouted to the pilot who flashed him a thumbs-up gesture. Hearn grinned and returned the thumbs-up. Daniel aimed his camera: *Saddack Thwip.*

He first heard the multiple rounds of AK-47 fire when the chopper had lifted to about two-hundred feet. Below, there was a confusion of activity as the men dropped their beers and scrambled for their M-16s to return fire. It would have been pointless for the men of Charley Company to run for the cover of the trees. The NVA had all fifty of them surrounded and in the open, and their gunfire was close.

Daniel watched the horizon tilt as the Huey banked hard and the door-gunner slapped open his machine gun's gate and tensed into firing position. A view down at nothing but the nappy clusters of treetops filled the open gunner's door, as Daniel was choked by nausea and the bile rising in his throat. Even so, he instinctively raised his camera and focused. *Saddack-thwip; saddack-thwip; saddack-thwip; saddack-thwip.*

Through his viewfinder, he could see dozens of puffs of AK-47 fire and rocket propelled grenades shooting from the trees surrounding the platoons. Three men already lay lifeless. Now a fourth wheeled back and fell to the ground. Hearn was shouting into the radio handset, probably calling in a napalm strike. He went down, but not out, as he crawled around the scurry of activity. Amid the tracer-threads from bullets being fired from all directions into the clearing, Daniel recognized the hulk of Battleship Washington, now diminished 150 feet below, standing near the center, firing steady bursts from his Mark-10. He charged the perimeter and went down by degrees, still shooting. In a moment he stumbled to his death in the flattened grass. Some of the men tried unsuccessfully to activate the Howitzer, but were picked off as they tried to get near it.

The big Chinook quickly lumbered into the air in two motions as its door-gunners fired into the trees. Daniel's chopper trembled from the recoil of the gunner's weapon as he continued firing. Bullet casings from the bursts of M-60's fire jangled hollowly on the metal deck. Daniel took some quick shots of the gunner in rapt concentration over his smoking machine gun.

The Huey started rumbling and vibrating as it took some metallic pings of 50-caliber bullets from the ground. Daniel sensed he was bolted to the deck, as the only action he seemed capable of was taking random pictures. Tony began retching what little he had left in his gut out the open gunner door; perhaps hoping his puke would land on some NVA soldier's head. The chopper suddenly jarred right. Daniel aimed his camera quickly up, long enough to see the pilot grasping his left bicep. Blood oozed out between his fingers. *Saddack-thwip.* "I've been hit! I'VE BEEN HIT!" He croaked toward his co-pilot. "Crocker, you've got the con!"

"Shit!" the co-pilot said as he grasped the stick. "Hang in there, Bert!" He righted the craft, increased the collective and they began to rise. Then the door gunner's firing stopped.

"FUCK! Shit!" Tony shouted down at the gunner's body slumped over his legs—his head bleeding into his lap. "FUCK! FUCK! FUCK!"

"Take the gun!" The pilot shouted back at him. "Take the fucking GUN!"

Tony contorted his expression. "You fucking *kidding* me?" He tried to shoo the gunner's blood-soaked corpse off his legs as if fanning away a swarm of mosquitos. "I don't know how work that

Goddamn thing! I'm just a fucking *newspaper writer!*"

The crew chief lurched across the bay to grab the two gun handles. He fired as the chopper lifted safely to height. The pilot took the communications mic in his good hand and keyed for Chu-Lai. "Bravo Six. Bravo Six. This is Hotel-Thirty. Can you read? Over."

Daniel cringed his shoulders as he lowered his camera and grasped his left thumb tight in his right fist.

"Bravo-Six. I read you, Hotel-Thirty."

"Bravo-Six, we're taking hits from some NVA troops firing on Charlie-Six and Whiskey-Eight from the trees. Hill 1282, about five kliks west of Phuoc Binh. Ak-47s and RPGs. Our guys are like sitting ducks! Request AC; Request AC! Over!"

"Hotel-Thirty, we're on it. Air cover's already been requested by the platoon lieutenant. Over."

"Bravo-Six. The L.T.'s down. Maybe dead. It's a fucking shit-storm down there!" He glanced at the body of the door-gunner. His expression sagged into dismay. "We have one casualty here in the air and three wounded. Heading to base. Out."

Bravo-Six's response was drowned by the thundering roar of two muscular Navy A-1 Skyraiders passing close overhead. Daniel followed them through his viewfinder. They split formation and flew in parallel low over the trees and dispensed a narrow, fiery trail of napalm over both sides of the clearing, now littered with limp bodies. There had to have been at least twenty wounded or dead. The Skyraiders arced up, then flew back toward the Huey for a second pass to throw more napalm.

Saddack-thwip; saddack-thwip; saddack-thwip.

CHAPTER TWENTY-NINE
Follies redux

The fragrance of yesterday's cigarette tobacco and mahijuana hung in the air around the press-briefing area. Wet stale scents of booze and beer wafted from the bar's darkness. There, a group of journalists lounged in rickety folding chairs, trying to reap some morsel of news from MACV's official bullshit. Hank Weller, a freelancer for the Associated Press, had taken on Barry Zorthian.

"But Barry. I thought the ARVNs were on our side, fighting for their country and all."

"They are, Hank."

"Well, fuck! One of these 'friends of ours' aimed his sidearm at my head. Bastard would've *shot* me!"

Zorthian offered up one of his professional, knowing smiles. "But he didn't. Besides, Hank. I heard about the incident. You drew first."

"Fuck you, Barry. I did not."

"What was the tenor of your interview, Hank? What questions had you asked him?"

"I don't know. Usual stuff, I guess. How do you like the food? How long were you out on your last operation? Stuff like that."

"And what else?"

"Jesus, I don't know. How many kills did your guys have? Did you see any NVA gooks in the jungle?"

"You said that: 'gooks'?"

"That's what the fuck they are, Barry."

"By 'they' you mean the Vietnamese."

"Yeah. Gooks."

"'Gooks' is a disparaging term for all Vietnamese. The ARVN are also Vietnamese on our side. So, you fired first. With your question…" he held up a pencil "…and with this. You gotta be careful how you frame your questions out there, guys."

Annie nudged Tony. "The pen as a weapon thing, again. Barry used that same example with Pete Arnett back in sixty-five."

"Any more questions?" Barry said as he gathered up his notes to call it a day. He glanced out at the correspondents, who seemed ready for this to rnd so thay could get back to their drinking. "Okay, then. Thus endeth today's briefing. Thanks again, ladies and gentlemen," he added in his usual sign off.

Tony restlessly raised his hand. "What about Phuoc Binh?"

Barry seemed apprehensive. "What *about* Phuoc Binh?"

"You didn't mention it. There was a firefight there at a place called Checkpoint Kilo. How many of our guys did we lose?"

After a thoughtful silence, Barry answered. "No one said anything to me. Besides if we report on every firefight…"

"This one was pretty big. I saw it up close. A platoon was penned in by the NVA. We had to have lost at least a dozen guys."

"I haven't heard anything about any firefight in Phuoc Binh."

Now Annie spoke out. "That doesn't mean it didn't happen, Barry…does it?"

"I'll check with Mac-Vee, Anne, but we don't have any record of it." He tread lightly with her because word was out about her carrying the recently promoted Colonel Frank Moss, his supervisor.

"Good, Barry. I'll check on it, too," she told him.

The Playboy Lounge was another one of those dim places lining Tu Do Street where American men hung out with their Vietnamese girls. The jukebox glowed like a dull jewel in the corner as it played another in the long list of Beatles' tunes. This time it was "I am the Walrus." Bian had recommended this place, and Tony had come to realize that for the virtuous person she claimed to be, she had some pretty raunchy tastes. That was fine with him.

He felt her little bare foot under the table carousing up and down his calf. He squinted into the harsh light that seemed to highlight their booth, as he regarded her smooth, high cheekbones, the hint of an overbite and the way her right eye drooped a little in fatigue. He mused at how frail she looked; as if she might blow away in the breeze from the floor fan, which did little but stir up the smaze of tobacco smoke.

"You remind me of a bird," he said through an easy smile.

She stopped moving her foot but kept it against his leg. Her eyes widened. "A *bird*? What you mean? Like a chicken?"

"Like a sparrow, Bian. You're so delicate."

"No. I strong. Like eagle." She sipped her beer. Then she lit the cigarette she had swiped from Tony's pack lying between them.

"I shot some Viet Cong a few days ago. From a helicopter," he said.

She stiffened as she drew her foot away from his leg. "You did? Why?"

"Oh, I don't know. Maybe because they were shooting at me?"

"Where did you do that?"

He leaned back and crossed his arms. "From a helicopter flying over a little place in the hills near Phuoc Binh. The door-gunner got shot and fell dead on my lap. I grabbed his gun and fired back at the VC that killed him. I might have taken out maybe ten of them."

One of Bian's cousins lived near Phuoc Binh. She grimaced a little smile to feign some interest. "Ten of them?"

He pursed his lips in pride. "You should have seen me. I was like John Wayne up there. The crew chief wanted to take the fifty-cal gun away from me, but I pushed him aside and kept firing. I told him that even though I was a journalist, I had it all under control."

The touch of her foot against his leg felt fainter as she held her hard smile. "You my soldier," she said hoarsely. "You numbah one reporter."

"Yup. I was thinking about you the whole time, Bian. You gave me the courage to take those bad guys out."

Her smile fell as she lowered her eyes to the table. "I glad, Ton-ney. You fight for me and my country," she said in a slight whisper.

"Really? You seem sad, somehow. I mean I get it—Vietnam at war and all that. But we're over here to make it right for you people," he placed his hand on hers, "right, Bian?"

She answered with a little shake of her head. "Yes, Ton-ney. You right. This war numbah ten. I hate this boo-shit war."

Tony reached over and stroked her cheek. "This bullshit war," he agreed.

The traffic was out in force on Tu Do Street. Peddlers hawked their wares: costume jewelry that glittered in the reflections from the streetlights and neon signs; rice balls smelling of curry and saffron and cooling in the remains of evening; left-over fish caught at least twelve hours earlier and beginning to smell like it; and, to sweeten it all, the clean fragrances from the carts and make-shift booths of fruit, jasmine, and orchids. As broad as the boulevard was, it seemed as though it was never meant to bear such a tight weave of chaos; but the well-lit street-side cafes and bar of the Continental Palace seemed far away from all that.

Annie was lost in thought while Frank sat across from her looking concerned. She ran her forefinger up and down the cool condensation on her glass of Jim Beam.

"You're awfully quiet, Gabbie."

She raised her eyes and offered up a coy smile that only bordered on sincerity. "Maybe I just don't know how to behave in the presence of a Colonel."

"I guess the same way you'd behave in the presence of a Lieutenant Colonel. You know when we're together like this, 'rank don't mean shit,' as my assistant sergeant says."

"I hope he doesn't say that to you."

He sipped his Scotch. "I hear rumors. Unease in the ranks, you know. Happens all the time when a new boss comes on board."

"Do you miss being over at The Rex? All the frivolity?"

"All the bullshit, you mean?"

"If you say so, Frank. I've just noticed you seem a little, I don't know, stiffer, in the last few weeks."

He raised his eyebrows in a coy show of optimsm. "*Stiffer*?"

"Oh, for Christ's sake, Frank. You know what I mean. More officious."

"I guess I do miss being at The Rex a little, and not having a

General or two breathing down my neck. You can't drink as much on the job there at headquarters, but the air-conditioning is more reliable, and the office furniture is nicer." He held up a finger to order another round as a waiter passed. "We'll have a couple of menus, too," he said, then he looked over at Annie. "Are we staying here for dinner?"

"I'd prefer something a little raunchier, but sure. Okay." The waiter nodded and left. "Frank. I need to ask you something, and I need you to be straight with me."

"Well, Gabb, as long as you're not asking me to marry you, I'll do my best to answer."

"I promise to keep it off the record."

"Sounds serious."

A passing jewelry vendor offered up a necklace for them to look at. He nodded toward Annie. "For prilly woman. Pure jade. Velly prilly necklace. I sell cheap."

"Yeah," Frank muttered. "Pure jade cast from an old Canada Dry bottle." He took it in his hands and then glanced at Annie. "You like this? I can afford it now."

"Velly cheap! And velly prilly!" the vendor insisted.

"'Very cheap' is probably not the best line for selling jewelry," Frank told him. "Maybe you should go back to marketing school."

"I give you twenny percent off!"

"I don't think he understood a word I said. So do you like this, Gabbie?"

"I don't know. Why don't you buy it for your wife?"

"Because you're here and I want you to have it."

She heaved a sigh. "I'm not exactly one for jewelry. It gets caught up in the jungle vines when I'm out on assignment." She lit a cigarette. "*If* I ever go out on assignment again," she muttered *sotto voce*. Noticing Frank's hangdog look over her rejection of his gift, she vigorously waved out her match. "Oh, for Christ's sake, Frank. Okay, go ahead and buy it for me."

He and the vendor carried out their fifteen-dollar transaction. The vendor pocketed the money then trundled, cart in tow, to his next victim.. Frank handed the necklace to her. "It'll go well with your combat fatigues."

"Thank you for being such a fucking romantic. Now I need you to answer my question," she said as she clasped the cut-glass necklace around her neck. "Off the record."

"I'll try."

"What do you know about Phuoc Binh?"

"What about it? Where is Phouc Binh?"

"Oh, I think you know. There was an ambush there. We lost about ten guys."

He tensed in apprehension. "I don't know anything about it…Even if I did, it didn't happen."

"Oh, come *on*, Frank! I have some of my photographer's pictures to prove it. Here:" She reached into her satchel, took out half a dozen of Daniel's eight-by-tens and handed them to him.

The low areal photos depicted eight bodies scattered around the open area of Checkpoint Kilo. Men were scurrying or crawling to get to the Howitzer, while the others were futiley trying to defend their position or rush the perimeter. He looked at the photos and shrugged. "This could have been anywhere."

"Thing is, Frank, it *shouldn't* have been *anywhere*. Those are men from two platoons of Charlie Company lying on the ground killed or wounded after they humped into a big nest of NVA and Cong."

He slid the pictures back to her. "It didn't happen, Gabbie," he insisted in a dry tone.

"You're fucking kidding me," she sneered as the waiter placed the menus on the table. "Are you gonna deny those are our guys in these pictures? You know they are. And there must've been dozens of NVAs in those trees picking them off like in a turkey shoot."

"Were *you* there, Anne?"

"Jeezuzz, now I *know* I've gotten to you, Frank. You called me by my real name, which I thought you forgot. Anyway, I hand-picked Tony and Daniel. They may be green, but they know how to do their jobs. They wouldn't have made this up. Anyway, from what we've heard through the Mac-Vee grapevine, the NVA wasn't really supposed to be in that area."

"The NVA is everywhere, especially in the central highlands and the DMZ. That's why we're over here in case you forgot."

"Not in that sort of concentration. It's almost like there's something in the works. An offensive or something. Are you guys at Mac-Vee putting our troops in danger by sweeping something you all know is going to happen under the rug?"

"Anne," he enunciated, "It didn't happen. And you can quote me."

"Oh yes it did, and yes I will…quote you." She stood up to leave. "Good night, Frank. Enjoy your dinner."

"I'm sorry, Gabb," he said.

She couldn't help feeling a modicum of pity for him. She knew he knew something was happening in the hills, but had orders not to say anything. Here was an instance where what was not said was the story. And that was the conundrum in mixing the press with Command. She leaned over and planted a light kiss on the top of his head. "I know, sweetie. I'll see you later," she glanced at her watch, "around eleven-thirty, in my cruddy little penthouse at the Caravelle." She caught the glitter of the necklace as she rolled it in her fingers. "And thanks for this, Frank. I really do like it."

CHAPTER THIRTY
The advancing herd

Thien's heartbeat rose as the herd of water buffalo gained upon him. He couldn't breathe, but he had to keep running toward the hut across the rice paddy where his aunt Nguyễn-Tay was with his cousins. Aunt Nguyễn-Tay had a solution for everything—she would offer him solace and the warmth of protection along with a bowl of sweet sticky rice. Maybe the sludge in the rice paddy would slow down the approaching herd, but the hut had started to recede into the far distance. His breathing had become painful, weighing him down, and he felt his lungs might explode. He looked behind at what must had been a thousand buffalo. They were joined now by a herd of stampeding rhinos, and then some giant tigers. Elephants trailed in the rear. He felt he was suffocating until he forced himself half-awake.

"Shit, Thien. What's the matter? You're kicking me in your sleep. You having some sort of nightmare?" Daniel slurred.

"Must find my Aunt Nguyễn-Tay," he mumbled, still hearing the thunder of the advancing stampede. He was jarred fully wake by the sound of an elephant's deep bray, joined by other warbling whinnies. The husky bawls dissolved into the wavering banshee falsettos of horses neighing.

"Thien?"

"I'm okay. Okay." he breathed as he rolled over to cling to Daniel. "I'm okay, Daniel. Okay." He cherished the silence until he heard the whinnying again, this time muffled through the wall behind him. "What the fuck is that?"

"What is what?"

"That sound. It's hideous."

Daniel heard what he'd become inured to over the nights he'd spent in his room adjoining Tony's. "Oh, that. It's probably Verdi or Puccini. Tony always plays opera music in the morning." He heard a triumphal male chorus holding the rumble of a note while a tenor rambled on in Italian. This morning it was louder than usual. "It is pretty awful, isn't it? Usually it's not this bad, because he plays Rossini—something a little lighter, at least."

A slight smile raised Thien's cheeks. "Why, Daniel. I never would have thought you knew opera."

"I don't. I've just come to know Tony," he said as he moved to swing out of the bed. "It's really annoying today. Now *I* have a headache."

"Where are you going?"

"Just next door to tell him to turn it down, or better yet, off."

Thien began to rustle himself from the bed. "I'll go with you."

Daniel knew Tony suspected he was with Thien, but didn't want to flaunt it by showing up at his door with his Vietnamese boyfriend. "It's probably better you stay here."

"Okay," he said as he slipped on his khaki shirt. He looked at his watch. "I've got to go, anyway. I need to be at work by zero-nine-thirty."

"How's that going, Thien? Is *Stars and Stripes* sending you out in the field, yet?"

Thien pulled on his pants. "Next week. They're sending me up to cover a Marine base in Nha Trang. It's a light assignment; more like practice."

"Hey. Don't knock it. It's an assignment. At least you won't be getting shot at."

"Probably not. Not yet at least." He walked to Daniel and kissed his cheek. "Tonight?"

"Of course."

"My apartment, then. No opera music."

"No opera music."

He smiled, then left the room carrying his shoes and closing the door behind him. Daniel was discomforted by another in a refrain of mental images of Johanna. She looked infuriated, as though she had just caught him and Thien in bed in bed together. He imagined her saying in her coarse little voice: *What the fuck are you doing to me, Daniel?* He felt a chill rumble through his shoulders. "Loving you, Johanna," he said aloud. "I…I can't love anyone else."

He opened Tony's door to a burst of two female voices coming through his mammoth stereo speakers. "Man? What the fuck is *that?*"

"'Attila the Hun'," Tony called over the music.

Daniel opened the door wide to see Tony waving his hands in the air to the flow of the opera, as though he was conducting it. Bian sat up against the headboard looking totally bored. She had her arms crossed high over her breasts as she puffed on a joint. Her bamboo *non-la* hung by its chin ribbon over one of the headboard newel-posts.

"Stop it, Antonio! Turn it down! Can't you see you're torturing this girl?"

"*You* go 'way! He not torture me!"

"See, Dan? Bian *loves* opera!"

She placed the joint in the bedside ashtray, took the *non-la* in one of her hands and held it over her lap as she rose to a kneeling position, and mimicked Tony's air-baton with her free hand. The sight of her breasts jouncing tightly as she moved led Daniel to miss Johanna all the more. He averted his eyes and went over and unplugged the tape player. The opera growled to a stop.

Tony ceased his air baton motions and frowned at Daniel. "Damn, man! What have you done? You've defiled Verdi! You're a real asshole, you know that?."

"I'm sure the rest of the people on this floor will thank me."

Tony lifted Bian's weed and took a puff, then suppressed a giggle. "You're a fucking killjoy, Dan."

"You numbah eight!"

Daniel tried to work his smirk into something friendly. "Why thank you, Bian. You've elevated me from a number ten."

"No. Then you numbah fifteen, so."

He wagged a finger at her. "Ah, ah, ah. Too late to rescind your opinion."

She looked over at Tony. "What he means, Tonney?"

"I have no idea, sweetheart. What *did* you mean?"

Daniel shook his head. "Never mind. That music through the wall was giving me nightmares."

"Of *course* it did, Dan. It's *supposed* to. It's 'Attila the Hun'."

Bian put her *non-la* on her head and reached down to the floor for her white *ai-do* blouse. "You no look at me," she warned Daniel, in order to call more attention to herself. She slid from the bed and grabbed up her black trousers.

"You leaving, Bian?" Tony asked. "It's too early. I was hoping we could hang out here a while longer."

She looked at her watch. "Time for church. It is long ride to other end of city." She kissed Tony on the cheek in passing. "I see you here tonight."

"It's kind of, I don't know, impersonal, here. How about at your apartment?"

"No! My sistah, she live with me. She kill you if she see me and you."

"I'll take my chances."

She tweaked his cheek. "You my brave Ton-ney. But you no know my sistah. She more dangerous than any Viet Cong." She made her way toward the bathroom "You thinner than my front yard chicken, numbah fifteen," she told Daniel as she passed him. Only then did he realize he was wearing only his jockey shorts.

CHAPTER THIRTY-ONE

Croissants in the basement

Wearing a traditional ankle-length white *ai-dao* over her black slacks, Bian blended in with the flow of similarly dressed women weaving through the clotted stream of pedestrians on Duong Pasteur, three blocks from the Catholic Basilica. Her face was shaded by her straw *non-la,* and her long ponytail swayed half-way down her back. She soon smelled baking bread from the French patisserie a half-block ahead, but she wasn't going there to buy a baguette. She was going to its basement to meet her sister, Trần Dao.

The shop was dense with the fragrance of bread. The shopkeeper, Nguyễn Lap, nodded his good-morning to her. She nodded back. "Is Trần Dao here yet?" she asked in casual Vietnamese.

He motioned toward the open basement door. "Waiting for you. Do you want a croissant? They're still warm."

"Okay, sure. Thanks, Nguyễn Lap." She flittered a smile of thanks as he handed her one from the tray. While munching on the croissant, disappeared down the creaking stairs leading to the cellar.

Despite the moist heat out in the street, the cellar was cool. Its stone walls gleamed wet in the low light. The room was redolent with the pasty scent of wet flour. Bian's older sister's shadow was elongated by the harsh glow from a goosenecked desk lamp on a plank board table. A severe-looking young Vietnamese man, dressed in civilian clothes, stood off drenched in the shadows to Trần Dao's right. She concentrated on a page in the notebook she held in both hands.

Bian finished off the croissant in one final bite. "Hello, sister."

Trần Dao held up a hand to silence her, then put the notebook on the table. Her voice didn't flow as smoothly as Bian's; it was coarse, clipped, and officious. "What have you found out? Anything?" Trần Dao asked Bian.

"Yes, maybe. My little news reporter said he saw a big fight in Phuoc Binh. Do we have fighters there?" She looked askance at the man standing behind her. "Who's he?"

Trần Dao glanced questionably toward the man in the shadow, who nodded. "I've heard about Phuoc Bihn. There was a company of our brothers fighting there," he answered "We had a small company surrounded. Four of our fighters were napalmed; three killed by American bullets. We killed perhaps ten or more of them."

Bian looked down at the notebook page that had preoccupied Trần Dao. It was a map of Saigon. A filigree of networks had been drawn around Binh Duong and Tay Ninh provinces north and east to the Cambodian border in red grease-pencil.

Trần Dao brought a hand to her chin. "That isn't good. For the Americans. I hope they didn't find any intelligence from our brothers fighting them."

"No. We wiped them nearly out, then retreated to ground up in the hills. The Americans later sent in reinforcements and have managed to establish a firebase there. I saw nothing in the American news about the attack."

Bian forced her glance deeper into the map. She sounded distracted as she spoke. "That's true. My little reporter is angry because the American news won't accept his story about it." She glanced again at the man next to her.

"Because the Americans do not like to report on their failures," the man said. "They need to give the impression that they are winning to keep up morale to recruit more men."

"Sister, who *is* this man?"

"This is Lieutenant Nguyễn Bon Do. He has been sent to help run our operations."

"Our…operations?"

"That's right, little sister," Trần Dao told her. "You've been serving the cause well just by listening in on the press briefings— at least as well as you could. Now that you have found your own personal source, even better. We want you to stay with him. Gain his confidence and report to us about what he has told you or written about. Now we're going to involve you a little more."

"Fighting for our people?"

"That will happen in time," the lieutenant said

. Bian detected a note of uncertainty. "I can do that. I *want* to help our cause."

Trần Dao placed a hand on her sister's shoulder. Her grip was rougher than tender. "I know you do, Bian. But there's a lot that must happen before we can even tell you what the operation is."

The lieutenant's expressoin into broke a handsome and relaxed smile, causing Bian to fall momentarily in love, but the feeling passed. "Even if someone told *us* what the objective is."

Trần Dao 's expression turned grave. She looked into her sister's eyes. "There is something we must have complete confidence about, little sister."

Trần Dao stared down at Bian. It was a way she used to intimidate her when they were children. "Of course, Trần Dao . Just like we used to keep secrets when we were younger. Like sisters must.

"This is much more than that. This is for your country. Before I tell you what we have in mind for you, can you promise we can place our complete confidence and trust in you? I only say this because of those times you betrayed your confidence to me when I was going out with that boy, Nguyễn Van Ngo. This is the same sort of thing, but much, much bigger."

Bian remembered all too well. She had confessed to her parents that Trần Dao had slipped out for the night with the boy, Ngo. She remembered he had buck teeth. For staying out with the buck-toothed boy, Trần Dao was beaten with a bamboo switch. "That was only twice. And we were young. I was just twelve. You were sixteen!" Bian defended. "Besides you made more than your share of mistakes, Trần Dao. What about that time you got revenge on our neighbor by peeing into his rice paddy?"

"Enough, girls!" Nguyễn Bon Do barked in the commanding tone that qualified him as a lieutenant.

Trần Dao heaved a sigh. "Bian, I need your absolute assurance that you will not get so emotionally close to your reporter that you become careless about what you tell him. You can sometimes act fickle when it comes to men"

"Sister, Trần Dao! You have my word. I have no feelings or interest for him beyond what you've asked me to do." She shivered her shoulders. "Ugh! He's not even Vietnamese. He's just another hairy dumb American. No better than a common *nguy*. Vietnam is always first with me." She stared directly at the lieutenant. "Above everything else," she enunciated.

Trần Dao glanced at Lieutenant Nguyễn, who nodded his assent. "Trần Bian, you are ready to begin your training for an offensive that's been in the planning since July." His tone had turned dour and professional Even I'm not certain of its scope, except to know that it will be large. This offensive will require a great number of troops, consisting of only the most loyal of our brothers and sisters. Trần Dao and I are committing you to the cause just by telling you about it.".

Bian bit her lower lip. She couldn't feel her feet but felt as though she was rooted to the earthen floor. Her voice was slight and trembling. "Of course, lieutenant. What do you want me to do?".

"First you are to begin military training."

"Really?"

"While still keeping your connection with the American reporter. Find out what you can from him, as you have been," Trần Dao told her. "But say your goodbyes to him for now. You'll be in training for the next three weeks. We leave the day after tomorrow.".

"Where? Where am I going for this training? The are American and ARVN fighter all around Southern Vietnam.".

Trần Dao looked thoughtfully at the lieutenant, then back at Bian. "You will be training in Cambodia."

"Cambodia? How will we get there?" She glanced again at Lieutenant Nguyễn. "I mean, the border is heavily guarded by the Americans and the *nguy*. They're bombing everywhere."

Trần Dao drew Bian's attention to the map. "Bian, you see these paths we've drawn on the map?"

"Yes. What are they?"

"Tunnels," said the lieutenant.

"*All* of these lines and drawings? They're *tunnels*?"

Trần Dao placed her hand on her sister's shoulder. "Yes, sister. They're tunnels, and that's how we'll get you into Cambodia. By going under the border. We have been moving our fighters through them for over a year. For you, we will drive to the Dai Holy See near Tay Ninh, here..." she pointed to a remote spot about six kilometers east of the Cambodian border. "and make our way through this tunnel to Krong Bavet in Cambodia. That is where our training camp is."

Bian pursed her lips to contain her excitement. "I'll just tell my American reporter I need to go back to our hamlet for a month because our uncle is dying."

"Which of our uncles?"

"Uh, Uncle Trần Nhin?"

Trần Dao took a polite sip of her tea and peeked over her cup at Lieutenant Nguyễn. "He's got to be one hundred and three by now. Tough old man, even without any teeth."

"My reporter won't question my leaving. Death is something everyone understands in this boo-sheet war."

The lieutenant lit a cigarette. "What does this 'boo-sheet' mean?"

"An American expression. Means 'The feces of a water buffalo'."

He shook his head in repressed amusement. "It is a stupid expression."

Trần Dao took another sip of ther cold tea. "That is because Americans are stupid."

CHAPTER THIRTY-TWO
The hill of angels

War had its way with the environment. Agent orange, the bombings, and napalm had done their job to make the landscape look post-apocalyptic all the way into the foggy horizon. What might have once been one-hundred-foot-tall canopies of rain forests were now reduced to scraggly twigs no higher than naked hedgerows, clumped in the barren swath of the McNamara Line. Much of this land had been graded as a mile-wide swath of soggy turf dotted with land mines, listening devices, and sensors. The project had been conjured up by Secretary of Defense Robert McNamara and a think-tank of techno-geeks. It was half-successful enough to be worth defending. Though the Line may have kept the NVA from charging across it, that didn't stop the artillery barrages from the north from pounding out consistent of damage ranging from annoyance to death.

Five marines manning a Howitzer ducked away from its ground-thumping recoil. It was just another shell fired into a void, but what the hell? It was aimed north, toward the equally non-directed fire coming back from across the haze of the demilitarized zone. Daniel shuddered with the ground as he took a close-up of one of the marines preparing to load another shell into the monstrous breach of the gun. His overall attitude had become as exasperated as it was now routine. When he'd arrived in Vietnam two months before, he saw some remnants of the will to win. Thien had told him that a thin veneer was masking something more pervasive and desperate. Now, in Con Thien, the collected will of the troops had sagged into open disgust.

Conversation in the trench was redundant:

"Fuck this shit!"

"Fucking A. I'm too short for this."

"Yeah? Wat'chu got, Malloy?"

A hardened sigh. "Twenty-three and a wake-up."

"Shee-it, man. You'll be home by Christmas."

"Won't do me no good if I'm dead."

A Howitzer down on the right fired another shell—a ground-shattering hollow ka-BOOM!! The sound left behind a paralysis of temporary deafness followed by a residue of ringing in the ears. Being in this moist pit of battle smelling of shit and piss—some on the ground and some in the pants—was like a life sentence in limbo. No one knew when it was going to end; no one remembered when it began.

Someone yelled: "INCOMING!", and a shell from three miles away in North Vietnam landed in the far wall of the trench. Its explosion sounded like a sibilant CRASH! Its impact spewed a rain of shrapnel and dirt. By now the guys could sense the incoming fifteen-pound shell even before they heard its muffled whistle overhead. Experience had taught them to take a face-down position on the muddy, urine-scented ground, prone on their stomachs with their hands covering their helmets. Better to lose your hands than your head. Daniel had just learned this tactic, but he was slow on the uptake, as the heated mud from the blast splattered on his face. A small, hissing bit of shrapnel lodged in the dirt three feet away from his cheek. Below the piss, the ground smelled like an open sewer. The Viet Cong artillery shell must have breached a latrine. Daniel opened an eye and spied a turd, or maybe it was a cigar butt, touching his chin.

The conversation began again. The voices were muffled by the ground in which the marines lay.

"FUCK this shit!!"

"Christ-sake, Jackson. You're fuckin' acting like a Army brat. You're a Marine. Be that."

"Fuck you, Henderson. I made the wrong goddam choice. I shoulda joined the Navy."

"Maybe you shoulda graduated high school first," came a raspy voice from further down. "Gone on to technical college and shit."

"Shut 'chure pie-holes, marines! We got a job to do here. And we do it." That was Gunnery Sergeant Dennet 's voice.

"An' what might that be, gunny?" Jackson said as he rose to his knees with the others. "Our job, that is?"

"Following orders, Jackson." Dennet groaned. "Following fucking orders."

"Only orders we got is to fuckin' sit here and fire at …I don't know fucking what. It's all the goddam same every fuckin' day. Been that way since like time began here. We need reinforcements."

"Westy says we're to hold position. We hold position. Them's the orders," Dennet said. His voice was drawn rusty by fatigue.

"Fuck Westmoreland," someone said. "I don't see *him* up here taking fuckin' fire. He prolly down in Saigon screwing some mama-san. That's prolly about his speed, anyways."

"Fuck Westmoreland," someone else echoed. It might even have been Dennet.

Daniel flicked the cooling mud from his cheek, spot-checked his Nikon, and took another shot of the mud-stained, unwashed marines down the line. *Saddack-thwip…Saddack-thwip.* Even his camera sounded tired. Daniel and Tony had been hunkering down here for three days now. Already it felt like thirty-three.

Jackson looked over at him. "Hey. Mister Photo. You come from the outside. What you think a all this shit?"

"Yeah," Malloy said. "You enjoyin' your little visit wid us? I mean like, are we being good hosts and shit?"

"Knock it off, Malloy," Sergeant Dennet grumbled.

"No," Daniel said. "I'm not liking it here at all. But yeah. Under these circumstances, I couldn't wish for better hosts."

A toothy smile bloomed white on Jackson's face. "Well, la-dee-fuckin' da!" He said and held up his M-16 between his thumb and three beefy fingers while extending his pinkie as though he were drinking a cup of tea. "Look at us. We good hosts!" He pointed at Daniel with his free hand. "I like you, Mr. Photo."

Tony felt the bump of his cassette-recorder against his thigh as he duck-walked through the trench. Occasionally he found a marine or two hunkering down in wait for the next south-bound barrage with their backs to a berm of the ditch. A few, their faces caked in mud, passed the time playing Blackjack. "Mother's Little Helper" bleeted from a battered cassette-player lying between them.

"…ah! Twenty-one! Pay up, mahtha-fuckah!"

"Asshole!" The other muttered as he handed him a Marlboro, then gathered up his soggy cards.

"Hit me."

The dealer with the cards slopped two of them down on the crusty blanket between them. The one showing was a jack of hearts. The other picked up the corner to peek at the face down card. "I'm sticking."

"Shee-it," said the dealer, fearing he was about to lose another hand, as he dealt himself a third card and peeked. "Shee-it!" he whispered again.

"Hey guys," Tony said. "Can I get a couple words from you?" He held his mike out.

"A couple, sure," said the dealer. "And here they are: Fuck you."

"Come on, Gavin," said the other. "Just 'cause you're losing don't mean you cain't make nice." The ash fell from his cigarette as he glanced up at Tony. "How can we help you, Jimmy Olsen?"

Tony offered up a little simper, "Jimmy Olsen was a photographer." He looked behind him toward Daniel, a dozen or so men off into the distance. "Jimmy Olsen's back there taking pictures."

"Yeah, right. Lois Lane, then. Anyway, you wanna know what we're doing here, right? And whadawe think about this fuckin' God damned, shit-eating, ass-suckin' war?"

"I think you just told me what you think about it."

"What paper you with?" Gavin asked.

"*The Los Angeles Tribune.*"

"Holy shit! Yeah?" said the marine with the winning hand. "I gotta mom and her no good step-husband in East L.A." He leaned closer to the mike. "Hi, mom! And hi to you, too, Renaldo, ya fuckin' no good lazy son'o'bitch! Go fin' a fuckin' *job!*"

"I'll make sure to print that" Tony said. "So, how long have you guys been here?"

"Here? In Con fuckin' Thien?" answered Gavin. "Too fuckin' long."

"I been here since July when the shit started coming down," said the other. "Now it's gotten worse. God damn shellin' at nothin,' all to hold the fuckin' McNamara Line. All that shit usta mean something, ya know? Now it all amounts to so much bullshit in a pile. I lost two buddies last week."

"Yeah," Gavin said. "We got bruthahs dying all over the place here. Ya know what Con Thien means, there, scoop? It means 'Hill of fuckin' Angels'. Well, this fuckin war's made a whole lotta fuckin' angels from all them marines it's went an' kilt."

The other squished out his cigarette in the mire near his boot. "Hill of Angels," he muttered with distaste. "Hill o' *shit* is more like it."

"You think you've taken down a lot of Viet Cong with all your shelling at them?"

"You been livin' in a hole, there, Scoop? How the fuck do *we* know? We can't even see what we're shootin' at. And they can't see us. Just ka-boom in one direction and ka-boom back at us. They mostly just make a mess outta our trench, here. We spend most our time just cleanin' it all up when we're not lying in the mud with our fuckin' hands on top our helmets. Then they might kill some o' our bruthahs here. I figger we luckier with us killing more o' them. But what the fuck do we know? We're just here. Followin' fuckin' orders. Shootin' at *nothin'*."

"I'm sure them body counts outta Saigon say we're winnin', but how can they know?" asked the marine with the winning hand, as he turned up his card next to the jack. An ace of clubs.

"Fork over another fire-stick, bro."

Gavin turned over the two cards next to his showing the jack of hearts: an eight of spades and a three of diamonds. "This time you owe *me*, dickhead."

"*Fuck!*"

"Anyways," Gavin continued. "There's no fuckin' way o' knowing how many Cong we hit. For all we know, half o' what we hit are prolly God-damn water buffalos."

"Saw a couple of them things wander onto the Line last week. One stepped on a Claymore. Fuckin' Ka-boom! Squish. God damn mess, buffalo guts everywhere."

"Buffalo guts. Got it.What do you guys think? We stand a chance of winning this war?"

"Who 'we'?" Gavin asked.

The other marine smirked as he lit another Marleboro. "'Bout as much chance as the Mets have of winning the Series next year. Which is to say 'no'." then he mumbled: "Freakin' Mets."

"I'm a Dodger fan, myself," Tony said.

The marine shook his head. "Fuckin' Dodgers. Never shoulda left Brooklyn."

"California baseball," Gavin said. "What a fuckin' sick joke."

"IN-COMING!" Someone shouted from a distance. They all ducked to the ground with their hands over their helmets. The helmet Tony had been given was too big and jostled from his head. No matter: he'd learned to take himself away with his recollection of the dying clown aria from *Pagliacci*. It kept him sane.

The shelling and firing had died down during the afternoon and through the night. Now about an hour before dawn, most of the guys in the ranks concentrated on cleaning and oiling their M-

16s as they complained away; lit and unlit cigarettes dangling from their lips. They realized that the cleaning might not make a real difference—the one sore distinction about the M-16 was that it was prone to jamming when you most needed it. The crews manning four of the seven big guns on the line were oiling and cleaning them, while the three guns in service remained trained toward the north.

The ubiquitous speakers on their poles spilled out Donovan's soft mantra, "First There is a Mountain...". It was one of many songs adopted for the troops' soundtrack of the war. Thus translated, it meant that combat units would fight for a hill in the central highlands only to lose it, then win it back, then be ordered to leave it and return to base, so the North Vietnamese Army could just walk in and reclaim it. As if it all had never happened: the hump of land that took their buddies no longer existed.

Daniel squinted through the dim light of the tent as he daubed off a fleck of mud off his camera lens. Tony blew into the workings of his tape recorder, then snapped the cassette compartment shut. The little snap of plastic hitting metal sent a tiny report through the odd silence lurking in their poncho-liner tents. Within their shelter they imagined themselves a world away from the menace lying in wait beyond their doorway hung with stinking military-issued towels.

Tony lit up a joint and caught the glint of the pistol holstered at Daniel's right hip. "Do you plan on ever using that thing?"

"What thing?"

"That gun you always wear. Your Colt .45 six-shooter, or whatever the hell it is."

"Maybe if someone tries to steal my camera." He held the lens up into the glare of the flashlight resting on the foot of his sleeping roll and daubed more dust away. "I've been practicing with it. Really, Antonio, you should have one of these."

"Why?"

"Well, for starters, there are some people out there who wish us dead. Not because we're soldiers or journalists, but because we're Americans. Most of our types have our cameras and pens, recorders and whatever. No guns, let alone the know-how to use them. It only makes sense." He blew over the surface of the lens.

"We got a whole bunch of troops out there with guns keeping us safe. Besides, they know how to use those things. I'd probably just shoot my foot off."

Daniel clicked the lens back onto the camera body. "Well, you *are* kind of a klutz, buddy."

"Fuck you, Dan. I am not. I know how to use an M-14, M 16, or whatever the hell it is. Remember back in that boot camp in August?"

"Where you shot at everything but the target? That forest'll never be the same. Who needs napalm when we have you?"

"You're an asshole., I actually have taken a few lessons over here. I can use an M-16. I just choose not to." An ash fell from his joint onto his bedroll blanket as he hunched over to tighten a bootlace. "Jesus. That boot camp feels like it was back in the Stone Age. It's really hard for me to fathom. It's only been, like what? Three months?"

Daniel picked out a telephoto lens and began to clean it "This place does have a tendency to make time go slow."

"Do you hate it? Now that we're in it?"

He thought about his answer as he looked toward the towels flapping in the tent door. He held open the towels and saw a rare clear night. The waning half-moon shone through, and he noticed the moving silhouettes of some marines leveling one of the Howitzers. "Honestly, Antonio? I don't know. I remember how gung-ho you were to come here. How are you feeling about it all, now?"

"I guess I'm still gung-ho…but now about not giving much of a shit. Anyway, do you miss Johanna? Don't see you getting too many letters from her."

"Jo's never been much of a letter-writer. She's more of a phone-talker."

Tony harrumphed out a laugh. "Not many phone booths here." He leveled a concerned gaze at Daniel's back as his friend continued to stare out the open tent-portal. "You two doin' okay? I mean, like, is Jo okay about you being over here? You never talk much about her."

"Doesn't mean I don't think about her…a lot."

Tony let a thoughtful silence gel between them. "Listen, buddy. You know I know about you, even though you never told me. But I think you know that. Shit. I had it figured out since Jared…" He noticed Daniel's back cringe. "…well, you know. I need to tell you. It's never bothered me. You're still like a brother to me, and that isn't going to change."

"Thank you, Antonio."

Tony detected a little choke in Daniel's answer. "I just need to know something that's been bothering me. Well, maybe not so much bothering me as poking my curiosity. Why did you go out and get hooked up so solid with her? I mean, you knew the *Trib* would send you here for six months." Daniel remained silent. "Look, man. If I'm getting too personal just let me kn— "

"You're not getting personal!" Daniel snapped sounding more annoyed than he needed to. "Sorry, buddy. I didn't mean to sound so—" He sighed away his anxiety as he hunkered back down on his bedroll to finish cleaning the lens. "The fact is, when I met Johanna, I felt something else. I could only think it's love. I mean, I love her, and she's pretty."

"Oh, yeah. She is that."

"And smart, even though she doesn't give herself much credit for it. But she was also needy. And I think that's what I came to love most about her. So, it was love for her neediness; someone to take care of in a way I never got the chance to take care of Jared."

"So, then, you were needy, too. You were bound by the necessity of need."

Daniel thought a little. "Yeah, Antonio. I never thought of it that way. 'We were bound by our necessity of need'. I like that."

"What can I say," Tony boasted. "I'm a wordsmith."

From outside came the tell-tale whistles. "IN-COMING!" And another from further down: "INCOMING!" And then a third call of "INCOMING!". Three distinct thuds and abrupt claps of explosive crashes shivered the ground. The improvised tent flaps blew open and dirt scattered onto their bedrolls.

"Shit! That was too fucking close!" Tony said as Daniel gathered up his gear.

They took up their helmets as they heard Gunnery Sergeant Dennet rush down the trench. "Okay, Marines! Off your sorry asses and man your weapons! We got more fire coming!"

"IN-COMING!!"

"IN-COMING!"

The calls of "IN-COMING!" sounded closer.

CHAPTER THIRTY-THREE
The foggy apocalypse

The activity seemed confused, but it was an organized routine all too familiar to the marines. Three of the Howitzers had already started firing at the sound of the first Viet Cong shell-fall. Two of the remaining four big guns, the ones being serviced, were slapped back together by five of their eight-man crews who then moved the big guns into firing position.

The spotlights had snapped on and had illuminated the camp enough for Daniel to snap his pictures on the run...*Saddack-thwip...Saddack-thwip.   Saddack-thwip...Saddack-thwip.   Saddack-thwip...Saddack...* His vision was caught not so much by the activity, but by eerie beauty of the tracer streams and explosions against the pre-dawn sky. He wished he was shooting color film. as A marine brushed by him and brought him back into the action. Someone had been tossed to his death by the impact of an explosion and lay three feet away from him.

Tony ran ahead, his recorder held high to capture the sounds of battle. Then he crouched down and held it to close to his mouth to deliver some commentary. He stumbled backward over a wounded marine, a gaffe which may have saved his life just as another shell hit close to where he'd been rushing. He raised himself to a stoop while still commenting into his microphone.

Another blast was enough to reel him backward to stumble and fall over a dead body.

"Shit!" he cried out, then jumped up to stand over the corpse. He stared down at what was left of the now steaming muck of the man's chest He became mesmerized by his expression. He cocked his head to examine the dead marine's composed features—not frozen in fear, but relaxed and serene. It was not so much an expression accepting death, but as one welcoming it. He saw a certain kindness caught in the marine's expression and felt an emotional inferno pulsing from within his own chest. *God damn this fucking war!*

He lowered his recorder and left it running as he leaned down and snatched up the marine's M-16. The gun felt colder and lighter than those he recalled practicing with, but he remembered how to carry it and release the safety. He stared at the weapon, wondering what to do with it. Recalling all that stuff he'd learned about the rifle, he checked the fit of a fresh magazine, then raised the gunstock to the crook of his shoulder. He emulated the stance of some guys down the line as they fired and shot out into the void.

Tony squeezed the trigger. His body jolted from the bursts of gunfire as he shot a stream of bullets over the ridge of the trench. He felt a hot rush of adrenaline swarm within his chest and then out through his fingers. He staggered back with the recoil, then steeled himself into a rigid stance. He fired again, this time remaining steadier on his feet. He pivoted to his right and fired a third blast into the void. He tapped his fingers against the smoothed ridges of the rifle's metal stock. "Ye HAH!!" he shouted as he ran further down the trench, now and again stopping to crouch and fire at nothing across the McNamara Line.

He spied a cartridge belt coalescing from the mud at his feet and stooped to pick it up. He draped it around his neck and felt the sharpness of its ridges digging into his shoulder. The weight of empowerment throbbed through the rigging he wore. *John Wayne! Yeeee-hah!* he shouted like he was on a thrill-ride. He fired again and again.

He nearly knocked Daniel over as he barreled past him, intent on shooting the M-16 out toward the treeline beyond the McNamera Line. "What the fuck?" Daniel groused. "What in holy shit are you doing, Tony? You're gonna get yourself fuckin' killed!"

"Yeee-HAH!!" Tony shouted hoarsely until his ammo ran out. "Fuck! Shit!" Not knowing how to load it, he tried to jam the end of the cartridge belt into the breach, as Daniel tackled him down and into the mud.

Then, from close down the line: "INCOMING!" A shell thumped into the trench wall next to them. Its muffled explosion shook the ground.

Tony felt no pain until he noticed a stain of deep red blood growing from his abdomen. The aching throb was dull and distant, and for a split-second he didn't realize he'd been wounded. Then he felt a surge of intense heat gnawing into his thigh. "I'm HIT!" he croaked, then looked over at Daniel crouched over him to protect them both from the blast. "Shit, Dan! I'm fuckin' hit, amigo! Those fuckers killed me! I'm gonna fuckin' DIE!"

Daniel gradually rose and opened his eyes. Blood from Tony's abdomen had seaped into his shirt. He was overcome by the same sickening wave of helplessness he'd felt when he watched Jared die. "No, man! You *can't* be! This can't be fucking happening! No again!" He placed his shaking hands on Tony's weakening shoulders and shook him. "You're NOT dying!" Tony's breathing had become shallow and staggered. "No! You are *not* gonna do this to me!" He peered through the fog of artillery smoke. "MEDIC!"

Tony spoke in a hoarse, faltering voice, as if it was some sort of requirement while dying on the battlefield. He began to fade away like he was doing a screen-test for war movie. "Shit…I'm dying. I feel the fuckin' life drainin' out of me, Dan." His voice ground down to a whisper as he groped for Daniel's hand. "Tell Annie…" Daniel dared a glance at the wound's source; a piece of shrapnel the size of a playing card jutting from Tony's right thigh. The puncture had sent blood pooling up near his abdomen. Daniel breathed a little sigh of relief—maybe Tony had not been struck in the gut, after all. "Tell Annie. I've always loved her."

Once he realized the wound wasn't as life-threatening as it was bloody, Daniel looked back into Tony's closing eyes. "Annie?"

"Yeah," he breathed heavily. "I've always wanted her to bear our children. Maybe in in a San Diego suburb somewhere." He swallowed mightily, as he continued to deliver his swansong. "Shouldn't talk too much while I'm here dying."

"You're not dying, Antonio. Your leg's a little messed up. And *you* can tell her that sappy crap. I wouldn't be caught…whatever…telling Annie any hokey bullshit like that. She'd beat me up."

"I'm not dying?" He brightened as he came back to life. "I didn't get hit in my vitals?" He stirred to venture a glance at his wound.

"Your leg. Just lie still. What about Bian? I thought she was your reason for everything."

"Oh. Yeah. She'll do."

Daniel shook his head and ruffled Tony's hair. His hand lingered longer than it should have as he felt its lamb's wool softness. He quickly withdrew it. "Just because I have sympathy for you and your leg wound, Tony, doesn't mean I still don't think you're a part-time asshole."

"Fuck you, Dan," Tony sighed through a breath as he relaxed into a rest.

A corpsman rushed in next to Daniel and leaned over Tony. "Can you hear me, buddy?"

Tony was slow in his response. He kept his eyes closed. "Ya don't gotta shout. I can hear you fine."

He cut open the pant leg of Tony's combat fatigues around the wound. "Okay what's the pain like?"

He opened his lids half-way. "Well, for one thing, it hurts."

"I get that," the corpsman said as he picked though his kit and pulled out a worn leather strip. "What kind of hurt? Ache? Searing pain? Bad sting? What?"

Daniel huddled off into the near background and started to take pictures.

"More like a burn. I feel it in my gut. I'm not supposed to die out here, am I?"

"Not on my watch. If it's a burn, that's good. It'll help cauterize the wound." He drew the leather tourniquet tight around Tony's upper thigh, then pulled out the shrapnel.

Tony winced hard. "Shit! Fuck you! Now THAT fuckin' *hurts*!"

"Good. You'll walk again," the corpsman quipped in haste. He held up the little piece of twisted metal that had done the damage. "Here. Have a war souvenir." He let it fall unto Tony's open fingers. It still felt warm.

"You're a real fucking comedian, aren't you? Here I could be dyin', and you're cracking fucking jokes."

"You're not dyin' there, Scoop. You caught a piece of shrapnel in the thigh is all." He tore open an envelope containing a morphine syringe. "Here, this might sting a little," he said as he poked the needle in near the wound. "Ain't too bad. Worst you'll get outta this is a little R&R and a scar." He was professionally quick in winding and securing a bandage around the wound.

"A war wound."

"Welcome to the fuckin' Nam," the corpsman answered as he packed his gear. "We've already called in an evac chopper for the wounded…and you. I've stopped the bleeding for now, but just lay still and keep that tourniquet on, no matter how much it'll begin to hurt."

"It's gonna hurt *more*?" Tony said.

The corpsman hadn't heard him. He was up on his feet hustling over to answer another call for "Medic!"

Daniel smiled down at him. "So now you can go back to Saigon and show your war wound to Annie. Maybe she'll fall in love with you and you two can go move to the Land of Nod in the San Diego suburbs."

Tony grimaced as the promised hurt settled in. "You didn't hear all that shit, Dan. I was just delirious with thoughts of my impending death."

"Yeah. Uh-*hunh*." Daniel said through a heartfelt choke. "You're still a sick fuckin' jerk, Antonio. You know that, right?"

"And fuck you very much, Jimmy Olsen."

CHAPTER THIRTY-FOUR
Honor among men

Confined to a wheelchair, Tony had been rolled to the rooftop patio of the Third Army Hospital. He inhaled a languishing draw from his Pall Mall, as he squined out over the tents and low roofs of the army base. Off in the distance like an impending doom was the MACV building. There, the generals sat on their asses and ran the war like a chess game, taking pawns without dirtying their manicured hands.

Daniel sat across the patio table from him in a rickety folding chair, as he thumbed through a pile of his out-takes from Con Thien.

"This whole war is one big fucking cluster fuck," Tony said. He inclined his head toward the MACV headquarters. "Those guys have no clue about what they're putting the field grunts through with their stupid, fucked-up orders."

Daniel's cheekbones rose a little through a vague smile as he picked out a photo. "Why, Antonio. I thought you couldn't wait to get into a foxhole with your typewriter."

"Yeah that was, what? Three months ago? Now I can't wait to get out of it. Since I nearly got killed, I feel like I'm here serving out a life sentence."

"You caught a little shrapnel in your thigh, and they found that parasite in your gut, is all. It's not like you've lost your leg."

"Yeah? Well, I did lose about a quarter of my small intestine. Fuck you, Dan! You try getting hit with rusty old shrapnel and then a tapeworm all in the same day and see how *you* feel!" He fell into a spasm of dry coughing, which sent a searing pain from where they had opened him up.

"It wasn't a tapeworm, and you should be happy they found it. Let that be a lesson for you to stop eating everything they serve you over here."

"Agh! It was probably something in Bian fed me. The things we ingest for love." He held his cigarette lengthwise and stared at it in disgust as though it were to blame. "I should probably give this stuff up, too. Cigarettes. I need to change things up a little. Maybe I need to get back to L.A. before I get fuckin' killed over here." He tamped it out in the overflowing foil ashtray on the arm of his wheelchair.

"Oh, Come on, Tony. You have this tendency to flick away your life like it's a foregone conclusion."

"More like Kismet. Anyway, I can't wait to get outta this place. The guy in the next bed kept me awake all night farting like a tuba. Here, let me see your photos."

Daniel smirked at him. "You sure you're up for it?"

"Anything to take my mind off this fucking hospital stay."

"This may not be it, then," Daniel said as he held one of his eight-by-ten photos out to him.

Tony took the photo and frowned at it. There he was, lying in the trench, his expression taut with pain as dark blooms of blood oozed through his combat togs. The corpsman was hunkered over him, tightening the tourniquet above the wound on his leg. "Fuckin' *great*. Is that what I look like when I'm about to die? I was hoping to depart into the hereafter with a smile on my face."

"Likely lying in bed next to Annie?"

"Would you shut up about her? I already told you I was fuckin' delirious."

Daniel poked the air with an index finger. "Ah. Delirium is the source of an inner truth, Antonio," he philosophized.

"You're an asshole, Dan. Who's that surgeon saving my life?"

"He's a corpsman. I didn't get his name. Things were a little busy for him."

Tony placed the photo on his lap, then looked back out at the MACV building. " 'Yondah lies the castle of my faddah,' " he said in a bad attempt to mimic Tony Curtis as the sheik prince in *The Son of Ali Baba.* "What are those guys trying to prove over there at Mac-Vee?"

"I don't know. That we can win this fucking unwinnable war? I mean, we're Journalists. We're supposed to have some sort of inside track on all this, and here we sit without a fucking clue about where to start."

Tony reached for another cigarette, then, reconsidering, pulled back his hand. "Yeah. Aren't we supposed to be purveyors of the truth? The truth according to the God-damned sycophants behind the podium at the Five-O-Clock Follies, preaching the words of the Holy Father, General Westmoreland. Shit. It's not about body counts, anymore."

"So, it's not John Wayne's war, like you used to think."

"Really? I'm sorry to hear that, Dan, but, yeah it ain't." He reconsidered and plucked up the pack of Pall Malls from the patio table and tapped one out. "This is fucking *Westy's* war. And that's what we have to report. Bullshit lies to gratify Congress's wet dream to carry this on."

"To no end."

"To no end. Am I right?"

Daniel lowered an empty stare at the stack of his Con Thien photos. "You're right, Tony." He smiled with half his mouth, He placed a hand on his good knee. "I'm proud of you, buddy. Finally seeing the value of all this."

"Which is absolutely fuckin' nothing," Tony replied through a plume of smoke.

"Nothing," Daniel repeated. "What do we do about it? What *can* we do about it?"

"Tell it like it is. The truth behind the bullshit. That's why we're here."

"You mean commentary? How do we get that through the Mac-Vee filter?"

Tony contemplated his cigarette as he assembled his thoughts. "Before we came over to this soggy jungle, I was an editor. And a damn good one."

"That you were. Are."

"I can spin the words through any maze. Leave that to me."

"But you'll be back in the field. Annie'll still have to tweak what you write for Mac-Vee's approval.

Tony offered up a subtle frown. "And she still sleeps with *Colonel* Frank Moss; the yogi of the Public Information Office."

"Sorry, Antonio. That's still true. You'll have to join the army and become a Colonel to compete with him for Annie. She may wear combat fatigues, but deep down inside she likes shiny things."

"And deep down inside you're a still an asshole, my friend. I guess you haven't heard—well, there's no reason you should—I just found out this morning. I'm leaving the field, indefinitely, because of my war wound. I'll be taking up Annie's slot as managing editor at the *Trib's* field office here. So there. I'll be in a position to sculpt the bullshit into truth."

"Shit, man. I *didn't* know that. Who are they bringing over here to cover the field?"

"No one. Annie's gonna do that. You'll be working out there with her." He took a sip of water and looked longingly at the cup. "I wish they served Scotch in this hell-hole."

"What the fuck? I'll be working with her? Not that that's a bad thing, but—"

"I think she's wanted that along. She started in the field in sixty-five. She's a combat reporter at heart and can't be pinned down behind a desk. Or by a man, apparently. Looks like she's defying old Frank, who wanted to keep her chained up in Saigon to mold her into his image of a concubine. So, see? There *is* hope in the wilderness for me and her." He shot Daniel a sly glance. "Whoops. I didn't just say that, right? I've got my beautiful little Bian, after all."

"Yeah. Right. Bian. Like that's gonna last. You watch out for her, Tony."

"Why? 'Cause you don't like her?"

"That, too, but no. Because she's sneaky."

Tony dismissed this with a pained little wave. "Have you heard from Jo? How's she doin' back there in the land of the sane?"

Daniel reflected on her last letter. "A few days ago. All seems well in San Francisco. It was raining there. She'd just spent some time in New York."

"Ugh! Disgusting place. I don't think I ever coulda been a right-coaster."

Daniel swiped a Pall Mall from Tony's pack. As much as he hated unfiltered cigarettes, he lit up and took in a short draw. "And I know now I love her more than I ever thought I would."

"Very healthy of you, amigo. She *is* your intended, after all."

"Indeed she is," Daniel said.

Tony breathed in the saline air filigreed with the fragrance of fresh and spent seafood from the booth of the fish monger behind where he and Bian relaxed on the beach.

It wasn't Santa Monica, but the waves were a lot wilder. Here at Dinh Coc Beach, twenty-five miles east of the thick, polluted humidity of Saigon, there were no boardwalks or adult jungle gyms festooned with musclemen. No clusters of bleach-blonded and tanned sun worshipers; no gaggles of middle-class family units announced by the screams and squeals of their uncontrolled kids. But, like the Southern California beaches, there were surfers. Here was a sweet spot where the waves of the South China Sea thundered down upon the sand after rewarding the boarders with a fantastic high.

His crutches were propped against the back of his beach chair. Gleaming with sunblock, covered with towels, and wearing a floppy combat fatigue cover, he felt as out of place as a fish in the jungle, but the last thing his wounds needed was a second-degree sunburn.

Though he and Bian spent some awkward naked sessions together since she'd returned to Saigon, their passion had been limited. He hadn't even seemed to notice her newly built muscle tone. Now she lay on her back, innocent as the kid that she recently had been. She was loosely veiled beneath the bamboo *non-la* covering her face, and her flimsy white beach robe; a lacy modesty uselessly covering the white string bikini she'd worn the first time

Tony had seen her. What was exposed of her naturally bronzed body glistened with coconut oil.

Tony adjusted himself in his creaky beach chair, causing one of his crutches to fall onto the sand. "Oh, great. Now I've got sand in my crutches."

"You should have of thought that before you went to got shot, Ton-ney," Bian muttered from a half sleep.

"Your logic confounds me, Bian. You want a beer?"

"Okay-yeah."

He reached into the Scotch cooler for two cans of local Beer 33. As she heard him pop the church key into the cans, she removed her *non-la* and sat up to take one. She was wearing her oversized sunglasses. "How come you still wear those sunglasses when you cover your face with your coolie hat?"

She soured her expression. "Not 'coolie hat' any more than you Eskimo. It is *non-la*. You racer or something?" She sipped her beer, then placed the sweating can to her sweating forehead.

"Racer?"

"Yeah…you no like people who not white like you?"

"Oh, racist. No. Of course not."

"Then you not call my *non la* a 'coolie hat.'" she scolded. "You numbah four for that, Ton-ney."

"Sorry. I'll try harder to be a number one for you."

She reached over and smiled coyly as she touched his cheek. "You keep trying. Okay?" She leaned toward him and pecked a kiss on his lips. "You be numbah one when you walk without sticks. When you take them off?"

He lowered a woebegone look at the sand-caked crutch lying at his side. "Doctor says another three weeks or so. By Christmas at any rate. Then maybe I'll have to use a cane."

"Christmas?"

"Yeah. It's one of those days when we white consumers get together with our families, so we can open presents and then argue over a turkey dinner."

"Turkey?"

"It's a big bird."

"That sound silly. Giving out presents then sit around eating big bird and to argue."

"Welcome to America." He stared thoughtfully at his beer can as he ran his thumb up and down its moist chill, leaving a beady little wake in its path. "Would you ever want to go to America, Bian?"

She smirked down at her lap. "Can I bring family? So we can argue over turkey big bird, too?"

"I'm serious. Maybe you can go back with me. Maybe we can…I don't know…get married or something, so you can."

She intensified her gaze. "You not mean that, Ton-ney."

"I'm serious, Bian. You might actually like it there."

"We get your movies over here. I see I would not like America," she replied, then slipped down her sunglasses to peer at him. "We have something like your turkey big bird day here. Like all our holidays in one. At end of your January. We call it Tet. This will be Year of Monkey."

"What does that mean?"

"They say it mean year of enlightenment. I no pay attention to that."

"What year is this?"

She smiled and brought her hands up to her ears and extended her slim index fingers to represent animal horns. "*Baaaa…*This is Year of Goat."

"That sounds not good."

"It alright. But next year be better."

"Let's hope so. This year has sucked. I never woulda thought I'd be shot up like this." He muttered: "This fucking war."

"It is fucking war. It is boosheet, all the killing and dying."

"Yeah. A month ago, I was in a swampy cold ditch in Con Thien trying to get stories from the marines to send home to America. And then I got shot." He rubbed the itch coming from the scar on his leg. "Fighting for fucking nothing."

"Where is this place, Con Thien?" she asked, although she already knew. Trần Dao had told her about the artillery fight happening back and forth across the Demilitarized Zone.

"Up north somewhere. We're trying to defend the God-damn McNamara Line."

Bian quietly absorbed what he had told her. Trần Dao hadn't said anything about a "McNamara Line." "What is 'Macanara Line', Ton-ney?" She sipped her beer while trying to act natural.

"It's some sort of invisible stretch of turf along the DMZ. The guys in the trench told me it had a bunch of sound-measuring wires and equipment and mines underground. It's all a bunch of technical boring stuff for anyone but the eggheads at M.I.T. and Cal-Tech who came up with it along with the blessing of Robert McNamara, our Secretary of Defense. Probably just so he could name it after himself. And our guys are getting killed over it for no reason." He did his best to roll over on his side to face her. She was looking intently at him. Tony knew she was just feigning an interest for his sake. "You wouldn't be interested, Bian."

"Who this M.I.T. and Kal-deck person you talk about?"

"Cal-Tech. They're just a couple of really smart science colleges. Outta my league for sure. I can't even do my checkbook.

Anyway, it's not our worry, Bian. Do you want a beer?"

She held up her nearly-full can. "You just give me one."

"Shit. Right. I thank my injuries for fucking with my short-term memory." He brightened: "Maybe I'm going crazy!"

She touched his lips with two fingers. "Shh! Do no think that, Ton-ney. You no crazy."

"Maybe not. Just pissed off, is all."

She took on a hurt look as she knit her eyebrows in concern. "You mad at me for something, Ton-ney? If you are, I will cry. I just want be good for you," she stated and took a sip of beer.

"Oh, no, Bian, honey." She cringed at the word: 'honey'. She'd already told him she hated cheesy 'so American' expressions like that. "I could never be pissed off at you. You're my anchor, here."

She drew back and glanced down at her body. "I not heavy like anchor!" She slipped her robe from her shoulders. "See? I *not* fat."

"Of course not. And I'm not pissed off at you. I'm pissed off at the generals and the American government—the way they're running this fucking war by killing off our guys for their own egos."

Bian let this sink in as she took another mental note. "Well, American G.I. don't think that, no?" she said. "They die for their country, like Vietnamese do."

Tony was perplexed by her sudden show of patriotism. "It's different for us. A lot of our guys in the field, who are out there getting killed over for something they don't believe in, are just as pissed off with the American Congress, the President and the commanding Generals as I am. A lot of them think this war is a lost cause. Besides, it's not like we're fighting for our country. We're fighting for yours!" His voice fell as he realized he had gotten too incensed over something that, when they were together, was none of her business. "Sorry. I get carried away over all this."

Her reply was long in coming, as she composed herself. "Who carry my Ton-ney away? I not let you get carried away."

"It's just a figure of speech—it means something like 'very upset.'"

Her expression relaxed into a smile as she stroked his cheek. "I no want my Ton-ney to be upset." She leaned over and kissed him, then surreptitiously drew his hand to one of her small, tight breasts. "There. Feel better?"

"Much. Thank you, Bian."

She kissed him again, stood up, shimmied out of her robe, and eased the *non-la* from her head. "I hate this boosheet war," she declared out to the sea. "I go swimming now."

"I'll watch…" Tony said, then looked down at his crutch lying in the sand. "Obviously."

Lowering sunlight flickered orange through a falling rain that cleansed the polluted grime from the air. The environment was sweetened from time to time with a speckling of apologetic train whistles from the station three stories below. Daniel lounged in a sling-back canvas chair near Annie's desk in the *Tribune's* Saigon field office. She had the drawn look of someone who was fuck-it/fuck-you disinterested. Out in the field, such a vacant expression was known as a "thousand-yard stare"— that of a passive seer who envisions a looming apocalypse and doesn't much care about it. *Fuck it all, fuck you all, anyway.*

It wasn't combat that had drained her dry, but the lack of it. She felt caged-in, and a yearning to be out in the wild. She even started to dress more like a soldier. Before, she would wear an army fatigue shirt hanging loose over a pair of faded jeans. Now she was garbed in a combat shirt secured by a marine-green web belt, and combat-camouflaged pants tucked into thick field boots, laced regulation-style. She had cut her hair and let it grow out ragged. Daniel was chagrined she'd done that to her beautiful, thick hair—a most alluring feature.

This was all meant to send Frank the message to let her go; to not keep her emotionally locked away for her safety and his amusement. It had worked—a little. He excused himself from seeing her in favor of more time at the office. It was just as well they were splitting. He'd started to use his power as a Colonel in the Joint U.S. Public Affairs Office to further sanitize her articles to favor the war effort. Another way to stifle her.

Well, no more. She had left him by degrees to pursue the quiet and forbidden night-long pleasures aboard an oversized, darkened sampan on the Saigon River canal. It had become her secret solace, as she inhaled opium and drifted off into an orgiastic world she could never describe once she woke from it. These encounters were made obvious through the faint shadows developing beneath her eyes, her sudden weight loss, and a thickening in her voice.

She selected one of Daniel's photos from a Mekong Delta reconnaissance mission. She wasn't looking at the photo's content—she trusted Daniel's eye for that—but searching for something beyond. She held the photo up to the sparse window light as though she was trying to look through it. She opened her mouth into a wide, jaw-breaking yawn, making him to cringe as he felt her pain.

"I like this one, I guess," she said, and she placed the photo down on her desk. "You know what's good here, Dan. Pick ten or twelve for the article. Take your time, it's not running until after Christmas."

"Sure," he said leaning close over the fanned-out photos to gather them up. "You okay, Annie? You look …over-tired."

" 'Course I'm over-tired, Dan," She grumbled. "It's a shit-faced war out there. How am I *supposed* to fuckin' look?"

"I don't know," he grumbled back. "Maybe not like shit?"

She flicked him a triumphant smirk. "You think so?"

"Jesus. You make it sound like I've just complimented you." He slipped the photos into his rucksack. "For the past few weeks you've been drifting away from, I don't know, life, or something. What'd you do? Take up drugs? Break up with Frank?"

"Yes," she responded, too abruptly.

"Yes, to *what*, Annie?"

She squinted her eyes shut in thought. "I, uh, broke up with Frank."

"I'm sorry, Annie."

"Don't grieve, honey-babe. I'm celebrating."

He snapped the flap of his rucksack shut, then heaved a withered sigh. "I never thought you two were good for each other, anyway."

"Now you tell me."

"At least Tony'll be happy to hear that."

"Why? Does he have a high school crush on me?" she asked. It was a rhetorical question.

"You knew that?"

"Of course," she said as she drew one of her little cigarillos its a frayed-edged pack.

"Tony swore me to secrecy."

"Honor among men, eh, Dan? Well, don't worry. Your secret's

safe with me." She lit up the cigarillo, then vigorously shook out her match. "That's why most women are born with intuition, sort of like prey, I guess. I'm just a woman pursued who can read men. Those wounded puppy dog looks Tony shoots at me? Come on, man!"

"You know, when he thought he was dying in that trench in Con Thien, you were high in his mind."

"No! Really?" Her lips broadened into a proud smile, which morphed quickly into a grimace. "That's corny, but charming. Like some sort of World War II movie when the dying G.I. says: 'Tell Annie I love her?' "

"Words exactly to that effect."

"Shit. Well, I'm sure all those sentiments went down the drain when I changed his post from field reporter to managing editor here in the *Trib* office and took away his chances to be a Hemingway on the battlefield."

"Actually? No. I think he lost that religion when he found out firsthand how ugly battle is."

"In other words, he grew up," she said.

"Exactly. He grew up. He's looking forward to getting back behind a desk to perform his wordsmithing. It's what he does best."

She blew out a tendril of smoke which meandered through the dust motes articulated by the hardening light. "I'm glad he's happy. It's not gonna be any cakewalk dealing with the *Trib*, now, you know. For any of us." She faltered at the thought of Frank marshaling her stories. "I've had to walk a real delicate line."

"You mean with Frank?"

She responded with a sad smile. "Because, and now in *spite* of Frank. That's why I'm leaving him. He's become the batboy for those sycophants up in Mac-Vee."

"That's a little harsh."

"He deserves it." She exhaled another stream of smoke to blend with the previous one. "You know the *Trib's* gone more right-wing. It's been pouring support into an effort to elect Nixon president. That's bound to hurt our integrity for sure."

"Oh, crap." His comment echoed into his coffee cup as he sipped. "I was hoping we actually weren't going to have Dick Nixon to kick around anymore."

"Yesterday's news. Anyway, you know politicians never keep promises…especially the good ones. Tony's gonna have his work cut out for him, trying to get his words through all those filters."

"I guess if anyone can to do it, Tony can. Present company excepted, of course."

"No need to qualify it, Dan. I just hope he can do a better job than me and not make the same stupid decisions."

Daniel showed her a little smirk. "Don't worry. Frank's not his type."

She tightened her look. "Or yours?"

"Shut up."

"Sorry. Anyway, probably the only honest editorial making it into the *Trib* will be yours. Photos can't lie." She cleared her throat with a dry cough. "So, you probably know I'll be replacing him in the field. We'll be working together out there, now."

"Like Burns and Allen."

She smiled. "I watch your back and you watch mine."

"Looking forward to it, Annie," he said standing to leave. "Oh. You won't tell Tony what I said about his dying words."

She squinted at him through one eye like a pirate as she held up two fingers in the Boy Scout salute. "Honor among men," she replied in a hoarse whisper, then winked at him with her other eye. "Say goodnight, Gracie."

CHAPTER THIRTY-FIVE
Darker sides

Bian bit nervously into the fresh-baked croissant she filched from the tray while Nguyễn Lap the baker wasn't looking. Now in the musty basement of the bakery, she stuffed another piece of the pastry into her mouth as Lieutenant Nguyễn Bon Do seemed to stare her down. She fixed her gaze on the pistol at his hip. Trần Dao tried calming her. "Now, now, little sister, relax. It is not as if we are holding you like a prisoner for interrogation," she said in succinct Vietnamese.

She wanted to tell Trần Dao that the lieutenant scared her to the bone, but she knew she was here in this grimy basement for a reason. A "higher purpose for the people of Vietnam," they had called it and told Bian that she was playing her part to "preserve her true birthright." She'd grown tired of "The Cause" and these words had become hollow to her. "My newspaper reporter has been to Con Thien, to write about the battle there." She paused to let this sink in.

"We know about the situation in Con Thien, Bian," Trần Dao said. "But tell Lieutenant Nguyễn what you told me."

"Okay," she reluctantly looked at the lieutenant. "He talked about something called the 'Makinara Line'."

The Lieutenant Nguyễn leaned back against the edge of the table and folded his arms. "The McNamara Line." he corrected. He nodded to Trần Dao. "We know about it. Did he say what it was?"

"He said it was a patch of land on the American side of the Demilitarized Zone. There are some wires underground for recording sounds and motion."

Trần Dao looked at Lieutenant Nguyễn. "This is true?" The lieutenant nodded. "Underground wires for testing sound? How does that work? Why do they do that?"

"My little reporter said that the American government worked with some colleges of science to put it there. N.I.T. and another along with the American, this McNamara person."

"M.I.T," Lieutenant Nguyễn corrected her again "A college of Technology in Massachusetts. Dign Lon Bao, our Communications Officer, attended there."

"He also told me that the American soldiers in are not happy with their generals and their government for sending them here. They do not believe they will win. They want to go home."

"The Americans are weak," Trần Dao said.

"Maybe not. Maybe they are smart for knowing they can not win." Lieutenant Nguyễn said. He turned his attention back to Bian. "You've done the cause well, Bian. You have brought us good intelligence. How much more do you think your journalist knows?"

"I think he is in a job where he might know more. His newspaper has put him in their office in Saigon, because he was wounded in Con Thien. He will be seeing more of other reporters' articles to edit and to send to the military headquarters."

"Well, you never told me *that*, Bian,"Trần Dao said

Lieutenant Nguyễn brought a forefinger to his cheek as he thought. "Then he will be seeing other raw reports before they are sent to be molded into American propaganda by the M.A.C.V.?"

Bien showed him a questionable look. Though she had heard Tony refer to something called the MACV, she didn't know what it actually did with the reporters' articles. "I suppose so, lieutenant."

"Then I want you to get very close to your reporter."

"What do you mean, lieutenant?" she asked apprehensivly.

"Gain his trust by whatever means to get more information from him," Trần Dao answered. "It sounds to me as though he loosens his tongue with you. The closer you are, the more he will confide in you. But we need you to be closer. Even if it means telling him you will marry him."

"*Marry* him?" She shot a frightened look at Trần Dao, as if to say: "*What have you gotten me into now, sister?*" She wondered if this was some sort of reprisal for her having betrayed Trần Dao to their parents over that boy she was dating when she was sixteen. "I cannot! I *hate* that person! He is only an American. I will be a disgrace to our family if I marry him."

"It is for the greater good of our cause. You can just *tell* him you'll marry him," Lieutenant Nguyễn told her.

Bian felt her stomach tighten. She now knew Tony wanted: to take her back to America as his adoring wife and be the mother of his children. She looked back at the lieutenant and balled her fists to her sides. "Fuck the cause, then!" she yelped at him as he winced "I will *not* marry that man. I will not disgrace my family; my village and my ...*heritage*!"

"You will not have to marry him, Bian," he assured her. "That might only have to be a final resort."

She glared at her sister. "You knew about this, Trần Dao?" Trần Dao answered her with silence. Of *course* she knew. "You would give up your only sister, from the womb of our mother, for this cause of yours?"

"Of *ours*, Bian; yours, mine, the Vietnamese. That is your true heritage: not you, our *country* is our heritage above all," Trần Dao scolded back at her. "All we are asking you to do is get more information from him however you can. Just keep up what you are doing, only do more of it."

She looked over at a dark corner of the room and imagined that gleaming ooze coating the walls was flowing out around her taut stomach and tarring her insides. "Tell me, Lieutenant Nguyễn. What is meant to be the result of this cause?"

"I cannot tell you that, Bian. I hardly know myself. I only know it will be complete and it will happen soon. Our army will catch the Americans and the South Vietnamese *nguys* by total surprise. Other than that, I know nothing more about it."

Trần Dao glanced over at Lieutenant Nguyễn "The apartment? It should make it easier." He nodded stiffly in assent. Trần Dao cast Bian a hopeful, sister-to-sister, let's-share-a-secret, look. "We have a single apartment for you off Dhan Yan Tri for you to meet your news reporter. Time could be crucial. You could—*should*—move in tonight or tomorrow morning."

Bian's hardened expression made it clear that this didn't move her, even though she'd been hoping for her an apartment of her own since she'd arrived in Saigon over a year ago. "Can I keep it after this, whatever it is, is all finished?"

Lieutenant Nguyễn thought for a second. "Yes, of course you can, Bian. As a gift from the Vietnamese People's Liberation Movement."

Until now, Bian didn't know the cause she'd been training for had a name. The lieutenant turned half his mouth up in a coy, uncharacteristic simper, which frightened her even more.

CHAPTER THIRTY-SIX
Independent women

Sleep. The body relaxes and passes into a space where nothing exists but dreams. The mind takes over and performs from the scripts of memories rewritten to the pleasure or pain of the dreamer. Here the dreamer watches a life that might have been experienced. If only it wasn't all a lie.

Annie sensed the ebb and flow of the canal beneath her while she lay on a hard-wood bunk which tonight felt more like a deep feather supporting her body. The wrinkled mama-san, cloaked by a wavering shadow, remained silent in respect, as though cherishing this holy moment along with her. In a delicate slow motion, the old woman held a flame to the glass of the glittering opium pipe and motioned for her to take another draw. Annie felt a warm mix of cinnamon and curry flowing down her throat. She sighed unevenly as a deeper sleep took her away.

The obscurity of the moist womb of the sampan's creaking hull took on the pulse of a frothy cuddle, syncing to her heartbeat. Warm and comfortable. Protective. The timid gold glows from the sparse candles and flame-light to the bowls of the other opium pipes around the greasy-smelling hold prickled in the expanse of the cool darkness like stars in space. No solid ground: no moment or place to trap and enslave. Just…space.

The faint current lapping against the sampan registered as the lighting of baby's kisses over her body. She sighed again while feeling soft oceanic surges from deep within her abdomen She drifted further into the tender paralysis of sleep and the oblivion of ecstasy. Nothing within nothingness. Weightlessness wrapped around an eternity.

Bian's apartment wasn't the Ritz, or even the Rex, but it was hers, thanks to the Vietnamese People's Liberation Movement. The little fifth-floor studio flat was set in a neighborhood far more open and less dingy than the one she'd left behind in the Chinon district. There, she'd shared a dank, three-room, cold-water walk-up and a hot plate with four other girls. This apartment smelled new, mostly from the fresh coat of paint that she had slapped on over two decades of caked-on color. She had inexpertly painted the walls in a dusty rose to cover the non-descript tenement beige which had dirtied the place with the depressing tint of old skin. Now there was a generous flow of morning light through a large, east facing window; a real premium for inner-city apartments.

One rickety stair-climb above was her favorite feature: a rooftop garden overlooking the low roofs fanning out to the Saigon River and its bustling fishing port. Cute little toots and the deep, hoarse farts of boat whistles and ship horns punctuated the street sounds that seemed never to cease. She would climb up there every night to take in the orchid and brine-scented air to gaze at the stars above the low-hanging smog misting the occasional glows of the Harassment and Interdiction fire. Though she was not a practicing Buddhist, in the garden she would carry out her own feeble variation of meditation more to relax than carry out a spiritual rite.

She didn't want to risk losing her apartment by angering

Lieutenant Nguyễn because she'd taken too long—nearly two weeks—to approach Tony. During her meditation a few nights back, she had decided that it was time to carry out her mission.

This morning she sat up on her futon with her back supported by a pillow. The small porcelain bowl of her morning tea had cooled to a comfortable warmth in her hands.

Tony lay on his stomach next to her with his bare arm draped across her lap. He had snored uproariously through the night, but now the snores had dwindled to muffled, apologetic snorts. She sipped her tea, looked down at him and saw that his wounds had nearly healed; the new bandages covering his incisions were only half the size they had been two weeks before.

She stiffened her shoulders at the thought of marrying him, even though Trần Dao and Lieutenant Nguyễn told her she would not have to take it that far. Bian's curse was that she could not see between the black and the white. She thought about how much she would disgrace her family, except for her older sister, if she married this Italian American man and all his opera music. He had nothing in common with her centuries of culture. A life of that? Numbah fifteen! Ugh! She cringed, then gazed at the stream of morning light through the window in front of her, as though trying to telegraph her feelings into it. She relaxed her shoulders, hoping that maybe he wouldn't want to marry her. But then her mission would be lost, along with her apartment.

She placed her tea bowl on the floor and gently shook him. "Ton-ney? Are you awake, Tonney?"

He stirred. "Uhhh…No," he mumbled. "I'm not."

She stroked his cheek. "Ton-ney, *be yeu oi*" she hated calling him: 'sweetie.' She never said that to any man because it was such a stupid expression. "We must talk. Can you wake up now, Ton-ney?"

Her uncharacteristically sweet tone caused him to open his eyes. "Okay, Bian," he said. He woke by degrees and winced as he sat up and leaned his back against the wall. He yawned and groped around the floor for his pack of cigarettes. "What do you want to talk about?" She hesitated, and then lifted her tea bowl with a quivering hand. "Oh, kitten. You're shivering. Are you cold?" He pulled the covers up to warm her.

She rose delicately from the futon. "I fine. I need more tea." She said and padded toward the corner that served as a kitchen.

"So. You woke me up to tell me you need tea."

"You want tea?"

"Coffee, if you have it."

"Just tea," she said as she worried over the teapot and the hot plate. "So, you get tea."

"I'm not too crazy about tea."

He saw the muscles of her naked body tense, as he stared at her taut little rear end. "I say tea. You drink tea," she defied him.

He lit his cigarette and blew out some smoke. "Yes, ma'am. Tea, it is, then."

She stilled her movement as she stared down at the teapot. Her tone became vague as she said to the pot: "Ton-ney. You remember at the beach when you say to me about getting married with you?"

"Uh…yeah," he answered cautiously. "I, uh, do remember that."

"You think it be …," she searched for the word, "possible?"

"You serious, Bian? I mean do you really want to get married?"

"Serious, yes. I think we need get closer to each other. And then I go marry to you." Her hands quavered as she pulled a second tea bowl from the shelf. She put a strainer heaped with used tealeaves over the bowl and began to pour. "Ton-ney. Did you hear m—?" She felt his hand light on her shoulder. She turned to face him where he stood naked, leaning on a single crutch.

"Yes, kitten. I heard you." She cringed again at his calling her "kitten." He leaned in to kiss her.

Her first impulse was to resist him, but she melted into his wish for a kiss. Already she hated what she'd done.

"What about the rest of it?" he asked.

"What you mean 'rest of it?'"

"I don't know…what I talked to you about. I can't just bring you back to America in April. We need to get married quickly. Or at least engaged. It should be a Catholic wed—"

Her dark eyes glared through a sudden rage. "America?" she shot back. "What you talk about…America?"

"You don't want to go back to America with me? You'd have to go back with me. I mean, as much as I like this place, and all—"

She kept her glare glued on him as she pushed herself away. "No! We stay here. Vietnam. I no go America. What the matter with you? We get married. You stay here."

"Here? In Saigon?"

"No, silly man. Peking. Of *course* Saigon. You not like it here?"

Now his anger flared. "Haven't you ever dreamed of leaving this swamp and living in America? Los Angeles? *Holly*-wood?"

"Where they make those movies? No, Ton-ney, I have not dreams about that. My home is here."

He reached toward her. "Kitten…"

She stepped back a pace. "No call me that! I not a baby cat! I am Bian, a Vietnamese woman."

She was so lost in their argument; she'd forgotten she was

naked. He looked her over. "And a very pretty one."

She crossed her hands over her breasts in defense of his stare. "Not for you anymore, silly man. You numbah ten, now!"

He smiled tightly. "You still want to get married, then, Bian?"

She thought for a moment to let her glower at him sink in. "Yes. But no America for me."

He rationalized that maybe he could go through an engagement to her, until the thought about going to live with him in L.A. gelled in her mind. He could always send for her after his return in March, or when the now-dwindling war was over. He also knew that not even the wisdom of God, Himself, would ever convince him to stay in or come back to Vietnam. "Let me think about it, then."

She picked up his bowl of steeped tea and handed it to him. "Here, Ton-ney. You go drink your Vietnam tea, now." Her voice had become choked with tears, as she imagined her fine new apartment dissolving away.

CHAPTER THIRTY-SEVEN
The call of the jungle

Daniel hunkered in the crook of two gigantic roots of a great banyan tree. He concentrated on swabbing a light coating of muck from one of his lenses with a tissue-wrapped Q-Tip. Whatever had fogged his lenses was as stubborn to clean as it was quick to return. Next, he would clean and oil his sidearm; a chore he had yet to perfect.

He looked out at the setting he'd last photographed. Shards of lowering sunlight, distinct through the sweat of the jungle, and clouds of ground fog, dappled the groundcover that smelled like rot tinctured by sewage. But the photo would be memorable. It was a chiaroscuro of soldiers silhouetted against the sun's rays fracturing the fog as they set up camp for the night. He knew it would be a fine opening spread for a feature on a typical Search and Destroy mission, this one being carried out somewhere in Bình Dương Province in the Viet Cong strongholds of the Iron Triangle north of Saigon. Ove the past several weeks, there had been sudden and intense flare-ups engagements in The Iron Triangle. So far, Daniel's platoon had been lucky; there'd been no engagements today. But there was always tomorrow, which promised to be hotter than the steamy, stinking one-hundred-degree heat of the jungle; heat trapped close to the ground by high levels of the dark canopy above.

He listened to the hum of insects rising to meet his tinnitus, which had grown increasingly severe recently, thanks to the sounds of gunfire and artillery. This was coarsened by the dry trill of crickets and other chirping tree critters. Occasionally he would hear the echoing scree of monkeys from high up in the canopy safely away from gunfire. Underscoring the chorus of natural sounds was the flow of music from a nearby lean-to where four soldiers crouched around a cassette player as they cleaned their M-16's. It was playing the ominous "For What It's Worth": *There's a man with a gun over there…Tellin' me I've got to beware…*

"No shit," Daniel whispered to his camera as he fixed the lens back onto the body.

He and Annie had been choppered in yesterday with the rest of the platoon and she was tensely joyful finally to place her boots back into the muck of it all. But there was something else; something in her glazed, wide-eyed stare and simmering restlessness that seemed to be hiding a darker truth.

She came upon him as he was crouched in the nook of the tree roots, cleaning his pistol. "Are you doing that right, Dan?" He looked up and saw her standing over him with her arms folded across her chest.

"Hell, I don't know. Probably not."

She lowered herself to sit on the root next to him. She smelled masculine, as if she must have just smoked one of her cigarillos. "Me, either. I was pretty good with a piece back in sixty-six." Sounding drawn-out through a mesh of fatigue, her tone had lost some of its former spunk. She pulled out her pistol, opened the chamber ,blew down the barrel, then held it like a spy glass to view through it. "Yep. Looks pretty good to me."

"Sure. Right, Annie. Did you oil it?"

She glanced at him and smiled whimsically. "Wow. I have to oil it, too?"

" 'Course you do, Annie. You know that." He reached out a hand. "Here. Give it over. I've got some gun oil here."

"I can do it, Dan." She slipped it back into her holster. "Man, it feels good to be back in the shit again." She angled her head back, closed her eyes and sniffed the air. "I even missed the rotten shit-smell of the jungle. All the damp darkness. This is what a womb must feel like." She looked at Daniel and showed him another coy smile. "I sometimes feel like I was born from the loins of the jungle; that I was separated at birth from it."

"Like Tarzan?"

She made a ritual of exhaling smoke from the cigarillo she'd just lit. "More like Jane; a woman in transition toward all that's unconventional and unholy." She stared straight up at the high canopy and the scant flickering sunlight through its leaves. "Actually, it *is* a holy place. I feel redeemed here, like all is forgiven."

"I just want to get the fuck back to Saigon," he told her. "I think the jungle is sinister. Especially here, for some reason."

"Scared, Dan?"

"No nothing like that. This is like a job for me. But I just want to do the work and get home."

"To Saigon," she stated.

"To Saigon, yeah."

"You know, I can tell you've caught the bug for that place. When we got on that plane to come here a few months back you seemed so…I don't know…*wanting* to leave San Francisco behind, like you didn't belong there. Since we've been here you've seemed to become so compliant with the environment. It's like you've started to pick up on its beckoning clues. You should stay. I know I could never go back to that cheesy Los Angeleeeze. I feel like my life began when I first landed in Ton Son Nhut three years and a century ago. I'm gonna stay. Maybe take up a room in the Continental like Graham Greene and write some novels."

"I can't stay here, Annie. For one thing, I'm with Johanna."

She knew better. She leveled a deliberate, sly stare at him. "*Are* you?"

"Yeah. I'm going back in April and give it my best shot."

"That can never work, Dan. There are too many invisible forces at work on you. Just tell me, to satisfy my intuition. *Are* you caught up in this place? I mean, if there wasn't this fucking war, wouldn't you wanna settle in here because you know it's something you need to fulfill you?"

He thought about it. Then nodded in surrender. "Yeah, maybe, who knows? If I did, I'd stay in Saigon, and never come out to these fucking mosquito-infested jungles."

A deep voice bellowed softly through them as if it rose from underground. "You ready, girl?"

She knew who it was. She kept her gaze trained on Daniel as she stood. "Then do it. Come back and stay. Maybe we could get a place together." She snuffed out her half-smoked cigarillo with a boot toe, then looked toward the sergeant who had approached them. "Yeah. I am. Very much ready. You, uh, got everything we need?"

He nodded solemnly at her. Daniel noticed the thousand-yard-stare in the roughed-up sergeant's eyes. It appeared permanent.

He also noticed the glimmer of the bowl of an opium pipe sticking up from the breast pocket of the sergeant's combat jacket.

"Catch ya later, Dan," she said cheerfully as she flittered her fingers in a parting "too-da-loo!" to him. She and the quiet sergeant then meandered by degrees into the privacy of the jungle she claimed to love so much.

PART FIVE
The Year of the Monkey

CHAPTER THIRTY-EIGHT

Going to Disneyland

Lost in thought, Bian twiddled a swizzle stick between her thumb and forefinger. It was the sort of thing she did when she was distracted or bored. She half-heartedly listened to the fatigued banter of Daniel, Annie and Tony going on around her. She should have picked up on comments like: "No reinforcements in Khe Sanh;" "Our guys are getting hit bad up there—*really* bad;" "Now the dickheads at the top are banking this will be the last fight before we win;" and other tidbits she could take back to Trần Dao.

But her mind wasn't on any of that. Instead, she had become increasingly distracted by her thoughts about Tony and how maybe she would like it if she went to America with him. Maybe she could become a famous Hollywood star like Raquel Welch, and she could send money back to Aunt Nginh. Then her whole family could live in their Phouc Long province hamlet like a movie star's family should. If she lived in California she could finally go to Disneyland. Maybe—just maybe—living a life there with Tony would finally make her happy.

She'd never fallen in love and wondered if this was how it happened. She pondered the swizzle stick she had twisted out of shape as she gazed at Tony. He took a break from expressing his points to look over at her and then wink over a reassuring smile.

As much as she tried not to like when he would do that, she did. She'd seen enough American movies set in lavish surroundings to know that was what she wanted — more than the petty politics motivating Trần Dao that had begun to bore her.

The three correspondents bantered on about the same bullshit propaganda served up from the Five-O-Clock Follies. Other nests of journalists hanging around at the Rooftop Bar were talking about the same thing. Some individuals had sulked off by themselves to sip their drinks and pout as though their cat had just died.

According to MACV and the Five O' Clock Follies, America was winning the war because the NVA body-counts were up from last month. In another sudden enemy attack on the marine base in Khe Sanh three days before, our valiant Marines had defeated the North Vietnamese in a two-day battle and had the NVA on the run. The correspondents were told that Khe Sanh was certain to be Ho Chi Minh's Waterloo — the end of the war was in sight.

"Bullshit!" Daniel said to Tony as they huddled over their bourbons.

Annie watched the dim bursts in the evening sky brighten the striations of clouds. "It was a God damned shitstorm up there," she mumbled. "It didn't look to me like the Cong and NVA were retreating."

Daniel's coverage of Khe Sanh had hardened his indifference toward the war. He'd begun to identify with the grunts in the trenches. The whole damn war had become a primal ego trip into the collective consciousness of MACV like some sort of thought-exercise. For the pawns in the field, it was all reduced to the simplicity of survival until their next precious poon-tang back in Saigon.

Daniel twiddled the soggy little pennants of the bandanna he had tied close around his head. The head-tie was a fashion he'd acquired during his coverage of Dac To, where his Army-issued fatigue cap kept slipping off his head. Also, instead of tucking his film canisters into the brim of his cap, he carried them in a reconditioned ammo belt he wore across his chest like a bandolier, giving him the appearance of a *Bandito* photographer.

His tone had taken on the rusty rasp of combat-speak. "Fuck it," he proclaimed, "I'm going back in tomorrow. I'm catching an oh-five-thirty transport back up into the shit."

"You goin' up with him, Annie?"

"Nothing to go back to, buckaroo. The NVA's taking it easy for the Tet truce next week, and I, for one, need the break. You're fuckin' nuts for going back up there, Dan. It's all going to be only mud and boredom. Take a break. Why don't you join me, Tony, Mike, Dana and the rest of us typo-jockeys and spend the truce getting fucked up on weed and booze?"

"I don't think a holiday is gonna keep those little bastards from fighting. I don't friggin' trust it."

"What's the matter with you, Dan? You've gone, like, all combat on us," Tony said.

"I've seen too much, I guess." Con Thien, Dac To, Hiep Duc, Tam Quan, Khe Sanh —in the last month alone, Daniel had seen dozens of soldiers turned inside out by NVA artillery and shrapnel making men into slushy bodies as others rushed to their aid only to arrive too late. He never realized intestines could be so tightly coiled or so easily loosened from the body.

Khe Sanh had done it to Annie, too. "After a while, we all get shell-stunned and numb in our senses," she said. She turned her attention away from the H and I fire and back to her Jim Beam. She sipped it, smacked her lips and showed a wry smile. "This stuff is the only thing that keeps me comin' back here to Saigon—into this vaudeville of civilization."

"And I thought it was me," Tony said.

"And of course, you, darlin'." She leaned over and planted a kiss on his forehead.

Bian, sitting in her creaky little chair next to Tony's creaky little chair, shuddered in a flick of jealousy. "You leave boyfriend alone!" she said.

Tony was stirred by her reaction.

"I know, Bian," Annie replied, "I'm just a thieving little Jezebel."

Bian tightened her expression, having no inkling what Annie had just said, but she knew it wasn't a compliment. "You numbah ten, girl!"

"Why, thank you, Bian." Annie said.

"Ton-ney mine. He go take me back to America with him."

Tony's shock over what she'd just said was matched by Daniel's scornful look. "No shit," he said.

"Tony's taking you back to L.A. with him," Annie stated sardonically.

"Yes. No boo-sheet. Then I will be movie star."

"Maybe. Who knows?" Tony said.

Annie stifled a laugh. "Sure she will. A real Gloria Swanson, ready for her fuckin' close-up."

"Let me know how that all turns out for you, Bian," Daniel said, then looked over at Tony. "You, too, Antonio."

"You shuddup, Doneeel. You still numbah fourteen!"

"Ah! I've been promoted." Then he turned to Annie in confidence. "I thought it was the opium that brought you back here."

She patted his knee and leaned closer to him. "No, Dan. That's what'll *keep* me here when this goddam war ends."

"Just like they told us it would end, making it safe for Little Red Riding Whore to go back into the forest," Daniel said.

Annie winced a smile, then kissed Daniel on the cheek. "Yuck. You need a shave. And a bath."

"No, darlin'. I don't."

"So," Tony said. "Mac-Vee tells us the war will end soon and the boys will be home by Christmas."

"Christmas was three weeks ago, so they're late," Annie said, and lit up one of her cigarillos. Daniel leaned back in his chair and rested his stockinged feet on the edge of the table. "Pee-eww! Jesus, Lilienthal! Put your shoes back on."

"Ah, jungle perfume," Tony said.

Bian scrunched up her face. "You feet stink like ol' water-buffalo, you!"

Daniel ignored their barrage of complaints. "You know, when the dudes at Mac-Vee talk VC body counts, they're just adding up the pieces of the Cong that've been blown up, and the other peasants who've been killed as collateral."

"Yeah, well: *duh!*" Annie said. She blew some cigarillo smoke at Daniel's socks to counter the smell.

"There aren't enough of our guys up in Khe Sanh to fight off what's hammering down on us from the VC artillery and rocket grenades," Daniel said. "We're outnumbered. And those dickheads at Mac-Vee don't even return their calls for reinforcements."

Annie shrugged her shoulders. "Same-old, same-old."

"Hell and damn," Tony said. "If Khe Sanh's supposed to be the VC swan-song, Westmoreland *should* be sending some support."

Annie took a languorous draw on her cigarillo. "Frank told me they're waiting until after the truce. Westmoreland is thinking about another draft call-up. You know: one big last hurrah from those ham-heads at the top to end this shit once and for all."

Tony reached down for a cigarette and let his hand linger on Bian's. "Jesus. Another call-up? How many more troops is he gonna throw into this mess? And then they're not even sent where they're needed. What powers those fuckers?"

"Self-interest and fart-methane," said Annie. "All Westy really wants to do is glimmer in his own glow."

"And to get his fucking picture on the cover of *Time*," Daniel said.

"I thought you weren't seeing him anymore, Annie," Tony said.

She greedily finished off her bourbon, then signaled the bartender for another. "Who? Westmoreland? Not my type."

"No. You know—Colonel Mister Frank Moss."

"I guess he got a sudden case of the hornies for me. And this time he told me he'd leave his wife. An added bennie."

"And you believed him," Daniel said.

"Of course not. But he called me at the right time. I was having a case of the hornies, too. My fingers were getting tired."

"Jeeezuzz, Annie! That's a little bit of intimacy you didn't need to share."

"What, Tony? You think men are the only ones who like to get off on themselves?"

"Well, yeah, I suppose. But we don't go around *broadcasting* it."

She looked intently at Tony, then at Bian stealing a longing look at him. "Hmm. Maybe you should."

Tony signaled the bartender for a beer to chase down his bourbon. "Not in mixed company."

Annie winked at him. "Mixed company? I don't see any nuns around here."

Tony flinched as Bian squeezed his hand. Taking the initiative to show that kind of affection toward him wasn't something he expected of her. Neither was the butterfly-light kiss she tapped on his cheek. She stood and slipped off her robe, revealing her bikini. "I go swim now, Mister America. You come too." She gathered her hair to the nape of her neck and secured it into a loose clump.

He grinned at her. "I will, babe. As soon as I find my swim-suit."

"No need that. I wait in pool," she said and then padded over to the rooftop pool glowing azure against the falling darkness.

Daniel crimped a hand like a tiger claw and swiped at Tony. "*Rrraaarr!*" he guttered at him.

"What, Dan? You think I wouldn't?"

"In front of all your comrades sitting around here?" Annie said. "I guess it *would* be a topic for your next confession. I dare you."

Tony started to unbutton his shirt. "Sweetie? I haven't been to confession since, like, nineteen-fifty-seven." He slipped off his loafers and continued to struggle with his shirt while he crossed over to the pool as Bian dove neatly in, hardly making a splash.

Her cooling tea untouched, Bian sat in a little web chair across from Trần Dao on the sidewalk in front of the bakery. She wondered if and when to tell her sister what she'd heard from the correspondents about Khe Sanh but didn't want to risk getting Tony into trouble. At the very least, she needed him. At the very most, she might have fallen in love with him. She felt a growing comfort in the idea of moving to Hollywood, becoming a star in American movies and then going to Disneyland.

What she'd heard may have been a moot point to Trần Dao, anyway, as she deliberately confined their discussion to benign, innocent things, like their family's preparations for the Tet holiday. Trần Dao had been vague about her own plans. She had hinted that she might not be going to their ancestral home out in Phuoc Long to visit the four generations of their family.

"We've got to go, Trần Dao! If we don't, Aunt Nginh will take it out on me!"

Trần Dao's expression relaxed into one of her rare smiles. "Don't be silly, Bian. Auntie Nginh is not about to take a switch to your behind. She's too old and doesn't have the strength to swat a fly."

"She won't beat me with a switch. She has a way of wounding with her words, instead."

Trần Dao shook her head. "You're not going either, little sister. You'll be with me."

"What are you saying, sister? Of course I will be going. What about our family? We've been getting together for the holiday since I can remember. And even before that."

Trần Dao thoughtfully sipped her tea, then shot her cup a scornful look. "Ugh! Cold." She put it back down on the table and placed her hand over Bian's. Her fingertips felt fragile, chilly, and damp. "I know, Bian. I already told Auntie Nginh we wouldn't be there. She was upset until I told her I was taking you to Wat Ounalom Monastery for three days."

Bian noticed Nguyễn Lap standing in the doorway of his bakery, taking in the sun. She signaled him to bring her another croissant and a tea for Trần Dao. "Phnom Penh is a long trip, don't you think? Besides, I'm no sort of Buddhist. Why would I want to go to a monastery for three days?"

Trần Dao swiped her hand away, then edged her empty teacup across the table so Nguyễn Lap could take it. "We are not going there, Bian. We are staying in Saigon. Lieutenant Nguyễn wants us to wait here. I've got us a room for the three days we'll be there."

"What would be wrong with my apartment? Can't I just stay there?"

Her sister's tone lapsed into annoyance. "No. We can't, sister. We need to stay close."

"Why? Close to what? Is Tet going to be when something happens? This big plan of his? When we should all be visiting our families?"

"I don't know why, Bian," she said sternly. "That's all he's told me. So that is what we will do."

"Pig shit! Okay. I'll do as you and he tell me. But it sounds really stupid," Bian mumbled as she looked toward Pasteur Street.

She thought it best not to be contrary, as she felt a sweat breaking out at the nape of her neck. This was the sacred Cause, after all: the grand invisible revoluion that would keep her away from the generations-old family tradition of sharing the Tet holiday. She sensed this Cause was all steam and no tea, but also realized this had to be the beginning of the plan that she, Trần Dao and Lieutenant Nguyễn had been meeting about in the sweaty basement of the bakery. She decided that there was no point in telling her sister what she had heard at the Rex Rooftop Bar. Their network was so dense, the Cause-planners probably already knew about it.

Bian breathed in and languished over the sweet, yeasty smells from the bakery, and felt a momentary peace. She looked past Trần Dao and to the churn of activity on the street. A graceful young woman with a practiced posture materialized from the crowd. She might have been a movie star. Maybe this was a sign for her future in America. The woman's smooth black hair hung from her *non-la* down to her waist and swayed in slow motion with each step. Bian wondered if she should let the length of her hair hang down free like that, instead of keeping it tied primly in her school-girl ponytail. Maybe she should attach a lime-green streamer to her straw *non-la*. She decided she must shop for a pink silk *ai-dao* like the one the graceful movie-star woman was wearing. No. Maybe a blue one.

Tony would like that because blue was his favorite color. She was overcome by a need to protect him; especially during whatever might happen in Saigon during the Tet holiday. By legend, The Year of the Monkey portended a time of mischief.

CHAPTER THIRTY-NINE

Sacrifices

Trần Dao swiped some grime from a third-floor window pane of The Sa_gon Star H_tel. She pointed at a van with oversized tires parked on Thong Nhut Street across from the American Embassy. She told Bian: "That is where you're going to be tomorrow night."

Bian squinted through the dim clearing and saw a innocuous-light grey panel van. It looked as though it had been heaped there since the war began. "I'll be sitting in that old truck, hidden from sight?"

"No, sister. You will be lying *underneath* it, hidden from sight."

Bian hoped that maybe she'd be held in reserve under the old vehicle while the Cause's organizers did all the dirty work so she wouldn't have to do anything at all. Once they were done with their little show of activity, she could crawl out into the sunlight, and go slip onto the fresh comfort of the futon in her apartment where she could truly sleep. Later, Tony and she would make plans to move to Hollywood, where she could leave all these silly warfare games behind.

She turned from the window and looked around the room Trần Dao had rented under an assumed name. It smelled putrid of old cooked fish that also permeated the hallway. There was only one lamp which glowed dimly and stirred up the darkness more than it brightened the room. She hated the idea of staying in this dingy place until she was called to hide under the truck. "Okay. Will I have something to eat while I'm waiting under the truck? I'll probably get hungry."

"No, Bian! This is not some sort of picnic out in the paddies! You will have a job to do as your duty to the National Liberation Front." Bian thoughtfully brought two fingers to her chin as Trần Dao went on in a crusty whisper. "You will know when it has begun, when our fighters waiting in the van get out. Once that happens, your job is to stay hidden and shoot at the feet of our resisters."

She drew her fingers from her chin to her temple. "Shoot out their feet? How will I do that, sister?"

"With your rifle, of course."

"How will I know whose feet to shoot off?"

"You will not shoot *off* their feet," Trần Dao snapped "You will stay hidden and shoot *at* their feet. To cripple them, while we attack them."

Bian stole another worried look at the van. It looked like the only things supporting the rusty heap were its slightly newer tires. She worried about how protected she would be. "Okay, then, sister, How will I know whose feet to shoot at, then?"

Trần Dao heaved out a frustrated sigh. "You will have clear sight, Bian. You'll be dressed as a resistor, and it will be easy enough for you to tell who is dressed like you and who is not. When the American and *nguy* fighters show up, they will be dressed in their uniforms. Shoot at *their* feet. Am I making that clear enough, now, little sister?"

"Yes." Bian replied sullenly, feeling as though she'd been

shamed. She thought about the used black pajama pants she would have to wear. Too large. Too scratchy against her skin. Maybe full of lice.

The orange glow from the neon sign for "The Sa_gon Star H_tel" above their window flowed some relief into the grey darkness of the room. For that, at least, Bian was grateful.

The ubiquitous spirit of war had made Saigon into one of those cities that always stayed awake as it kept watch. Here it was, 2 a.m. again, and sleep seemed as impossible as it was useless. Down the corridor, civilian advisors and correspondents lolling around in room 310–the "Caravelle Kasbah," —were having their nightly boisterous and directionless chatter about the folly of the war. It sounded more like a camp reunion now that so many correspondents had claimed their down-time during the lull of the Tet Holiday. The pitches of their voices dribbled down the hallway like a muffled Greek chorus. Daniel knew that there were more people in the room than voices. Some of them, probably including Annie, were stoned-out into a quiet submission to visions of real and imagined finer things.

Daniel lay drenched and fevered on the tangles of his bedsheets and hoped for rain to cool the humidity. Pulsing frizzes of neon from the street throbbed like a heartbeat through his open window. The sounds up from Tu Do Street were speckled with the quip of bleating car horns, the tingling of rickshaw bicycle bells, and the echoing voices and catcalls of soused American soldiers.

Tonight, though, it wasn't the humidity, the noise or his apprehension about his latest three-day tour among the smoldering husks of buildings and worn-out men in Khe Sanh that kept him awake. It was Johanna's letter; a massage from a more rational, more grounded netherworld beyond his grasp. The letter lay neatly folded and sheathed in its envelope on his bedside table. He flicked on his light and hoisted himself up against the headboard, then reverently lifted the envelope. He picked out the letter, slipped on his glasses and began to read it for the third time since he'd received it yesterday morning. The pages penned cautiously in Johanna's tight handwriting, were fragranced with the residue of hospital ether.

January 16

Dear Daniel,

Sorry it has been such a long time since I wrote, but a lot has happened since New Year's Eve, and I have been busy trying to ease my father's pain (more about this later). I finally told Dad about my cancer, and he collapsed into my arms sobbing. I hated to see him cry like that, being so vulnerable, and so unlike him. I am seeing him in a whole new way now and have gotten much closer to him—just like it was before Tamara showed up, and the shit began to fall. I think I'm surprised to finally realize that he is just as fragile as the rest of us. Somehow, I am glad to know this, because we're now at the same level and I feel for him more than ever before. Or maybe it is that I feel differently. More compassionate. It is a kind of love I have learned through you—through us. There can be no real love without sacrifice—it is the thing that reveals how alike we all really are. And how short life can be. We've sacrificed for one another, Daniel, and I love you all the more for it.

I guess Dad thought I needed a change of scenery away from San Francisco for the holidays while he's spending some time here in New York City visiting a Yale classmate; some sort of famous doctor from the Sloan-Kettering cancer hospital, who will be treating me for my...I still have a hard time saying what it is...cancer. I'll be in the hospital at least until mid-February, so you can write me there.

Anyway—how stupid of me for keeping this from Dad. If he'd known all along, we might have treated this sooner. Apparently, it's more severe than

I'd been told by Doctor Kornfield and his golf buddy, the oncologist. There are no guarantees this will work, but the doctor here wants to try me out on a new and aggressive treatment for brain cancer. It will require heavy chemo treatments, but that doesn't scare me. First, they have to take this fucking tumor out. They have a master brain surgeon here who I'm told is a miracle worker. That is going to happen in a few days, and by the time you get this, the operation will have been done. I hate to tell you this, hon, but my time frame may be shortened if this doesn't work—and maybe even if it does—by as much as a year. I can only pray to God that it works.

You were right all along to suspect Kornfield's casualness in treating me. If I had accepted this cancer more responsibly to begin with, I would have gotten a second opinion. I was probably in deep denial or didn't want to hear the truth. I am so sorry, for both of us. As it is, Dad's out there trying to build a case through his law firm against Kornfield, who originally diagnosed this fucking thing and has done really nothing since then. Dad could win this case, but I'm not hopeful.

He's been under a lot more stress since New Year's. Tamara made the decision last September that we should go and spend the holidays in Vermont with her sister, Alexa. You know: a real fucking New England Norman Rockwell kind of experience. Maybe Vermont reminds her of Russia, or something—it's a beautiful place, but far, far, away from San Francisco, and it only made me miss home —and you—more. Anyway, when Tamara got together with her sister, she turned even more toxic than usual! They talk only in Russian like they are speaking in tongues.

It seems she and Dad had decided to finally (!!) divorce last October and she got totally soused and really abusive (mostly in Russian) toward us. I never realized how much she hated ~~Jews~~ us all, but I guess that was at the bottom of her anger. She got more drunk and more abusive, then violent. Even the cops showed up and dragged out of the hotel with her sister. We haven't seen her since, probably will never see her again, and it is just as well.

Dad has seemed so lonely and sad since. And it is not because he misses Tamara—we're even relieved about that. But on the news of my cancer, he remembered Consuelo, my mother. We both loved her very much. Dad needs me now, and I need him to fill the hole in my heart until you come home and once again fill it. The thought you are returning will keep me going, and it will keep me hopeful.

I miss you so much, Daniel. Now, more than ever. I am counting the days until you return to me on April 22—ninety-six days, six hours and fifty-four minutes from now. Give or take. Please, hon, stay safe and save yourself for me. And please, Daniel-love, try not to worry about me. I will do my best to be heathy by then. And there are so many things I need to discuss with you— mostly about how much I love you.

Take care, sweetheart,
Johanna

P.S. Nathan came by the hospital yesterday and says to tell you hello. He's studying at Columbia now and has a new girlfriend. I'm happy for him. And I'm happy for me to be free of all of what happened six months ago, so I can go back to being just his friend. You and Dad are the only two men I really need and love. Outside of that, my feelings just become confused.

———

Daniel was seized by with a sensation he hadn't felt since Jared was killed; a helpless kind of feeling that came on with a need to vomit. He lunged toward the bathroom and braced himself against the sink, not to puke, but to burst into tears. He stood in place, with his forearms against the the basin for what seemed an eternity as he released his silent frustrations.

He gazed at his reflection in the mirror, and saw a face that Johanna would not recognize, or not even imagine. Even though he was in Saigon, he still looked roughed up for the trenches. His cheeks and jaw were covered by an amber stubble of beard, and his wild, darkened red hair rambled around the green head-tie he hardly ever removed. He hadn't bathed in a week. He brought a sinewy hand to his cheeks to wipe away some of the dampness. His nails were fringed in black. His nose and forehead bore traces of mud, maybe leftover from Khe Sanh. His lips were set solidy in an angry scowl. His dimmed eyes were sunken into pits of shadows and set in a five-hundred-yard stare into obscurity. His breath smelled rotten, and he felt as if he was decaying from the inside out. The war had sunk into his pores and defeated him.

But the message in Johanna's letter made him realize how much he'd thought about her all these months. Of course, he had loved her in words, but now, after reading her letter, their meaning welled within him. He bowed his head and braced himself more firmly over the sink. Finally, he went to the shower and turned it on to clean up before writing her back.

He spent the better part of an hour pacing around his room and composing his letter. Now, an hour shy of dawn, the talk from the Kasbah still filtered down the hall, but much of it had mushed into the soft sanctities of marihuana, coke, peyote, hashish, and LSD. As usual, most of the correspondents would turn in around 10 a.m. and wake up for drinks at around 6 p.m. as the cycle continued.

He stopped pacing and stood at his hotel-quality scratched-pine desk, staring down at his ancient little Royal typewriter as though it was challenging him. He chewed his lower lip, then sighed as he sat down to type:

January 29, 1968 —5 A.M.

Dear Jo,
I love you.
I've been surrounded by so much of the muck of war over the last 4 months. I've seen things. Ugly, horrible things. These are things you'll never know, but I'll remember, and they will probably haunt me for the rest of my life. What I've seen here has changed me and has darkened my attitude. But

through this darkness; when I can no longer seem to care about anything, the light that you have given me glows through and encourages me with the hope and strength to go on. And I love you, Jo, more than I might detest the person I've become.

Outwardly, I've also changed. I've become as combat hardened as any marine. I have seen more and more death; more courage, all for the preservation of...something. The Viet Cong I have seen and photographed killed in combat have ceased to become sentient beings like you and me. They are merely "The Enemy," as I am learning the lesson we all are being fed from the top: We win this war through V.C. body-counts, and not through the virtue of any higher purpose. This is not John Wayne's and Audie Murphy's War—this is Johnson's, McNamara's and Westmoreland's war. We fight for their egos, not medals. And I feel like I've become no better than the rest of them.

I love you, Jo. I love something deep in your core, which has touched something deep in mine. I can't explain it, but I feel you within me now, and when things seem darkest for me, the thought of you always pulls me through. You've saved my life every day, even if I hadn't realized it all the time...

...Until I found you within me again when I read and re-read your letter. You're right: love is all about sacrifice; and the more we sacrifice, the deeper we feel the love. I've let go of my integrity over here. A life in the breach is one you must be prepared to give up in the trenches when the bullets are flying inches from your head. But my love for you and knowing you love me has been shielding me from harm. I refuse to lose that shield, and I promise to remain safe...for us.

My love for you fills me as much as the hope that you are in the best hands at Sloan-Kettering. Jo, don't you think for one second that I will not stand by your side and fight like hell to see you through this, even while I'm here. Hon, we <u>will</u> beat this, no matter what. Actually, I'm encouraged that they're going to take out that tumor, and maybe the cancer with it, to make it controllable. And then you'll be rid of it, and we will live our lives as lovers, and not two people in fear of when the other shoe will drop. So, though I'm here for now, I'm still by your side, as I feel you near me. I'm glad Roberto *knows, and he'll look after you until I come back to you and we will look after you together. Yes, we will beat this thing.*

Anyway, I've done some thinking as I wrote that last paragraph. I've decided I'm going to come home to you now. On Monday, once this Tet Celebration New Year is over here and things get back to shitty-normal, I'm going to hop a flight to New York for a few weeks to see you for myself. And to be with you.

I'll send this letter in the Trib's *overnight pouch to our New York office, and they'll messenger it over to you at the hospital. I may be already winging my way to you when you get it!*

I love you, Jo. I love you so deeply.

Daniel

P.S. Can't say I'm sorry to hear about Tamara. I always thought there was something rotten in her. I only remember her being drunk every time I saw her. Roberto needs you now, so stand with him. It's so important to have a solid relationship with your Dad. In the short time I've known him, I've often thought of him as more of a father to me than Roger ever has been. Send him my best.

See you soon, hon...

With love...

CHAPTER FORTY
'My One and Only Love'

The quiet squelch of saxophone music crippled the very air of the room as Tony lay on the bed, trying to listen with a straight face. He found it easier to focus on Annie, nestled there on the windowsill, with her instrument glittering in little flecks of gold and bronze. "I never figured you for a sax, Annie."

She stopped playing and looked blandly at him. "Shut up, Tony. I'm trying to play."

The shrill tones on the up notes sounded terrible; like a goose being strangled. "What are you trying to play?"

Backlit by the sun, she was haloed in silhouette. He'd never been in her hotel room before, except to stick his head in. Now he was lying on her bed, and she was there playing her saxophone. With the door closed. "Don't you like it?" she said.

"No. What is it?"

"You couldn't tell?"

"Well, you know..." His voice came out in tightened gasps as he fought back a swell of nausea. "Me being so tone deaf to anything but my opera. Maybe my hearing's a little off."

"It's Charlie Parker. 'My One and Only Love'."

"Okay." He propped himself against the headboard.

The last hour or so had been a blur. He remembered they were drinking at the Caravelle Bar. Then someone offered him some cocaine. He sniffed deeply…and now he was here.

"What the fuck happened to me?" he asked. "How did I end up in your bed?" It was a question he'd never dreamed he would ask her.

She stopped playing. "You don't remember? You passed out."

"Oh, fuck!"

"I had some of the boys carry you up here. You really don't remember?"

He sighed, and then emitted a polite cough. "Uh, no. Probably because I passed out."

"And you hit your head."

"What?" He reached to the back of his head and felt a moist spot. He looked at his fingers pink with blood. "Oh, shit. This country is bound to kill me."

"What the hell? It's Vietnam, Tony. Death is an occupational hazard."

"It's a fucking toilet is what it is."

"Shh, hon. Try not to talk," Annie told him as she came to his bedside. She poured some water into a Dixie cup and plopped in two Alka-Seltzers. She held the fizzing concoction to his lips. "Here. Drink this. It's the best I could come up with. Now drink it, or I'll send you on your way."

"Pickee-pickee…" he groaned, downed in one gulp, and then issued a little burp. "Shit, sorry. How fucking embarrassing."

"You were embarrassing down at the bar, is what. You were kinda drowning in your stupidity."

"Oh, yeah."

"Oh, yeah," she mocked. "And for the record I never was a

Playboy Bunny."

He pursed his lips in thought. "Well, you *coulda* been."

"Thank you but no fucking thanks."

"I'm sorry I said that, Annie."

"That among other things." She lit up a joint. "Anyway, I've decided to look after you until you've recovered a semblance of your sanity."

He looked at her, then down at himself lying in her bed. "I, uh, don't think I'm sane yet."

"Tony, honey? I don't think you've ever been sane."

"You didn't have to do that, Annie. Take me in like this."

"Don't worry, buckaroo. You're not staying." She slid from the windowsill and came over to the bed. "Here. Move over."

They lay there looking at the scarred ceiling until she realized she needed him tonight. She tamped out her joint, rolled toward him, and nestled closer.

He loudly sniffed in the hempy, marijuana scent of her hair.

"Why are you sniffing around like that?"

"Sorry," he gasped in a whisper.

She stroked his cheek.

"Thanks," he said. "I needed that."

"Shut up and don't go all hokey on me." She leaned in and kissed his lips. "And I needed *that*."

They continued to gaze at the ceiling as though it housed the cosmos. He looked at Annie's sax and conjured up a small smile. "So now I know what that mystery package was."

"Huh?"

"When we first got here. Dan and I rode in that jeep from Ton Son Nhut to meet you and ... *you* at the Continental. I had to sit in the back next to this big wrapped-up package digging into my ribs. It was that saxophone." he coughed again. "Who ever thought that rough, tough Annie Farrell would ever play something like 'My one and Only Love' on a sax?" He stroked her hair. She nestled closer. "I guess you're just a fluffy little kitty-cat, after all."

"Oh, shut up," she murmured into his shoulder, "and let's just lie here."

The throbbing brought on by the lightness in Tony's head magnified the subtler one below. He jiggled his legs to try to nudge the lumpy weight of his penis to a more comfortable position from where it had folded over upon his thigh. The memory of Annie's nimble fingers gently fondling and massaging his works a mere four hours before left a soothing rapture behind. He couldn't remember feeling this lucky and wondered if he'd been the victim of a happy coincidence.

She had revealed the softer side of her emotions with a kind of grace Tony had never imagined in her. He thought about how she had mounted him twice during the night, welcoming him into her with the moist throb of pressure; ever so slowly; ever so tenderly. She raised and lowered herself upon him: tensing and relaxing in a gentle conflict of pent-up longing and release. Tough girl turns tender.

She soothed the taut muscles of his face with her feather-light, dewy kisses. Her kisses came as a soft barrage as they climaxed. His breathing tightened, as he stroked the curves of her body. As they were coming together, her irregular breaths became soft, plaintive gasps. When they were done, they lay there for a while in a breathless silence, which seemed to lift them into a sort of zero-gravity, until finally, she pulled his face to hers and spoke first.

"If you tell anyone about this, Russo. I'll feed your fucking dick and balls to the Saigon River."

"Does that mean we won't do this again?"

"No. Of course it doesn't mean that." She reached below the twisted sheets and started to massage him some more. She then stopped and relaxed into a doze.

He looked over at her as the grey morning light seaped into the room. She had nestled her head into her lumpy pillow as she faced him. Her mouth was contorted open, and she breathed out some indelicate snores, accented rudely at times with a snort. The right side of her face was quite unattractively mushed where it rested against the pillow; her hair matted messily over her cheeks. She was the most beautiful sight he had ever seen.

She blinked awake after he reached his hand over to brush a strand of hair away from her mouth. "Wha' time izzit?" She asked in a whisper rasped by sleep.

"Around five a.m.," he said. "I have to pee."

Her lips broadened in in a smile. "What a line. You are the sexiest man alive." She reached over and brushed some sweat from his forehead, then busied herself to sit up on the bed. She slid from the tangled sheets and emerged like Aphrodite dressed only in a fatigue shirt, which she pulled modestly across her breasts. "Fine, but I need to use the crapper first."

He huffed a little laugh. "Yeah, well. You're pretty sexy, yourself."

"That was fun last night, sweetheart".

"I'm telling you, Russo, don't go all schmaltzy on me. You've been warned. And if you call me 'sweetheart,' again, I'll feed your balls to the fish. Again."

"And I will, yours." He told her as she closed the bathroom door.

When she was done brushing her teeth and splashing some cold water on her face, she emerged from the bathroom, buttoning her shirt "You know, Tony. As much as I'd like you to stay, and all, I've got to kick you out, now."

"Oh, okay, I guess," he said as he slipped from the bed. "Uh, So. How did I do last night?"

"How did you do…what?"

"Last night. Was it good for you?"

"Oh, for shit's sake! Russo? You ask me that again and I'll drop you right there where you're weaving in place."

"I was just wondering…Jeezuzz. All these conditions of yours."

"Will ya just shut up?" She looked over and smiled a knowing, feline smile. "Yeah, sweetie. You did fine."

CHAPTER FORTY-ONE
The Sa_gon Star H_tel

Annie hated holiday truces. They took all the excitement out of being out in the rough, and all that seemed left to do was while away and waste her mind in the Kasbah. Tonight, a malaise of boredom had settled in like the musty gloom of the place, and even Mike Herr and Sean Flynn had left a few hours ago in pursuit of something sane, like drinking.

And then there were the newbies, those cub reporters on their first assignment, who treated the experience more like a thrill ride than a war. She was pissed off with herself for having decided to hang out with this group of kids as they left the Caravelle to stagger down Tu Do street toward the Saigon River docks in search of some action. To her, they all seemed to be fourteen and she'd begun to feel like their den mother. The only action along the river she might had wanted was the Opium-Den Junk. Yet she'd managed to stay away from that dank place to imbibe with her own cultural type in a more uptown manner, which was a lot more fun and a lot less trouble.

She gradually lagged behind the kids, as a couple of marines joined them, and they all began to whoop louder into the distance. As she wove her way around all the street life toward the Continental, a berserk rickshaw tricyclist wearing an oversized *non-la* swerved close to her to avoid hitting a fruit vendor. "Jeeezuzz fuckin' *Christ!*" she blurted. "Shit, man!" she called after him. "What are you? A fuckin' KAMAKAZEE?"

It was nearing one a.m., and Daniel and Tony were among the last hangers-on at the Continental. A lonely guy at the bar hunched over his martini to guard it like a hidden treasure. Tony stared at him as he sipped his third Budweiser and Daniel still nursed the same now-tepid Michelob he'd ordered when he first sat down. Earlier, he had dropped his letter to Johanna in the overnight pouch to New York and was now feeling a little more relieved.

The Continental was a posh respite from the war, and for a moment he imagined himself here with Johanna. He then recalled those sultry San Francisco nights they'd drink at a patio-bar. He imagined the smooth neon glows from the surrounding restaurants on Fisherman's Wharf—only to realize it was just another burst of New Year's fireworks…in Saigon. No place could be farther from San Francisco, but he had come around to Annie's sentiment. Here in Saigon, was beginning to feel somewhat more at home.

Tony turned his gaze toward the glimmering rain-dampened street. "Shit, man. I feel like I'm sitting here drinking with a corpse. What's eating at you, hunh?"

Daniel tried to sigh away his grief and offered up a feeble smile. "Nothing, Antonio. Absolutely nothing."

"Yeah, sure, buddy," he grumbled. "I can tell by your voice." His attention was diverted by the sounds of overzealous "*Whoops!*" followed by a bellowed "*Boo-yah!!*" from across the street.

He looked at the passing cluster of kid-correspondents, intern contractors, and Marines meandering toward the action that would bristle until dawn. Lost in their souped-up babble, they continued their jagged journey toward the Saigon River in search of one of those scruffy late-night dives to drink their way into the Lunar New Year morning. The Tet holiday meant nothing more to them than another opportunity to get stoned, then plastered, then stoned again. And, tonight, if they were lucky, score some poontang to keep them busy past sun-up. "Amateurs," Tony scoffed.

Daniel's smile flattened as he glanced across the street. "We were all that age once, not so long ago," he said. "And I never want to go back there," he mumbled.

Tony hadn't heard him. "Don't you think those kids are a little young to be journalists over here?"

Thier faces were illuminated in red in the bloom of another flare of fireworks. "No younger than a lot of the grunts being shot up out there in Westy's war."

"Yeah," Tony said. "The kids are probably just mercenary freelancers for their high school newspapers or something." He looked over Daniel's shoulder and squinted into the distance. "Damn! There's Annie! The Cavalry has arrived." Daniel looked over at her as Tony made a finger-gun with his thumb and forefinger and pointed at her. She did the same back at him.

"Christ, I need a drink," she said as she pulled up a stray chair and called the waiter over to order a neat Jim Beam. Tony ordered another Lowenbrau. "Nothing for you, Dan? It's your last chance before this place folds up for the night."

"Little Danny's not drinking tonight. He's too depressed about I don't know what."

Annie furrowed her brow and leaned across the little table. "What's up, man?"

He continued to brood.

"Oh, come on, Lilienthal! Your expression looks like it's just been dug up from underground. What's buggin' you, honey?"

Daniel wet his lips, then downed of the warm remains of his beer. "I got a letter from Johanna. She's in some hospital in New York City."

"Shit, Dan. Jo?" Tony said. "She okay? And what the hell is she doing in New York?"

Daniel let out a deep sigh. He had to tell someone. "She's at Sloan-Kettering. She has brain cancer."

"SHIT!" Tony said. "Jo has cancer? Fuck!"

Annie placed her hand over his and lowered her voice to just above whisper. "Oh, Dan. I'm so sorry."

Tony placed his hand upon Daniel's shoulder. "How long have you known about this, buddy?"

"She's had it for a few years. I've been trying to play it down with you guys. Maybe I was hoping it was gonna go away, or something."

Tony looked over at Annie and saw her eyes brimming with tears. He moved his hand from Daniel's shoulder and over to hers. He took a quick sip of his beer, then stared at the label like he was ready to have a talk with it.

"There was something else in her letter that threw me," Daniel said.

"What was that, honey?"

"I don't know. Something about sacrificing for love…and how life is too short."

"Well, it is. I guess. Just look around us. What's our our chance of survival here? Like, fifty percent?"

"Somehow I don't think that helps, Tony." Annie said and

then leaned in closer to Daniel. "There can't be love without sacrifice, honey. That's what makes it love. Anyway, I'm always saying things like life's too fuckin' short, like 'live while you can'."

"…for tomorrow we die," Tony said as he toasted the air with his bottle. "Welcome to the freakin' Bubonic plague."

"Shut up, Tony, you dumpster." She squeezed Daniel's hand. "Is there anything I can do, Dan? Would you like to go see her for a little while? I can cover for you."

"Could you, Annie? I mean, I was gonna ask you about it."

She saw how Daniel's appearance had softened from one of those G.I. Joe he'd become a few weeks before—the combat-stunned guy who craved going back to Khe Sanh to kill the approaching dinks. She'd seen it before. Too much, too soon—the war had gotten in the way of his purpose for being here. He needed a dose of R&R: a short trip back to what mattered, and to Johanna.

Annie needed him to come back as the devoted photojournalist she'd hired in the first place. "Sure, hon. I'll cut you some stateside transport papers on Friday to get you out on the afternoon flight."

"You'd do that?"

"Of course. Maybe I can get Sean to fill in for you. He'd like that. He's a crazy bastard."

"I love you, Annie."

She patted his hand. "I love you, too, sweetie. Just go home and get some rest and be with her. Okay? Then come back and do your best work."

"Can I go, too?" Tony blurted.

"No. Because you're an asshole. Besides, you don't wanna leave your little Geisha behind." She cast him a private but telling look. "Right, Russo?" she threatened.

He nodded and winked at her. "Right, Annie."

"Thanks, Annie," said Daniel.

She kissed him lightly on the forehead. "You're welcome, hon." She smiled. "Happy New Year. Happy Year of the Monkey."

Tony raised his bottle again. "*Yeah, yeah we're the MONKEES!*" he sang.

Annie rarely had an opportunity to allow herself to show compassion, and she felt good about it. Maybe she'd found that instinctual woman within, after all. Tony glanced around at the sound of a chair scraping against the terra-cotta floor tiles a few tables away. A waiter was stacking glasses and dishes on a cart. "Looks like they're shutting this gin joint down for the night. How about let's order a liter of something rich and gold to see us through to morning?"

Four G.I.s meandered down Nguyễn Dinh Street. "HAPPY FUCKIN' NEW YEAR!" One of them bellowed out into the street as they passed.

Tony and Annie answered his shout with a toast of their Dewar's bottle-in-a-paper-bag as fireworks streamed and popped in the night sky. "Ahh, these Asians and all their fireworks," Annie groused. They kept on, weaving their way toward the newly built American Embassy. She looked up at the branches of a neat line of tall trees lining Thong Nhut boulevard, then took another swig from the bottle. "Hey out there! Keep it DOWN!" she said to the sky. "We're trying to get some SLEEP down here! It's fuckin' TWO-A.M. in the fuckin' morning, already!" She was answered with an over-loud barrage of pops followed by one big boom of a vivid red explosion erupting into tendrils of bright orange. "Jeeezuzz!"

"Aw come on, Annie!" Tony said. "It's their Christmas and Fourth of July piled into one big New Year's celebration. Let the kids have their fun."

Annie squinted at him. "Russo? If I didn't know any better, I'd think you've been Vietnam-ized by your little girlfriend. *Hey*! You're Italian! Man-up to it!" She grabbed up a paper bowl of soggy nuts from a street side cafe table. "Here, buddy have some nuts. *Mangia*! *Mangia*! And stop looking like your dog just died.".

Tony tried to keep up the front of hiding his night with Annie. "I miss Bian. I wish she were here. She's been gone for two days now, and I have another week of this lonely shit."

Annie took another sloppy slip. "Jeee-zuzz! Come on, man. I know that a fuck is a terrible thing to waste, but it's only been a week. I'd gone without for about a month now, so I don't feel the least bit sorry for you." Then she added: "Right, Russo?"

"I suppose…"

She stopped again and peered into the sleepy darkness of "*La Bohemia* Saigon Bar," another one of those squalid early-morning dives with an open front and a fancy name. From its clammy gloom, dimly brightened by a blinking Jukebox in the back, came the overloud sibilance of "For Your Love". Two scrawny whores barely out of their teens slouched indolently near the entrance as if they were held prisoner by the place. The carnival colors of their tight, sequined dresses glittered while they waited to persuade a passing John to buy them a champagne glass of Canada Dry and a half-hour on grimy, sperm-scented bedsheets in a dingy room of the Sa_gon Star H_tel above the bar.

"Ah, my long-lost sisters," Annie slurred. "Hello, little girls!"

One of them answered back in a tiny voice toward Daniel.

"You want fuggie-fuggie, Joe?"

"I show you numbah one time you nevah forget, you!" the other one chimed at Tony.

"There you go, Tony. It's there for the asking. Only ten bucks a throw. And they're all virgins," Annie said. "Ain't that right, girls?" she called into the bar. "You're all virgins!"

"Me. I virgin, yeah!" The first one said.

"Me better! Me virgin better than she is!" said the second girl. She leveled a gaze at Tony. "I show you real *good* numbah one time, Joe!"

"See, Tony? You've got a way with women," Annie told him.

"Oh quiet, you lush," Tony laughed as he ushered her along.

"Man, woman, no different!" one of the girls called after them.

"Hell," Annie mumbled as she followed along. "Maybe *I'll* try one of those little girls. Been a while since I've been with a woman."

Tony tugged at her sleeve to pull her back. "You stay with us, you. God knows who or what those girls have contracted."

They walked further down Dai Lo Thong Nhut toward the embassy, then sat on a stoop in an alcove. Daniel lit a cigarette and tweaked a little smile down at it. He glanced over at the dull-gray van across the street. "What about your colonel, Annie? You told me last week that you…"

"Frank? He doesn't count. He's just research. I've demoted him to ingrate since he stopped feeding me information after that Phuoc Binh incident he kept denying."

"We were there." Daniel said. "It fucking happened, and I have the pictures."

"Well, Frank said it didn't, so it must not have, as far as Mac-Vee is concerned." She leaned back and took in the fireworks.

Some sounded closer than others.

Then a mortar screamed overhead and crashed into the front of the embassy, collapsing a dusty hole next to the entrance.

"Shit!" Tony gasped. "Some fucking fireworks!"

CHAPTER FORTY-TWO
Chia tay, Chị Gái

They heard crashing glass as a second mortar hit the front of the building. Annie ran her hand down to the cool steel of her side-arm as sirens blared from the embassy and a couple of Military Police came rushing out to the park fronting the building. A third mortar shell whistled from above and scattered up clumps of concrete from the sidewalk, uprooting one of the street-side trees, which crashed down by degrees to the pavement.

The three glanced dumbfounded at one another as Daniel quickly grasped the butt of his Colt .45. Annie did the same, as she rushed in a crouch to a nearby cafe table and kicked it on its side to serve as a shield. She saw five Viet Cong rebels in their black pajama-uniforms and red armbands scramble from the back of the grey van across the street. They held their AK-47s at tight aim as they headed toward the embassy. Daniel scurried in the other direction and took cover behind a concrete flower box. Tony remained in the shadow of the alcove and watched as one of the army M.P.s fell to the street writhing as he grasped his bleeding shins. A killing shot came diagonally from above and struck him in the heart.

"Fuck! SHIT!" Annie seethed as she fired a few random shots toward the five rebels. They had already scattered into the in park in front of the embassy, taking down a few embassy marines. A dozen more soldiers and marines in varying degrees of dress and sobriety zigged and zagged down Mac Dinh Chi Street from The Saigon Lounge and Emporium half a block away. Three officers staggered before them with pistols drawn. As they approached the van, one fell to the ground clutching his calf with one hand. He turned to fire at another swarm of about twenty rebels who had rushed behind them. Then another fell, as he grabbed his ankle. Each one shot in the leg took a shot to the head from the snipers posted somewhere above. Daniel waved his pistol in the general direction of the snipers as he squinted for clues—any barrel smoke or rustling from where they might be. But he was blinded by the streetlights, and the snipers were too far above in the darkness.

Tony looked toward the van and saw a little flare from beneath, as another round was fired wildly toward the melee. Whoever was shooting from there was a real rookie V.C. Most of the bullets missed their mark, another few scraped up or plowed into the pavement. "Annie!" he shouted as he feverishly pointed to the van. "Under the grey truck! Under the grey truck!"

"WHERE?!" She shouted back.

"There's someone shooting from under the fucking TRUCK! Right there!" He rolled over on the ground to where she was. "There. Under the truck."

"I see it!" She said and leveled her .45 to where the shots were coming from twenty-five feet away.

"God damnit, I need a gun!" Tony shouted,

"You'd shoot your fuckin' foot off!" Annie groaned tightly as she fired another shot.

"Yeah, well that's already happening to a lot of people out

there!" Tony said. Another flash lit up the underside of the van." There's another one...right there!"

"I see it, damnit!" She shouted over her right shoulder. "DAN! Aim under the *truck*!""

Instead he'd had taken a bead on where he thought a sniper was coming from; too far away for the range of his .45. "What? WHERE?"

"Right there!" Annie pointed anxiously. Her experience had taught her the difference in the sounds of gunfire. The M-16 gave off a metallic, muffled pop; a Soviet-issued AK-47, more of a distinct *click*. "That AK-47 fire's coming from under that fucking truck! Across the street!"

Daniel peered in that direction and could just make out someone coalescing from the shadow under the van. Through his eyes had been conditioned by photography to see detail through density, it appeared to be a woman. A skein of her smooth black hair swooped across half of her face. Another marine from the embassy grabbed his thigh as he went down. He lay there on his side, firing his M-16 up at The Sa_gon Star H_tel, a half-block down the street. Then a bullet from the sniper exploded his head.

A grenade from an M-80 streamed whistling into the embassy gates, collapsing one from its hinges. "Fuck *this*!" Tony shouted as he jumped up and ran erratically in a crouch toward the body of the dead marine and grabbed his M-16. He had no time to remember how to use it.

"SHIT! Tony! Come BACK here!" Annie shouted.

He didn't hear her, or pretended not to, as he crouch-ran toward the van with his rifle aimed.

"God fuckin' DAMNIT!" Annie squawked as she shoved a fresh clip into her pistol and tore after him. She kept clear of the range of fire from beneath the van, then pivoted and shot toward the roofs.

Tony crouched protectively out of sniper-sight behind the van. Then the shooting from underneath stopped. Something felt eerily familiar during the silence that seemed to ooze time into slow motion. The AK-47 skittered from beneath the van onto the street. Though the pandemonium going on all around him, Tony aimed his weapon under the van. An unsure, frightened wisp of a voice came from the shadow. "Ton-nee?"

He could find only one stupid answer. He whispered only loudly enough for her to hear as he squatted lower: "Bian? Honey? I thought you were spending the week with your family."

He heard her voice harden into a choke. "I so sorry, Ton-nee! I had to do this. I wish I din't, but I had to."

He allowed himself a few seconds for this surreality to sink in. "Why, Bian? Why did you have to?" he whispered back.

"Are you gon' kill me now?"

"No, Bian. Of course not. Now you come out from under there."

There was another silence until an RPG exploded in front of the van, scattering concrete and dust. Her frightened voice was choked in tears. "Will you bring me to Hollywood and Disneyland? I want to go there with you, now."

Tony choked back some of his own hurt. "Sure. Let's you and me go to Hollywood." He placed his rifle on the pavement and extended his hand toward her. "We'll catch the next flight out to L.A. Come on, kitten. Take my hand."

"You sure? No boosheet?"

Feeling caught somewhere between pity and anger, he felt entirely numb. "No boosheet, Bian. You're number one for me.

Please. Take my hand." After a moment's hesitation, he felt the fragility of her fingers upon his.

Annie's frantic voice seemed to come from a half-mile behind him. "TONY! What the fuck are you DOING?"

He looked over his shoulder. "Shh. It's *Bian*," he said anxiously, as if hoping, under the circumstances, that Annie might understand.

She looked at the bodies scattered in the street; many made possible by the spray of bullets from Bian's AK-47. "Fuck shit, Tony! *She* did this?" She crouched down next to him to squint into the shadow. She saw only little glimmers through the gloom but heard Bian sniffing through her tears. "Get her out of there, Russo!" she snapped, then stood back up and held her pistol at a rigid downward aim in Bian's direction.

"Come on, Annie," Tony said. "Tuck your piece away. You're gonna scare her."

"*Scare* her? What the fuck's the *matter* with you, Russo? Bian! Get your scrawny little ass out from under that truck!"

She squeezed her fingers tight around his. "Ton-neee?"

The gunfire had become more intense, as a five more Viet Cong emerged from a Renault taxicab like clowns from a circus car. Paying no attention to the grey van, they charged in loose formation through the blasted-open gates of the embassy.

"It's okay, honey," Tony said; his voice tightened in uncertainty. "It'll be fine. I'll protect you, come on out."

"Jesus Christ, Tony!" Annie seethed harshly.

"Okay, Ton-ney." She clasped his hand. "We go Hollywood, now?"

He looked up at Annie. She relaxed her shoulders and lowered her piece, still holding it in both hands as she saw Tony's anguished, pathetic expression. Helpless. Tears now smeared his cheeks, as she nodded.

His tone was uneven; just as frightened as Bian's was. "S'okay hon. The plane's waiting at the airport to take us to L.A. Just you and me. I've already got us a house on the ocean, there. Come on now. Come on. There, you got it." He helped her gently from under the van.

The black pajama garb of the Viet Cong hung loose over her body like the old clothes of a street urchin. The wrinkled material was thinned at the knees. The red armband had slipped down to her elbows. They fell into a loose embrace. "It's okay, honey," he reassured her. "It's gonna be fine."

"No, Tony," Annie enunciated. "It's *not* going to be fine."

Bian's little voice was muffled as she settled her head into the crook of his shoulder. "I did no want to hurt anyone, Ton-ney. I no want to hurt *you*." She engulfed him in an embrace. "I *do* love you, Ton-ney."

"I love you too, Bian," he whispered.

Daniel had crouched his way across the street while tightly grasping his sidearm. "What the *fuck*?" he gasped as he took a protective position behind the open back door of the van. "God damnit Tony! What the *fuck*?"

"It's Bian".

"Shit, man. I can see that. But what…? She's—she's a fucking V.C.?"

Annie remained still and said nothing as Tony rested his head protectively on Bian's shoulder. A rocket grenade sizzled low overhead and blasted out the stoops where they'd been sitting moments before. Daniel could see the bottle of Scotch in the bag explode. Its glass fragments glittered suspended in the air, then showered down onto the sidewalk.

"Waste of a perfectly good bottle of Scotch," Annie muttered.

For an eternal few seconds, there was a hard silence, then Daniel heard a blurt of static from the front seat of the van. He squinted into the gloom of the van's bay and saw the glow of a transmitter. He heard sibilant, anxious whispers in Vietnamese, then spied a human form dressed in black crouched low in the passenger seat. He didn't have to think twice. He raised his pistol and fired point blank. An explosion of blood spattering against the windshield glittered through the darkness.

Daniel might have killed some people before from the trenches of Khe Sanh, but they were hidden in a tree line maybe seventy-five feet away and his kills had been as obscure as they were anonymous. But this was different—he'd never seen anyone he'd shot get hit at close range. He remembered what Thien had told him about the close range kill from a pistol. For a moment, he felt an affinity for his victim, now draped lifeless over the still-sizzling radio. There lay a man with maybe a wife, kids, sisters, aunts, a mother—and dreams of a better future. All taken away by his hand.

Behind him, Bian tried lunging for the open door as though she could help her fallen comrade: someone she had met for the first time only hours before. Tony restrained her and drew her back into an embrace as he moved her further away.

He then froze as a bullet tore through his bicep, then another almost immediately into his chest and lung. He collapsed to the street. Bian knelt with him as he fell. "No. Ton-ney! NO!" She shielded his body with hers as though trying to prevent his soul from drifting away into the sky. His labored breathing was light and watery; more like whispers than breaths "No, Ton-ney! We need go to Hollywood…get married. You cannot die!" She clasped him tighter as Daniel and Annie rushed toward them. Then Bian fell back to the street upon him; the blood from a wide gash in her face mingling in full force with that of Tony's against the rain-dampened pavement.

Annie aimed her pistol in the direction the shots had come from but saw nothing.

Hidden by the high ledge of the roof of The Sa—gon Star H—tel, Trần Dao felt the feathery flow of heat wafting from the barrel of her sniper rifle. She breathed in the smooth scent of cordite from the bullet she had just fired. She felt no remorse as she fixed her gaze on Bian's body draped over that of her American lover. She felt nothing at all.

"*Chia tay, Chị Gái,*" she said in a crusty whisper. (—Farewell, little sister—).

CHAPTER FORTY-THREE
Incapacitated

Tony felt the sting and a slight swelling in his cheeks. It hurt to look at anything, but through the blur of his vision he saw Annie sitting in his hospital room chair near the window. She was staring out at the distant, dissipating smoke over the Ton Son Nhut airbase. He tried to shiver away the throbs of pain lingering in his chest. "Annie?"

She glanced over at him. "Hey, Russo. Welcome back." Her voice sounded weak, and her eyes were reddened as though she'd been crying.

"What the fuck happened to me?" He said as he winced from the pain in his shoulder.

"You were shot."

"*Again*?" he sighed, and then emitted a weak cough which sent a jagged stab of pain through his right side. He tried to lift is arm only to realize its bicep was closely bound to the side of his chest. "I hope the guy who did this to me is in worse shape than I am."

"Shh, hon. Try not to talk," she told him. She came to his bedside, poured some warm orange juice into a Dixie cup, and held it to his lips. "Here. Take a swig."

He strained to sit forward. He coughed again and winced at the pain. "What is it?"

"It's orange juice. Now drink it, or I'll finish the job on you."

"Jesus H…more of your threats," he managed to say though more coughs, then sipped reverently from the little cup. He made a sour face and coughed again. "Fuck! Shit!" he spat as he felt a searing pain stab through his lungs. "Damn hospitals can't even do orange juice right," he croaked. "So, what happened to me and how long ago?" He heard a crackling of gunfire in the distance. "Is Saigon still under attack?"

"At least you remember that much."

"Oh yeah."

She touched the back of her hand to his forehead to feel for a fever. "Do you remember seeing Bian?"

"Vaguely. Where is she?"

Annie sighed as she withdrew her hand. "She was under a truck firing an AK-47 at our guys. Tony—she was V.C."

He wet his lips as he absorbed this. "No," he decided. "She wasn't."

"Sorry, hon, she was. And you were shot in the leg and chest by a V.C. sniper. Dan and I kept you covered. We bound you up the best we could to stop the bleeding and carried you to the back of the van until the shit died down. It was almost four hours before we could get you to the hospital. They operated on you and patched you up."

"Operated? It was that bad?"

"They had to take about a quarter of your right lung."

"What th' *fuck*?" He coughed again and cringed to his core. "Shit! First part of my intestine, and now my lung. This fuckin' war's taking me apart piece by piece!" He tried to sit up, but a ferocious surge of pain brought him back down to the pillow.

"I was gonna tell you: don't try to move. Doctor's orders." She brushed a strand of hair from his forehead, and let her fingers linger on his temple. "Anyway. You were pretty delirious when we brought you here. I've been looking after you since."

He took her hand in his. "You didn't have to do that, Annie."

"It was either me or the nurses, and they're all too busy with all the shit that's been coming down."

"How long have I been here?"

"I don't know. Maybe four days. I've lost track of time." More bursts of gunfire crackled and sizzled off in the distance. The stiff, leftover scent of gun oil though the open window joined the ammonia-either-shit smells of the hospital. "The Cong launched a surprise attack on the Tet holiday. They tried taking the American Embassy and the Presidential Palace. We pretty much put them down. They also tried to take over the radio station and Ton Son Nhut airbase. That one was a little dicier, but we took them down there, too, eventually, a couple of days ago."

Tony brushed a wisp of cigarillo smoke away. "What? They thought they could catch us with our pants down? Like Pearl Harbor on a Sunday?"

"Yeah, well, at the last minute, Westmoreland let this Colonel Weyand guy mass a few troops here, because the Colonel sensed something fishy coming on. Otherwise, we wouldn't have been so lucky." She looked out the window as more gunfire sounded. "Shit's not over yet. We're still trying to hold them off in the Cholon District."

The room seemed to absorb the mounting silence as he gave Annie's hand a feeble squeeze. His question was deliberate and pained, as though he knew the answer: "What about Bian?... She okay?" he asked.

Annie relaxed her shoulders as she slid her other hand over his. "Honey. She was killed."

A glisten shone in Tony's eyes as he silently took in her news. For a moment, he felt no pain. He sunk his head deeper into his pillow.

"I'm so sorry, Tony. It had to be. She was Viet Cong. She would have been shot, anyway."

"We shot her." Tony stated. "Our side shot Bian. She was unarmed, and we shot her."

"No. We didn't. She was killed by a Cong sniper—from her *own* side. Not ours." The silence became stifling. Annie wished she could be anywhere but here, but she knew here was where she had to be.

"We were supposed to get married in L.A."

"No, honey," she said hoarsely. "You weren't. It could have never happened."

"I know, Annie," he reflected sadly.

He sniffed back another tear and breathed in. "Sorry," he gasped in a whisper, then offered up a pathetic simper. "He-men like me aren't supposed to cry."

She stroked his cheek. "Sure, you are. Crying helps to make you real. And if you're nothing else, sweetie, you're a real, and wonderful, man."

"You mean that, Annie?"

"Right. Now *I'm* the schmaltzy one. Go figure that out."

He winced again. "Yeah. Well right now I need the latrine. Like I gotta puke or something."

"Damn, man! There you go, getting all sexy on me again. You really know how to turn me on."

"Well, if that's all it takes…"

"You are a real pain in my ass, Russo," she quipped as she moved closer to the bed and started to ease him from it. "Come on, cowboy. Up you get...one...two-three, *Heave!*" He groaned to a wobbly stand, and she guided him gently to the bathroom as he dragged his I.V. pole clattering across the tile floor.

He grabbed onto a towel rack to steady himself. "Thanks. I can take it from here, sweetheart."

"I warned you about that 'sweetheart' shit, so knock it off."

"Yeah, anything you say, commander." He pulled the I.V. pole behind him. Grasping anything that was bolted to the wall, he groped his way to the toilet and hunched himself over it, as she eased the door closed.

It turned out to be just a case of the dry heaves. He labored to his feet and reached for a bottle of aspirin on the edge of the sink. The bottle fell to the tile floor, scattering its contents underneath the sink and around the toilet. "Fuck, shit!" he whispered sharply.

"Everything okay in there?" he heard Annie call. "I mean, I'm not coming in there unless I absolutely have to. It'll ruin my moment to see you leaned over the john."

He hoisted himself around, wincing against a hot shot of pain blaring from his chest to his arm. "I'm fine...," he groaned.

Once done, he opened the door to find her leaning against the wall with her arms folded loose across her stomach. "You know," she said, taking his arm to support him as he staggered toward the bed, "Now that you're on the mend I gotta to split for Hue and help Daniel out. There's a lotta shit going on up there."

"Who'll nurse me back to health?"

"There's a whole staff here to take care of you. You'll probably end up in that rehab over at Ton Son Nhut."

"Oh, fuck. Not *that* place, again."

"Yeah, well, there are plenty of bitchin'-pretty nurses to take care of you until I get back." She looked down at the floor.

"Whenever that'll be," she mumbled.

"Well, Annie. You got the 'bitchin' part right. Last nurse I remember was straight off a casting call for the Mongol Hordes." His voice had tightened, and he broke off into another spate of painful coughing. His face turned red.

"Jesus, Tony. You okay?"

"Huh? Of course not!"

"Yeah, well, suddenly you look sunburned in your face."

"Must have stood up too quickly. I do feel a little lightheaded."

"Come on, hon. Let's get you to your bed and get some meds into you."

"Oh," he said as he leaned against her shoulder. She patted his head as she helped him into bed. "Annie? Once you get back, let's talk."

She processed what he'd said as her lips quivered to fight back some tears. "You just get some rest, now, honey," she told him.

CHAPTER FORTY-FOUR
The sod of chaos

Daniel huddled in the bay of a troop truck with sixteen combat-ready marines and five other correspondents. It had been an ass-numbing, twelve-mile, one-hour trip down Route One, now the most dangerous road on earth. At times, the troop truck picked up speed, but mostly it slowed to hump its way over potholes and craters shot into the two-lane highway. With each jostle, Daniel clenched his two cameras as their straps dug into his neck. North Vietnamese Army bullets pinged and thudded against the side of the truck, while their mortors flew close overhead then hit the ground near them with their muffled explosions. At least sitting next to Thien made it all a little more bearable.

It had been a clusterfuck in Da Nang since Sunday, when reporters started queuing up for a trip into the action in Hue. Daniel had been surprised and happy to run into Thien after he'd been waiting four hours to hitch a ride to Phu Bai, then on to Hue, which had been under intense attack since Saigon was hit five days before. Thien had tapped him on the shoulder and guided him from the anxious clutter.

"Come on, Daniel," he confided. "I'll get you up to Hue."

He restrained himself from drawing Thien into a hug. "Jesus,

Thien! What are you doing here?"

"Same as you. Reporting on this fucking war." He simpered. "But I'm on the right side of getting you where you need to go."

"Christ, man. It's good to see you." Daniel said, then lit a Marlboro and made to slide the pack into the breast pocket of his flak jacket.

"Thanks. I'll take one."

"You don't smoke."

"I do now. Terrible habit; but when among the jungle savages…"

Daniel noticed how the glint in his eye had dimmed as he'd hardened to become combat-blinded like the other journalists. He flicked the pack against his right hand to expel some cigarettes. "Here, man, take as many as you want."

"Thanks," he replied He took four and slipped them into his breast pocket. "For later. When it gets hot."

Daniel raised his cigarette in a toast. "For later. Now do you want to tell me how you think you can get me into Hue when my colleagues over there storming anything with wheels like barbarians at the gate?"

Thien's smile turned a little wicked. "I've got clout. I am a 'Snuffie' and I speak the language. Ergo, I rank."

"Snuffie," Daniel repeated.

"Yeah. I report from the grunt's side of things for *Stars and Stripes*—I tell the troops I need a story and promise them I'll send it to their hometown paper to make them look like heroes. They love me, and I can go just about anywhere. And, because I work for Mac-Vee, I only write the inspiring stuff. Not like your mainstream media trying to make this war look as bad as it really is."

Daniel shifted the weight of his backpack. "You believe that? What you write?"

Thien thought about it for a second. "Well, I have to if I want to keep my cushy job and get through this garbage heap of a situation alive. Here's our ride." Daniel glance into the bay of an ancient troop-truck packed with marines bound for Hue via Phu Bai. "Smoke on the Water" blared from within.

"Yo! Tin-man!" said a Marine from the darkness of the bay. "We're off to fight in that fucking battle. You wanna ride along with us?"

"Tin-man?" Daniel said.

"My reporter-handle. 'Tin-man'—Thien—get it?" He squinted into the bay. "Who is that in there!"

A corporal with a jagged, gleaming scar down his cheek poked his head through the open rear flap of the canvas cover. "It's me! Alfred E. Newman. What...*me* worry? Get your ass up in here. I gotta tell you about how my main squeeze back in Bayonne reacted to that article you wrote. They published it in our paper! I got a major fuck waiting for me when I get home. You saved my relationship, dude!"

"Sure. Okay, Newman. But I gotta bring my friend, here, along. He's a reporter, too."

Daniel felt the earth tremble as the engine of the truck powered up, and a puff of black exhaust smoked billowed from the exhaust pipes sticking above the cab. "The fucking more, the fucking merrier!" Newman shouted above the grinding gears. He extended his hand and helped Daniel and Thein haul their gear into the bay just as the truck jostled and rattled into motion like a dilapidated rhino.

Once in Phu Bai, they were herded with three other reporters, seven marines and a lieutenant colonel into the bay of the half-track they would take into Hue. The closer they got, the more the North Vietnamese Army's bullets thudded like hail against the sides of the truck stinging it like a swarm of bees.

The other reporters, CBS News' Jack Laurence, his cameraman, Keith Kay and UPI photographer Dana Stone; veterans all, took the rude jostling in stride. "This bumping around keeps up, I'm gonna shit my pants," Stone groused in his Vermont accent. He glanced over at Daniel and Thien. "Who's your buddy, Tin-man?"

"I'm Dan Lilienthal. With *The L.A. Tribune.*"

"Ah…La-La Land's official rag. How's Annie Farrell doin'?"

"You know Annie?"

He smiled wryly. "Intimately, you might say. Since sixty-six. We're part-time classmates in the Kasbah."

"Yeah," Daniel huffed a nervous laugh. "She does get around."

"Aye-yuh," Stone agreed. As he nodded, little glints of light reflected from his wireframe glasses.

The driver's rusted voice skwalked through the tinny-sounding speakers blaring Rock music from the truck's cab. "Flaps open, marines! We got some major V.C. shit coming up ahead."

Two marines ushered the lieutenant colonel to the metal floor of the bay.

The five others on each side dropped to their knees and flipped open some wooden slats above the benches of the bay. The light flowed through the openings as dusty shards into the semi-dark. The crackling of gunfire grew louder and more intense. Daniel blinked his eyes tight with each hollow ping against the truck's armor. The marines braced themselves, elbows on the benches, and poked the barrels of their M-16s and two M-60 machine-guns through the openings. "Locked and loaded, Gunny," Alfred E. Newman called out to his sergeant from his machine gun.

"Guess we're getting close to the Mac-Vee compound," Thien said. He casually guided Daniel to hunker down next to him on the deck.

"Okay. Open up!" The gunnery sergeant barked. The marines aimed and fired. The deafening reports from seven M-16s and bursts from the two 60 caliber machine guns reverberated through the bay. There was an eruption of gunfire from close outside, and an AK-47 bullet ripped through the canvas cover and tore through the side of Alfred E. Newman's neck, nearly exposing his esophagus. He collapsed near Daniel, and his blood pulsed onto Thien's pants. He tried stemming the flow of Newman's blood with his bandanna, as Daniel cupped his hands tightly over his ownears to muffle the rattling clamor.

The firing mercifully died down and two marines eased Newman from Thien's lap. The truck jostled and squeaked twice to a halt. Thien nudged Daniel. "We're here."

Daniel had hardly heard him through the ringing in his ears. "What?" he shouted.

"We're here," Thien enunciated, as he unfolded himself into a crouching stand. "The Mac-Vee compound. We're here."

Blessed light flowed into the darkened bay, as a marine flung up the canvas flap, and two others rushed Newman's heaving body from the truck and into triage. The rest piled out, blinking in the light as if they'd been holed-up underground for months. A familiar-looking petite woman with a thick, dirty blonde ponytail swaying across her back rushed to Jack Laurence and exuberantly kissed him, Keith Kay, and Dana Stone on both cheeks. Daniel heard her say in a shaky French-accented voice as tiny as she was: "...Oh, God! I'm glad to see you guys! You know I love zees fuckin' marines. Zay saved my life!"

"Who is that?" Thien asked. "Do you know her?"

Daniel remembered. "Oh yeah. That's Cat Leroy, a photographer with *Paris-Match*. She likes to take chances out there. She probably got caught by the V.C., or something."

"And they let her go?"

Daniel smiled as he recalled the one time a few months back that Cat, Annie and he had drinks at the Rex after another Five-O-Clock Follies vaudeville routine. "She probably drove them crazy."

They hustled into the relative protection of a the nearest building. "Fucking hell of a ride!" Dana Stone said to Daniel.

Daniel cringed a smile. "Yeah it did suck a little, Dana."

Dana held out a cigarette to him, and Thien reached to take it. "You're welcome, Tin-man."

"Okay, thank you, Dana." Thien said, then turned to Daniel. "I'm surprised Tony or Annie didn't make this trip with you."

"Yeah," Dana echoed. "Is Annie coming up?"

"Eventually. She stayed back in Saigon to...look after a wounded friend. She told me she might be here tomorrow or Tuesday." He tugged at his bandanna to secure it closer around his head.

"Well, it seems like a month since I was with her in the Kasbah last Thursday. Shit. Has all this only been going on for, like, five days? I miss her, already."

"I do too, Dana," Daniel replied.

The cesspool stench was the first assault to Daniel's senses as he fell into the grim reality of life in the compound. It smelled like shit because there *was* shit piled up into two-foot mounds in the non-working toilets. Then came the ammoniac, sour stench of urine that had been pissed into the piles of the shit in the toilets and in the corners. To go outdoors just to take a leak was to take your life in your hands. The stink of piss and shit brought on some rages of vomit, and the fragrance of bile permeated the weighty air.

The scent of cordite weaved its way through the open windows and doors, adding to the moist, musty smell of the corpses. All the body bags had been used up after the first day, and now the dead were stacked outdoors in the courtyard, partially exposed through undersized canvas tarps flapping in the chilly-wet wind gusts.

Thien seemed not to notice, as he dissolved his thoughts away into his Zen Buddhist exersizes. He'd managed to find a closet, and closed the door to spirit himself quietly away for a moment. Once Thien finally set foot out among them from the little closet, Daniel noticed his eyes were red and heavy with fatigue, as if he were emerging from something deeper than meditation.

When Thien wasn't wandering around in a semi-daze, he whiled away the time writing in his correspondent's journal — most likely reporting some public relations bullshit about how the stalwart American forces had easily gained control in Hue, and the boys could be home by Easter. Of course, it was all crap, but that was his job, regardless of the surrounding stink of the truth.

The crowd thickened with each arriving truck, and Daniel started to feel even more closed in as day one slid into day two. Food had already dwindled down to one soggy C-ration a day, and the water was stagnant and far from potable. It had to be boiled over little fires from chips of C-5 explosive, the fuel of necessity, as most of the wooden furniture had been broken up for kindling.

Still, he realized that being holed up here was safer than the street. Out there, the air was dense with gunfire and the stench of rotting bodies. Scores of NVA and ARVN corpses, some not recognizable as human, lay blackening and bloated on the steaming sidewalks. Finally, to escape the unwashed stifle of humanity in the compound, Daniel, Thein, and six others decided to venture out through the two-block frontier of havoc in the street to the damaged structures of Hue University. Still standing, its classroom building coalesced like a phantom through the chilly humid mist.

They left as the gunfire had died down and dawn was creeping through the waning moonlight to shed some light against the walls of the compound. The scene was made more surreal by the blare of pop music into the compound from the Vietnam Armed Forces radio station. The saccharine song, "Love is Blue," was as out of place here as Vermont maple syrup. They filed crouched low across the rain-glimmered, pocked remains of Dui Tan Street, toward the entrance of the university where some marines, a handful of correspondents and many Vietnamese civilians had found an unreliable refuge. From there they could see the dim glow of fires across the Huong River; its grey chop shimmering in reflections from the burning Citadel in the city's center.

The Citidel was now being rigorouisly defended by the North Vietnamese Army. The walled fortress—the target of many attacks in Hue—was key to taking back the city. Red and green tracers arced through the brightening sky as the NVA exchanged fire with the pockets of ARVN soldiers and US Marines huddled in doorways and windows blown out into jagged holes.

The ransacked classrooms of the university offered a thin protection, but at least there were overturned desks to shelter behind. Some of the chalkboards were scrawled with messages in Vietnamese and English. Most of them had been smudged to chalk-smears, but Daniel made out a few—"Fight for Peace"; "Surrender or Die Trying"; "Pray for Us Sinners," and the simple one: "Class Dismissed." In time Daniel heard a familiar voice from behind one of the corner desks. "This fuckin' sucks, guys!"

Thien identified it. "Holy-beJesus. Is that Annie back there?"

"Where?"

Thien motioned with his head. "Back there. Hiding in the corner."

"Well, hot shit!" Daniel exclaimed. "Annie? Annie Farrell? Get yourself over here."

Her voice sounded breathless. "Is that you, Dan?"

"No, woman. It's my freakin' doppelgänger. Come on over and join us. Drinks are on Thein."

"Shit. Thien's here, too?" Her voice got closer with each word.

"The very same," Thien said.

The building shuddered with recoils from the 50-caliber machine gunfire from the next room. It made a hollow, clackity-clackity-clackity sound, which subsided into a hard silence, and left another ringing in Daniel's ears that caused his head to throb. More popping bursts of gunfire and the piercing swoop of a mortar grenade tore through the air close above them. Annie hurried over hunkered down next to them. Her fatigues smelled of rust. "Damn, it's good to see you guys! I just ran out of cigars, and I need a smoke!"

Daniel reckoned she must have been temporarily deafened, too, as she shouted over the residual sounds that had died down. Even so, her words sounded light through the ringing in his ears. "I'd never smoke those damn things, Annie! You know I only smoke Marlboros," he shouted back at her.

She lifted the pack sticking out of his flak jacket pocket. "I guess I'll just have to settle, then." She tapped one out and lit it with the enormous flame from her Zippo. Flicking her lighter closed, she blew out a thin ribbon of smoke, then leaned close to kiss Thien on his cheek, and then Daniel on the forehead. "Long time, no see, Desperado. How are you liking editorializing for *Stars and Stripes;* telling the real world all the good stuff about this God-damn war, and how we Americans are winning it single-handedly?"

Thien offered a weak smile and then sighed. "It's a dirty job but somebody's got to do it."

"S'okay, honey-bun. Just don't lose your sense of objectivity."

"Right. This war sucks." He looked around at the empty classroom. "Hue sucks."

"Atta-boy!"

There was another muffled burst of AK-47 fire from down in the street.

"Why, I think they're trying to kill us," Annie said, then shrugged her shoulders and flashed a *who-gives-a-shit-anyway?* grin at Daniel.

"You sound chipper in all this Armageddon," Daniel observed.

"You're kidding. Really?" Annie said, then pursed her lips. "Well, I'm not."

"How's Tony doing?" Daniel asked.

Her pout bloomed into a secret smile. "He's safe in the

hospital. At least as safe as a guy can be in Saigon, nowadays. Anyway, they had to take part of his lung."

Thien looked up from his journaling. "Damn! Tony got shot?"

Annie glanced over at him. "He'll survive. It just made him grumpier."

"Jesus, the way they're taking him apart piece by piece in that hospital, he may just as well be out here in the shit," Daniel said.

"That's what he says. But he has no urgent desire to be here. Here, or in Saigon."

"The war still raining down, there? Christ, Annie, what the hell happened?"

"Looks like they caught us with our panties down, Dan. This wasn't just any random hit. Last count, the V.C. coordinated about a hundred strikes at the same time. If it wasn't so fuckin' rude, I'd fuckin' envy them. Here in Hue is about the deepest I've seen it, though. How long you guys been here?"

"About three days and six years," said Thien. "And you?"

She took a languishing inhale. "Came in from DaNang last night."

"Rough trip," Daniel said.

"Yeah. Tell me about it." She pinched the remains of the cigarette between her dirt-smudged thumb and forefinger. Another round of gunfire shook the room. "This whole goddamned week has been a rough trip," she said then crushed the butt out on the bottom of her boot. Daniel snapped a close-up of her in the wash of the morning half-light breaking through the holes in the wall. Her expression was a mix of sad, yet happy, reflection, showing her relief to be back in her chosen environment created from sweet, blessed sod of chaos.

CHAPTER FORTY-FIVE
Drowning in Hue

Daniel braced himself against the splintered frame of a second-story classroom window as he photographed the flow of events below. Another marine was down, deliberately shot in the legs by a Viet Cong sniper as bait to draw out other marines to help him. Which they did. Two of them ran in a zig-zag pattern to try to carry their crawling comrade to the safety of the shadows from which they'd come. Daniel aimed his black-taped Pentax down at the street and held the view tight upon them until they converged on the man down to help him to cover. Orange tracers of machine gun bullets from a third-story window across the street struck the eviscerated concrete with little puffs. *Saddack…thwip….*

One marine folded his arms like a forklift under the armpits of the limp, wounded one to drag him to safety, while the other returned fire vaguely in the direction of the sniper fire. *Saddack-thwip…*then dragged him, off leaving a thin trail of blood on the street…*Saddack-thwip/saddack-thwip.* Through it all, the two marines seemed to be protected by some higher power that kept them from being hit. Until the last second, when the sniper's bullet caught the marine covering them in the heel. He grasped at it and hobbled to safety, his foot wobbling under a power of its own. *Saddack-thwip.*

A tug of film signaled the end of the roll. Daniel quickly rewound and set in another cartridge. He was so concentrated on this that the snap of the camera back closing was all he heard, despite the surrounding mix of rock music and gunfire. Another marine ran a straight line across the street, followed by tracers and bursts of sniper fire. *Saddack-thwip…saddack-thwip.* He was lucky and made it across.

Even through all the ammo fire, he heard Cream's "White Room" flowing from a boom box in the corner. This wierd attempt to make it all seem familiar only further dimmed any concept of comfort. The US and AVRN troops had been backed into a corner by NVA forces that for now appeared to have gained the upper hand. The marines weren't trained for street fighting; they were used to shooting out into the tree line, not up or down—as was the tactic in this urban combat.

Daniel jolted at another close burst of 50 caliber machine gun fire through the blown-out window to his right. The machine-gunner, a short, wily Black kid, lowered his weapon and wiped the sweat from his forehead. "Shit! Man? If I wanted this fuckin' shit I woulda stayed back in Southeast fuckin' Chicago. At least then I were shootin' at some bad-ass brothers from a differnt hood."

During a momentary silence; hardly ever a good sign, Daniel peered across the street as a few more marines ran safely for cover. "Looks like you mighta got 'im," he said hoarsely. His speech sounded dried out, which was pretty much the way he felt. He cleared his throat and took a few more pictures.

Another round of sniper fire spit up the concrete around two marines crossing the street for cover. "I guess the fuck I din't," said the machine-gunner. "There must be a whole shit-load of them snipers in there."

"Make a hole, marines!" shouted a lieutenant directing two grunts wearing noise-suppressing headsets and carrying a 106 MM cannon toward the window on Daniel's left. It looked more like a bazooka: just a big, squat tube with a chamber at the back end. It was meant more for the field than an enclosure like a classroom. "And clear out unless you wanna get deaf!"

The Chicago marine looked over his shoulder at the gun, then folded his weapon sharply against its tripod. "Shit! Man? If that one-oh-six cain't take out them muthah-fuckahs, then they be ghosts who cain't be kilt." He snapped the breach of his weapon closed. "Putcha hands over your ears, muthah-fucks," he calmly reminded his brother marines as he left the room as his gear clattered against him like so many car-keys.

Daniel watched the gun carriers position the canon in the window. The Lieutenant met Daniel's stare with a wry, knowing smile. "Better do as he says," he advised. "This thing makes noise." He slipped a noise-cancelling headset up from around his neck to cover his ears as the other two opened the breach and slipped in an immense shell. Daniel took the advice and slipped back into the corridor. He braced himself against the He undid his bandanna from around his head and wrapped it twice tight around his ears, then aimed his camera to set up a close-range shot of the marines preparing to fire. doorjamb and undid the bandanna from around his head and wrapped it twice tight around his ears. He then aimed his camera to set up a close-range shot of the marines preparing to fire.

The two Ka-BOOMs!! of the 106 shook the building. The first

concussion coursed the old plaster of the walls into networks of cracks. The second seemed to have destabilized the structure of the building, forcing puffy cascades of dust to funnel down from the ceiling and through the edges of the door and window jambs. Catcalls and shouts from the marines in the hallway and in other rooms echoed down the hall. "Take that, you motherfucks!" "Four-fuckin'-*oh!*" and "Nice to meet you, *Charles*!!"

"Got 'em," the lieutenant proclaimed as he calmly lowered his headset back down to rest on his shoulders. The air had been softened to a murky cloudiness, and thickened with the mellow, unctuous scent of cordite.

Daniel snuck back into the room and to his window to photograph the resulting carnage. A solid quarter of the building across the street had been blown away into nasty-looking jagged holes edged with chunks of concrete; some still falling to the street. The exposed floors were littered with the dead, and where the sniper nest had been, North Vietnamese fighters hung in pulpy parts—two torn torsos pulsed out bursts of blood through the hanging blobs of what was left of them. Daniel felt a rising clump of warm sour bile course up his throat as he took a series of pictures with each of his two cameras. His nausea had distanced him from his emotions which zig-zagged crazily between the shallow victory of revenge to and the shame of what this had all come to. Shooting pictures was all he could do, even if he'd be the only one to see them. He couldn't imagine such gruesomeness on the pages of the *Tribune.* He backed out of the room as stealthily as he'd come in and took one last shot of the two marines packing up the big gun.

He glanced through the blown-out doorway of a fire exit. The wide steps were piled with lumpy body bags stacked like sandbags against the colorless walls. At the base of the stairs, on top of a pile of rubble, lay the bodies of a marine and ARVN soldier, both with their faces blown away. The South Vietnamese soldier was missing an arm and both legs. The marine's body was draped across his as though he'd been trying to protect him. Daniel was transfixed by the macabre sight for what seemed to him hours, but in reality, was only the time it took him to void phlegmy blobs of vomit upon the top step. The shooting had gone quiet. Through the ringing still in his ears, all he heard was "Purple Haze" pounding from the big boombox speakers.

The firing finally died down by nightfall, as if both sides had finished another workday of trying to kill one another in the name of blindly followed ideologies. In any more rational environment, the marines would be out sharing a tall one and boasting about their kills. But here it was just pure fatigue. No one cared about who was winning, or who was short and would be home by the end of the week. That would have been too normal. And nothing about Hue was normal, not even in the context of combat. This was something else. This was about dread in the absence of confidence.

Things seemed to make a little more sense up on the roof, where Daniel and Annie—she draped in an Army blanket— relaxed against a ledge wall while staring up into the cloudy night sky. "I see the Big Dipper," she said.

Daniel passed her his joint. "Where?"

She took a lingering hit, then handed it back to him. "I don't know. Somewhere. Stars. They all look alike to me."

He leaned back and gazed up at the dim clouds and combat haze against the backdrop of night. "I don't even see any stars."

"Use your imagination, then, Dan. They're up there behind all those clouds."

"I would, but tonight's weed isn't working for me." He couldn't get the day's carnage out of his mind as he pinched the reefer between his thumb and forefinger and stared sadly at it. "'Alas, poor Yorick…I knew him well, Horatio…'" He tamped it out on the tarpaper deck, and watched it smolder.

Annie shivered and nuzzled up against him. She felt tense. "I'm cold."

"It is that, Annie. Cold." He settled his body next to hers and drew half of her blanket over his shoulders. "Who woulda thought the tropics could be this fucking frigid?"

"Umm. Who knew?" She took his hand in hers and squeezed it. "Your hand's cold, too." She stared out toward the Citadel glowing across the river. Orange tracers arched over and around it. White sparks of soundless gunfire splashed from its little windows. She sighed. "It's the God damn Fourth of July over there. I wonder how many people will die before this is all over?"

"This fuckin' war. You still wanna stay on in Vietnam after the rest of us have gone home?"

"Mmm…You bet'cha. I *love* this place. The only thing fucking it up for me is the war." He knew that wasn't it. Annie lived for the chaos of war. If it ever ended, she wouldn't know what to do with herself except grow old and bored. She cuddled closer. Daniel wondered if it was not so much from the chill as her yearning for the warmth of companionship. He reckoned for himself it would be both. Combat is, as any step toward dying, the loneliest place of all to be.

Daniel concentrated on "A Whiter Shade of Pale" filtering up through the open hatch. He fell into its softness.

"Ya know, Dan," she said dreamily, "when the smoke dies down, the sun comes out, and we're all safe out of firing range, Vietnam is the most beautiful place on earth. Who'd ever wanna go back to L.A. after this?"

His lips slipped into a tight smile. "Who'd wanna go back to L.A. after anywhere? You should try San Francisco."

"Been there many times. I was at the Be-In last year. What bullshit. But then, I was never the Ginsberg-Leary type. That's amateur stuff. I prefer my opiates more directly from the bush." She settled in some more and rested her head against his chest. "Natural and pure," she said, sounding as though she was falling asleep.

"You still doing that, hunh?"

"When I can. It used to be a much more enriching experience in the Kasbah until all those cub reporters and thrill seekers started showing up. Now that the children have brought in their LSD, it feels to Dana, Sean and me like we're running a kid-care center. Not that LSD is a bad thing, when done right."

"He asked about you."

"Who?"

"Dana Stone. When we got here a few days ago."

"Well, great. Tell him I asked about him, too. I really miss those clowns."

He nodded. "Anyway, I guess I'm just old fashioned. I like sticking to the stuff that's smoked or drunk."

She kicked him lightly on the leg. Her gentle blow was softened more by the blanket; as worthy a protection as any concrete bunker below. "You *are* old fashioned. Don't knock it 'til you've tried it. A little Honey from the Golden Triangle from time to time can really put all this in perspective. Somehow it leads a person to believe this shit won't go on forever. Someday this war will be over. And yes, Daniel-me-boy. When it does, I'm staying right here."

Daniel tried to let the conversation lapse into the light flow of the music.

"Dan?"

"Yeah, Annie?"

"I'm sorry you couldn't get back to Johanna. I was gonna cut your papers for home until all that shit came down in Saigon on Wednesday night."

He tightened his arm around her shoulders. "It's okay, Annie…I mean, given the situation."

"Soon as all this smoke clears, okay? You need to be with her, and she needs you with her, now. Okay?"

"Thanks, Annie."

"Mmm," she said through another shiver, then leaned over and kissed him on the lips—nothing sexual, just an affirmation of their common bond here among the ruins. She leaned back against the ledge. "What's gotten into Thein?" she wondered. "He's really changed since he stopped being Frank's lackey."

"This war happened to him."

"Mmm. It gets to all of us after being out in the field for a few rounds. Especially if your job is to report on America's-winning rah-rah stuff for the Mac-Vee propaganda machine."

"I know it's gotten to him. He wanders off on his own a lot to hibernate in whatever corner he can find. He does what you do, which is something I never knew he did before."

"Okay, Dan. You've won. You've confused me."

"Opium. He takes opium. Tried to get me to do it with him back in the compound a few nights back."

He felt her stir under the blanket. "And you didn't? Man? What is *wrong* with you? Does he have some on him now? Let's get him up here!"

Daniel reached under the blanket deep into one of the many pockets on his combat fatigue. He pulled out a little transparent plastic bag containing a small brown slab of opium and a kit of paraphernalia. He held it up to show her. "He gave me this, just in case I changed my mind. I have no idea how to fire up this stuff. I figured you'd get better use from it than I could."

Annie concentrated her gaze on the bag. "Jesus, how considerate of him! He gave you a kief large enough to stone Minnesota for a week! What's Thien doing? *Mining* this stuff?" She rustled herself from the blanket. "Come on, cowboy. You have *got* to try this! Don't worry, momma will show you how."

"Annie? God-damnit!"

"God-damnit, nothing. Man up and let's do this thing." A stray concussion mortar broke the silence of the night. Annie glanced up at its blue-white glow, then back down at him; deep into his eyes. "This shit is the only way you can win over this God-damn situation; you and me zoning out into euphoria someplace far away from here."

Daniel thought of all the smeared blood and death and ugliness of the day. He sighed deeply. "Okay, Annie. Show me the way."

CHAPTER FORTY-SIX
The million-pound cloud

Daniel and Thien leaned back against a muddy wall of sandbags and stared into a raggedy row of foliage thirty yards away. They were safe for now. There had been nothing to see since some scattered bursts of NVA harassment fire had come from across the way about fifteen minutes before. Now the marines lolled against their weapons as they smoked cigarettes and listened to the music filtering out from a double-sandbagged hooch. Good rock music was sacred in this place. *You can blow away my head, but don't take away my Hendrix music.* Every so often the chatter of a sub-machine gun would break through the the sappier stuff, especially if it was something like a Burt Bachrach tune.

"Fuck *this* shit!" a gunner said.

Daniel arched his head further back to take in the view of the sky—a hazy blue field with a puffy cloud or two. He'd heard somewhere that one of those innocent-looking, medium-sized fluffy things that seemed so weightless in the sky can weigh around a million pounds. How would someone know that? "Did you know that, Thien?"

"Did I know what?" he said as he worried over changing the ink cartridge in his ball-point pen.

"That a cloud could weigh as much as a million pounds? I

mean, how would someone go about figuring that out? You think they go up there with a big scale, or something?"

"Shit, Daniel, how would *I* know? I was a communications major."

"And see how that's paying off for you? Our journalistic talents could get us killed out here."

"Or maybe your million-pound cloud will fall down and crush us all." A private smile drifted up from memory. "Anyway, speak for yourself, my friend. I am going to get through this thing, even if I have to run in the opposite direction to do it."

Daniel gave him a light punch in the arm. "Coward."

"Hah. If being a coward will keep me alive, then I'm a coward and proud of it."

Daniel raised his camera and took a picture of a marine stoking up a mortar cannon. He was neatly silhouetted by the fiery fringe of the deepening sunset—a pleasant shot amidst an ugly scene. Somebody had turned up the speakers as Jimi Hendrix sang "Hey, Joe."

"*Yeah!*" came a shout from the near distance.

Another chimed in along with the words: "…'*Hey Joe, Where're ya goin' with that gun over there?*'…"

A routine burst of AK-47 fire crackled back at them through the silence of a tree line sixty yards away.

"Why *thank* you, Charles!" a marine shouted toward the sound. "For a while I thought you was fuckin' sleepin' out there!"

Daniel felt a hand on his shoulder, and he relaxed into Thien's touch. He had forgotten how warm and comforting it felt, and how much he needed it now. "So, brother. What's this I hear about your Jody? She's sick or something?"

"Johanna," Daniel corrected him. "How did you know about that?"

"Drug up Annie enough, and she'll tell you anything. I hope for all our sakes she's never taken prisoner. They wouldn't need to torture her; just give her a shot of Jim Beam and a few hits on the opium pipe. Anyway, something like she was going to send you home for a time to see about her, before all this happened?"

Daniel leaned further back against the cool stack of concrete-stiff sandbags and lit a cigarette. Through habit, he handed one to Thien. "Don't know for sure. I got a letter from her a few weeks ago. She was in a hospital in New York with a stomach thing. For two weeks. She thought she might be there for another couple of weeks."

"For a stomachache?"

"Yeah. Crazy, hunh?"

"Why is she in New York and not 'Frisco?"

Daniel twitted a slight smile. "Don't ever call it 'Frisco' to a San Franciscan. They'll think you've time-traveled from the Gold Rush."

Thien blew out a long stream of smoke: translucent white against the sky. "Well, I hope she'll be okay. She's good for you."

Daniel felt a tinge of sadness. "I think the best person ever to happen for me." Another intense round fired from the distance, and the marines answered with rattling bursts from their own machine-guns. A rocket-grenade whistled overhead, but no one stirred. It had all become routine. If it was close to hitting them, they would have scattered for shelter, or covered themselves. This one struck harmlessly into the dirt seventy-five yards behind them with a muffled explosion.

Thien's voice was weighted by fatigue. "Looks like the NVA is getting tired as we are here, fighting for this plot of nothing,"

"Westy thinks it's important, I guess," Daniel said.

"Him. What a dick. He's controlling this war from a toilet bowl."

"Is that the basis of your story, Tin-man? You finally coming around to the 'sensible press' way of thinking?"

"I got to write what I see through the eyes of propaganda, man. Complete with flourishes and flowers."

"Bambi and Thumper…"

"Cinderella and her fairy Godmother…"

"…Ozzie and Harriett."

"Who?"

"It's an American thing."

"Sadly, this is *all* our thing. Now the best we all could do would be to fade away into that million-pound cloud of yours."

The Viet Cong come up from their tunnels after the sun goes down, so as the sky grew darker, the firefight intensified. Twenty-five feet down the trench, a marine shot through the chest was bleeding out into the mud as his buddies tried in vain to revive him. It didn't take long for him to die. Two marines bowed their heads in prayer over the body, then one of them removed his poncho. With a ceremonial reverence, he covered the corpse. Daniel tensed himself until a chilly quiver took over.

Thoughts of Johanna comforted him through the chaos swirling around him. He hated himself for being here. Among all the muck, gunfire and death, he suddenly felt so alone. He closed his eyes tight to take his mind far away into the warmth of Johanna's embrace and the solace of her tender kiss. The sting of dry tears heated his eyes. The music drew him back.

Janis Joplin belting out "Piece o' My Heart" seemed to come from deep in the soul of the big speakers. Sounds of machine gun bursts etched into the night and rattled the air. Everything was futile, as nobody really knew what he was shooting at. One of the marines was firing as enthusiastically as a maniac. Daniel reckoned that maybe he'd been pushed over his edge by the war, perhaps bucking foe a Section-Eight discharge..

He edged himself away from the marines at war. He searched his mind for a merciful, mythical zone of quiet. He stepped back and felt his boots slop into a thickness of mud that momentarily anchored him in place like quicksand. He raised his Nikon with its strobe-flash attached, and snapped a picture of four marines hefting a 106-MM canon in an Iwo-Jima-like pose. The strobe burst out its light in a flash preceding the diminutive *pop* of light it made. One of the marines jolted. "What the fuck you doin', man? Shit! I thought you was a shot from the rear!"

"Sorry, man. I should have warned you."

"Fuckin' A, you should have!" He pivoted to face Daniel as he supported the cannon on its end and draped his arm around it like it was his prom date. He held up his M-16 like a scepter and eased his helmet back on his head as he found the bravado to relax. "Okay, brother. *Now* you can take my picture."

Saddack-thwip-flash-pop….

"What the fuck you doin', Jonas?" One of his buddies barked. "What? You think this fuckin' shit is some sorta picnic? Let's get this one-oh-six set up, pronto!"

Saddack-thwip…

"Aw, c'mon Hart. We gotta show the world we was here," Jonas said as he lowered his rifle.

"Fuck, man! I think the world already knows that shit," Hart said, as an NVA bullet hit a marine in the chest five feet away. "SHIT! C'mon! Let's fuckin' MOVE it!"

Two men hustled to arrange the gun against the edge of the trench, while Daniel and Jonas bent over to help the wounded marine. The 106 went off with a deafening, ground-jarring report as the marine quickly bled out.

"FUCK!!!" Jonas erupted, then drew the marine's helmet over his face to cover it. "Fuck, fuck, FUCK!!!"

"Sorry," was all Daniel could say as he stood, aching from his crouch.

Jonas rose to help the others hurridly reload the gun to fire another futile shot into the night.

Daniel could do no more today. His feet felt leaden as he struggled to lift them from the mud and trudge toward the flappy little tent he and Thien shared. He was shaken back into reality as he heard a whoosh near his temple, and felt a hard, gritty spray of sand and muck against his cheek. A Viet Cong bullet had slammed into the trench wall where he'd just been standing. It burst apart the mud-encased sandbag as if it was a sack of flour.

The tiny chunk of kief had boiled down to a thick, simmering clear liquid, in the pipe-bowl, ready to be imbibed. Daniel leaned forward to hold the pipe over the timid flame from Thien's lighter as he held it steady under the bowl. The the old wooden pipe stem warmed his lips as he puffed more vigorously until he sensed the smooth, smoky stream of heroin massage his throat like waves of silk flowing down to soothe him. He eased back as he felt the calming, hypnotic release. Annie had been right. Once you get used to it, opium does taste as sweet as Kahlua.

He found himself in Johanna's arms; felt her kisses on his cheek tenderly work their way to his lips. He felt the nimble trifling of her fingers within his. Her coy smile; her gentle touch;

the way she eased down upon him; how gentle she was. He had been crying more lately, and the thought of her released more tears. He smiled. "Johanna…" he whispered through his rapture.

"Ummm," Thien mumbled, now calmed into his own enchantment as he lay next to Daniel's cot on the dirt floor of the tent.

Daniel floated further away. His new-found bond with opium drew him into a feeling of helplessness. What hell Johanna must be going through. He recalled how soft her hair felt to his touch, and he felt a tightness of tears. "Hey…" he whispered in a quivering voice. "Thien…"

"Ummm?"

"I need to be held." He felt Thien's fingers fidget along his inner thigh. He lowered his hand to stroke Thien's cheek; a feather stroking sand.

More Burt Bachrach music filtered through the air and into the sunshine no one would have thought possible six hours before.

"Just a little lovin';

Early in the mornin'… "

Life had eased back into a semblance of tench-warfare normalcy. Daniel slowly opened his eyes and came into the day. The smells of breakfast: fresh coffee, eggs and sausage tinctured the envioronment. He was lying on the dirt floor of his tent in Thien's light embrace.

"Just a little lovin' ,

When the world is yawnin';

"Turn that shit DOWN!" cried a groggy voice from a few tents down.

"Yeah! Play some Goddamn Steppenwolf, or somet'in'!"

"Good morning, trooper," Thien whispered to Daniel through an easy smile as he stroked his cheek.

Daniel could only grimace a smile back, not quite knowing what to feel, as his lingering thoughts of Johanna faded away into guilt. He nervously swiped his fingers across Thien's hair and eased himself to a stand. "I think that fucking ground broke my back. I must've slept on a tree root, or something."

Thien took on a worried look. "That was nice last night, Daniel."

"Umm," Daniel said. "You smell that? Fresh coffee; breakfast cooking. A *real* breakfast."

Thien eased back down into his sleeping bag. He tried keeping a level tone: "Yeah. There must have been a lull in the action. I heard a Chinook with supplies come in a few hours ago. It didn't wake you?"

"I musta been totally drugged out," Daniel said as he pulled some tooth powder and a razor from his ditty-bag. He brushed his teeth with his index finger, then dry-shaved his face, leaving behind a little cut on his chin. "Oh, crap!" He daubed it with a bit of toilet paper, then rushed to slip on his crusted field fatigues, now embedded with the smell of sweat, cordite and musky wet earth tinctured by the coppery scent of blood. He wrapped his bandanna around his head, and tied it tight. He then took up a camera and looped the film bandolier over his shoulder.

"You okay, Daniel?"

He considered his answer as he stared through the breezed-up tent flap at the early-morning light. " 'Course I am, buddy. Why wouldn't I be?" He planted a cursory kiss on the top of Thien's head. "Come on, now, get your ass out of that bag. There's a war a-waitin' out there and it's a beautiful fucking morning." He managed an uncertain, jagged smile.

His concern eased when he scooted from the tent into another world of sunshine and relative quiet. *It's all so fucking surreal*, he thought as he headed toward the mess-tent. A passing corporal hailed him. "Yo, Jimmy Olsen! I was just on my way to your tent. Finally some fuckin' mail came in this morning. Here's a letter for you."

He glanced with caution at the envelope as though he'd been sent a failing report card. Johanna's penmanship looked so tentative.

He needed a cup of coffee first; more to calm than to stimulate his nerves. He filled a grimy mug and sipped. The coffee was warm for a change. "Not bad today, Riley," he said.

"Yeah. This time it's the real shit; not yesterday's grounds mixed with butt ashes to kick it up a notch."

"Shit. You've been mixing grounds with cigarette ashes all this time?"

Riley showed him a wicked smile. "That ain't the half of it, Scoop. You don't even wanna know. Butcha din't complain yesterday before this morning's supply drop, so I guessed you liked it enough."

Daniel thought back on yesterday morning's coffee. Actually, it hadn't been that bad, whatever it was. He nodded and started to move on.

He settled onto a bench far off in a corner, tore open the short edge of the envelope and blew in it to balloon it open. He was met with the fragrance of lemon, Johanna's favorite. With trembling, aching hands, he unfolded the letter.

"February 10, 1968

Dearest;

I love you, I love you, I love you. I just wanted to start with that.

I'm back from New York City and finally resting in our apartment. I look around, and it reminds me of you more than it ever has. That ridiculous Australian trail hat you made me buy at Abercrombie's when you were picking out your backpack still hangs where you left it on that hook in the living room. Next to that goofy picture you took of me; next to the one you had someone take of us. I stare often at that picture. You look so relaxed and confident; I look as happy as I remember ever being as I stand next to you. Wishing you were here now by my side.

Also, I don't know whether to feel sad that you are still over there now that things seem to have gotten worse, or happy that by April you will be back in my arms again. Please, take care of yourself, dearest. And return to me soon.

I don't know exactly how to put this, so I'll come right out with it:

The treatment in New York didn't work. My cancer is worse than they had originally thought, and this is mostly because I waited too long, and Dr. Kornfield didn't act quickly enough. They took some more tests and told me that the cancer has become aggressive and made its way into my lymph nodes. It may be spreading to my bones. They also found another smaller tumor in my brain. The funny thing is that I feel good, no more headaches or throwing up like before. I'm still dropping things, though, and yesterday I let your favorite coffee mug fall to the floor and shatter. I'm so sorry, hon, I know how you loved that mug.

Dad's become obsessed over trying to press charges against Dr. Kornfield. I think he is taking this whole medical case over the top. We found out that this charge isn't a first for Kornfield, and his lawyer is some sort of Shyster who specializes in winning malpractice cases against "killer-doctors" (Dad's words) like Kornfield. I've never seen my father dig so deeply into one of his cases.

I love you, I love you, I love you, Daniel. I know this all sounds like shit, but please try not to worry, as hard as that may seem. And Please keep yourself safe. We'll be together again in less than two months—that's what keeps me going.

I love you, I love you, I love you

Jo

He felt lacy tingles through his nerves. All he could do was stare at Johanna's letter and let the tears billow in his eyes. He wanted only to hold her to him and never let her go. He gazed down at her weak, uncertain handwriting and could see the toll the cancer was taking upon her. A few loose strands of her hair clung to the page. He read it again and was helpless with the harsh understanding that there was nothing he could do. Fate had taken over.

Ten miles off in the distance—actually, ten feet away, right outside the mess tent—someone shouted: "Incoming!!" And the air of what started out as a beautiful fucking morning was seared by the hard whistle of a rocket grenade.

Daniel's nerves had been frayed by the acts of heroism and death he'd spent the week photographing in Khe Sanh. He was further devastated by Johanna's letter, and needed a few days of R&R. It would start all over again the day after tomorrow when he was to fly up to Quang Ngai Province. There, he was to cover of the heated action in "Pinkville," so named because the area was always colored in pink on the maps. But for today, he needed to latch onto a little bit of sunlight and the tonic that Saigon could offer, even amid the sporadic street fighting still going on. He felt a strong apprehension about what might be waiting up in Pinkville. He'd gone into countless firefights by now, but he sensed something different about this one. He wondered if it was some sort of premonition about dying.

PART SIX
The Weight of Indifference

CHAPTER FORTY-SEVEN
The boy-soldiers

Thien the Tin-man, every G.I.'s reporter-friend, wrangled a chopper ride for himself, Daniel, and Annie to Quang Ngai Province in the flatlands of northeast South Vietnam. At any other time, this would seem like a cushy assignment in a rough area: cushy because the Tet Offensive seemed to have quieted since the defeat of the NVA at Hue. It was rough because it landed them near a wide cluster of hamlets in Pinkville where the grunts had been taking on rashes of fire from NVA snipers who'd been there since the beginning. Often the NVA, led by the Viet Cong, would trek down from the mountains at night and take up positions in the small settlements populated by peasant farmers who wanted only to survive.

Three months before, the Marines had turned their position here over to the Army's newly formed Americal Division. The uneasy truce within Pinkville had the sustainability of one of those urban neighborhoods protected by street gangs, as the Americals were like renegades stationed within their element to be left to their own prejudicial judgements.

The Huey transporting them made a chaotic, grinding, guttural-popping landing like a steam-punk machine out of a Jules Verne story. It thumped down hard on a dirt clearing at LZ

Dotti, an artillery outpost near Son My village located in the heart of Pinkville. The chopper had settled down at a forty-degree angle on its right skid, then crashed with a grating, rattling bang on its left just before the engine died.

Daniel and Thien glanced at eachother. "Auspicious beginning, this," Daniel told him, then swallowed his anxiety to slip out the gunner's door. Annie seemed to have taken the jolting ride with a charge of excitement. She noticed a Private trying to hide against a pallet-load of C-rations and supplies about ten feet away.

He raised a sleepy-eyed look at the pilot. "Shit, Denkins. That was some bad ass, fucked-up landing. Your bird okay?"

"I got a bird for you, Price," Denkins replied, showing him his middle finger and easing himself from his ragged seat at the controls. "We took on some sniper fire over Co Lay, but that din't matter much. This thing turned to shit about ten kliks out of Da Nang. Maybe we caught a fuckin' seagull in the turbines, or something."

"Tell Crocker so he can tell The Spook to take a look at it." He grinned and showed an array of uneven teeth. "Who the fuck knows? The Spook'll eat anything. Maybe he can have your chopped-up seagull for dinner." He then leaned back against the pallet and took a mighty draw on his joint.

"Well," Daniel said to Thien. "*This* looks like it's gonna be another fun trip."

Thein's expression darkened. "Hardly. I know about these guys. Let's just ask our questions, snap some pictures and get the fuck out of here."

Everything was dry, even now in the waning monsoon season.

Annie lay on her cot smoking a cigarillo, as "Hey there, Little Red Riding Hood" hissed out from the distant P.A. speakers around the little base. She blew out a thin stream of smoke as she contemplated the weave of the canvas ceiling of her tent. The pant legs of her fatigue trousers were rolled up to her pronounced knees. Her calves were randomly crisscrossed with thin scratches as if there'd been a cat fight around her legs. But these marks were left by the thick elephant grass she ran through the other day to catch yet another chopper shuttling her from one un-remembered place to another. She felt a rare and merciful breeze cool the soles of her bare feet.

"Thein doesn't seem to like these guys very much," Daniel said from his seat on an empty ammo case across from her.

"Yeah, well he has a right to. Dana calls these Americal Division guys 'The Animal Division.' Most of them have been scrounged up from street gangs and the illiterate South. You wouldn't want to mess with them in real life, so no telling what *this* place has turned them into. Keep your cameras as close to you as you hold your side-arm, Dan. Mike Herr warned me last week they'll rob you blind while you're sleeping."

"They're not too smart then."

She took a long draw. "Hell, no. They're the ones who only the sub-cellar of the Army wants. I think the combined I.Q. of this division is about eighty-four. I heard their Lieutenant is as dumb as a bag of hammers. And worse. He's a butt-boy to a Captain Ernie Medina who thinks he's some sorta Lee Marvin to these guys."

"Who's the Lieutenant?"

"He's fresh outta some podunk college in Florida. His name is something like Caulley. No. Calley."

"You've done your homework, darling."

She cast him a sideways look. "We journalists call it research. You should try it sometime, cowboy."

"Don't have to. I'm living in it."

"Well, your term here for the *Trib* is about up, anyway. For all intents, you're a journalistic short-timer."

"What about Tony? His term's up, too, then."

She looked back up at the canvas. Her lips formed a furtive smile as she tamped out her cigarillo. "Oh, I think I've convinced him to stay."

"You make it sound like you tortured him."

Her smile broadened. "Maybe. Depending on how you see it."

The ensuing silence betrayed her little secret. "Oh, Jesus, Farrell, you didn't. You granted his wish?"

"What wish?"

"His wish. To get into your combat fatigues."

She simpered. "Well. That's one way of taking the charm out of it. But yes."

"When did you all find the time to get *that* going?"

"It didn't take much time. We started a few months ago just before Tet, before he was shot up in front of the embassy."

Daniel huffed a little laugh. "Well, nothing stops true love, I guess."

She flicked him a glare. "I never said anything about love."

Daniel frowned. "Then you're just playing with his emotions, because he certainly has those feelings for you."

She thought about it for a moment. "Dan. This is getting too deep. Can we talk about something else? Okay? *Shee-it,*" she sighed, then rolled her head toward him and saw a sad expression beneath the day's accumulated grit on his face. "Hey. How's everything at home? Have you heard from Johanna?"

"Yeah…I got a letter last week."

"Johanna's a pretty name. I wish I had one like it. How's she doin'?"

He looked out into the lowering sunlight, and remembered what he was supposed to forget, for now—how he felt so bound to her needs. "I don't think so. I think it's spreading. At least she's back in San Francisco."

"Oh, fucking shit! God-damnit, Dan! I should have gotten you out of here weeks ago. How come you didn't tell me? I woulda put you on a transport from Ton Son Nhut, myself."

He looked at her and at the rare glisten in her eyes. "There's nothing you could have done, Annie. Besides, I was up in Khe Sanh when I heard from Jo. I couldn't just excuse myself to go back to Saigon, like this is some sort of office job."

"Alright, you shithead. You listen to me. As soon as we rotate out of this fucking wherever we are, I'm cutting a temporary transfer home for you."

Daniel piqued a smile. "I thought you said I should stay here in Saigon. Remember?"

"I said a *temporary* transfer. You've caught the fever for Saigon, just like I have. You'll be back. For now, though, Johanna comes first."

He lowered a solemn glance down at the camera on his lap. "Thanks, Annie. Really, I appreciate it."

"Nothing stops true love," she said, throwing his platitude back at him.

"Not even death," he whispered mostly to himself. He heard the metallic click of her Zippo's lid as she flicked it open and closed. Open and closed…. She was apprehensive about something, for sure. He looked out at the retreating light, and then concentrated on fixing the lens onto his Nikon's body. He thought about Johanna's letter, then realized how much he needed to take some pictures right now to put his thoughts right. "I guess I'll go do some photography while there's still light."

A couple of G.I.s were gathered around cleaning their M-16s, caught in a nice sidelight which shone off the barrels and stocks of their weapons. They at least pretended not to notice Daniel, as he overheard them muttering about "…fucking gooks, dinks and slope heads and how they were "going to pay big time for taking out Sarge Cox with their fuckin' booby-trapped landmine." Daniel raised his camera. *Saddak-thwip; saddack-thwip.*

One of them swung around at the sound and glared. "What the *fuck*, Slick!"

"Sorry, guys. I'm a journalist for *The L.A. Tribune.* Give me your names and I'll get you some copies."

"I don' want no fuckin' snapshots of me. Get ridda what 'chu just did!"

"Okay," Daniel said, and pretended to rewind the film to remove the images on the negatives. "Done. All gone."

"Don't 'chu go 'round takin' them fuckin' Kodaks lessen' you axe us first," another said. "We don' cotton to that kinda shee-it."

Daniel wanly smiled. "Thanks. I'll remember that." He felt a nudge against his shoulder and turned around to face a young lieutenant with a cherubic face, dark brown fly-away hair, and a failed attempt at a mean squint. He looked barely old enough to shave.

"You're the photographer from *The Tribune.*" His voice was soft with an undertone of growl.

"That, I am."

The lieutenant's look turned more offensive as he tried to drill his stare into Daniel's soul. "Well, I'm Lieutenant Calley," he announced.

Daniel smiled away Calley's glower. "Hi," he said. "I'm Dan Lilienthal."

The lieutenant thought for a minute. "Lilienthal." He thought a little more. "Jewish, right?"

"Uh, yeah," Daniel said guardedly.

"Just wondering. Just so you know, I'm the boss here; and what I say goes, so no back talk. Anyway, the captain said for me to tell you guys to keep what you do confined to this outpost area."

"Uh, okay. I'll pass that along."

"So, no following us out on patrols, or anything. We're goin' out on a restricted mission in a few days, and don't need a bunch of reporters gumming up the works."

This guy really was stupid to tell a reporter about a "restricted mission." It was like an open invitation. Daniel grinned and shook his head. "Okay. We'll just stay here. Thanks, lieutenant."

Calley tried on a smile, which only puckered up his face. "Good, Lilienthal. We understand each other. Enjoy your visit." He turned and walked away.

"Yes, sir," Daniel said to his back. "We understand each other completely."

"Yo! Scoop! Over here! Take my fuckin' pitchure!"

Daniel turned to face a bald shirtless grunt with a well-defined set of muscles caught in the warm half-light of the setting sun. A weave of scars veined his pock-marked, roughly-shaven face. He showed a menacing grin displaying three missing teeth. "Yeah, okay...." Daniel became transfixed by a weird necklace made up of strung together things resembling dried apricots. He raised his camera. *Saddak-thwip...saddack-thwip.* "What's that hanging around your neck?"

The grunt took hold of the necklace and held it out. "This? It's a bunch of gook ears I chopped off up in Chu Lai. Some of 'em while they was still alive and squirming."

Saddak-thwip. Daniel sensed the guy was stretching the truth. Renegade marines were known to do such things, but these army guys weren't quite salty enough. He might have swiped the necklace off a dead marine. "Jesus, man!" he said. "That's fuckin' brutal."

The scar-faced G.I. scowled with the triumph of a tough guy. "Yeah. I fuckin' love the screaming a dink makes while you go an' cut out their ears. It ain't like a human scream, more like some sorta fuckin dog-whimper. Makes you feel like you're in control of things, like you own a life."

Saddak-thwip...saddack-thwip. "Okay man. What's your name? So I can make some extra prints for you."

"What's yours?"

"Dan Lilienthal. I work for *The L.A. Tribune.*"

"Lilienthal." He let this sink in. "Me? I'm Crocker. I sorta run things around here."

Daniel flicked a wry smile. "I thought that lieutenant was the boss here."

He huffed a scornful laugh. "Calley? Shee-it...he can't even control his own dick. He don't run nothing, not even hisself. Only thing he knows is how to get us all kilt. Now the captain, 'Mad Dog' Medina...most o' us would follow him just about anywheres. The only thing Calley knows is his way up Medina's ass. Most of the guys, here? They listens to me."

Daniel doubted that as well.

He found Annie a few hour later sitting off by herself away from some grunts huddled around a fire built from twigs and rope. A few of them were straining to take in the effects of the warmth and the burning hemp. Some of them seemed stoned, or at least acted like it through the miracle of wishful thinking. Others were smoking weed and still others, mostly the "shit-kickers," chugged from cans of Pabst Blue Ribbon and belched between sips to the morbid sound of "Together Again" squelching through the little speakers. The drunker ones slurred loudly and miserably off key to the refrains.

"Shut the fuck up, shit-kickers!" one of the potheads threatened.

"What? You got somethin' against Buck Owens?"

"I got *everythin'* against that fuckin' shit country music, you fuck head," said another.

"Malloy? You ain' got the sense God gave my mule," said one of the shit-kickers. His Alabama drawl was so thick it sounded put-on.

"You a fuckin' beetle-brained shit-head, Pritchett," Malloy slurred loudly. "Marryin' yo' lit'l ten year-ol' sister give you a attitude, or sumpthin'?"

"I'll show y'all some fuckin' *attitude*, boah!" Pritchett threatened, and then swung his body around the hemp-fire to grab Malloy's neck. He pushed his face toward the fire.

"You watch out there callin' me 'boy,' you fuckin' cracker!" Malloy croaked, as he tried to fend the big Alabama farm boy away. The rest cheered on the tussle, happy as long as one of them got the shit beat out of him. Malloy forced his way free then bloodied Pritchett's mouth with a downward punch that skewed his jaw. Little Malloy, cast from the mold of a street gang, wriggled away from Pritchett and sat on top of him to pin him. Blood slathered from his mouth as he landed a tight succession of blows to each side of the Alabaman's jaw. He didn't stop even when Pritchett's mouth had been pulped.

Finally, Crocker stepped in and pulled Malloy away. "Okay, you pecker-heads, tha's enough. Save that shit for the fuckin' dinks when we goes after them."

Malloy stood over Pritchett breathing heavily with his fists still balled. Pritchett lay prone and looked dead, but his chest was heaving. Finally, he roused himself and broke into a round of snotty chortles. "Okay, douchebag," he croaked, "go ahead an' change the tape to your rock shit."

"Now, don't you feel better?" Crocker said to Malloy. "You got wha' chue wan-ned."

"Yeah, Crocker," Malloy mumbled dejectedly and headed toward the "entertainment tent" housing the tape-player that fed the speakers. "I fuckin' *guess* so."

"An' none of that fuckin' Harlem jungle-bunny horseshit I been hearin' you listenin' to, boah!" Pritchett called after him, then spat out some blood.

Malloy held up a bony-fingered bird as he walked away.

"Okay now, Pritchett. You get up an' get me another beer. I spilled mine all over the fuckin' place when I came over to help you out," Crocker told him as he dragged him to his feet.

"These guys are such a *pleasant* bunch," Annie told Daniel. "I can't wait to get the fuck out of here."

"Just don't forget to take me with you, Farrell. I got a feeling we're gonna need as much civilization as we can get after this assignment."

"And you, my friend, are going *home*. Temporarily." She stood up and stretched this way and that, to ease out the stiffness in her body from sitting for such a long time.

A couple of guys watched her aerobics from the behind the firelight. Daniel noted their stares. "Be careful, hon. You've woken the jungle."

"I'll be fine, cowboy. Don't worry, okay?" She kissed her fingertips, touched them to his forehead, and then went off to her tent.

Another voice rose from the darkness, this one with a Spanish accent: "Yo! You! Meester photographer." Until now, Daniel felt protected by the darkness that had deepened as the fire died to embers. The murk was punctuated by little glows from the tips of the refers. "Come on an' join us."

Doused in trepidation, Daniel made his way over and hunkered down. He conjured up his most amiable smile.

"You wan' some weed? My cousin, he send it special to me alllll de way from my home in Tijuana."

"No. Thanks, anyway."

"'*Thanks, anyway,*'" another scoffed. "Well ain' *you* the polite one. But maybe not so for dissin' a gift offered to you by a friend."

"Here." It sounded more like a threat as the grunt offering the weed reached across the embers. Daniel thought it best to accept. He inhaled timidly, and held in the gritty warmth of its smoke, which sent him into a spasm of dry coughing. The grunt smiled wide. The gold fillings in his mouth glimmered in what was left of the light. "See? Ees good."

"Yeah," Daniel coughed through the burn in his throat, then

reached to hand the joint back to him.

"No, meester photog. You keep. I got more."

"Those fuckin' gooks," someone lamented. "They went and killed Cox."

"I heard he thought he disarmed the mine, and it went off when he fuckin' picked it up."

"You *would* think sumptin' like that, Wingo, you freakin' Guinea. Cox wouldn't do nothin' stupit like go an' pick up a mine, like, from the ground. He too smart fo' that shit."

"Fact is, he fuckin' died from it. Fuckin' guy was a legend," said another.

"Hah!" Crocker's voice was coarse. "Legend, my ass."

"He was, by the way Cap Medina talked about him at the funeral today," came a long, Texas drawl from across the dying fire.

"Shee-it, Sawyer," Crocker slurred back. "Don' you get it?" By the way he was drawing out his speech, Daniel could tell that the mix of beer and the Tijuana weed was having its way with him. "The Cap jus' wan-ned to fuckin' fire us up for this mission he has for us day after t'morrow. It's like our first real chance to go out an' kill gooks."

"Yeah, like the man say," the Mexican said. "He wan' us to kill everythi' on two legs or four, anythin' with them fuckin' slanty little eyes."

"Fuck yeah! Death to the slopes!" someone bellowed.

This was followed by a hearty, but sleepy round of agreement. "Yeah! Death to them slopes!"

"Yeah! Remember Sarge Cox!" the Mexican said.

"Aw, come on, Alvarez," Crocker told him. "You ain' got the senze God gave a dog's foot."

"Sense ee-nuff ta know Cox saved my ass a coupla times."

"Sheee-it! I think every swingin' dick here in Charlie Company saved your ass a coupla times there, Killer Joe. Fucked up as you are." From Crocker, Alvarez took that as a show of affection. Crocker glanced at Daniel sitting next to him. "Well there, Slick. You been awful quiet. Wha'd you think 'bout our Sergeant Cox? You best not go writin' 'bout all this in your paper, now."

The Tijuana weed had taken its toll on Daniel, too, by breaking down his defenses. "I dunno, corporal. I never met the gent'man."

Crocker bellowed out a sudden, phlegmy laugh through the open chasm of his toothless mouth. "*Gent'man!* Tha's fuckin *rich!* Cox a *gent'man!*"

"Hardly not," someone with a New Jersey accent said. "An asshole, maybe, but no fuckin' damn gentleman."

"Well, ain' *chu* puttin' on th' aires, Slick. Callin' our guy a gent'man." Crocker said. "You know, man? You got it dicked. You can leave this kick-ass war at anytime you want to fly back to Las Angelees, while we gotta maybe get fuckin' kilt over here cuttin' up an' killin' slopes, gooks and dinks."

"Sorry, I—"

"You ain' sorry for *shit*, dickhead. We ain' got no choices. You do. Tell me. You married?"

Daniel didn't want to answer that, but his sullen reply came out of fear. "Yeah. I'm married," he lied.

Crocker fondled one of the ears on his necklace like a worry-stone. "Okay. So you're married. An' you din't sound none too happy tellin' me that. What you do? Find out she was out there in Las Angelees boinkin' some guy she knows is better n' you? Or maybe because she got tired waitin' for you? Or maybe she decided she don' like sheenies like you. Maybe wha' chu need is to to go out an' get some *decent* poon-tang in Saigon."

"You fuckin' shit Cretan!" Daniel shouted as wheeled toward Crocker and tried to force his head down into the embers. Crocker didn't resist much, as he chortled over Daniel's feeble attempt to bring him down. He felt two sets of hands grab him by his shirt and film bandolier. Alvarez and Sawyer flung him down on his back and started to pummel his stomach.

Sawyer tried to grab his Nikon, but Daniel held it tight to him, caring more for its safety than his own. He grasped his Nikon in both hands and banged hard it against Sawyer's face. The force caused something in the camera to rattle around. The tall Texan fell away, pressing a hand against the deep gash in his cheek. "You son-ov-a-*bitch*!" he screamed. "You are fuckin' toast for that! You are fuckin' *toast*!"

Another voice, sounding only a little more sober, came from behind. "HEY! Hey! What the *fuck* is this about?" Lieutenant Calley pulled the two privates away from Daniel. "Jesus, men! Save it for later, okay?"

"Th' son v'bitch wen' after Corporal Crocker...sir," Alvarez said.

Calley glared over at Crocker, still giggling as he crouched near the ember-fire. "Why, hel-*lo*, lieutenant," he said. "How're *you* this fine fuckin' evenin?"

Calley shook his head in disgust as he glared over at Sawyer. "Then Crocker probably deserved it," he said. He then glanced down at Daniel. "You okay, son? Sorry about these soldiers they're just a little hyped up over our next mission." He looked up at the cluster of men before him. "Which commences on Saturday at the LZ at zero-seven hundred. Sharp! V.C. action has heated up over in Son My. The captain wants us frosty for it. So be up for it."

"Oh, we will, lieutenant," Sawyer drawled, as he pulled his hand from the bleeding gash near his eye. He stared at a burn in his open hand, then leveled a menacing glance at Daniel. "We already fuckin' are. Ready for it. Frosty, yeah."

"Fuckin'-A!" someone said.

Calley nodded sharply and helped Daniel to his feet. "We can't have my boys roughing up the press like this. You'll keep a lid on this, right, Lilienthal?"

Daniel looked across the fire pit and noticed the two grunts who'd been leering at Annie talking privately while occasionally looking up at him and then at Sawyer. He pivoted from Calley's weak grasp. " 'Scuse me, lieutenant. I've got to go turn in, now."

"Take your time, son," he heard Calley call after him.

CHAPTER FORTY-EIGHT
Things that go bump in the dark

Given Charlie Company's prejudice against his kind, Thien had made himself scarce. He either stayed in his tent or at a meager desk and a percolator set aside in a damp corner of the Operations tent for the visiting public affairs reporters. Often he would stray off to a cluster of rocks he'd found, to scribble his commentary for *Stars and Stripes*: Gung-ho Army! Our overpowering force! One of the operations that could end the war; routing out Viet Cong insurgents from South Vietnam—again. Bottom line: gung-fucking-ho Army.

It was a story best composed from a distance. This morning he had managed to sneak out—past the enemy in the camp—a little after dawn to meet for coffee with his confidant, Nguyễn-Moy, an ARVN chopper pilot out of Da Nang. His little four-passenger observation helicopter was being worked on here in LZ Dotti to be in operation by the afternoon. Nguyễn and Thien had developed a brothers-in-turmoil relationship.

Daniel rested fitfully and alert with one eye open during the night, not falling asleep until after sunrise. He told Thien nothing about his futile assault upon Crocker, realizing some things were better left alone.

He woke at eleven-thirty, as he heard some movement outside the tent. "Thien?" he called from the shallow depths of his fatigue. "You out there?"

No answer; just a repetitive clinking followed by a swish.

"Hey, Thien?"

"He ain't here," the voice was a slow grumble. "Is jus' me."

"Oh, shit," Daniel said, recognizing Crocker's slur. "Corporal Crocker."

"One an' the same. Invite me in, why don'cha?" He didn't wait for an invitation as he slipped through the tent flap carrying his M-16. He seated himself on the edge of Thien's cot as Daniel swiveled to a sit on his. He fiddled around in his blanket for his pack of Marlboros and a lighter. "I'll take one of those, Slick. Thanks for offering."

Daniel reluctantly passed him one of his three remaining cigarettes. "You're such a gracious fuckin' guest, Crocker."

"Ain' I, though?" he said as he took the cigarette. He flicked and fired up wooden blue-tip match against his gun stock.

"That looks a little dangerous, striking a match on what could be a loaded weapon."

"Not if you know how to do it, an' are suicidal at heart, Slick. So? Sleep well?"

"Well as can be, I suppose."

"Good. We aim to please here at the Americal Hotel." He raised his gun as if to clean it, holding the end of its muzzle near Daniel's heart. Daniel jolted back. "Aw, don't worry, Slick. She ain' loaded. Yet." He opened the breach and concentrated on picking at its mechanics with the point of his knife. "Ya know? We got some fuckin' rules here in Charlie Company."

"Uh, yeah? What are they?"

"Oh, you'll fin' out soon enough." He stared down into the breach as he picked away at a stubborn speck of something. "Jus' know that it's a, like, a privilege for you reporter-types to be here. Your type ain' too, welcome-like, here." He waited for a response.

Daniel stared nervously down at the gun barrel rustling against his chest. "I gathered that."

The ash fell from the cigarette dangling from Crocker's mouth into the rifle's chamber. "We got important shit to do here, an' don' need no snoops from th' outside." He blew hard into the breach and roused up some of the ashes. "'Specially if they be reportin' on our doin's here."

"Okay."

"Jus' remem-mer that, Slick." He leveled his gaze at Daniel as he raised his knife. "So, the sooner you get outta Dodge, the better."

"I couldn't agree with you more."

The glimmer in Crocker's black eyes flared through the shadow cast by his hairy brow as he brought his knife blade to Daniel's cheek. "Get it?"

"Yes, Crocker, 1 get it."

Crocker flicked the tip of his blade near Daniel's temple and drew a bead of blood. "That was for pissin' off my man, Sawyer. He's Jonesin' to mess you up." He brought his knife back and snapped the rifle-bolt closed. It sounded like a crackle of gunfire in the small space. Daniel winced again as Crocker finally stood to leave. "Long's we understand each other, Slick." He stopped at the tent flap and faced Daniel again. "Oh yeah. Couple my guys wanna know. What's the deal with the chick?"

He seared a gaze toward Crocker as he measured out his answer: "She's a reporter. Why?"

Crocker's fat lips bloomed into a half-smile. "Is she hot?"

"No! And she's off limits."

"Uh-*hunh*," Crocker muttered. "Thanks, there, Slick. I'll let 'em know." He turned and left Daniel trembling where he sat, needing a cigarette but too numb to reach for his last one.

Daniel kept a furtive vigil on Annie's tent across the way from where he sat on a campstool outside his tent. Tonight would be another sleepless night. He had kept Crocker's visit to himself, hoping it had been merely an empty threat, but kept his side-arm locked and loaded and at the ready, just in case.

The clacking of Thien's typing inside their tent offered a comforting rhythm for now. He stared off into the misted low hills to the north as he tried easing himself into a serenity that was a culture away from here.

"Daniel," Thien called out. "I need you here for just a minute."

Daniel groaned as he stood and slipped into the tent. "Yeah. What do you need?"

"Well, I need you to read what I just wrote, but I also want to know what you've been doing out there for the last hour. You seem intent on something."

"It's nothing, really."

"Man? I know you well enough. Something's on your mind. You know what's on mine…getting outta this God-damned hell hole. So now, tell me. What's on yours?"

Daniel heaved out a sigh. "I'm worried for Annie. I don't trust these guys by the way they've been leering at her."

"You don't think she can handle herself? She's probably been in worse situations than th—"

"Not like this. I have a really bad feeling here, Thein."

Thien paper-clipped his article together. "Anything I can do?"

"I don't know. Maybe get us back to Saigon in a hurry. I need a Scotch."

He relaxed Daniel with one of his warm smiles. "Got us covered, there. Once these guys leave for whatever that mission is they keep talking about, I know a Loach pilot stuck here who can chopper us out. We should be back in Saigon by fourteen-hundred tomorrow afternoon."

Daniel eased his shoulders in relief. "I'll order a late lunch for us at the Continental. On me."

"You go ahead and do that, friend. Meantime you look a little worse for wear. You get some rest. I'll keep checking on Annie if it'll make you feel any better."

It was not until after midnight, when Thien was deep asleep and Daniel remained half awake, that he heard some rustling and muffled anxious voices. The hubbub was punctuated by something that might have been a restrained scream coming from Annie's tent. He shot upright, grabbed his pistol and kicked the leg of Thien's cot.

"Wha' th' fugg, Dan?" Thien mumbled.

"It's Annie. Something's happening. Grab your piece."

Daniel slipped through the tent's door, loaded pistol in hand, as Thein slid from his cot to follow him. Annie's tent walls looked like they were breathing heavily as she thrashed about. Her cries became louder and more distinct. A loud slap cracked through the air as Annie let out another abrupt, frightened scream. Then a voice drawled: "Shut up you fuckin' cunt! Open wide for Big Mike! He's fuckin' hungry!" Another scream from Annie. "Will you shut the fuck up, woman? Lundgrun! Hold her down, gawd-damn it!"

Then another male voice growled, "She keeps fuckin' moving aroun'! *Shit!*...You fuckin' *bitch*!" This was accented by another slap. Then came a sharp cry of pain from one of her attackers. He rushed from her tent, shirtless, as he clutched his bleeding hand.

Then came a third voice: "*Fuck*! Sawyer! She's packing heat!" Just before a pistol shot. The bullet billowed out the roof of her tent as it passed through.

He heard Annie scream: "Get outta my tent, you fuckin' assholes!"

"Fuck *this* shit!" the third soldier barked as he tumbled out through her tent door. He was followed by Sawyer, whose cheek still gleamed from the deep welt where Daniel had clouted him with his camera. His running was awkward, as he tried pulling up his pants—his little pink prick still half-erect in the crisp moonlight. Daniel caught up with him and tackled him as Thein ran after the others with his pistol drawn. Daniel held the muzzle of his gun to Sawyer's temple. "You fuckin' shit, Sawyer! I should fuckin' kill you right now!"

"Fugg, you Lilienthal, you Gawd-damn sheenie!" he sputtered, then spat in Daniel's face. Daniel hauled off and pistol-whipped him hard across his other cheek. Twice. Sawyer let out a feeble laugh before he groaned into unconsciousness.

Right now Annie was more important than Sawyer.Daniel pushed himself away and rushed into her tent. The place looked like it had been subjected to a police raid. Annie was trembling in fear as she uncharacteristically cowered on a corner of her cot with her knees drawn up to her chin. Her shirt had been ripped open to expose one breast. She was bleeding from her mouth. Daniel went to comfort her. He reached out his hand and she slapped it away, screaming: "Get AWAY from me! You son of a BITCH!"

"Annie. It's me. Dan," he said.

She angrily slapped his hand away again as he moved closer, then she pounded his chest again and again in a surrealistic silence. He kept his arms around her in a tight embrace until she stopped fighting him away. She sobbed onto his chest. "Those mother-fuckers tried to *rape* me!"

Daniel stroked her ruffled hair. "Shhhh, hon. It's gonna be okay."

"No, Dan! It's *never* gonna be okay," she sniffed.

Thien caught up with one of the other two who had stopped in his tracks. He raised his .45. "Turn around, asshole."

He did. He relaxed his shoulders as he showed Thien a sneer and raised his M-16. He drove the bolt home in its chamber, which resounded in a metallic click. "My gun's bigger n' yourn." His drawl came somewhere from deep down in the American South. His chin had an ugly sore from a fight he'd been in recently. He broadened his smile as he realized Thien was Vietnamese. "Well. Lookee here…looks like I got me a bonified *gook* in my sights." He held the tip of the gun barrel to Thien's chest. "Now, y'all go ahead and put down your li'l ol' cap pistol, gook, afor'n I drill a forty-five-caliber hole through y'all's li'l V.C. gut."

Thien lowered his pistol.

"Tha's rahght, y'all. Good boah. Now drop that li'l ol' thing to the dirt, an' kick it away."

Thein did.

"Now, doan' y'all go home and tell no mamma-san wha'chu saw here. An' you go an' tell your li'l newspaper buddies to keep

---

this *all* away from their stories. Rahght?"

"Right," Thien whispered.

"Good boah. Now ah'm gonna back away while ah keep you in mah sight, yeah. You jes' stan rahght there where ah'm a-leavin' you."

Thien breathed unevenly as he stood his ground and watched the deep-southern farm boy back away into the darkness.

When he felt safe, he picked up his pistol and moved dejectedly toward Annie's tent. He found her trembling in Daniel's embrace, with her shoulders heaving as she cried and sniffled into his shirt. He then looked down in disgust at his pistol, wanting to throw it away for all the good it had done. "We're gonna crush those mother-fuckers," he muttered.

"Yes, Thien," Daniel said, as he continued stroking Annie's hair. "We are."

The question was how.

CHAPTER FORTY-NINE
Pinkville

Annie writhed sweating in Daniel's cot. Through the remains of the night she cried out in her sleep. "Get off me, you bastard son of a bitch!" "You fuckin' ape!" "I'll cut your fuckin' DICK off!" And "I'm gonna KILL you! I'm gonna fuckin' kill you ALL!"

Daniele never left her side, as he tried to soothe her by daubing her forehead with the warm stale water from his canteen. Thien offered to watch over her while Daniel got some well-needed sleep, but he wouldn't leave her. "Daniel, you didn't sleep last night. You really need to."

"No, Thien. I need to be with Annie. There'll be plenty of time to rest once we get back to Saigon."

"I hope so."

Daniel placed his hand on Thien's and offered a benign smile. "Maybe you could scrounge up a cup of coffee? Bad as it is."

"Sure," Thien said, then swung himself from his cot. He went toward the door and gazed at Annie sweating in her fitful sleep. He leaned over and stroked her cheek, offered up an understanding smile, then left and went to fire up the percolator on the little press desk in the Operations tent.

Daylight soon began to sift into the tent. Daniel sipped his coffee from s well-worn mug, as he watched Annie finally settle into a deep sleep. He glanced trough the open tent flap into the relentless morning sunlight. Today was going to be a hot one—weather-wise, at least. He heard the fifty men of Charlie Company readying to leave for their mission. Beyond the clink and rustle of their gear, they were eerily quiet. He reasoned that maybe their fear of dying in combat had finally overcome their bravado.

Thien sat on the other cot worrying over his boots. "Shit," he muttered as he broke a lace.

"What's wrong?"

He examined the broken strand of leather. "On top of everything else, you mean? There was a message for me over in the Ops tent. I've got to provide back up to a public information reporter and photographer they're sending up from battalion headquarters in Duc Pho. I guess this monster-ass so-called secret operation has extended beyond the camp, here."

Daniel smoothed out a wrinkle in the blanket covering Annie. "Man, I'm really sorry to hear that. Do us a favor and don't get shot, okay?"

"I've always been pretty good at avoiding the Viet Cong. So don't worry."

"I didn't mean by the V.C.," said Daniel. He took a brisk sip of his cold coffee. "Ugh," he frowned. "Sometimes this stuff actually does taste better cold."

"Come on with me. I want to introduce you to the pilot who's flying you you guys out of here."

Daniel glanced down at Annie as she puffed out little snores.

"Come on, Daniel-San. She'll be fine, now."

The sound of rotors firing up and whining to full was

thunderous as it reverberated through the ground like a San Francisco earth tremor. The troops, armed twice to normal, milled around eight ominous-looking black assault choppers as Lieutenant Calley and Captain Medina herded and organized them to load onto the helicopters. The two officers moved through the troops separately as they ignored one another.

Daniel coughed away some rising dust as Thien introduced him to Nguyễn-Moy, the pilot of the light observation helicopter that would fly him and Annie to Saigon. The little Loach Looked kind of cute among all the big, bad war-choppers.

"You're not coming along, Tin-man?" Nguyễn asked.

"No. I was tagged to back up some reporters for *Stars and Stripes* who are covering this."

"Shit. This mission is gonna be that important? I thought it was just a search and destroy kinda thing." Thien shrugged his shoulders, as Nguyễn turned to Daniel. "So. You're from *The L.A. Tribune?*"

"That we are."

"Ah. Real-world big-time stuff."

"To some, I guess. Me, I just wanna get the fuck outta here."

Nguyễn gave an easy grin. "You and me both, chief. You and me both."

A nearby assault chopper feathered down its engines a little, and Daniel was able to decipher The Doors' "Break on Through" coming from a sound system within its hold.

"War, drugs, and Rock 'n' Roll," said Nguyễn.

"None other," Daniel agreed.

"Yo, Tin-man! You're with us," said a passing pilot on the way to another Loach with a shark-grin painted on its nose.

Thein clasped Daniel's bicep. "My ride. I gotta go." He turned to follow the pilot.

"Don't get shot, buddy!" Daniel reminded him.

"I hear you!" Thein called back with a half-hearted wave.

"Tin-man's a good guy," Nguyễn said. "He's becoming sort of a legend among us. Even though he reports for that dip-shit goodie-two-shoes rag of his."

Daniel felt the hard, deliberate brush of a shoulder against his arm and glanced over to see Crocker leering at him, singling him out. He said nothing but pointed an accusing finger at him like a gun. He turned the back of his fist, raised his middle finger, and then slogged toward his helicopter. Sawyer followed close behind his knight like some sort of squire. He scowled at the ground, refusing to look at Daniel. A huge bandage covered his left cheek. Sawyer's reaction—or lack of it—was more unsettling than Crocker's.

"Friends of yours?" Nguyễn asked.

"No." Daniel looked up while some assault choppers gathered up massive clouds of dust as they lifted from the ground to circle overhead then arc forward toward the east to join the others. Daniel had heard that their destination was a placid rice paddy one hundred and fifty meters east of My Lai 4. "Just get us away from here, Nguyễn."

"I'm right the fuck with you, chief."

When he got back to Annie's tent, Daniel found her fully awake, as a sullen version of her usual self. "How're you feeling, Annie?"

She lifted her gaze from her bare feet to him. "I'm not going back to Saigon," she announced. "Not yet."

"You sure you're up for staying? After last ni—"

"God-damnit, Lilienthal! I'm *fine*! We're gonna follow through on this. We're here to do a job. Right?" Daniel said nothing. "*Right, Dan?*" She slipped on a ragged pair of thick socks, then eased her feet into her boots.

Daniel realized she had a point, but the fiery look in her eyes telegraphed revenge. He knew she wasn't ready to follow Charlie Company into their mission, but he let it slide. "Right."

She stood briskly, took her sidearm from its holster and jammed in a clip.

"But you remember we were told by that idiot lieutenant not to follow these guys off the base."

"Unh-hunh," she said. "Which is exactly why we need to." She stood and wriggled her arms through the straps of her rucksack. "If they've got something to hide about this thing, we need to fucking cover it." She pulled her holster belt tight around her waist and jammed in her Colt .45. "Okay." She smiled menacingly at him with a cock-eyed grin. "Ready to go, now?"

The assault choppers had all left by the time Daniel and Annie found Nguyễn oiling the engine of his Loach. Annie's mind was focused on whatever dark thoughts she had as she coolly introduced herself to him. They tossed their stuff into the little four-seat cabin, and Daniel crammed himself with all their gear in the backseat as Annie took her place in the co-pilot's seat next to Nguyễn and buckled in. He wasted no time taking off.

"Where's the action, today?" Annie shouted over the soft whine of the rotors trembling the cockpit.

"A little east," Nguyễn called back. "Place called My Lai, I think."

"Take us there."

"*What?*" Nguyễn said. "That's nuts, Anne. I'm not flying my little bird into that shit!"

Annie hated to be called "Anne." It reminded her of her parents. "Just take us to My Lai, Nguyễn."

He looked over his shoulder at Daniel. "You sure you guys wanna do this?"

"If that's what she wants!" Daniel said back.

"Damn! Okay. But listen. I'll drop you close, but after that, I'm landing my 'copter far enough away to not get my ass shot off. This baby's acting up too much to be taking fire from the V.C.!" He fumbled around between the seats and handed Annie a communication handset. "When you're ready for me to lift you out of there, call me on this. Channel's already been set up. I'll be no more than five minutes away, eating my three-day-old tuna sandwich for lunch."

"You're a sweetheart, Nguyễn!"

"You mean that, honey?"

"I do!"

"Well, then, let's go!" He banked the Loach around to the east then lowered the nose to pick up speed.

Around a half-hour later, a little after 8:a.m., they approached My Lai from the south, at about one-thousand feet—close enough to see what was going on. Nguyễn's Loach was only another helicopter in the buzz flying over the attack already fully underway. Huey gunships strafing the hamlet circled below them. There, and in the lush paddies around it, the black-clad Vietnamese inhabitants were scurrying everywhere to avoid the gunfire from the sky. Some stood in position and held up their American-issued badges meant to identify them as noncombatant farmers. Annie cringed as she saw one of them shot down where he stood. Another, resolutely holding up his badge, was gunned down in cold blood by a Charlie Company soldier, who then marched forward to shoot an old woman running to escape.

Tears dampened Annie's cheeks. "Jesus wept! Those fucking *animals!*"

Another elderly farmer numbly continued harvesting some crops as though none of this was happening. He collapsed from a shot directly in the head. Daniel leaned forward through the open door of the cockpit and started snapping pictures through a long lens.

Annie pointed to a thick clump of trees next to a knoll about a kilometer ahead. "Set us down there, Nguyễn. Up ahead near those trees."

Nguyễn throttled back and flew lower to ready for a landing. Daniel recognized Lieutenant Calley, who, having rounded up some villagers, seemed to be berating a soldier holding his M-16 loosely pointed toward the ground. Daniel spied Captain Medina circling throughout the carnage in the nearby distance, brandishing his .45. He cringed as Medina casually raised his pistol and shot an old farmer in the head. The force of the shot sent his *non-lo* flittering ten feet away. Medina then swiveled around, shot a young boy in the chest, then calmly walked on.

Annie stared in disbelief. "Holeee fuckin' *shit*. Holeee fuckin' God-damn *SHIT!*" She wiped more tears from her cheek. "Those fucking sons of bitches!"

"Set us down *now*, man!" Daniel barked. "*Now!*"

Nguyễn circled the Loach, then throttled back to pitch up for a landing. It hovered about two feet above the ground as Annie slid from the cockpit.

Daniel had critically damaged his Nikon when he'd hit Sawyer with it and was using his own Pentaxes. They weren't as automatic as the Nikons. He had some trouble getting into position, since he had to gather his gadget bag of lenses. He slung his two cameras around his neck, then pushed the passenger seat forward to jump. As soon as he hit the ground, he ran in a hunker toward some trees, while he held one of the cameras poised to shoot. Annie waved off the Loach. Nguyễn waved back, then swiveled the helicopter away and high-tailed it back in the direction they'd come.

By the time Annie reached him, Daniel had found a spot between a couple of bushes from where to take his pictures. He took a bead on Calley, and focused. The lieutenant was still yelling at the private who had apparently disobeyed his order. He stood looking down at the dirt with his rifle leaning against his side, as Calley was red-faced in anger. Daniel steadied his camera.

Saddack-thwip, Saddack-thwip.

The lieutenant puffed out his cheeks like an angry blowfish.

Saddack-thwip.

He raised his pistol toward the group of old men, children, and women he had rounded up. Two of the women, their cheeks soaked in tears, pleaded for their lives.

Saddack-thwip.

Calley calmly raised his gun and shot the women dead.

Saddack-thwip, Saddack-thwip

The camera in Daniel's mind seemed to take control, telling him: *"I've got this."*

Calley then fired again into the group.

Saddack-thwip, Saddack-thwip

The taller old men fell first upon the children as though to shield them. Calley fired his repeatedly into the human pile…

Saddack-thwip, Saddack-thwip

…until he reckoned they were all dead. He then slipped another clip into the butt of his gun and fired at the pile of the dead again, to make sure.

Saddack-thwip, Saddack-thwip

Daniel raised his second camer with its long lens to get a close up of Calley. His face was expressionless—he'd done a job and was ready for the next one. But the truth showed in his eyes, open wide to show the white around his pupils, revealing a deranged obsession for more.

Saddack-thwip.

Several feet, away, the reluctant private stood in awe of what he'd just seen his company lieutenant do. Calley turned to him. His normally cherubic face bloomed into a benign smile. He said something to the private—probably something like: "See, boy? That was easy."

Now in his own sort of trance, the private slowly raised his M-16 and turned. He fired at an old woman running erratically away.

Saddack-thwip.

She fell to the ground, blood oozed into the dirt from beneath her displaced straw *non-la*. The close-up view of the young soldier revealed a glisten of tears on his cheeks.

Saddack-thwip.

Daniel turned to see Annie scribbling in her notebook. Her shoulders heaved as she sobbed uncontrollably through her writing.

Saddack-thwip.

He looked over his shoulder to another knoll about a quarter of a kilometer away. It was dense in elephant grass and overlooked a ditch and a dirt road. It seemed closer to the activity in the village. "Hey," he whispered.

She looked up at him. "Yeah," she croaked.

"I'm going over to that knoll, there. I think I can get some closer shots."

"Yeah. Go. I'm staying here." She looked back down at her notes.

"Annie?" She said nothing. "Hey! Farrell!"

She looked up at him and wiped her cheeks. "Yeah?"

"We're gonna get through this, okay? We'll never forget what's happening here. But we've got to get through this. We gotta do our job and get this story out. Fuck these guys! Fuck all of them!"

She fluttered a sad smile and went back to her notes.

Daniel rushed in a zig-zagging crouch through the rough elephant grass to the spot he'd chosen as his photographer's roost. He itched from perspiration that had seeped into the grass cuts on his arms and cheeks. He took up a position behind a rough hedgerow overlooking a clearing in the hamlet. He screwed a 135-mm lens onto his Pentax and began shooting some pictures of the burning straw hooches below. The dead villagers had been left where they lay. He counted at least thirty bodies, including the ten taken down by Calley, who was now at the edge of the village, encouraging his men to kill more "slopes, gooks, and Cong." More peasants collapsed to the street. Someone had set up a boom-box to blare out "Helter-Skelter," like a soundtrack.

In the middle of it all, he spied Crocker, open-shirted with his ear-necklace fluttering against the blood and perspiration glistening his chest. He stared down an old man's body as he slid his Bowie knife from its sheath. He then casually stooped down and began to carve the old man's ears from his head.

Saddack-thwip.

Daniel's camera lens must have glinted in the sun because Crocker glanced up toward where he was hiding. He looked around, then back down at the bloody ear in his hand. Daniel reminded himself to aim his lens lower and away from the sun next time.

From the road, Daniel heard a rebel yell, then two pops from an M-16. And then a third. He saw that Sawyer chasing two teenaged girls running away toward the far end of a roadside ditch stacked with bodies. He fired once and took down one of them down. He let out another rebel yell, again, twice. He fired again at the second girl as she limped ahead. She finally fell backward into the dust.

Daniel had to look away. He had seen enough in the 45 minutes since they had arrived, and he knew that through the level of their frenzy Charlie Company was not yet finished.

Time had become meaningless. He huddled away from the carnage, wishing he could sleep so he could wake from this horrible nightmare. He was brought back into the moment by crackling sounds and the stinging smell of smoke. The men were torching the village using their Zippos and a backpack-mounted flame thrower to smoke out whoever might be left in the hooches. Villagers escaped from the spider holes in their burning homes only to be murdered as they ran. Mothers carrying their children were shot dead. For the most part, the very young children had been spared, because they weren't old enough to be Viet Cong like their parents and grandparents.

Daniel lifted his gaze away and toward the road. Sawyer was nowhere in sight. He aimed his camera at the ditch piled with bodies.

Saddack-Thwip.

"This can't be fucking happening," Daniel whispered to himself, like a mantra to the cadence of his picture-taking.

Saddack-Thwip.

"This can't be happening."

Saddack-Thwip. Saddack-Thwip.

"This *can't* be fucking happening!"

Saddack-Thwip.

"This isn't happening!"

Saddack-Thwip.

"This is *not* fucking happening!"

Saddack....

Then he smelled gunfire cordite and felt the barrel of a rifle moving over the contours of his shoulder until the heated tip of its muzzle rested firmly near his cheek.

"What the *fuck* are you doin' here, Lilienthal?"

He froze as he recognized the long Texas drawl. He breathed in the ugly scents of combat: ammonia, gunoil, moist sod, and the blood, piss and shit of the dead, along with the smell of his own vomit on his boots. "My job," he said. "Taking pictures."

"Well then, me, too…following orders. Stay still, asshole."

Daniel heard the rifle's bolt being snapped into its chamber. He knew this was going to be it for him—the end of his life. What he'd witnessed here in this hell had been enough for a lifetime, anyway. He was ready to go, but not to leave Johanna. He felt the barrel dig into his cheek. Sawyer was going to torture him by not killing him right away, to let him think—to allow' his reminiscences haunt him.

Then: "Say your fucking prayers, dickhead."

"Hey, there, big boy. Miss me?" Annie's voice was breathy, seductive, and close. Daniel sighed with relief as the rifle muzzle eased away from his cheek.

"Jesus! Fuck shit!" Sawyer rasped.

Daniel turned to see Annie standing behind Sawyer with her hair tumbled free and her combat shirt unbuttoned to her navel. Her look might have been a wanton, come-on kind of look if there hadn't been so much hatred lurking behind it. "I think you left my tent too soon last night. I was just gettin' started." She gritted her teeth behind her hard smile and reached out to run her left hand down Sawyer's cheek, as she held her right hand casually behind her back.

Sawyer relaxed into the moment, not believing his luck. "Really, bitch? *Now?*"

Annie cringed. "Oh, yeah," she breathed. "I *love* it when guys trash-talk me like that, especially in combat. I can't wait any longer. I'm throbbing down there."

"Really?" He eased his M-16 to the ground and moved his hands down toward his fly. "Okay, cunt…let's you and me head off into them trees over there. It's been a whole half-hour since Big Mike n' me had us some poontang, and that w'aint none too lively."

"Sure, big guy," Annie said. She clenched her jaw, then produced her right hand holding her .45 pistol. She shot his knee-cap.

"You fuckin' CUNT!" he shouted as he reached to grab his knee as he fell into the grass.

"Oh. *Yeah!* I just *love* that fuckin' trash talk!" She shot him in the foot. "Keep it coming," she sneered. "It's so fuckin' *sexy* coming from a big boy like you."

"BITCH!"

"Oh YEAH!" She shot him in his right arm.

"Jesus, Annie. That's enough!" Daniel shouted. "You made your point."

"Really, Dan?" Her angry gaze was locked upon Sawyer's squirming body. His skin had turned so red that the welts on his face blanched white. "I don't think I have." She leveled the barrel of her pistol toward Sawyer's groin.

"Farrell! Don't do it!" Daniel cried. "Don't fuckin' DO it!"

Annie's glower into Sawyer's twitching eyes turned into a wicked smile. "Oh, I think I will. So long, Big Fuckin' Mike."

BANG!

The bullet hit his inner thigh and probably grazed scrotum. A bloom of blood seeped slow as lava from his groin through his trousers. Sawyer shivered in too much shock to cry out.

She turned to Daniel and relaxed her smile. "There," she said. "I feel better now. Don't you feel better, Dan?"

All Daniel could feel was a sympathy pain in his own groin. "Fuck, almighty, Farrell! Do you know what the fuck you just *did*?"

She glanced back down at Sawyer and thought a little. "Yeah." She slid her pistol into its holster. "He'll live." She then picked the handset from her belt and called Nguyễn to get them the hell out.

His voice squawked thin over the little speaker. "Thank freakin' Buddha! I'll be there in five."

They were safely away now. The smoke rising from My Lai 4 was still visible two miles back to the east, and three-thousand feet below as the Loach chuddered south-southwest toward Saigon.

Daniel huddled silently in the backseat and stared out at the tops of the broadleaf trees flickering by. He couldn't look at Annie, at least not yet, as she gazed calm and expressionless ahead. Vindicated.

He reconstructed what he'd seen that morning, trying to filter the facts from his imagination. The worst of it simmered to the surface of reality and it was horrible. He caught a glimpse of Landing Zone Dotti streaming below. It seemed ominous and empty, with one lone Huey on the tarmac being serviced by a small repair crew. The rest of its swamp-life was still about eight kilometers east and most likely burning, killing, raping, and gouging out ears of the dead for trophies. Daniel felt a chunky scratch of bile surge up his throat. He swallowed it away.

Annie finally broke the ice of the silence. "We have to report this," she said as she remained staring ahead.

"Report *what?*" Daniel asked sarcastically, trying to decide if her sin was any worse than those committed on the now barren and bloodied dirt roads of My Lai.

"What we saw this morning." Her voice was dried out.

"Yeah," Daniel replied. He huddled up against the sacks of their gear as though he might try to doze it all away. He wondered if she'd already blocked out what she had done just a half-hour earlier. *Well,* Daniel reasoned, *she did save my life—So there was that.* And what she did to Sawyer could be almost forgiven because Annie often took situations to extremes, and because of the despicable thing Sawyer had done to her the night before.

She looked back over her shoulder. "No, Dan. I mean it. What happened there. It has to be told."

"It's what this war has always fuckin' been behind the scenes, Farrell. They just don't want us to know about it."

"Which is exactly why we have to report it. It's our duty."

"Duty to who?" Daniel asked. He really didn't know anymore.

CHAPTER FIFTY
Hard choices

Annie knew she could never shed the remembrance of what she had witnessed in My Lai 4, but the story had to be told. She'd spent the past few days trying to ease back into her routine in Saigon, but remained emotionally drained. She'd taken three showers today to try to wash away the residue of horrors in her mind.

She looked out at the busy riverfront from the roof of the Majestic Hotel and breathed in the familiar scents of Saigon. She concentrated on the glitters of dusk-light on the wavelets, barely disturbed by the silent passage of junks and fishing boats churning home to their docks. The elixir of smell, sight, and sound; the reminders of her adopted reality, soothed her.

Tony, breathing shallow and heavy due to his partial left lung, ambled over from the bar and set his cocktail on the glass table. The hollow ring of glass-on-glass jarred her back to the moment, as he struggled to ease himself into the chair next to her with the help of his cane. She reached over, squeezed his hand, and smiled briefly as she felt his kiss on her forehead.

"You're feeling a little better, Annie?" Tony asked.

A sullen smile. "A little."

Thien spoke up from across the table. "Jay Roberts submitted his coverage to *Stars and Stripes* yesterday. He hated having to tone it down for them."

"They took it?" Tony asked.

"Yeah," Thien answered. "To give to their editors to sanitize."

"Figures," Annie said.

"They slanted it in true Mac-Vee tradition: *In their mission to clean up Pinkville, the heroic boys of Company C swept in and wiped out a nest of Viet Cong. Almost a hundred V.C. killed.*" He sipped his tea.

"Rah-rah, America," Tony said. "Making Vietnam safe from its own monster."

"There were far more than a hundred killed," Annie said.

"I heard more like *three* hundred," said Thein. "Maybe there were a hundred children."

Daniel found their table and pulled up a chair for himself.

"Nice of you to show up, buddy," Tony said.

"I was souping out some prints. I thought I was gonna puke after a while. My photos told me far more than I wanted to fuckin' remember."

In what had become her mantra over the last forty-eight hours, Annie again said: "We gotta let this thing out. Just gotta." She took another sip of her tea and cringed as she gazed disdainfully into her cup.

"Sure," Thien said. "Through your *Tribune*. At least they're more open to this sort of commentary."

"Hardly," Tony said. "Once Johnson dropped out last month, the *Trib* decided to endorse Nixon, which is like endorsing the war."

"Not that the *Trib* ever backed Johnson to begin with," Annie said. "They even tried to convince Reagan to run."

"Really?" Daniel said. "I never knew that."

Annie flinched a smile at him. "That's because you still don't do your research, Dan."

"You should do that more often, hon," Tony said.

"What?" she said, turning her smile toward him. "Research? I do it all the time."

"Smile. You look good in one."

Her expression fell into a brief sulk. "Yeah, right, Russo." She mussed his hair. "Such a fuckin' romantic."

"So, Annie," said Thien. "How are you going to get your story out?"

"First, it's gotta be written. Then, If the *Trib* doesn't want it, we shop it."

"I'll write it," said Daniel. "I'm ready to, now."

Annie contemplated her cold tea. "No *you* won't write it, Dan. *We* will. Thien? You were there. You in on this with us?"

Thien's drew his lips up into a benign smile as he shook his head. "No, sweet flower. I can't. Not if I want to keep the only job I have with Public Affairs. You three have choices. I don't"

"Not me," Tony said. "I may not hold with all that Nixon is about, but I'm married to the *Trib*. So I choose to play the poltroon on this one and keep my name out of it." He looked over at Daniel. "Aren't you guys taking a job-risk, here?"

Annie's eyes glistened over the decision she'd been struggling to reach. "To me, this story is more important than being a typewriter jockey for *The Los Angeles Tribune*."

"Hey!" Tony complained. "That's *my* typewriter-jockey job you're taking about!"

"And I need my bread-winner to pay our apartment rent." She gave him a kiss on his cheek.

"You two are moving in together?" Daniel asked.

Annie nodded. "I'm tired of the jungle life. At least for now. Tony's had his eye on a flat on Phan Thanh Gian overlooking the channel."

"Near the zoo?" Thien asked.

"No worse than the zoos we've been slogging around in the up-country," Annie remarked.

"I put a deposit down on it last week, when you guys were—last week." Tony said as he halted his instinctive reach for one of Daniel's Marlboros. Daniel wondered how Tony would react to Annie's probably shooting off Sawyer's balls—an incident she seemed to have already expunged from her memory. Tony slid the cigarette pack more toward Daniel and put his hand over Annie's. "So, you have that fallback you were talking about, then?"

"What fallback?" Daniel asked.

She put her hand on Daniel's so that she, he and Tony were chained together in an show of friendship. "Dan, honey. I haven't told you this because I wasn't sure, myself until we got back two days ago. Dana has been trying to get me to become a free agent like him. He's already secured a paid post for A.P. I think now I have to do it."

"Shit, Farrell—"

"Just hear me out, okay? You fly out in a few days for San Francisco. I want you to stop off to see Larry in New York and pitch him the My Lai piece we'll write tomorrow. Show him your photos. The *Trib* won't wanna risk a story like that; and I have a strong feeling he'll reject it. But they do have the right of first refusal."

"What's this got to do with you going to the A.P.?"

"When Larry rejects it, I think it'll be a good time for you to call on your conscious. You can either say, 'Okay, Larry. I just thought I'd give it a try, and now you can put me on to my next gig.' Or 'Okay, Larry. I'm getting this story out there. You suck, fuck you, and I quit.'"

"Well, Farrell, that's kinda putting me on the middle of the fuckin' Bongo Board. Besides I'm going home to take care of Jo, and I'll probably need the *Trib's* health care. Why the hell would I wanna do a fool thing like quit?"

"You won't lose your benefits," she told him. "Because I'll be taking you on with me."

"You're *what*?" Daniel said incredulously. "You think I should be a post photographer for A.P.? No freakin' way!"

She squeezed his hand. "Where I go, you go, cowboy. And Sean and Dana like your stuff. You'd be an asset. I mean A.P. may pay for shit, but their hazardous pay benefits are great."

"Yeah, Tony scoffed, "That's why they call it 'hazardous'."

Her look deepened. She could tell Daniel's gears were churning over her suggestion. "Dan, hon. We gotta get this My Lai thing out before anyone else who wasn't there does."

Daniel lit a cigarette. "I don't know, Annie. First things first." He blew out a hefty swirl of smoke. "Why's Larry in New York, anyway? He hates New York."

"He's there for a Nixon fundraiser at the Waldorf Astoria, and for an audience with his highness, the Trickster himself," said Tony.

"Shit! I got to deliver our story-ultimatum at a fucking *Nixon* party?"

Annie sputtered a laugh. "Don't get yourself all twisted up over it, buckaroo. It's not like you're gonna have to get done up in a tux, though it might be cute to see you like that. All you gotta do is meet Larry in the bar at the Waldorf and hand him the story and your pictures."

"Or not," Tony said.

"Yeah. Or not," Daniel agreed. He glanced over at Thien who was taking the conversation. "You've been quiet through all this Tin-man. What's your take?"

He showed an easy smile. "My take? Well, Daniel, once you're back here working under a contract with Associated Press, you can move in with me at my place."

Thien had learned to read Daniel beneath the surface. But he also knew that Daniel needed to be with Johanna first, to sort it all out.

The Weight of Indifference
By Anne Farrell and Daniel Lilienthal, filed March 22, 1968

On March 16th— an endless week ago—we witnessed a more egregious assault against men, women, and children than we could have ever imagined. We'll forever be haunted by the memory of bodies of women and old men among those of children and infants piled haphazardly in a roadside ditch, while still others were left to die where they had been raped and mortally wounded. Most of the wounded were so badly violated they would likely be dead before nightfall, when and if any help might reach them. Women and children—many were too innocent to realize what was being done to them by the G.I.s of Charlie Company, U.S. Army Americal Division, led by Captain Ernest Medina and Lieutenant William Calley. Many of the boys of Company C were teenagers whisked up the mean streets and dirt farms of Forgotten America. They were new to war, and followed the orders from their two commanding officers to shoot to kill anyone who looked Vietnamese. North or South; it made no difference.

This was Charlie Company's first mission. They had been processed quickly though basic to provide more American troops for the war. They were insufficiently trained on how to conduct themselves in combat. Many of them were conditioned by Medina and Calley to hate the Vietnamese people as being sub-human in their own country. The men were sleep-deprived. Some had been kept awake by amphetamines and other drugs.

March 16, 1968—

My Lai 4 is a small hamlet on the central coast of Vietnam. It consists of six-hundred peasant-farmers whose family lines stretch back centuries deep, but no wider than the five-mile radius of their village. Most have never been farther out than Son My, a town less than a mile away, where they bartered their crops to feed their families.

It is almost eight a.m. on a Saturday morning. There's a kind of a festival atmosphere in the little hamlet as its inhabitants ready their buffalo-drawn carts for the traditional Saturday trip to Son My. There they will set up their stalls and tables to trade or sell their monthly produce of rice for fish and other staples. It is also a way for them to connect with neighbors and friends they haven't seen for a while. More important, it is a way to get away from the war raging around them, and the raids that have been stepped up the area dubbed "Pinkville" by the troops. The name refers to the military maps, which usually show the area in pink. In the past, there had been sniper fire at U.S. troops operating in the area.

The preparations to leave for Son My are interrupted by the thunderous, earth-shivering sound of army helicopter gunships swooping down from the vivid blue spring sky. The firing from three hundred feet above begins immediately, and lives are snuffed out in the town and its surrounding fields. And then, through the lush, green rice paddies, come the fifty soldiers of Charlie Company, firing their M-16 rifles point blank at anyone—young mothers; old mama and papa-sans and their children— many of them infants carried in their mothers' arms, or in papooses on their backs. Some of the victims are holding up their allied-issued identification badges as proof that they are friendlies. They shout out the only American words they know and are trained to use in situations like this: "No V.C.! No V.C.!" They are killed where they stand.

The troops are primed to believe that these folks eking out their simple lives are Nationalist Army Viet Cong, and that instead of stooping down to tend their crops, they must be planting mines. Blood and bodies are soon scattered in a swath through the fields leading toward the hamlet of My Lai 4. Charlie Company forges its way unopposed into the small plaza, where Lieutenant Calley has begun rounding up about ten old men, women, and children as they continue to cry out: "No V.C.! No V.C.!" At least one soldier resists Calley's order to kill them in cold blood. Angered by this disobedience of a direct order, Calley sets an example for the soldier by shooting his rounded-up victims execution-style. One by one. The children, protected by the bodies of their mothers, take longer to kill. He fires at them again.

Off in the distance, Captain Medina wanders, casually shooting civilians trying to flee as he directs his troops. The soldiers of Charlie Company, now obsessed by the spirit of their commanding officers, begin to kill more of My Lai's villagers. The attack is only fifteen minutes old, and already about thirty unarmed peasants lay dead. The carnage is to continue for another three hours.

August of 1965, CBS reporter Morley Safer dispatched a TV spot as he stood in front of a peasant's straw home in Cam Ne. A marine behind him calmly held his lit Zippo lighter to a perplexed old Vietnamese man's straw-thached home. Here, too, there had been rumors of Viet Cong activity. Here, too, the victims were women, children, and elderly men. The assault on Cam Ne yielded no Viet Cong, and no dead, only a burned-out village and a population of displaced peasants. 'This is what the war in Vietnam has become,' Safer said. For his comments, he was barred from following any more marine operations in Vietnam. What were we trying to hide in 1965? Now, perhaps, we know. This is what the Vietnam War has become—and perhaps has always been.

We thought we would win this war. We will never win. The Americans and their allies are sucking the culture out of Vietnam, which has always been a sensitive, often changeable one. But it has never been wiped out as we are now trying to do. As for the men of Charlie Company, Americal Division, they will claim that they were just following orders. The official story proclaims they are heroes for wiping out a nest of one-hundred or so

Viet Cong. The real story is that over three-hundred helpless civilians (by the most current count) were killed in cold blood. None of the peasants was armed; none was Viet Cong; none of military age; and none suspecting that three hours earlier that they would be dead—murdered—by noon."

Annie yawned and stretched out the fatigue she'd developed over the six hours it took her and Daniel to compose their dispatch for Larry Graham. "Well, Dan?"

He sipped his scotch. "Well, Annie?"

"I believe we have it."

"I believe we do."

"We make a good team."

"Yes, Farrell, I believe we do."

She glanced over the commentary once more. "Okay, honey. Let's roll with it." She stood up and stretched again, then leaned down to face him. "Hey," she said.

"Hey, what?"

"Shut up." She took his face in both her hands and drew him closer for a heartfelt kiss. He felt a quivering energy through her lips. "I'll miss you, cowboy. We'll *all* miss you." She mussed his hair. "I don't believe in saying goodbye," she said, then left his room for some much-needed rest.

He folded up the dispatch and placed it on top of the clothes in his duffel bag. He stared at the bag, remembering for the first time since September how Johanna had balked at its size and wealth of pockets when they picked it out at Abercrombie & Fitch.

CHAPTER FIFTY-ONE

Back in the U.S. of A.

t was dawn when the TWA flight touched down at Kennedy Airport. Daniel felt little more than the jolt of the wheels touching down on the runway. He had first started feeling detached when the 707 landed at Paris's Orly Airport for a three-hour layover before his midnight connection to New York. On the way to Paris, he'd decided not to call Johanna right away, and to consider himself still on assignment until he left New York. He wanted to get this thing with Larry done first.

He spent much of his brief stay in New York City camped in the tiny dispatch cubicle at *The L.A. Tribune*'s office down on West 12th Street. Phone communications with Annie and Tony were sketchy. He spent the balance of his time in the *Trib's* remote darkroom developing some of the photos he would show Larry.

He viewed the prints coalescing through the watery, safe-lit developer solution, still horrified over what had been depicted. Just before midnight, he'd head back to his Best Western hotel room on 14th Street, where he would crash on his squeaky bed for some fitful hours of sleep. His hotel room smelled of Lysol and air-conditioning turned too cold. He'd wake up confused by his surroundings six hours later in time for a dry shave and a chilly two-minute shower, followed by an institutional cup of coffee at a local Chock-Full-O'-Nuts. If he'd sniffed hard enough, he would have picked up the residue stink of the recently ended city-wide garbage strike. Still, a garbage strike was better than a mortar one.

After four days back in America he sat hunched over his Scotch in a heavy dark-oak booth in Waldorf Astoria's Bull and Bear Bar. The feeling of being a stranger in a strange land dug deep into his core. The place seemed sanctified by some delusion of normalcy; a lie away from the fragile world he'd inhabited for the last six months. This place was just wrong.

Larry sat across from him, uncomfortable in the three-piece suit he had to wear. Back home he would be dressed in the required and prefered uniform of Los Angeles: lightly stained sport-shirt, chinos, and sock-less Weejuns. He had loosened his Republican-red tie down to the second button of his shirt, which was already flecked with pasta sauce from lunch.

Daniel and Annie's article had been with him for two days. There had been plenty of time for it to fully fester in his mind. He concentrated on re-reading the last paragraph. Daniel sensed it was a ploy to ease the tension.

"I just had lunch with Nixon's front guys," he said to the pages. "It was Italian.".

"I can tell, Larry. You're wearing it."

Larry peered up at Daniel. "Hunh?"

"You've got a tomato-sauce stain right—" Daniel pointed to his own breast pocket.

Larry laid Daniel's article aside and strained to look down. "Oh, shit. I can't take me anywhere." He tried daubing it with a wet napkin, which only made it worse. "I can just see sitting at that fucking fundraiser tonight with a goddam pasta-sauce blot on my tit pocket."

Daniel tried on a smile. "I don't think Nixon will notice."

"I don't know. There's not much that slips by ol' Dick Nixon. I think he's got another set of eyes in his ears." He let the stain be. He looked back up at Daniel. "I read your thing, here."

"That's why I gave it to you." Daniel said as he braced himself. "What did you think?"

Larry often played dumb while he framed his answers. Daniel reasoned it was his way of putting the questioner on the defensive. "About what?"

"About Annie's and my article? About our account of what happened in My Lai?"

"It stank. Don't get me wrong, kid. The piece is really good, but what you say happened there stank."

"It more than stank, Larry. It was a fucking tragedy. A total fuck-up of all the hearts and minds shit we went over there to do."

Larry pushed the article aside. "We can't run it," he said blankly.

"You want proof, Larry? I brought some of my photos along." He pushed the thick manila envelope he'd been holding at his side across the table.

Larry blanched at the realization of what he might be viewing. He re-lit his cigar and opened the envelope. He thumbed through the photos slowly at first, then nervously quickened his pace. They depicted groups of My Lai villagers being rounded up; Lieutenant Calley aiming his .45 service revolver; shooting a woman crying as she desperately tried to protect her child; an old papa-san being shot execution-style; a young G.I. shooting a pre-teen child in the back the child was trying to run away; burning hooches with their inhabitants tied up in front of them; bodies in a ditch—many of them children; Corporal Crocker cutting an ear from a corpse...

He laid the pictures face down before him. "This is what you saw happening?" His voice had weakened to a hoarse croak.

"I didn't stage them, Larry.

"This is fucking hideous! Horrible!"

"Newsworthy. It has to be told," Daniel insisted as he stared down at the pile of overturned photos. A flash of red out in the hallway caught his eye. A banner: *"Richard Nixon for President 1968!"* And underneath in big, black block-face type: *"Nixon's The One!"* A husky workman was on a ladder positioning groupings of red balloons. Daniel thought back on his time in Saigon and how it was a different surreality than this one. He longed to finally be back in San Francisco, holding Johanna close and making sense of it all through her warmth against his.

Two Republican Party revelers in straw boater hats emblazoned with *"Nixon's The One!"* on their paper hatbands stopped by to stand over Larry to ply his concentration away. They were weaving in place, already plastered by three in the afternoon. Larry winced as one of them slapped him on the back. "Hey, Larry! Big night tonight!"

"Yeah," Larry said. Normally, he'd try his best to assimilate with goons like these. His tone sounded sheepish; out of place even for his often-rudimentary social graces.

"Dick Nixon checked in an hour ago. He's here!" The other said. Daniel felt a numb wave of chill that Nixon was in the same building.

Larry smiled. "Bully. Hey guys, I'll check in with you later, okay?"

One of them pointed at Larry and gave an exaggerated wink. Larry returned the gesture. The other glanced down at the one up-turned photo. By itself the subect looked innocuous enough. It depicted the cluster of confused villagers just before Calley would execute them. "Must a been one helluva party," he said. They then moved to a distant booth to join some other drunk Nixon fans.

"What do you intend I should do with these, Dan?"

"Pick out a few and run them with the story."

"God-damnit, kid!" he exploded. Some patrons looked up. "The *Trib's* a respectable paper, not a *Police Gazette* gossip rag like some sort of penny dreadful!"

Daniel relaxed at Larry's expected response. "Okay, Larry."

"What the fuck do you mean, 'Okay'. You should have known we wouldn't run gruesome shit like this. And your story? Where's your back-up? Your sources?"

"Annie Farrell. She was right there with me. You can see she helped write the story. Wrote it, actually. And of course the photos."

"Farrell works for us, and she can be hot-headed about this fucking war. We haven't heard anything else from Saigon that—*this*—happened. Only a report that our guys wiped out a nest of Viet Cong in My Lai. It was a notorious hotspot for our troops over there. It was a victory, for Christ's sake. And that's what we reported."

"And you, Larry Graham, believed it," Daniel replied, unaware that he and Larry shared the same basic convictions about the war. Larry said nothing as he seemed to quiver, buffaloed in place by his photographer. "Aren't my photos proof enough for you?"

Larry heaved a sigh. "I still can't run this in the *Trib*."

"Can't, or won't?"

"Frankly, Dan? Both," he said, after some thought. "Look, kid. I know it'll be hard for you, but why don't you try to forget this happened?"

"Forget?" Daniel grabbed the stack of photos and the envelope. "No, Larry. There's no way I can forget this."

"It's best for you, and for the *Trib*. Tell you what. What if I promoted you to Photo Editor?"

Daniel knew this was a ridiculous suggestion, a ruse, even, but Larry had to offer something. He tightened his lips. "Photo Editor."

"Yeah, why not? There's a 30 percent salary kick in it for you."

"Culling out other photographer's stuff for the Sunday Supplement and the Fashion editions? I don't think so, Larry. My place is back in Saigon—in the thick of it—not editing out photos of celebrities, cute puppies, and this year's purses. You know me better than that."

"I just thought I'd try."

"Nice try. But no thanks."

Larry seared a look at him. "You know, I gotta tell you, you can't take this story anywhere else."

"I can't?"

"Not if you wanna keep your job."

"Oh, good. A threat."

"Not a threat."

Daniel slid the photos back into the envelope, then rose to leave. "Okay, then, Larry. I guess I'd better resign."

"Bullshit! You wanna risk Farrell's job, too?"

"She said to tell you she's got that covered. She wants this story out as much as I do."

"What? She's got an offer from another paper?"

Daniel summoned an innocent smile and shrugged his shoulders.

Larry shook his head. "What about Russo? I suppose he's in on this."

"Actually, no. He isn't. Tony likes it where he is."

"At least *one* of you three clowns has some sense left." He took a deep pull on his cigar, then huffed out a sigh. "Okay, Dan. You insist, so I accept your resignations. You and Farrell. You can leave the photos with me. You took them under the *Trib's* watch. We own them."

"I don't think so, Larry. I took them with my cameras using my film. I'll pay you back for the developer and paper. That stuff belonged to you guys."

Larry thoughtfully considered this. Daniel could only hope what might be running through his mind. Before anything, even the *Los Angeles Tribune*'s political leanings, he was a reporter. He might have been seeing something of himself in Daniel's conviction. "Look," he sighed. "Though you know we own any photos taken for the Trib, just forget the fucking protocol and hang on to your pictures. Annie's story, too, okay?" He flicked his hand toward the door. "Okay, kid. Go." Daniel nodded curtly and then gathered his stuff. "Hey, kid…Hey, Dan."

"Yeah, Larry."

"Now that you no longer work for us, can I tell you something off the record?"

"Sure. You know we'll always be friends."

Larry's smile tightened. "I hope you get this done. I really mean that."

"Thanks, Larry…and I really mean *that*."

"Okay. Noted." Larry looked out into the hallway. *Nixon's The One!* The drunks in the booth at the end had become more boisterous. *Rah, Rah, Dick Nixon!* Larry stared ruefully at Daniel.

Daniel recognized the look on his face. "What, Larry?"

He nodded toward the envelope tucked under Daniel's arm. "Don't give up this fight, kid. Remember. Despite all the bullshit, I wasn't wrong about you. You'll always be a photojournalist. You're a natural. And this story *has* to be told. Somehow."

"Somehow," Daniel said, flicked a nervous smile, then walked out toward the hall where the Dick Nixon sideshow had already begun.

As soon as he resigned from the *Los Angeles Tribune,* he left the Waldorf with his duffel bag to catch a cab to Kennedy and his seven-p.m. flight to San Francisco. There was a more important matter than his leaving his job waiting for him there.

PART SEVEN
Going Home

CHAPTER FIFTY-TWO
Homecoming

Johanna's body began to betray her long ago. The edges of her vision had darkened and blurred. Her breathing had become torturously tightened, and she'd wake from a fevered sleep gasping for air. At least the gasps dulled the hot, swirling metallic shots of pain, which would mercifully swell into numbness, only to attack again. She felt the frequent little volcanic eruptions of her lymph nodes spew their fatal warmth throughout her dried-out body. She knew it would all be over soon, but she refused to acknowledge that intuition. Especially not today.

She sat stiff in the couch like a schoolgirl wallflower who was not sure how to compose herself. She tried listening to the baritone flow of "Some Velvet Morning" from the stereo. She curled her fingers into her palms and examined her nails. They were chipped, dry and had yellowed beneath the polish. She'd had her visiting nurse paint them over in glossy pink, after helping her into a puffy blouse and loose-fitting jeans to help hide her frailty.

When Daniel had left, she'd weighed about a hundred and fifteen pounds. Now it had become a stuggle to maintain her weight at eighty-five. Her ankles and feet were swollen within her tightly bound, white-white Keds sneakers. Her eyes had sunken into her wrinkled complexion like darkened pools of shadows.

There were no longer any of her characteristic laugh lines, as though laughter was not permitted. The nurse had done what she could to moisturize her face. It was all about camouflage as Johanna had tried to turn back time to the way she looked six months ago before. Beneath the makeup, she had the appearance of someone forty years beyond her age. The laudanum the nurse had given her had helped, but she still felt lightheaded, and was afraid of collapsing if she stood.

Cancer had taken more than her life and looks. It had taken away her dignity. The doctors at the clinic poked and prodded a body that no longer belonged to her. Despite it all, she practiced a smile. And then another, which froze in place at the buzz of the doorbell and the muffled sound of the voice she had longed so deeply to hear: "Jo! I'm back. I'm home!" Her eyes ached as they swelled with tears, and it took all her effort just to stand to trundle like an old woman to the door.

"I'm coming, Daniel!" Her whisper was more like a croak. She cleared her dry throat and tried again. "I'm *coming*, hon!" That effort tightened her breathing into a dry cough. With a quivering hand, she grabbed the doorknob, maybe more for support than anything else. *No! Don't let the pain show! Not now!* She straightened herself and opened the door to the man she loved so much. She collapsed against him into a tight, but fragile embrace. He smelled of Ivory Soap. The material of his clothing felt rougher against her cheek than it should have. She hoped he had not seen how hideous she looked.

He too was trembling. "Oh, Jo…Jo! I missed you so much."

Her voice was muffled as she rested her head in the hollow of his shoulder. "Oh God! I missed you more." She sobbed, but there were no tears.

"Come on, hon. Let me get a look at you." He tried to push her back, but she held on more tightly to the lifeline he had become.

His tone was so much more tender than she had remembered. She burrowed into him, never wanting to let go. "No, let's just stand here like this." She delicately cleared her throat. "Let's just hold each other. Okay?"

"Okay, Jo, sure. But let's get out of this hallway first." They held their embrace like a close dance as he walked them into the apartment. "Come on now, Jo," he said. "This view of your pretty neck has lasted long enough."

She sighed her way from the embrace and stood trying to look at him, while trying to avoid his expression upon seeing her like this. She felt like running away. Then she saw how easily his smile rose, as he locked his view upon her.

"Beautiful as ever," he said.

"You mean it?" she said through another sob and a sniff. "Do you really mean it?" she gasped.

"Fuck, Jo. After all we've been through together? Why would I lie to you now? Of *course* I mean it. You're the most beautiful sight I've seen in six months."

She stepped away, held out her thin, trembling arms and stared at him. "I—I-uh. Think I've lost a little weight."

His smile broadened. "It looks good on you. I like your new hairstyle, too."

At that she blanched. "Uh-okay, Daniel. Thanks. I'm glad. Uh, do you want me to make you a drink or something? . I could—"

"No, hon. I'm fine. Actually, it's been a long flight. I could use a shower and a shave. Some kid kept kicking the back of my seat."

"Oh. Then you need a rest. Why don't you take a little nap, then, okay, hon? I had brand new sheets put on the bed."

"Jo. I didn't fly ten thousand miles to you just take a nap. No way. I just need to get my stuff out of the hall and clean up." Before he turned for the front door, he kissed the crown of her head. She feared he might sense how synthetic hair smelled.

He felt cleaner than he had in six months after taking a warm shower—the kind that steamed the mirrors. Johanna had the cabinets stocked with fresh new things; soap, toothpaste, and shaving cream—all the comforts of home. He stroked his patchy stubble, which had lately started to itch, then lathered his cheeks and luxuriated in a slow-motion shave with a fresh blade.

Dressed in a loose, button-down shirt hanging untucked over a pair of clean khaki shorts, he stepped barefoot out onto the balcony, grasping a blessed bottle of Lowenbrau. Johanna lounged in the wicker couch which overwhelmed her diminished frame. He tried not to notice how everything around her seemed just a size or two too big. He loved her for her attempts to make it all seem normal, when she probably wondered as he did: *Who's kidding who, here*? He kissed her cheek. It felt dry to his lips. He felt the feathery touch of her fingers upon his forearm.

"Umm," she said. "You found the beer."

"In the fridge, just where I left it six months ago."

"No, sweetie. I threw that out last October. These, I got for you last week."

He eased down next to her, trying not to disturb anything. "Thanks, Jo."

She nestled closer to him. He felt her cough reverberate through her entire body like a chopper shuddering through flak. "Shit, I missed you. I never worried you wouldn't be back, but I missed you so much, Daniel. That sounded bad. I did worry for you, but something told me, that you were too smart to get shot or…"

"Killed?"

"Yeah, I guess, hon. That, too."

He draped his arm around her shoulder and felt her shiver. "You cold? I could grab a blanket."

"No, sweetheart. I've got one here. Right here next to me."

He noticed it was a struggle for her to speak. "Let's just sit here okay, Jo? Just look out at the night and relax?" He stared out across the bay at the throbbing lights of Fisherman's Wharf. Even those weren't the same as he remembered. The night-lights of Saigon were more vibrant, yet simple. Here, the setting seemed more manufactured, like a tableau. Johanna's shallow breathing, registered through his own body. She leaned against him. Except for her being with him he felt more like a visitor here, and no longer a participant.

He pulled his gaze away from the bay toward the patio table where he saw a battered package the size of a shoebox. It could have come only from the war.

"What's in the box?"

"Oh, yeah," she said. "That came… That came for you yesterday, from the *Tribune*. It looked important."

"I'll open it later." She shivered again and nestled closer. "You sure you're not cold, Jo? Maybe we should go—"

"No. Let's just stay here. I love it out here. Looking out at the lights. Aren't they beautiful?"

Her tone sounded desperate, like the voice of someone trying to soak it all in for one last time. It reminded him of the dying men he had often tried to help in places like Khe Sanh and Con Thien, who had accepted death: *God! That mortar fire!*

They would mutter. *Those tracers! So beautiful, sooo beauti—*

"Stop it!" he croaked aloud.

She stirred against him. "Hunh? You okay?" He felt her tenuous touch on his cheek; her nimble fingertips feeling like the brush of a bird's wing.

"I'm fine, Jo. Fine." He took her fingers in his hand and kissed them.

"Did something happen over there to spook you? I've heard about that happening."

"I'm okay." He settled back with a sigh. He felt more in love with her than ever. "I'm more worried about you."

"I'm feeling okay, Dan." Her breathing tightened around her words. "I'm really okay."

"No, hon. You're putting up a good front, but I need to know."

"There's nothing to say. I'm feeling so much better." She sat up and took his face in her hands. "Look at me." Her smile was contorted in an attempt to look genuine. "See? Nothing to worry about."

He smiled back at her. "Your smile, Jo. It hides a truth." He stroked her cheek. "All you have to do is tell me how bad this really is. Don't try to hide it. It won't work."

She hauled in a deep, uneven, breath and sat away from him. She brought her hands to her hair and removed her wig to expose her bald skull. "It was the chemo. Daniel. It didn't take because the cancer had metastasized so badly."

"Oh, Johanna!" he cried as he buried his head into her chest. He felt her labored breathing and grasped the reality of it all. "God, I love you so much!" For a while, she said nothing while he held her as though she was his life.

"I'm so sorry…so sorry, Daniel."

"How bad is it?" he said into her shirt.

"The doctor said no more than six weeks. This time I believe him. I can feel…I can feel it."

He moved away and gazed at her trying to stay strong as her lower lip quivered. "You're more beautiful to me now than I ever thought you could be."

She tried on a smile. "You're just…… you're just saying that, Daniel. Always searching for just the right thing to tell me."

"No. Jo. I mean it. You are beautiful."

"Bald and all?"

"Oh, come on, Jo." He leaned forward and kissed her hard. Then he kissed the smooth baldness of her head. He pulled her close to him and rested his head against her chest. "I'll never leave you. Never."

"I'm so tired, Daniel," she whispered. "Mind if I go to bed, now?"

"Sure, Jo."

She made a painful effort to stand but fell back down into the couch. 'Shit. How embarr—embarrassing. Sorry, hon." She tried to stand again, but he rose first to help her to her feet. She shook her head and tightened her lips. "Dizzy." she breathed.

"Let me carry you, Jo."

She ran her knuckles lightly up and down his chest, as she gazed down at her feet. "I'm not an invalid, yet. I do this every night. I'll manage."

"Bullshit, Jo. No more," Daniel said as he lifted her body into his arms. He needn't have tried so hard— she was much lighter than he had imagined. Skin and bones lighter.

She looped her arms around his neck. "Oh…my hero." she kissed his cheek.

"No, Jo. You're my hero…heroine."

She let out a tenuous sigh, and she leaned her head against his neck.

He put her to bed, tucked her in, got a beer from the fridge, then went back out to the patio. He slumped into one of the four canvas-backed chairs around the table. The package from the *Tribune* caught his eye again and he dragged it toward him. It was from Thein. Inside, a letter rested on another box. He took out the letter and read:

3/26/68

Dear Daniel,

It's only been a day and we miss you already here. Anne is worried sick about your meeting with Larry Graham, and how he took to your article and photos. I am so proud of your commitment to the truth about what is happening in the field. As bad as My Lai was, we are now hearing about more isolated incidents, and that they aren't confined to Pinkville. You and Anne have done a major service by exposing all this shit.

I know you have your priorities now, though. Johanna comes before all else, and I pray for her. I also know how much you love her. Your photo of her shows a beautiful woman with a beautiful mind. I can tell.

He felt the trickle of a tear easing down his cheek.

I have a feeling you will not return here to stay, as Anne and Tony keep predicting you will. Love for another is a stronger bond than war. But, in case I am wrong (and I can be, as you know!) and you do return to stay, you have a place here at my apartment. As you already have a place in my heart.

Take care, brother.

War Sucks,

Thien

P.S. I've enclosed a little gift for you. Think of me if you can use it.

He lifted the smaller package and undid its rice-paper wrapping. It was a tin box containing a neatly prepared opium kit with three thick Hershey-bar sized kiefs. He fingered them lightly between his thumb and forefinger. He thought about Saigon.

He placed his elbows on the table and nestled the heels of his palms against his temples. He closed his fingers into tight fists, then began to pound them lightly against his head.

CHAPTER FIFTY-THREE

Honey from The Golden Triangle

The days seemed to scramble together into a weird sort of time salad, marked only by Daniel's carrying Johanna to bed. Each time he lifted her he could gauge the way her life was ebbing away. But her attempted smiles had brightened to that same innocent, wide-eyed child's one he remembered from the first time he met her. It was that smile that drew him to her since the beginning; the one he had kept tucked away in his memory while he was in-country — the memory-smile he drew out when he needed it most.

He was pricked by a pang of the inadequacy he had sensed in My Lai, and before, when he saw Jared'a body being heaved into the ambulance. Now, watching Johanna slip away bit by bit, he felt the same sort of uselessness. He hadn't the strength to tell himself that he couldn't control a life, or its fading away. With Johanna, as with Jared, it was another cost of love paid with tears. He leaned over her, as he sat on the edge of the bed while she slept fitfully, pursing her lips in her sleep like an infant. His helplessness could not aid hers. A kiss and a stroke of her cheek was all he could provide. Perhaps to her, it had seemed enough.

"Daniel!!" She woke screaming, grimacing and convulsing

---

tightly a few nights later. "Dan! I can't...!"

He bolted upright from where he had been lying next to her, sometimes drowsing, as he kept his nightly watch. "Shit! Jo! What?"

"I feel these hot pains. Like needles in me."

"Where?"

"Everywhere. Like every pore of my body.

He swung out of bed. "I'm calling an ambulance."

"No! Not that! Please. I'm not ready. Not yet."

Neither was he.

She heaved a deep sigh to compose herself. "No," she breathed, willing herself on. "Not ready yet...not ready."

"Okay, hon." He flicked on the light and could almost see her pain. Her skin was blanched white. He bit his lower lip in thought. "You sure you don't want me to call anyone?"

She grimaced that smile he loved and tried to hold it, then reached out, brushed his arm, and stared at him—just stared—trying to hold her smile, which soon fell. She licked her lips, lacking the strength to do anything but lie still. "I think......I need a glass of water. Can you......get me a glass of water, hon? And some pills? Two......laudanum pills? In the bottle on the sink," she breathed laboriously and closed her eyes. "Two laudanum...please?"

He'd come to realize that the doses of laudanum were now no more than a placebo. He would try again to talk to the nurse about it, but expected her usual reply: *"I know. I see her in pain, but this is the highest dose we can give without getting hospice involved."* Tomorrow he would tell her to get hospice involved—anything to ease Johanna's pain. But, like her...he wasn't ready, yet.

"I am sorry, hon...." she said. "I prayed that you would never see me this way. This must be like a night--nightmare for you."

He kissed her lightly on her hand. Even its trembling had withered away. "No, Jo, no. Every time I'm with you is like a dream."

"Dream on, then, . Dream…on." Her voice faltered.

"There's something else, too. And this really means something to me. I've seen a lot of shit over there. Bad shit. And, I've seen a lot of bravery and heroism. Real bravery. The kind I never thought I'd see anywhere else. Until now. Until you." He cleared his throat. "Jo, you are the bravest person I've ever known." He glanced over toward the dresser, where he'd hidden Thien's opium kit wrapped in a pair of boxer shorts. He knew the laudanum was really a mild dose of opium, but it was far less potent than the stuff Thien had sent. "I think I might have something better than your pills to ease your pain."

He padded over to the dresser, opened the top drawer, and lifted out the bulky pair of boxers. Religiously, as though preparing a Communion Host, he liquified a small chunk of a kief with his Zippo and dripped it over another piece packed in the bowl of the ornate little pipe to soften it. He drew on the pipe stem to get it started, and felt its sweet warmth roll down his throat.

He brought the smoking pipe over to Johanna, who now lay shivering though waves of pain. "Here, Jo. Try to sit up, okay?" He carefully placed his free hand on the small of her back and drew her close to him. He held the pipe to her dry lips. "Here. Take a little inhale." She did. "Woah…gently, gently. Let it work on your pain."

He soon felt the tension ease from her body as she went limp. "Oh… that is goood," she whispered. Though her voice was drenched in fatigue, her speech had returned to a lazy semblance of normal. She drew in some more from the pipe. "Wow, Daniel…my pain is going away… awaay. What *is* this?"

Daniel offered up a paternal smile. "It's a gift from a dear friend—something you can't get here. It's called 'Honey from the Golden Triangle'."

"Honey from the Golden Triangle," she repeated dreamily and then fell into a deep sleep. Daniel stared at her as he took another puff for himself. He then gently positioned her head back into the thickness of the pillows.

CHAPTER FIFTY-FOUR
Permission to pass

The high bright light through the kitchen window indicated that it was probably around noon as Daniel braced himself over the sink and stared at the water flowing from the spigot. He realized that Johanna's time had just about worn down. The cancer had reduced her voice to a croaky whisper, sometimes just gasping for air in the form of soundless words. There was so much they needed to tell one another, but no time left to say it. He turned off the faucet then carried his cold coffee to the kitchen table and sat. He traced the flow of the grains of its wood while trying to empty his thoughts somewhere— anywhere—else.

Johanna hadn't been the only setback in the last three-and-a-half weeks. He had heard from the *San Francisco Chronicle*. Though they were interested in his My Lai piece, they couldn't run it without the back-up of a corroborating witnesses. They called his story "Your account of the incident in Vietnam," reducing it to mere hyperbole. *Rolling Stone*, a San Francisco-based indie which had just started publishing a month before to big national numbers, seemed very interested. In a personal call from Jan Wenner, *Rolling Stone*'s upstart publisher, he said that it was a "dynamite fucking piece," but they were committed only to covering the music scene. A.P., U.P.I., and Reuter's all wrote to say the story might have gone too stale for their brand of breaking news, though it needed to be published...somewhere. *The Los Angeles Times* wrote that it was too incendiary, sticking to their hard-line stance of social conservatism.

He felt reduced to being the keeper of a truthful story about an ugly incident, which was either too hot or too cold. Except for *Rolling Stone*, all the rejects had been through letters. They came along with the bills stacking up on the front door side table. Nothing good comes through the mail.

But finally, a call came through from an unlikely source—U.C. Berkeley's *Daily Californian*. They would accept it and run it as a front-page lead. Corroborating back-up be damned. Daniel had a proven track record with them from his coverage of Jerry Rubin's Vietnam Day Committee protests, along with the separate stories and commentary he'd done for them on the Be-In and the Monterey Pop music festivals. The editor told him they'd run it in three-week's time and requested some of his pictures. He told him they had a deep handle on the network of university newspapers that would want to run it before the Democratic National Convention in Chicago in August, which was already promising to be a hotbed for SDS protests. "Your article is fucking right-on to build up student awareness of the atrocities going on in that fucking war," he added. He had the voice of a thirteen-year-old. During the call, Daniel had been distracted by Johanna's light moaning from the bedroom, so all he told him was he'd send the photographs by messenger, and, oh yeah, thanks.

As he placed the receiver back in its cradle, the stack of bills on the table caught his eye again, making him feel more helpless. He stared at the ominous envelopes, some emblazoned in red ink with: "Did you forget?" "Second Notice" or the more threatening

"PAST DUE." On top was a letter from Annie, stamped: *"Par Avion."* That didn't mean much; it still took air mail a week to get to the states from Saigon. He carefully picked it out.

As another pot of coffee perked with its *swish-blub* sound in the background, he sat back down at the kitchen table and opened the envelope:

May 15, 1968

Hey, there, cowboy!

Haven't heard from you in a while—actually since you left, which has been a long *while—so I thought I'd break the ice.*

"First of all, how's Johanna? Is she recovering well? You know they're making huge advances on cancer research, and I'm sure as much as I hope she'll get better. Our thoughts are with you, Dan. We all miss the hell out of you.

"Any luck in getting our article published? I guess not, otherwise we would have heard from you. I'm really sorry it had to end for you the way it did at the Trib. I've known Larry a long time—too long—and I knew how he might react. He can be such a dick. He sent me a real pissed-off letter, but I could see through his bluster. Now that Larry's as old as he is, he looks back thirty years and wishes he could be us. All good correspondents gain their stones through the hard knocks of their convictions. If you don't go that route, then you wind up towing the line for The Institution of the Press. Larry chose that way. He did add a P.S., though, one of his 'Off the record, okay?' pundits. He said I was a good journalist and blah…blah…blah. But he also said you were one of the finest young photojournalists he'd ever worked with. 'Kid's got a shitload of talent,' he said. I believe he meant it, and really, that's a lot of currency, coming from Larry Graham, one of the world's greatest gum-shoe editors. If you don't believe me, ask him!

Anyway, enough of that. I'm working for A.P. now with Dana, and sometimes Sean tags along with his camera. We have permission to go just about anywhere we want as long as we bring home a story. Sort of like a big game hunt—speaking of which—Sean was chased down by a tiger last week while we were up in the central hills covering the Montagnards. They are tribal primitive, loin-cloth-wearing, spear-chucker types with excellent aim and camouflage skills. Those guys really know how to become the bushes they hide in. From day to day, you never know who they're working for. Probably even before the French came along, they were farming their skills out to the highest bidder. When we were there, they were caught somewhere between the North and the South, and I'm not sure whether they were looking closer at us than we were trying to look at them. Sorta scared the shit outta me. We brought back a great story, though— the kind the Trib *would never run— and Sean's photos are nearly as good as yours.*

"Which brings me to this: though you've never met him, Sean likes your work, and Dana remembers meeting you that time on the way to Hue. He likes you, and your 'hidden independence' (funny, I never saw your 'hidden independence'—maybe because I was trying too hard to be overtly so.). The three of us have lobbied and finally succeeded what I'd hoped - getting you into the A.P. ranks with us. Really, Dan, working with them is a fucking blast. Pure reporting —no restraints. You can be as independent as you want. We told our office here about your situation, and they said for you to call their San Fran office on Market Street as soon as you're ready. They'll talk details with you and give you papers to come back over here—where you belong. If you need me to, as much as I hate San Francisco and just about all big cities, I can fly out there and back you up...then hopefully take you back here with me. Sound okay with you?"

Yes, it does!

Tony and I have moved in together up west of the city. The guy's a real homemaker. Makes me sick. And if I hear one more fucking aria, I'm going to jump out our first-floor window. Anyway, we love each other in spite of it all, and I've found a comfort zone with him (away from the hard drugs, you'll be happy to know—at least for the most part). I don't know if a marriage is in the works...Shit! Wait! Did I just say *that?!* won't *marry him or any other* *bastard! What's the <u>matter </u>with me? On the other hand, though, who knows? I love him so much he numbs my thinking.*

Dana helped me to pick out a bike—a Suzuki rough terrain model—and is teaching me to ride it. I've taken down only two rickshaws, so far. A motorcycle is the kind of vehicle we need to get into the tight spaces we do out here, and faster than most choppers. We just toke a few joints, pack up some more and we're on our way out into the hinterlands for our next story. We'll get you on one when you get out here, you'll need it. Tony's too chicken-shit to ride one, says that he needs to keep his stable job at the Trib—my old job, actually— to support my health care when I break my leg riding into a banyan tree. Motorcycle riding makes me feel so free—and independent.

Well, sweetheart. Enough out of me. You take care of Johanna, then get your ass back here. Okay?

Love,

Annie

Daniel felt a glimmer of hope, as, for a moment, he allowed his thoughts to move from Johanna. He heard a timid knock on the countertop, and glanced up to see Jainie, the visiting nurse, wearing a look of deep concern. He felt a flush of paralysis, realizing he hadn't heard Johanna's cries for maybe twenty minutes. She'd been eerily silent.

"Uh, yeah, Jainie?"

"She's worse, Dan. We need to get hospice involved."

All he could do was nod his assent. "Okay," he whispered. "We'll call hospice."

Jainie left her usual shift at the usual time after Daniel made his usual lunch of two wheat-bread peanut butter and jelly sandwiches and a Fanta orange soda. He stared out the patio window with its view across the bay toward that foreign city he used to call home.

He pondered over being stuck between a rock and a hard place and wished for a miracle to emerge from a sudden medical breakthrough that would restore Johanna to better than she had ever been before. Then, they could move back to a miraculously war-free Saigon and live in a beautiful place over-looking the river. A triple-fantasy. But these had become the dreams that kept him going, as he chomped absently into his usual wheat-bread peanut-butter and jelly sandwich.

Two hospice nurses had come by after Jainie had left, and things suddenly happened fast. It was more like an ambush on the world he'd built around Johanna when they took over.

Betsy, the senior of the two, went to the bedroom, took one look at Johanna, then instructed her assistant, Sue, to give the patient a shot of morphine. As Sue did this, and then straightened out the bedsheets, Betsy left the bedroom to talk with Daniel. She recognized the vacant look in Daniel's eyes. It was the kind of look that accompanied the helplessness of one who'd not yet to come to terms with the dying of the one they love. Betsy was trained in the game of loss—it was her job. She guided him to sit on the living room couch.

She started out empathetic. "You're not okay, are you, Daniel? Can I call you Daniel?"

"Dan is fine."

She smiled easily. "Okay, Dan. Obviously you know what's happening here."

"Yeah, Betsy, I'm aware."

"You may think you are. But you're not."

He glared at her for her impertinence. "Of course I know.

Johanna has advanced cancer. She's dying."

"Wrong on both counts. She doesn't have cancer—it's had *her* and has done its job. It's taken over her body, but not her mind. So, she's not dying, either. She's passing. Do you understand the difference?"

Daniel cringed, fearing that Betsy was going to lay some sort of philosophical religious bullshit on him. "Uh, no?"

"Passing," she said. "Think of it as going through a doorway. Someone comes to your house today, right now, and knocks on your door." She demonstrated with two knocks on the coffee table. "What do you do? What do you say?"

"Uh…'Come in?'"

"Okay. That might have been two weeks ago. I'm talking about today, Dan." His look became perplexed, and she read it— read him. She eased her shoulders and settled back on the couch, hoping he would follow her lead and relax. "No. You don't say 'Come in'. Not today. Today you say something like, 'Get the fuck away and leave me alone. My beloved Johanna is dying, and I don't want anything to do with anyone else.'" She canted a look at him. "Isn't that pretty much what you're thinking now? Even though the person might be offering to help, all you can say is 'Get away from me?'"

"Pretty much, I guess."

"Okay. Now passing is different. Passing says, 'Come in. I need your help. Johanna needs your help.' So, we are passing into your life, and into what is left of hers. We're here to help. You made the decision to call hospice in, Dan. You gave us permission to help Johanna pass because you both need us. And, I promise you, we are good at what we do." She placed her hand on his trembling knee. "You are no longer alone in this. Neither of you. We're here now."

This resonated with him. All that had blurred around him in the past few weeks began to clarify. "Thank you, Betsy. I appreciate that."

"Okay, Dan. Now here's what's going to happen. Us helping to make this easier on Johanna is gonna make it tougher on you. How tough is your choice, but not you or anyone else can get in the way of what we're doing for her. Okay?"

He tensed up at this. "You're, like, taking over."

"We're taking over," she agreed. "But we're going to involve you every step of the way. Not for you to tell us what not to do, but for you to let us do what we do best. I've done this for over twenty years now, and it's never easy on the grieving."

"What are you going to do?"

Sue came through the bedroom door. She seemed like a meeker version of Betsy. "She's resting now. I gave her ten CCs."

"Okay. Another ten just before we leave at six, and she should sleep well through the night."

Daniel stiffened again, as he hoped that whatever they gave her wouldn't react with the "Honey" he'd given her two nights before. "Ten CCs of what?" he asked.

"Morphine," Betsy told him. "That laudanum she's been taking is no more effective than an Alka-Seltzer for her condition now."

"Oh, okay. I kind of thought that," Daniel said. He vowed to check into the effects of morphine against the pure opium. He remembered seeing more than a few tripped-out soldiers treated with morphine for their wounds. Some circus acts even mixed the two for recreation.

"Sit down, Sue," Betsy said. "I was just explaining things to Dan." She turned her attention back to him. "Okay. Here's the plan. Sue will come at nine each morning to check Johanna and give her a shot, then leave. At one, I'll be coming by with another dose and I'll spend some time with her until five or so. I'm closing the bedroom door, and you may hear us talking. Please don't listen or come in. This conversation is between Johanna and me. Okay?"

"Okay, sure. I get it. Nurse-patient privilege."

"You can call it that." She glanced around at the few empty pizza boxes, Daniel's half-eaten sandwich on the dish and the dust devils on the floor. Most of the time, house cleaning was the last thing on the mind of the grieving. "Sue. We should get this place cleaned up. Today, maybe?"

"Okay. I'll call Marie." She stood and went over to the phone. "Okay to use the telephone, Mr. Lilienthal?"

"Please. Call me Dan. And yeah."

Sue dialed and soon was talking to someone on the phone. Her distant little voice was a soothing tonic.

"I noticed your mail. And some over-due bills when I came in."

"I'm sorry, I—"

"No need for that. Paying bills has probably not been a priority for you. We know people who can extend your time to pay them. It's a service we provide."

Daniel started to imagine the dollars all this would cost. "Wait how much do we have to pay for all these services?"

She smiled and pondered this as though she was figuring it out. "Ah. Let's see. For you? *Nada.* Nothing. We're a volunteer service, Dan, not a money pit."

Daniel sighed in relief. "Man. You guys are angels."

"We try to be. But as I said, this won't be easy on you. Starting with the hard facts. One is that Johanna doesn't have long."

"How long?"

"Hard to say. My gut tells me maybe a week."

Daniel suddenly felt as if he'd turned to stone. He blanched and shivered in another bolt of paralysis.

"I know, Dan. It's hard to hear. But no one can will Johanna to live. As I said, her cancer has done all it wanted to do in her. Now there's just time, and little of that. So, I'm urging you to accept my putting in for her to be transferred to the Hospice Wing at U.C.S.F. Medical Center. It's a nice place. Peaceful. But there's something you need to understand before I do this."

"What?" His voice sounded hollowed out.

She put her hand on his knee again. "She won't come home again."

He choked out some dry sobs, and she hugged him. It felt plush, like Johanna's hugs had once felt. He choked up more with the memory.

"Can she…?

"Can she what, Dan?"

"Can she hear me when she's like this?"

"She can hear everything you say." She stroked the back of his neck. "Hearing is the last sense to go."

"Can she talk? I mean now, she can barely — "

"The morphine'll take care of that. By morning she'll be reciting 'War and Peace.' This is going to take a lot of patience on your part, Dan. You'll have to show her how strong you can be, even if it takes everything you've got. You can't let her see your weakness. Be strong at her bedside, then go out onto your porch and howl into the night if you have to." She flicked a little smile. "This is San Francisco. You can get away with crap like that."

He pulled away and swiped some dampness from his cheeks. "A week?"

"It's up to you. You have to show her how much you love her."

"How?"

She leveled a benign, but serious gaze at him. "By giving her permission to pass. She has to have your permission."

CHAPTER FIFTY-FIVE

Release

Daniel hadn't left Johanna's hospital bedside. She lay there engulfed by the bulk of pillows and coverlets making her look like a delicate doll with her head wrapped up in a white turban. Her complexion was dulled and dry—the color and consistency of parchment. Her veins and capillaries showed a faint blue tracery beneath her translucent, pale skin, which outlined the hollow structure of her skull. What remained was the semblance of her wide-eyed expression, sometimes punctuated and brightened as she gifted that innocent smile.

Roberto came into the room often to wait silently with him. Sometimes he laid a reassuring hand on his shoulders. Daniel was withered away with concern and impending loss, saying little, but leaning closer over her to whisper: "I love you, Jo," into her ear. Him telling her that provoked her beautiful smile to bloom. She often touched her tongue to her dry lips. Daniel responded by daubing them with wet cotton; a simple ritual that helped her to relax. Occasionally she mustered the strength place her hand upon his—cool against warm—soft upon tense.

Every so often, Betsy dropped by, and encouraged him to take a break. Get something to eat; walk around the halls for exercise. She knew he wouldn't. Sometimes she would whisper words about letting go, and subtle urgings to give Johanna his permission to pass. Betsy understood that he couldn't let her go, yet. He would solemnly shake his head as his eyes glistened with tears. He wasn't ready.

Sometime around dusk, Johanna stirred then stiffened. Her breathing became labored. Daniel felt another one of Roberto's grasps on his shoulder. He turned to Betsy.

'What's happening to her?" Daniel asked anxiously.

Betsy just shook her head. "She's getting closer to the end — entering a new phase of letting go. I need to increase the morphine drip a little." She stood and adjusted the intravenous flow. "She needs more to keep the pain under control."

"She's in more pain?"

Betsy nodded. "She is. I'm sorry."

Daniel gazed around the surrealistically cheerful room, then out the picture window overlooking Golden Gate Park. The tops of the tall pine and eucalyptus trees cluttered around the edges of open fields were glazed in orange from the settling sun. like a Maxfield Parrish illustration. Off to the far right, the bright orange spires of the Golden Gate Bridge rose stoically above the wisps of bay fog.

Looking back at the park, he tried to single out the clearing of the Polo Grounds where the Be-In had been held a year and a half before—back when Johanna seemed her healthy self, masking the secret of her cancer. She had known even then it could take her away. He recalled the way she held him close. "I wouldn't know what to do if I ever lost you, Daniel," she had told him. He'd answered: "You're not going to lose me, Jo. Not ever." She had never said anything about him losing her this way.

Johanna relaxed back into a sleep. Betsy brought him aside. "She's sleeping peacefully, now," she said. "Let's go out into the hall."

The corridor reminded Daniel that he was in a hospital, not a fake hotel room designed for the dying. The smells of ether tinctured by that of death hung like a shroud. The air-conditioning was too strong and Daniel shivered from it despite Betsy's arm around his shoulders. "You can see she's struggling, now, Dan."

"Yeah."

"It's time for you to tell her she can go."

"I can't Betsy…not yet."

"Dan. Please hear me," she said as she turned him around to face her "You're not giving her your blessing to pass is not…"

"Not what?"

Betsy sighed. As long as she'd been dealing with death, this was still the hardest thing to say. "…Not making it any easier for her. It's making things worse. She loves you so much, Dan, she's holding on for you. She needs for you to tell her it's okay for her to go. That you will be okay. That you'll carry your love for her with you always—even though you're no longer together in this world. She has to know you're committed to loving her."

"I don't know. I just don't know."

She held him with her steady gaze. "There comes a time when loving someone can become selfish. Don't let that happen to you and Johanna. Do what's best for both of you. Permission, Dan—permission. Show Johanna how much you love her by making this sacrifice."

Daniel's lips began to quiver. "I—I can't."

"I'm gonna tell you a hard truth, now. I just increased her

morphine again. Any more, then the morphine takes over and brings her away. As it is, I'm certain she won't live through the night. Without more morphine to ease this along, she could die in pain. You do not want that for her. I know you don't. And I can't up the dose without your permission. Now is the time to say your good-byes, Dan…and let her pass, knowing she loves you more than anything. You have to help her let go."

Daniel thought for a moment as he brushed a stray tear from his cheek. "I need to be with Jo, now, Betsy."

Daniel said nothing to Johanna; he just took her hand and held it into the night. Her breathing became increasingly labored and shallow. Roberto dozed off in the easy chair near the window. Toward midnight, reruns of "The Beverly Hillbillies" flickered silently from the TV to chop into the darkness. It was then that Johanna's breathing started to become a phlegmy rattle as she lay with her mouth open. Daniel flagged the floor nurse as she passed. She hurried to the bedside and checked the morphine, then left to get another bag for the IV.

Betsy, yawning heavily with fatigue, followed the floor nurse back in. Roused by the commotion, Roberto stood on the other side of the bed near the I.V. stand "Her breathing sounds rough," he said. He knew what that meant from when Consuelo was dying. He looked over at Daniel and could see the fear in his bloodshot eyes.

"What does that mean?" Daniel asked, hoping for reassurance.

Roberto solemnly shook his head.

"It means her lungs are filling up," Betsy said.. Her system's shutting down." She looked at Daniel. "It's time."

"No. It can't be!" He'd seen one person he loved die already.

He refused to let it happen again.

"Dan," Roberto told him. "I've been down this road, and it was the hardest thing I ever had to face. I loved Consuelo just as much as you love Johanna. But it's time. We will not be losing Johanna. In a very big way, we will be gaining her. She'll become a part of us. I know this. I feel Consuela within me all the time."

"Roberto?" he gasped, as though looking for his approval.

Roberto turned to Betsy. "Turn up the morphine. As her father, I'm giving you consent."

Betsy turned to Daniel. "Dan?"

Daniel leaned close to Johanna. "She can hear and understand what I say?"

"She can," Betsy answered.

He leaned closer. "Jo. I love you, Jo," he whispered. "You will always be a part of me. I love you. You've been so brave. Fought so hard. But now it's time to let go." He choked up hard. "You can go, now. I love you, Jo." He felt the fragile squeeze of her hand around his. Her fingers felt so cold.

Her voice was a nearly inaudible tremolo. "Dad?"

"I'm here, sweetie. Loving you as much as I always have," Roberto said through his own pain.

"D-Daniel?"

"I'm here, Jo. I'll always be with you."

"I-I love y-you both," she gasped. "Dan? H-hon?" She daubed her lips with her tongue.

"Yeah Jo." He rested his cheek against hers. "I'm still here."

"Th-Thank you, hon," she whispered delicate as a sigh. "Thank y-you."

Roberto nodded to Betsy to up the morphine.

Daniel watched as Johanna's eyes closed, ever so gently, and she she slipped away he saw the tender rise of her smile. That beautiful, innocent smile.

CHAPTER FIFTY-SIX

Epilog

(July 10, 1970)

Johanna's essence had not just passed into the night two years before. It had settled fully into Daniel's heart. He needed to read her letter once again. The edges of the sealed envelope Lynda handed to him at the funeral had softened and grayed through time and use, and now he yearned for the balance it provided. He had almost memorized it, but Johanna's tight penmanship served out another reminder that she was still with him:

February 11, 1968

Dearest Daniel,
There's so much I want to tell you, but I can't, so I've given this to Lynda to hand to you later.

—And Lynda: <u>If you opened this envelope to read this because of your stupid curiosity, stop reading now! This is between me and Daniel!</u>—

Daniel, this cancer is something I have known about for two years, but never wanted to face, so I stored it away in the back of my mind. I knew about it when we first met, but my love for you helped to dissolve the thought away to a point where I stopped believing it, myself. You and our time together gave me hope.

My love for you has always been real. And now the cancer is real. I had tried to will it away in secret despite the headaches and all the "toilet sickness" (to be delicate!). When I told Dad about it, during that time Tamara marched away back to her Soviet Union, or whatever, he rushed me to Sloan-Kettering Cancer Center.

Maybe because I acted on my cancer too late, their experimental treatment only made things worse, but I was aware of the risks. The cancer spread rapidly from my head into my lymph nodes, and now it has gone into my bones and maybe my blood. I have been told I may have three to four more months, if I'm lucky. My only hope left is that I have a chance to hold you one more time.

I just want us to hold each other again—to tell you that wherever I am, I am never going to be far away from you. When I am gone, I want the power of the love I will always hold for you to convince you to promise me something.

This one last thing:
Hon—I want you to live on. Anywhere, any way you want, and with anyone who will make you happy. You have my full permission to live your life fully. Doing this will keep our love alive. No matter who you choose to spend your life with, never give up on love. I will always be there with hugs and kisses. Lots of hugs and kisses. No matter where I am, I could not go on without them, or the memory of you.

I love you, Daniel, now, as I always will,
Jo

He folded the letter and placed it back into the envelope to store it safely away where he could always find it when he needed it again.

Thien had gotten the call from Tony earlier this morning confirming what they all had suspected for over a month. Back in

April, Annie joined Sean Flynn and Dana Stone on one of their notorious motorcycle jaunts to some undisclosed destination with the excuse of covering another random skirmish in the hills. In fact, they had ventured into Cambodia, now rife with the Viet Cong who had enormous influence there.

Normally, the three rogue journalists would have returned from their jaunt to Saigon a few days later, scratched up and tired, but ready to bluster on about their adventures over shots and beer. The few days after this last trip had stretched into weeks, then into months. Word started to filter back that they were taken by the burgeoning Khmer Rouge Army led by Pol Pot, the brutal Cambodian leader now on his rise to infamy. Concern solidified into the truth that the three were dead, through an official statement issued from the Associated Press through Saigon's MACV offices.

Tony's feelings had not been expressed through tears, but through fits of rage. He blamed himself for not being more adamant about Annie going off on her fool's errands with those two renegades. But this was Annie Farrell. How could she not test the risk of getting a story?

Thien's voice came from behind Daniel, who stood staring out the window at the canal. "Hey, brother. You doing okay?"

He took Thien's hand, the one holding a Lowenbrau, and kissed it. "As well as I can, under the circumstances."

"Yeah. We all loved Annie. How could we have survived this war without her… what?

"Acerbic wit?"

"That, too, I suppose. I was thinking more along the lines of her encouragement," Thien offered the beer he'd brought. "Here take this. It'll cool you down. It's hot out here."

The bottle slid from his hand into Daniel's. "Not as hot as it used to be."

"Yeah," Thien said. "Who knows what's next? I hope not those fucking Cambodians."

Daniel sipped his beer as he gazed into the view outside their apartment. Fishing boats and junks churned silently through the canal, barely stirring up a wake, as if they floated above the canal rather than within it. Life in Saigon had fallen into a cautious new normal routine. It was quieter here in this part of Cholon than it was in mid-town as where people churned and prattled through their day. It was all so peaceful as Daniel relaxed against Thien's shoulder, thinking he'd never, since his time with Johanna, felt so much at home.

"The Weight of Indifference" Playlist

Prologue   (March 15, 1968)   Daniel in My Lai
We Gotta Get out of This Place   Eric Burton and The Animals

Chapter 7 – "Swimtime" (May 1966)   Johanna by the pool
Summer in the City   Lovin' Spoonful
Rainy Day Women   Bob Dylan
Good Lovin'   Young Rascals
Kicks   Paul Revere and the Raiders

Chapter 12— "Peace, Love and Loneliness "(January, 1967)
                                Be-In at Golden Gate park
Beat it on Down the Line   The Grateful Dead
Somebody to Love   Jefferson Airplane
Bye-Bye, Baby   Janice Joplin—Big Brother and the
                                Holding Company

Chapter 15 — "Down in Monterey" (July, 1967)
                                Monterey Pop Festival
Punky's Dilemma   Simon & Garfunkel.
I Think I'm Fixing to Die Rag   Country Joe and the Fish
One (Is the Loneliest Number)   Al Kooper
Grooving is Easy   The Electric Flag

VIETNAM

Chapter 24 — "Hunting buffaloes" (Late September 1967)
                On the River Patrol Boat in Mekong:
Paint it Black   The Rolling Stones
                Chopper form Me Tho to Saigon:
Highway Sixty-one   Bob Dylan

Chapter 26 — *Operation Wallowa* (Early October, 1967)
                Arrival at Que Son:
Alabama Song (Whiskey Bar)   The Doors

Chapter 29 — "Follies redux" (Mid-Late October, 1967)
I am the Walrus   The Beatles
                Tony and Bian in the Playboy Lounge, Saigon:

Chapter 32 — "The Hill of Angels" (Mid November, 1967)
                Card-playing marines at Con Thien:
Mother's Little Helper   The Rolling Stones
                Marines cleaning rifles at Con Thien:
First, There is a Mountain   Donovan

Chapter 37 — "The call of the jungle" (Early January, 1967)
For What it's Worth   The Buffalo Springfield
                Daniel and Annie in the Iron Triangle:

Chapter 41 —
"The Sa_gon Star H_otel" (January 31, 1968–Tet Offensive)
For Your Love   The Yardbirds
Music from a street side bar:

Chapter 44 —"The Sod of Chaos"(Early February, 1968)
                Thien and Daniel on way to Hue:
Smoke on the Water   Deep Purple
                                Crossing the compound in Hue:
Love is Blue   Paul Mauriat

Chapter 45 — "Drowning in Hue" (Early February, 1968)
White Room   Cream
Purple Haze   Jimi Hendrix
                During Street fighting in Hue:
A Whiter Shade of Pale   Procol Harem
                Daniel and Annie on roof in Hue:

Chapter 46 — "Khe Sanh, again" (Mid-late February, 1968)
                Daniel and Thien in a Khe Sanh trench:
Hey, Joe   Jimi Hendrix

Piece o' My Heart   Janis Joplin (Big Brother ...)
    Morning in Khe Sanh:
Just a Little Lovin'   Dusty Springfield

Chapter 48 — "The boy-soldiers"(March 13, 1968)
    Annie at LZ Dottie:
Little Red Riding Hood   Sam the Sham & the Pharaohs
        Charlie Company around hemp fire:
Together Again   Hank Williams

Chapter 50 — "Pinkville" (March 16, 1968)
      Charlie Company departing for My Lai:
Break on Through   The Doors
      During the My Lai attack:
Heater-Skelter   The Beatles

Chapter 53 — "Homecoming" (Late March, 1968)
    As Johanna waits for Daniel:
Some Velvet Morning   Nancy Sinatra/Lee Hazlewood

Chapter 56 —"Epilog" (July, 1970)
Let it Be   The Beatles

About the Author

David (D.H.) Robbins has been actively writing fiction for nearly 30 years. His first novel is a family saga centered around the 1960s, "The Tutone DeSoto" (2014), introduces eight teenagers growing up in Iowa during the veiled turbulence underlying The Kennedy Years (1960-63).

This second novel, "The Reverend" (2019) is set in New York City in 1963-64. The Greenwich Village Scene, Lower East Side and the New York World's Fair are featured settings.

The third in the saga, "The Weight of Indifference," is set place during the counterculture years (1965-68).

He's co-authored two media design books, "Motion by Design" (Lawrence King, 2007), and "Visual Effects Artistry" (Elsevier Press, 2009). He has also created and produces a 5-part lecture series, "The 1960's—Revisiting a Crucial Decade." Robbins has taught learning module design and is now teaching a fiction-writing course/workshop.

Robbins was born in Darien, Connecticut, and currently lives in Simsbury, Connecticut where he continues to type away on his short stories and novels.

www.ingramcontent.com/pod-product-compliance
Lightning Source LLC
Chambersburg PA
CBHW071932130726
47908CB00015B/133